Selected praise for T P9-DNZ-140

Against the Wind

"This is definitely a page-turner full of compassion
and love shared by two unlikely souls. This is a 'don't miss' read....
Kat Martin is a very gifted writer who takes you
from the beginning to the end in total suspense."
—*Fresh Fiction*

Against the Fire

"After reading the first book about the Raine brothers,
I knew Kat Martin would have to do something pretty amazing
to make her second book as much of a joy to read.
As soon as I opened the book, I realized that she has succeeded....
I simply loved this book. I didn't want to put it down."
—*Suspense Romance Writers*

Against the Law

"4 ½ quills! Ms. Martin has struck the motherlode....
Against the Law is by far the most powerfully intense
romantic suspense with its charismatic characters,
[and] a story line that defies gravity."
—*Romantic Crush Junkies*

Against the Storm

"Fans of Martin's Raines of Wind Canyon trilogy are going to
love meeting more of this testosterone-and-honor-laden family."
—*RT Book Reviews*

Against the Night

"*Against the Night* is not like anything else I've read.... I love a
good suspense story and this one packs one heck of a wallop."
—*Long and Short Reviews*

Against the Sun

"[Martin] dishes up romantic suspense, sizzling sex
and international intrigue in healthy doses, and fans
are going to be the winners. Readers better set aside a block of time
to finish this unputdownable tale of adventure and romance."
—*RT Book Reviews*, Top Pick!

Also by Kat Martin

KAT
MARTIN

AGAINST THE
EDGE

HARLEQUIN® MIRA®

Recycling programs
for this product may
not exist in your area.

ISBN-13: 978-0-7783-1443-1

AGAINST THE EDGE

Copyright © 2013 by Kat Martin

For questions and comments about the quality of this book, please contact us at
CustomerService@Harlequin.com.

Printed in U.S.A.

To my sister, Patti Johnson, and my brother Michael Kelly.
Miss you guys!

One

Houston, Texas

His head was pounding. Too much Jack Daniel's last night. When Ben Slocum pulled his big black SUV into the driveway in front of his garage, the only thing on his mind was getting a couple hours of sleep.

Reaching up to hit the garage door opener on his visor, he spotted a silver Buick with Hertz rental plates parked in front of the house. His gaze swung to the porch, where a woman in a conservative yellow business suit stood rapping on his door.

Ben groaned. Last night two of his best friends, Alex Justice and Sabrina Eckhart, had gotten married. Alex, one of his fellow private investigators at Atlas Security, had fallen hard for the pretty redhead. Ben had never seen a guy look happier about getting hitched.

Their early-October wedding had turned into good news for Ben, who'd gotten lucky with a slinky little blonde from Dallas he had met at the reception. He'd spent the night in her bed at the Marriott, and neither of them had gotten much sleep.

Still dressed in his black tuxedo, Ben glanced at the porch, shoved the Denali into Park and turned off the engine, cracked open the door and slid out from behind the wheel. His pants were wrinkled, his white pleated shirt haphazardly buttoned and opened halfway down the front. His black bow tie hung loose around his collar.

Company this morning was the last thing he wanted.

He took a long look at the woman whose attention was now fixed on him as he crossed the front lawn. She was tall and slender, with dark brown hair clipped back at the nape of her neck, and a very pretty face. High cheekbones, a heart-shaped face and full lips. Too bad they were currently thinned in a disapproving line.

He wondered what she was selling. Whatever it was, he wasn't buying. He just wanted to hit the sheets.

Ben strode up on the porch. "'Fraid nobody's home," he said, hoping she would just go away. He wasn't in the mood for another female, no matter how good she looked.

"I can see that," she said. "I'm looking for Benjamin Slocum. I presume that's you?"

He lifted a black eyebrow. "And you would be?"

"My name is Claire Chastain. I need to speak to you, Mr. Slocum, on a matter of extreme importance."

"I'll be in my office this afternoon. Why don't you stop by…say three o'clock? We can talk about anything you like."

"This can't wait."

Of course not. She was a woman. Everything was a matter of critical meltdown. "Is this business or personal?"

"Personal."

He let his gaze drift over her, taking in the soft curves. Slender and elegant, but there was plenty of female wrapped up in the pretty package.

"Do we know each other, Ms. Chastain?" *As in, have we spent the night together? Maybe I drank too much and don't recall?*

But he hadn't done much of that since he'd left the SEALs. Since then he had behaved himself. Well, more or less.

"No, we've never met. Please, Mr. Slocum. This is important, and I would rather not discuss it out on your front porch."

Irritation filtered through him. "Angel, this had better be good." Reaching into his pocket, he pulled out his house key, stuck it in the lock and opened the door. He went in and turned off the alarm, stepping back to allow Claire Chastain into his living room.

Ben closed the door. "Look, lady, I just got home from a wedding and I need a shower. There's a coffeemaker on the counter in the kitchen. Coffee's in the cupboard overhead. If you want to have a sensible conversation, I suggest you make us a pot."

The woman's dark eyebrows shot up.

"And don't be afraid to actually put some coffee in the pot."

Her mouth dropped open. Ben chuckled to himself as he turned and headed for the bedroom.

Of all the nerve! Everything she had heard about Ben Slocum appeared to be exactly correct. The man was arrogant and overbearing, downright rude. In his rumpled tuxedo and smelling of sex and perfume, it didn't take much imagination to know he had spent the night in a woman's bed.

He was a navy SEAL, she reminded herself. That had to count for something. They had a reputation for being tough, brave and honorable. Still, from the information she had, he had been out of the military for the past five years, a medical discharge at twenty-eight after a combat wound in some godawful jungle in the Philippines.

She had no idea the sort of man Ben Slocum had become. One thing she *did* know: he looked even better than the photo she had seen of him when he was twenty years old. At least six-two, maybe a hundred ninety-five pounds of pure masculinity.

Beneath his black tuxedo jacket, a set of ridiculously wide shoulders tapered down to a narrow waist and a pair of long legs. Jet-black hair cut short enough to hide a faint curl, and the stubble of a night's growth of beard just made him more handsome. She tried not to think of the glimpse of chest hair she'd seen beneath his unbuttoned shirt.

And those eyes. So pale a blue they looked otherworldly. She had seen a pair like them, but on a nine-year-old, the effect just wasn't the same.

Thinking of the little boy and the help he so desperately needed set her feet in motion. Making the arrogant jerk a pot of coffee tweaked her ego, but that was hardly important. She took down the can of Folgers and began the steps necessary to get a pot brewing. Once the coffee was looked after, she took a moment to check out the house.

Neat was her first impression. The dishes clean and put away, no crumbs on the round oak table in the kitchen. No messy stacks of papers on the white ceramic tile counters. *Decidedly male* was her second thought. Brown leather sofa and chairs in the living room, oak end tables and pottery lamps. A big flat-screen TV on the wall, and a stack of hunting and fishing magazines sitting on the antique oak coffee table in front of the sofa.

She felt something soft brush against her and looked down to see a big gray tomcat winding between her legs. His golden eyes looked up at her as she bent down to scratch his ears.

"Well, aren't you a big fellow."

The cat began to purr. Ben Slocum was a cat person? She was more a dog lover herself—not that she actually had one—but she liked all animals. From the look of the cat's glossy gray fur, he was definitely well cared for.

The sound of a door opening caught her attention. Claire looked up to see Ben Slocum striding down the hall, towel-drying his not quite wavy black hair. In jeans and a black T-shirt that stretched over the muscles on a very impressive chest, Ben was a formidable presence. Claire had to force herself not to take a step back as he walked into the living room.

"Smells good." He paused long enough to lean down and run his hand over the big cat's thick fur. "I see you've met Hercules."

"You like cats?" she blurted out before she could stop herself.

"I like animals in general. I tend to prefer them to people." He continued on to the kitchen. "Coffee looks ready. You want a cup?"

She definitely needed something to bolster her courage. "Yes, I think I do."

Ben took down a pair of mugs and poured them full, handed one to her. He didn't offer her cream or sugar. He took a sip, seemed to approve.

"What's so important it couldn't wait till this afternoon?"

"Why don't we sit down?" She started for the oak table, but Ben caught her arm.

"Why don't you just tell me what the hell is going on?"

Her patience was thinning. "Why don't I just show you?" Ignoring his request, she marched over to the table, set her coffee mug down and sat in one of the captain's chairs. Pulling the strap of her purse off her shoulder, she reached inside to retrieve Sam Thompson's fifth-grade class picture.

Slocum walked over, crossed his arms over his impressive chest and stood eyeing her from a few feet away.

Claire looked up at him. "I'm here, Mr. Slocum, because of your son. His name is Sam, and he needs your help." She didn't show him the photo. She wanted to choose exactly the right moment.

"I don't have a son. I'm a lot of things, lady, and careful is one of them."

"Do you know a woman named Laura Schofield?"

"No."

"Her name was Laura Thompson when the two of you were engaged."

A muscle tightened in his jaw. "If Laura has a kid, it isn't mine."

"I'm sorry to tell you that Laura Thompson is dead, Mr. Slocum."

The color drained from beneath his swarthy complexion. He pulled out one of the chairs and sat down facing her. "What happened?"

"Breast cancer. She passed away two months ago."

Ben leaned back in his chair. Clearly he was upset. She hadn't expected him to take the news so hard. She thought maybe it was a good sign.

He took a drink of his coffee, seemed to steady himself. "I'm sorry to hear about Laura. But as I said, if Laura had a kid—"

She turned the photo over and slid it across the table. "This is your son, Mr. Slocum, Sam. He's nine years old."

Ben stared at the photo as if it were a hand grenade about to explode. He was shaking his head, but those pale eyes remained riveted on the pair staring up at him from the smiling face in the picture.

"Do you remember a night nearly ten years ago when you went to see Laura? The two of you had ended your engagement years earlier. You were still in the SEALs, home on leave in San Diego. Laura was living in L.A."

She could see that he recalled. He reached over and picked up the photo. There was no mistaking whose child it was. With Sam's black hair, strong jaw and ice-blue eyes, the two were nearly identical.

He didn't look away from the picture. "She didn't tell me." He glanced up. "Why didn't she tell me?"

"It's a long story, Mr. Slocum. If you give me a chance—"

"Ben. My name is Ben."

"All right, *Ben.* The important thing is that you have a son and that Sam is missing."

Ben came up out of his chair. "Missing? What do you mean, *missing?* He's nine years old. How can he be missing?"

"Sam disappeared ten days ago. I've been talking to a detective named Owens in the missing-persons division of the Los Angeles Police Department. Unfortunately, the police believe Sam's a runaway. Which is what his foster parents believe."

He carefully studied her face. "But that isn't what you believe."

"No. I believe Laura's ex-boyfriend, a man named Troy Bridger, took the child. The police have looked into it, but so far they haven't been able to find any trace of either one of them. That's why I'm here. I need your help, Ben. I know you're a private detective. I need you to help me find your son."

Ben was blown away, his mind in disjointed pieces.

Feelings of unreality that this could be happening. Disbelief that Laura would have his child and not tell him. Anger at her and everyone else who had kept the boy's existence a secret. Those emotions and a dozen more sliced through him with brutal force.

He had a son. There was no mistake. The boy looked just like him. And the timing was right. He had been stationed in San Diego with SEAL Team One. He'd come home from a mission and found a letter from Laura. She wrote that she was living in L.A. and that she would love to see him. It was an opportunity, he'd thought, to find out if there was any chance of rebuilding the relationship they'd once shared.

He and Laura had met in his first year of junior college and he'd fallen hard for her blond beauty and outgoing personality. He had asked her to marry him and Laura had eagerly accepted.

A few months later, he had caught her in bed with one of his best friends.

Laura's betrayal had stabbed like a knife, cutting out part of his heart and soul. For years, he hadn't been able to stop thinking about her, unable to get her out of his head.

At first it had been like old times, laughing, talking late into the evening. That night, Laura had invited him into her bed and he wasn't about to turn her down. The sex was great as always, but his feelings were no longer the same. The resentment was still there, buried deep inside him, the old animosity. He hated her and he loved her. And he hated himself for loving her. That hadn't changed.

It was the last time he had seen her.

He looked over at the woman sitting across the table. He needed to get moving, take some kind of action. Do something to find his son. But he needed information first. Without it, his efforts would be useless.

He called on his years of training and self-control and forced himself to sit back down. "Exactly who are you?"

She kept her fingers wrapped around her coffee mug. He thought that she was more nervous than she wanted him to guess.

"As I said, my name is Claire Chastain. I'm a social worker in Los Angeles County. I worked with Laura and Sam a few years back. They became more than a case to me. Laura and I were friends."

He thought of the woman he had loved. Blonde and beautiful. *Sparkling.* That was Laura. Everyone adored her. But she was never what she seemed.

"You think this guy Bridger took him. Why would he do that?"

"To get even with Laura. He knew how much Sam meant to her. He was furious when she kicked him out."

There was something in her eyes, the way they couldn't quite meet his. "Laura's dead," he said. "I don't see how taking my kid is going to hurt her. What aren't you telling me?"

She returned her eyes to his face. "There's a good

chance he's also trying to punish me. I disapproved strongly of Laura's relationship with Troy. I think he blames me for the breakup. And he knows how much I care about Sam."

"What kind of a man is he?"

"Not the sort you would want Sam to have for a father. He's an alcoholic. He gets mean when he drinks. I never knew what Laura saw in him. Maybe his tough-guy persona appealed to her." She looked up at him. "She loved you, and you were a SEAL. Troy Bridger looked a little like you. Maybe he reminded her of you in some way."

"She never loved me. I was just an amusement to her."

He could tell she wanted to argue. Instead she took a sip of her coffee. "Laura was trying to get sober, but Bridger was a drunk and he pulled her back to the bottle. She ended the relationship when she started getting sick."

"How long did she live with him?"

"Only a couple of months. I can't imagine why she stayed even that long."

"He isn't some kind of pervert? Some guy on the sex offender's list?"

"The police checked. They said he wasn't on the list. At least not under that name. The few times I talked to him, he never seemed inclined in that direction."

"But you don't know for sure."

He didn't miss the guilt that moved across her features. "No, I don't know for sure. But my guess is his motive was more about revenge against Laura."

"And you."

The guilty look returned. "That's right."

"Because she dumped him and he blames you."

"Yes. And Troy has this men-are-superior thing. He doesn't value women very highly, and Sam's a boy. He would go on and on about boys becoming men...real men. As if he could make it happen for Sam."

Ben's insides were churning. How could Laura have brought this kind of loser into her house? But he hadn't seen Laura in years, and if she had been drinking the way Claire said... "How long have you known I was Sam's father?"

"Laura told me two years ago. She wasn't drinking then. She begged me not to tell you unless there was no other choice. She said you lived a life of adventure, that it was the life you wanted. She said you wouldn't want to be tied down with a kid."

He felt like punching something. The woman across from him was his closest target. Too bad he had a rule against hitting women.

She was watching him, sizing him up. Did she really think he would shirk his duties as a father? Did Laura really think that? "Just proves how little she knew me."

He took a drink of his coffee, but his adrenaline was pumping and he no longer needed the caffeine. "Los Angeles was the last place Sam was seen?"

"That's right."

"You headed back there?"

"So you've decided to help me?"

"I'm going to find my son. It doesn't matter if he's run away or if this guy Bridger took him. The minute I saw that picture, I had no other choice."

Two

Claire felt those pale eyes boring into her like twin laser beams. When she had come to Houston, she hadn't been sure Ben Slocum would help her. But then she saw his face as he looked at his son for the very first time, and she had believed nothing would stop him from finding the boy.

"What other information can you give me?" Ben asked, shifting restlessly in his chair.

"I left my briefcase in the car. I have copies of Laura's file. She wouldn't want me to show it to you, but—"

"I don't give a fuck what Laura would want. She kept my son from me. She should have come to me years ago. Now her silence has put him in danger. I need to know every damn thing the woman did since the day Sam was born."

Claire's fingers tightened around the coffee mug. She wasn't afraid of him—well, not exactly—but she didn't doubt he was a dangerous man.

"I don't know everything. Just what's gone on since she filed for financial assistance and I was assigned her case three years ago. And what I know as her friend."

"What about Bridger?"

"I was able to get a copy of the police report. They looked into finding him. Came up with nothing."

"Why not?"

"The police think the name Troy Bridger is an alias."

Ben leaned back in his chair. "You're kidding me, right? You're telling me the cops don't have a damned thing on the guy who may have abducted my son?"

"They don't know who he really is, and they don't know where he's gone. They know his address before he left town because Laura knew where he moved after they broke up. I was able to give them the information. Laura also told me he worked as a crane operator for a big construction company, but the police talked to his supervisor and he said Troy quit a couple of weeks ago."

"What about fingerprints? There had to be some in his apartment."

"They didn't find a match. I'm sorry. I wish I knew more, but I don't."

"Why are you so sure Bridger has Sam?"

"Troy drove a beat-up Chevy pickup. Sam's foster parents said he came to the house to see Sam a couple of times. I talked to the neighbors. One of them saw his truck in the area the day Sam went missing."

"You got a plate number?"

"No."

"Have the cops got a BOLO out on the guy?"

"Yes. They're looking for him as a person of interest, but so far they haven't found any trace or him or Sam."

Tension rippled across those wide shoulders. "So there's nothing under Bridger's name, no driver's license, no registration, no plate number. Nothing."

"The police say his driver's license was a forgery. There's no real proof Troy Bridger ever existed."

Ben raked a hand through his thick black hair. His now-cold coffee sat nearly untouched in front of him. "You think this guy Bridger took him, but the police and Sam's foster parents think he ran away. Why would he do that?"

She wished she didn't have to tell him. She wished it weren't true. "Sam was wildly unhappy in the Roberson house. I promised him he wouldn't have to stay there forever. I tried very hard to get custody myself, but the judge thought Sam would be better off with a couple. I told Sam I was going to keep trying. If that didn't work, I'd make sure he got moved to a family he liked."

"But Sam didn't want to wait," Ben guessed.

"That's right." Just thinking about the betrayal she had seen in Sam's eyes made her heart hurt. "He threatened to run away a couple of times, but I don't think he really would have. He was just so impatient. You know how kids can be—or maybe you don't remember."

He cast her a glance. "You don't think I can remember that far back?"

She smiled. "I know you're only thirty-three. I just meant some people kind of block out their childhood."

"Well, I remember mine way too well."

She mulled that over, knew from Laura that he'd had a tough, lonely childhood. "Sam was unhappy. I think that's the reason he left with Troy. Troy had known his mother. That was the connection. And Troy has this dog. Pepper. A black Labrador retriever. Sam's crazy about that dog."

"I want to see those files, but we need to get on the road. In a missing-child case, time is crucial. You should have called me the day he disappeared. Hell, you should have called me two years ago when Laura told you my name."

Her chin inched up. She didn't know Ben Slocum, only what Laura had told her about him and what she'd been able to dig up on the internet. "Maybe I should have. I guess that remains to be seen."

His jaw went hard. He looked as though he was fighting to stay in control. He released a slow breath. "I keep a bag packed. Old habit. I'll grab it and we're out of here. It'll take a little longer to get through airport security, since I'm traveling with a weapon."

"A weapon? You're taking a gun?"

"We don't know what we're dealing with here. I'm not going empty-handed."

She didn't know how she felt about that. He was ex-military, though. If anyone ought to know how to use a weapon, she supposed it would be Ben.

He wasn't gone five minutes, returning with a black canvas duffel slung over a heavily muscled shoulder. Ben put out a new batch of dry food for the cat, who had his own high-tech security cat door into the backyard, checked the auto-watering bowl, then went outside and drove his Denali into the garage. Then they headed out to her rental car for the trip to the airport.

"You drive. On the way, I'll go through the files."

She didn't argue. She didn't like his high-handedness, but she liked his take-action attitude. So far the police had come up with nothing. They believed the Robersons, believed Sam had run away.

Claire didn't believe it for a minute.

As she drove toward the airport, Ben sat in the passenger seat poring over the files she had brought in the hope that if he decided to help her the information might be useful.

"Laura Maryann Thompson," he read. "Born in Pittsburgh, Pennsylvania, December fourteenth, nineteen eighty. It lists the schools she attended. Pittsburgh Community College is where we met."

"She was your same age, right? You were both sophomores? You were putting yourself through school, planning to join the navy when you graduated."

"That's right."

As the car rolled along, Claire flicked him a sideways glance, saw him studying her face.

"So she talked about me," he said. "What else did she tell you?"

"She said your father was a steelworker. That you worked with him at the mill part-time to put yourself through school. She said your mother left when you were nine years old."

"That's right. The same age as Sam. She tell you my dad worked like a dog just to put food on the table? He was a good man but he was a lousy father. Mostly I had to fend for myself. It wasn't the kind of life I'd want for a kid of mine."

Claire made no reply. Laura had told her Ben had been pretty much on his own since grade school, since the day his mother walked out of the house. She'd said she admired what he had made of himself.

"What happened to Laura's parents?" Ben asked as she merged onto the 59 Freeway heading north. "They were nice people. Samuel was her father's name."

"They died in a car wreck six months after Sam was born. I think that was part of the reason she started drinking. She wasn't good at handling responsibility."

Ben's jaw looked tight. "I would have helped with the boy. All she had to do was ask."

Claire didn't tell him that Laura hadn't asked him for help because she didn't want to burden him. The reckless, devil-may-care boy she had loved in college wanted excitement and adventure. He hadn't been ready for marriage or fatherhood. Even years later when he had come to L.A., he wasn't ready to settle down.

Or at least that was what Laura believed.

Ben looked down at the file. "Says she married a guy named Tom Schofield in 2001. Divorced a year later. No kids. Why not?"

"Laura said she didn't love him. She said she tried to, but it just wouldn't work."

He looked up as they took the turnoff to the airport. "That night in L.A….she told me she was on the pill."

Claire could feel those icy eyes on her. He was waiting for her to say something, but she didn't want to betray Laura's trust.

"Tell me the truth," he pressed. "Did she get pregnant on purpose?"

A shaft of weariness slid through her. "Laura wasn't on the pill, if that's what you're asking. She wanted your baby. There was no way to be sure she'd get pregnant that night, but she was happy when she found out."

"Son of a bitch."

"As it turned out, she wasn't well suited to be a mother. She loved Sam, but the responsibilities of raising a child were just too much for her to handle."

Ben fell silent, but she could feel the anger rolling off him in waves. Laura had borne him a son. She had needed his help, but she had refused to ask.

Neither had Claire. And some of his anger was definitely aimed at her.

They missed the 11:10 flight out of Bush International, but got tickets for the 2:20. Ben had wanted to stop by the Atlas Security office, where he worked as a freelance P.I., and put the company computer whiz, Sol

Greenway, to work digging up something—anything—on Troy Bridger. But it was Sunday, and after Alex and Sabrina's wedding and late-night reception, everyone was sleeping in. No one would be at work till Monday morning.

If he found anything that would give Sol a place to start, he'd call him at home. The kid was always willing to help.

While they waited in the busy terminal for the later flight, Ben went through Claire's files a second time. The information on Sam tugged at a place in his heart he didn't know he still had. His son was a straight-A student. He played baseball and soccer. His teachers liked him and he had lots of friends.

Clearly Sam was a lot more outgoing than Ben ever had been.

A document he had missed the first time slid out from behind another piece of paper. Sam's birth certificate. The father was listed as Benjamin Slocum. It made him mad all over again.

"Why didn't the welfare department call me? I thought they went after deadbeat dads for child support."

Claire's gaze swung to his. She had big green eyes, he noticed, though it was hard to tell with a pair of reading glasses perched on the end of her nose as she read the paper.

"You weren't a deadbeat dad. You didn't even know you had a son. And they didn't go after you because Laura stopped taking assistance after just a few months. She thought it was demeaning."

"I'm not surprised. Her mother was a member of the DAR."

"Daughters of the American Revolution."

"That's right. She was always proud of her family

heritage. She had a lot of self-esteem—at least back then."

The terminal buzzed with noise around them, making it a little hard to talk. "So if she wasn't getting assistance, why were you still involved?"

"I told you, because we were friends. Better than friends, if you want the truth. I can't explain it. I was a couple of years younger. At first I felt sorry for her, raising a kid by herself. As I got to know her, something just clicked between us. And I admired her for trying to make it on her own."

"Did she?"

"She worked as a secretary in an insurance company. She drank too much, but she managed to control it enough to keep her job." Those big green eyes zeroed in on him. "And there was Sam. He's really special. Smart. Tough. Yet amazingly loving. He took care of Laura more than she took care of him. You can be proud of him, Ben."

His throat felt tight. He had a kid named Sam. A son he could be proud of. He was out there somewhere and he was in trouble.

"I'm going to find him. I won't stop until I do." He felt Claire's hand on his arm, looked down to see long, slim fingers, no wedding ring.

"*We're* going to find him, Ben. I promised Laura I'd make sure Sam got a good home. I intend to keep my word."

With the time change, the plane landed at 6:00 p.m. The October weather wasn't much different in L.A. than in Houston, eighty degrees, clear skies and sunshine.

"There's no reason for you to stay in a hotel," Claire said to Ben as she wheeled her carry-on along the crowded corridors then took the escalator to the ground-floor exit. "I've got an apartment in Santa Monica. You'd have your own room. We can brainstorm, work the leads you come up with."

She shoved through the terminal doors and stepped out on the sidewalk, where a heavy gust of wind hit her, plastering the narrow skirt of her conservative yellow suit to her legs. A few feet away, buses and taxis rushed past. Cars crawled along and limousines darted in and out, picking up the rich and famous who frequented the L.A. airport.

Ben shook his head. "Look, Claire, I'm a private investigator. Finding people is one of the things I do. The information you've given me is going to help. If I need something else, I'll call you. Just give me your cell phone number, and—"

"No. That isn't going to happen, Ben. You don't seem to understand. I promised Laura *on her deathbed* that I'd take care of her son. I failed to do that. Now I have to make this right. I promised Laura—and not you or anyone else is going to stop me."

Something shifted across his features. Might have been a hint of approval, but probably just a trick of the light.

His voice softened. "Look, I get it. You're trying to do the right thing. But I'm a professional, Claire. Aside from that, I'm the boy's father."

"You're his father in name only. Sam doesn't even know you exist. He isn't going to just fall into your arms. Dammit, he might not even go with you if you find him."

"What about your job? Don't you have to work?"

"I…umm…took a leave of absence. I have a small

inheritance from my grandfather. I can afford to take some time off."

Those icy eyes were filled with turbulence, his features hard.

"I need to be there," she pressed, "to make sure he understands what's happening to him. For God's sake, Ben, he's just a little boy!"

Ben tipped his head back and stared up at the cement overhang above them. He seemed to be trying to pull himself together. "All right. We'll try it your way. But I'm not letting you slow me down. If I need to move fast, I will."

"Okay, that's fair enough."

"I'm gonna need to rent a car."

"You can use mine. If I need to, I can borrow one from a friend."

He hesitated a moment more, then nodded. "All right, then I guess that's it. Let's go." He didn't like it, she could tell, but he was a smart man and her logic was sound. Sam didn't know him. He wouldn't trust him. But he trusted Claire.

And she had let him down.

Her heart pinched. She'd failed him and now she had to make it right. Claire just prayed Ben Slocum was a different man than the reckless heartthrob Laura had portrayed him to be.

Ben found Claire's car parked in the overnight lot. A nearly new red Honda Accord. Interesting, since Claire Chastain didn't strike Ben as the red-car type. Those women were fiery-tempered. Impulsive. Passionate. Then again, it was hard to figure the currents running beneath a female's facade.

As he plucked the keys from her hand, he took another long look at her. In the sunshine, her dark hair had deep red highlights. Mahogany, he'd call it. He wondered what it would look like unbound. Her cheekbones were high, her skin smooth and clear, and there was a tiny cleft in her chin.

He'd been so angry, so worried about the child he never knew he had, he hadn't looked at Claire Chastain as a woman. A very pretty woman. Now that he did, he wished he hadn't.

Under different circumstances, it would be fun to discover what lay beneath her cool reserve. To find out if she would be a red-car woman in bed.

Not this time. He had more to think about than his sex drive—or hers. And though he clearly interested her in a number of ways, he wasn't sure that interest included sex.

If it did, it didn't matter. He had a son to find. And after that—

For the first time it occurred to him that from this day forward his life would be never be the same. If he didn't find Sam, he would always think about him, worry about him. Wonder where he was. Wonder if he was alive. If he was happy.

If he did find him, he would have to be a father to the boy. He'd need to make a home for him, see him properly raised. Ben's life would be completely changed.

"It's almost seven o'clock," Claire said as he loaded his canvas duffel and her carry-on into the trunk of her car. "What should we do first?"

"I want to talk to the family Sam was staying with. See what they have to say."

"The Robersons. They live in Calabasas. It's a pretty long drive. Shall we call them? Let them know we're coming?"

He shook his head. "I don't want them showcasing. I want to see the way they live. And I don't want to give them time to put up their defenses."

"All right. Why don't you let me drive since I know how to get there?"

Ben tossed the keys back to her, rounded the car and settled himself in the passenger seat. As she slid behind the wheel, he tried not to notice the length of pretty thigh exposed when Claire's yellow skirt slid up.

He leaned back against the headrest. "I could get used to having a female chauffeur."

Her gaze swung to his. "Was that a joke? Did Ben Slocum just make a joke?"

His mouth edged up. "Not much of one."

Her features softened. "We're going to find him," she said with an amazing amount of determination. "Troy Bridger, or whatever his name really is, thinks he's gotten away with stealing Sam, but he's wrong."

"You're that sure that's what happened?"

"I know Sam. Troy used his dog to get Sam to go with him."

Ben studied her face. The set of her jaw and the steel in her voice made him wonder if he'd been shortsighted when he'd formed his initial opinion of Claire Chastain.

Three

The Robersons were a decent family who earned money by being part of the foster care program. They had two kids of their own and two or three fosters at any given time who were waiting for permanent placements.

Sam had been one of those.

The trouble was that twelve-year-old Kenny Roberson and his ten-year-old sister, Tammy, were spoiled and somewhat selfish. And Kenny was often a bully. Since the Robersons tended to take their kids' side over the other children in the house, the environment could be stressful.

From the start, Sam had refused to take Kenny's guff. He'd stood up to the older boy and because he had, he'd had a tough time getting along with the family.

Claire's gaze fixed on the highway stretching ahead of her. It was dark now, rows of taillights as far as she could see. "I have a feeling you're as stubborn as Sam. If he'd only waited another couple more weeks…"

Ben's hard look sliced toward her. "You should have called me. I would have come for him."

"I didn't know that. I'm beginning to think some of the things Laura told me were wrong."

"Some of the things? She hadn't seen me in years."

"No, but she sort of kept track of you. That's how I knew where to find you."

Ben's black eyebrows went up. "How'd she do that?"

"She had a Facebook friend in Houston. A woman you slept with."

"Jesus! Who was it?"

"I don't know. I told her someone like that wasn't a reliable source."

Ben didn't say more. She thought he was wondering, thinking about the life he'd been leading, wondering what it would be like to have a son.

Claire was wondering what kind of a father he would make.

She continued along with the stop-and-go traffic heading north. It wasn't five minutes later that she glanced over to see Ben sound asleep in the passenger seat. Watching those thick black lashes resting so peacefully against his cheeks reminded her that he had been awake half the night having sex. A little tremor of awareness slipped through her, which Claire firmly ignored.

Her mouth thinned. That she was thinking about Ben Slocum in any context other than Sam's father irritated her more than a little. Claire jammed her foot on the gas, then slammed on the brakes as the taillights brightened on the Cadillac in front of her. The Accord jerked to a sudden stop, but Ben Slocum didn't wake up.

Or at least he pretended not to.

Ben sat up the minute Claire turned off the engine. The brief nap had at least cured his headache. They were parked at the curb in front of a beige two-story stucco house in a subdivision northwest of L.A. The neighborhood the Robersons lived in looked family friendly.

Ben cracked open his door and so did Claire, and both of them got out. An overturned blue bicycle and a deflated basketball lay in the grass in front of the porch. Ben climbed the stairs and rapped on the door.

A woman answered, mid-forties, bleached blond hair and a plus-size figure. "May I help you?"

"Hello, Mrs. Roberson," Claire said when the woman recognized her. "I'm sorry to come by so late, but this is Sam's father, Ben Slocum. He wanted to talk to you and Bob, ask you some questions."

"I thought Sam's father was dead."

Ben stepped into the porch light. "Unless your eyes are playing tricks, I'm just as alive as you are and I need to talk to you about my son."

He felt Claire's hand on his arm, warning him to take it easy. She returned her attention to the woman and managed a tentative smile. "Ben's a private investigator, Martha. He's hoping you can help him."

"It's getting late," Martha said. "You should have called first. Tomorrow's a school day. I have to get the kids to bed."

"This won't take long." Ben brushed past her, making his way into the house. There were toys scattered around, but no kids in sight. He could hear them playing somewhere upstairs. The living room was neat, with sturdy furniture and inexpensive lamps. He could see into the kitchen, and it was clean, too. He couldn't complain about that.

"I just wish you had called," the woman said.

Ben caught the sound of heavy footfalls and turned

to see a burly man, bald and grim-faced, thumping down the stairs.

He walked into the living room. "What's going on in here?"

"Bob, this is Sam's dad, Ben Slocum," Claire said. "He's hoping you and Martha can help him find his son."

"It's late. Come over tomorrow when the kids are in school."

Ben's blood begin to simmer. "My son is missing. Since it was your responsibility to watch out for him—which you failed to do—I would think you'd be interested in helping me find him."

"Listen, mister. Sam ran away. The police are looking for him. I don't care who you are—I want you out of here."

Claire gasped as Ben grabbed a fistful of Bob Roberson's white T-shirt and slammed him up against the wall. "My son is out there. He's only nine years old. You're going to answer my questions. Now. Right this minute."

From the corner of his eye, he spotted the wife slipping toward the cell phone on the kitchen table. Claire stepped in front of her, blocking her way. *Score one for the lady.*

Ben slammed Roberson once more against the wall. "You hear what I'm saying?"

Roberson swallowed. "Yes. Fine. What is it you want to know?"

Ben let him go and stepped back out of his comfort zone. "Did Sam take his clothes when he left?"

"Yes, most of them, anyway. That's how we knew he wasn't taken against his will."

"Did you or your wife ever talk to Troy Bridger?"

Martha answered, her face a little pale. "I did. He said he was a friend of Sam's mother's. He asked if he could speak to the boy. I told him he could but they had to stay in the living room."

"Did he mention any plans he might have had, something he was going to do? Any place he was going or where he was originally from?"

"No."

"How about after that? Did you see him again?"

"He came over one other time. It was a Saturday. I was busy making lunch…that's how I remember. I figured he would keep Sam occupied. The boy was always underfoot, causing some kind of trouble."

One of Ben's eyebrows went up. "Is that so?"

"Yes, it is. Sam couldn't get along with the other kids."

"You mean he couldn't get along with Kenny and Tammy," Claire corrected. "Your two kids. Sam got along fine with Suzy and Tim."

"Just because that's what Sam told you doesn't mean it's true."

Ben looked at Claire, noticed the mutinous set of her chin and figured it must be gospel. "The day Sam went missing…did you see Bridger that day?"

"No."

He turned to the husband. "How about you?"

"No. Look. Sam's run away once before. He came home the same day. That's what happened this time. He left on his own."

Ben chewed on that. He didn't know what the boy might do. He had to trust Claire's judgment. He just hoped he was trusting the right person.

"How long did you wait after Sam disappeared before you called the police?"

Silence fell in the living room.

Ben's jaw tightened. He moved into Roberson's space. "How long?" he asked softly.

"Two days. We figured the kid was having a tantrum, all right? We thought he'd come back when he got hungry."

Ben's hands fisted. "You don't know what a lucky man you are, Roberson. You're lucky I'm smart enough to know that if I started pounding on you, I wouldn't be able to stop."

Turning, he strode out of the house. He didn't hear what Claire said, just the sound of her heels on the sidewalk behind him as she hurried to catch up.

"I'm driving," he said. "Give me the keys."

"You're too angry to drive. I'll get us home."

"We aren't going home. Give me the goddamn keys."

Claire tentatively placed them in his hand, and his fingers closed around them. A few minutes later, he was heading down the freeway toward Hollywood, working to keep his speed under control and his temper in check. He hadn't gotten much out of the Robersons, but he had a friend in L.A. who owed him a favor.

It was time for Ben to collect.

By the time he turned off the Hollywood freeway onto Sunset Boulevard, Ben's temper was under control. He'd been stationed in San Diego during his days with the teams. He knew his way around L.A. enough to get by. And to help, Claire had a GPS mounted on the dash. He had plugged in the destination street address before he'd pulled away from the curb.

"I can't believe you did that," Claire said after a lengthy silence that told him how much she disapproved of his behavior at the Roberson house.

"No wonder Sam ran away. What a pair of a-holes."

"Yes, well, if they call the police, it'll only cost us more time."

"They won't call the police. Roberson's too scared I'll come back and beat the crap out of him. Which I'm more than tempted to do. The man waited two days, Claire. Two days."

"I know. I knew you'd be angry if I told you."

"I missed it in the police report. Probably a good thing."

The corner of her mouth curved up. She had a very pretty mouth when she wasn't scowling. Nice full lips, glossy pink lipstick.

"Laura said you had a temper."

His gaze moved from her mouth to her eyes. "I'd never hurt a woman. I wouldn't hurt a kid, if that's what you're thinking."

"I wasn't thinking that. I was thinking that Sam wouldn't put up with Kenny's bullying. That's why the Robersons didn't really like him. He's three years younger than Kenny, and yet he was the leader in the house, the one the other two foster children looked up to."

A trickle of emotion slipped through him. He wasn't sure what it was. Pride? How could that be? He didn't even know the kid.

He amended that. With Claire's help, he was beginning to know his child, at least a little.

"I'm surprised you didn't ask to talk to the other foster kids in the house," she said.

"There was no way that was going to happen without a fistfight, and even if the Robersons agreed, the kids would be afraid to say anything."

"I talked to them the day after Sam was reported

missing," Claire said. Ben glanced in her direction. "They told me Sam didn't say anything about leaving. They didn't see him pack his clothes, but Tim said he took the photo of his mom he kept on the nightstand. He also said Sam and Kenny had a fight a couple of days before. Apparently since then, Kenny had been making Sam's life hell."

"So he might have run."

"Or he met up with Troy, the way I think he did."

"What about the kids at school?" he asked. "You talk to them?"

"The police did. He was still pretty new. He hadn't really made any friends. No one knew where he might have gone."

Ben returned his attention to the road. "The cops will be looking for Sam. I'm going after Bridger. You better be right about Bridger having my son."

He drove down Sunset Boulevard, stop-and-go, bumper-to-bumper traffic, lots of restaurants and bars, people with weird-colored hair and nose piercings ambling along the sidewalk. The GPS showed a turn up Laurel Canyon Road. He made the turn and followed the directions up the mountain.

There was a wrought-iron gate at the bottom of a hill in front of a private driveway. He pushed the intercom button and a familiar woman's voice came over the line.

"Yes, may I help you?"

"Hi, Amy. This is Ben Slocum. I need to talk to Johnnie. Sorry it's so late, but it's important."

"Ben! Oh, my God, of course. Come on in."

Claire flashed him a look. "One of your old girlfriends?"

"That's Amy Riggs. She happens to be my friend's wife."

The electric gate swung slowly open. Ben drove the Accord up the hill, parked in front of the first building he came to and turned off the engine.

It was a modern structure, white stucco with a flat roof and a garage off to one side. Farther up the hill, a much-bigger version looked out over the Los Angeles basin. Amy and Johnnie Riggs walked out on the porch. Amy ran down the front steps and into his arms for a hug.

"Ben! It's so good to see you."

She was a tiny little thing, long straight blond hair and big blue eyes, the woman John Riggs had fallen madly in love with. From the sappy grin on his face as he looked at her, he still was.

Johnnie walked over and clapped him on the shoulder. "Good to see you, Iceman."

"You, too, Hambone." Riggs was a ranger. He could out-eat every man in the platoon and never gain weight. Or at least it was said that that was how he'd gotten his nickname. Ben turned, introduced Claire to Amy, then the muscular, dark-haired man with the perennial five o'clock shadow. Only Johnnie's wasn't for effect like most of the Hollywood crowd's.

"Good to meet you both," Claire said. They were sizing her up, Ben could tell, wondering if she meant more to him than the women he usually dated. She meant more, all right. She was the key to finding his son.

The group went into the house, and Ben spotted the bulging suitcases sitting in the entry. "You going somewhere?"

Riggs grinned. "We're off to Hawaii, my friend. I've

been promising Amy. We're leaving first thing in the morning."

Not good news. "That's too bad. I was hoping you could help me find my son."

Johnnie's eyes widened. "You've got a kid?"

"Looks that way. I just found out this morning. Unfortunately, he's gone missing."

"The hell you say."

"Hey, Johnnie! We gonna finish this? I need to get going."

Ben didn't recognize the lanky, dark-haired kid in scuffed cowboy boots and a Dodgers baseball cap who came up the stairs two at a time from the floor below.

"That's Tyler Brodie," Johnnie said, tipping his head toward the man striding toward them. "He's smarter than he looks."

For the first time that day, Ben almost smiled. Because the kid, with his crooked, lady-killer grin, looked about twenty-five years old.

"Sorry, man," Brodie said. "I didn't know you had company."

"It's all right, I'm glad you're here." Johnnie made introductions. "Ty, meet Ben Slocum. You remember me telling you about him? Helped me in Belize when Amy and I went down to find her sister."

"Ex-SEAL, right? Johnnie said he owed you big-time for helping him out of a jam. Nice to meet you." The kid's handshake was solid and strong. Johnnie introduced him to Claire.

"Ty's not only smarter than he looks, he's older. Almost an old man of thirty. He's a former jarhead, and I just made him my partner."

"Johnnie's been working way too hard," Amy explained. "And Ty's really good at his job."

"Which is?" Ben asked.

"Doing the same thing I do," Johnnie said. "Digging up information. He's been working for me a couple of years. Ty's a licensed P.I., and like Amy says, he's good."

Ty grinned. "Thanks, boss...I mean partner."

Ben looked him over. He trusted John Riggs. If Johnnie said Brodie was good, he must be very good.

"Since Johnnie's heading out on vacation, it looks like you're the man I'm going to need. My son's missing and the police don't have a clue where to find him. I've got the name of a guy who might have taken him. I need you to dig around, Ty. See if you can come up with a lead."

Brodie nodded. "I can handle that."

"You want a beer or something?" Johnnie asked. "Claire, you want a glass of wine or maybe some iced tea?"

"Wine sounds great," Claire said, getting a smile of approval from Amy.

"I'll have a Coke if you've got one," Ben said. He was still recovering from a hangover and he'd only had a couple of hours' sleep. He needed to stay focused, keep his mind sharp.

Riggs and Amy led them into a living room dominated by a wall of glass that looked out at a sea of colored lights in the valley below. Johnnie opened a small refrigerator in the built-in bar, took out a couple of beers and handed one to Ty, poured wine for Amy and Claire, took out a Coke for Ben.

"Flight's not leaving till 9:00 a.m. We got plenty of time. Why don't you fill us in?"

Ben didn't hesitate. Johnnie could sleep on the plane. In the meantime, he could use all the help he could get.

Ben started talking, and an hour later, they were still making plans.

"I need to know what the cops are doing," Ben said. "A detective named Owens at the LAPD is in charge of the case. I'd rather work things on my own, keep a low profile. You guys got any connections in the missing-persons division?"

Johnnie tipped his head toward Brodie. "Ty's got half the females in the LAPD swooning over him. He can find out pretty much anything you want to know."

Ben arched a brow. "That so?"

Brodie's mouth edged up. "A smart man never reveals his sources, but I can find out what's happening with the case."

"That'd be great."

Cell numbers were exchanged. "I'll call as soon as I've got something," Brodie said.

It was late when Ben and Claire left the house and headed for Claire's apartment. Ben tried not to think where his son might be spending the night.

Four

Claire's eyes felt gritty and her neck hurt. It was one o'clock in the morning by the time Ben pulled her car into the carport beneath her Santa Monica apartment on Sixth Street. With the time change, she'd been up for more than twenty hours.

Ben had been up even longer. She ignored a little niggle of curiosity about the woman he'd been sleeping with the night before she'd met him, and led him toward the guest room. He tossed his duffel on the bed.

"Your bathroom's at the end of the hall," she said. "There's soap, shampoo and toothpaste, and the towels are fresh. If you need anything, just let me know."

"I need to get on the internet, see if I can find anything on Bridger. I hope you've got Wi-Fi."

"I've got it. Sunrise452 is the code. But you need to get some sleep, Ben. You won't be any good to Sam if you're dead on your feet."

He scrubbed a hand over his face. He'd been clean-shaven that morning; now a rough shadow darkened his jaw. "You're probably right. I could use a couple of hours."

"I usually get up early. If you're not up, I'll wake you."

He nodded, turned to survey the queen-size bed, looked at it with longing.

"By the way. Johnnie Riggs called you Iceman. That's your nickname? From the SEALs?"

"Yeah."

With eyes like his, there was no mistaking where the name had come from. "Good night, Ben."

"Good night, Claire. See you in the morning." Ben disappeared behind the guest room door, and Claire went into her own room to shower before going to bed.

She yawned as she headed for the bathroom. With so much on her mind, she wasn't sure she'd be able to get any sleep.

Surprised to find the sun shining brightly through the curtains over the windows, Claire yawned as she climbed out of bed the following morning. She needed to wake Ben and make some coffee—strong, she remembered, was the way he liked it.

Slipping into her robe, she opened the bedroom door and stepped out in the hall, heard footsteps an instant before she collided with Ben. His arms went around her, steadying her before she took a fall.

"Easy."

"Sorry. I—I didn't know you were awake." He was returning to his bedroom, freshly showered, a towel slung low on his hips, his black hair wet, drops of water beaded against his tanned skin.

Claire's mouth went dry. She couldn't take her eyes off the thick pectoral muscles, flat stomach and six-pack abs. A patch of curly black hair spread over his chest and arrowed down his stomach to disappear beneath the towel.

She couldn't seem to breathe.

"You okay?" he asked in a voice that sounded a little gruffer this morning.

Claire stepped back as if his skin had burned her. "Fine…I'm just… You just took me by surprise."

"I've been awake for hours. Wanted to see what I could find on the net." His gaze ran over her, taking in her sleep-tangled hair, traveling over the nipples that had hardened under her short silk robe, down the legs exposed below the hem, all the way to her bare feet.

How those icy eyes could look burning hot she would never know, but her stomach contracted beneath that heated gaze and her nipples hardened even more.

In an instant, his demeanor changed, the heat disappearing as if it had never been there.

"I need some coffee, doll. How 'bout you make us a pot?"

Her mouth dropped open, then snapped closed. Before she could tell him to keep his pet names to himself, he had walked on down the hall, disappeared into his room and closed the door.

Ohhhh, the man was infuriating! Ben Slocum was rude and arrogant, a complete macho jerk. How could Laura ever have fallen in love with him?

But she had, Claire knew. Laura had loved Ben desperately. And she had never gotten over him. Loving Ben Slocum and having to give him up had ruined her life. Even having his child hadn't been enough to save her from the depression she felt in losing him.

Claire glanced at the door of the guest room. Laura had called him a heartthrob. He certainly had the most incredible male physique she had ever seen. Even the jocks in the gym didn't look as good as Ben, whose hard-muscled body just seemed more authentic.

As a former SEAL, it actually was. It didn't mean she had to like him. Still, for Sam, she would try to keep an open mind as much as she could. Laura had loved him. There had to be something good about him.

Then again, for a while, Laura had thought she was in love with Troy Bridger.

Ben went back to work on the laptop he'd set up on the kitchen table at 5:00 a.m. that morning. Claire was on the computer in her bedroom, digging for information same as he was.

Her place was nice. Just a few blocks from the beach. It was an older building, condos rented as apartments, but the unit was in good condition, the living room comfortably furnished with a pale green sofa and chairs, a glass-topped black wrought-iron coffee table, cream and pale green throw pillows.

There was an area with a glass dining table and upholstered, pale green high-back chairs. Lots of beach paintings hung on the walls. Overall, it was simple and elegant but not stark. The kitchen had white cabinets and a round white table with a butcher-block top. Lots of cream and pale green in the dish towels and pot holders, knickknacks on the walls.

He glanced toward her bedroom. Aside from handing him a cup of coffee, Claire hadn't said more than a couple of words since he'd run into her in the hall.

He almost smiled. In only a thin silk robe, her thick mahogany hair curling around her shoulders, her bare legs exposed, she was one sexy lady. Since the last thing he wanted to feel was any sort of physical attraction to a woman he was trying to work with, he needed to keep her at a distance.

It was working even better than he had planned. Which should have made him happy, but didn't.

He was beginning to like Claire Chastain. Yesterday, when she'd stood up for Sam, then stepped in to stop Martha Roberson from calling the police, that feeling had crept up another notch. Hell, he'd even felt a twinge of admiration. Claire was one determined woman.

He still wasn't sure if he wanted her to be right about Bridger having Sam or whether it would be better if his son were wandering the streets of L.A.

Ben gazed down at the computer screen. He'd been surfing the net for hours, trying to find out about the people involved in the case. That was how he needed to look at it—as a case instead of a situation that involved his own flesh and blood. He had to be objective or he wouldn't be able to do his job.

He'd started with his ex-fiancée, Laura Thompson. She'd married Tom Schofield less than a year after he and Laura had split up. So much for her broken heart.

Then again, Laura clearly didn't have a heart, since he had found her in bed with another man just days after he'd given her an engagement ring.

He tracked her through old newspaper articles: her engagement, her wedding to Schofield, their divorce six months later. Old courthouse documents filed not long after changed her name back to Thompson.

He tracked her to Los Angeles where he had hooked up with her again. Her Facebook account was still open. He read personal posts, saw photos of Sam when he was younger.

It was oddly surreal to see a smaller version of his own face staring back at him. Surreal and surprisingly emotional. When he thought of all the years he had missed with the boy—the Little League games, the parent-teacher meetings, Christmases and birthdays— anger bubbled up inside him.

Even he hadn't known how much he would regret not being there for those things.

What he didn't find was a single damn thing connecting Laura to Troy Bridger.

His office in Houston was open by now. Picking up his cell phone, he punched in the number for Atlas Security, got Annie Mayberry, the receptionist and manager.

"Annie, it's Ben. I'm in L.A. Long story. I need to talk to Sol. He in yet?"

"You sound tired, Ben. That little blonde you took home after the wedding keep you up till the wee hours of the morning?"

Ben ignored the gibe. Annie knew everything that went on in the office. Hell, the woman knew everything that went on in Houston. She had a tongue like a viper and didn't hesitate to use it. She was also a mother hen and everyone's confidante, even his.

"I've got a son, Annie. I just found out. The boy's missing. I need to talk to Sol."

A heartbeat passed. "You got it, Iceman. Anything you need just let me know."

"Listen, I may be gone for a while. Will you check on Herc in a day or two, make sure he's okay?" Annie had a key to his house. One of the few people he trusted with his security codes.

"No problem."

"I've got a couple of cases I was supposed to start working this week. The files are on my desk. Maybe you could ask Jake to take them. Or maybe Trace could work one of them for me." Trace Rawlins owned the company, and Jake Cantrell was another P.I. who worked freelance in the office. Both men were ex-military, Trace a ranger and Jake a Force Recon Marine sniper. They were among his closest friends.

"Don't you worry," Annie said. "We'll handle it. You just find your boy." She spoke to Sol on the intercom, then patched him through. Annie was a real busybody, but she knew when things were serious. "Good luck, honey."

Sol picked up right away. He was only twenty-four, but when it came to computer know-how, Sol Greenway was as good as it got.

"Hey, Ice, Annie says you got a kid?"

"That's right. He's only nine and he's missing. I need to find him, Sol."

"Just give me what you've got and I'm on it."

Ben gave Sol the few details he had, including info on the Robersons, Bridger's name and last known address, that he'd been employed at Warner Construction. "I've also got some photos I can send."

"Great," Sol said. "I'll try facial recognition. Take a look at the registered-sex-offender list, too, see if there's something somebody missed."

Ben's stomach tightened. "Thanks."

"I'll start digging, just prowl, see what I can find."

"That'd be great. Keep me posted."

"Will do." Ben ended the call and went to work. Using the portable scanner he'd brought with him, he sent Sol the photos he had of Sam, along with a picture of Bridger with Laura that Claire had given him.

Finished, he came up out of his chair just as Claire walked back into the kitchen dressed in jeans and a crisp white cotton blouse, a pair of gold sandals on her slender feet. Her toenails were painted a fiery red, he noticed, and thought again about her car and taking her to bed.

Which wasn't going to happen. He took a last glance, appreciating her feminine curves. At least not anytime soon.

"Have you found anything?" she asked.

"I need to talk to the people Bridger worked for."

And he needed to get into the bastard's apartment, which the police report had said was vacant. He needed to see if the police had missed something, but he wasn't going to cop to breaking and entering to Claire. "I'll be back when I'm finished."

"I'm going with you. And I think we should go to his apartment. It was empty when the police went in, but they might have missed something."

His mouth edged up. "Glad you thought of it. His address was in the police report. I'll stop by before I come back."

Those determined green eyes fixed on his face. "I said, I'm going with you."

He could see by her stubborn expression she wasn't going to back down. Since it wasn't worth an argument, he just walked over, took the keys down from the hook on the key rack and started walking.

"After you," he said, and pulled open the apartment door.

Claire followed Ben up the metal stairs into the Warner Construction trailer next to a big high-rise building site. They walked over to the Formica-topped counter, and one of the female employees left her desk and came to greet them.

"May I help you?"

"Any chance you knew a guy named Troy Bridger?" Ben asked. "I understand he worked here."

Claire didn't miss the way the redhead smiled at Ben.

"Troy was a crane operator, but he quit a couple of weeks ago." She gave him a long, slow once-over, clearly liking what she saw. "He didn't give us any notice, just picked up his check and said he wouldn't be back." She was wearing tight jeans and a navy blue T-shirt with the words *we dig you* stretched over a lush pair of breasts.

"Did Troy usually pick up his paychecks?" Ben asked. "Or did you mail them somewhere?"

She tossed a red curl over her shoulder and gave him another smile. "Troy always picked them up." To his credit, Ben didn't seem to be taking the bait, but the redhead was definitely interested. Claire couldn't fault her taste in men.

"Did he say anything about taking another job?"

"He said he was going to be moving," the woman said, "leaving the state. He didn't say where he was headed. I figured maybe he was going home."

Claire's interest picked up. "Do you know where he was from?"

The redhead's gaze never strayed from Ben. "He never said, but I think it was somewhere in the South. He talked about having brothers and he said he liked to hunt. Once in a while, I noticed a Southern drawl."

Ben turned to Claire. "You notice it?"

"We didn't talk that often. I hadn't thought about it until now, but yes...I think he did have a slight Southern accent. Not too much, but some."

Ben returned his attention to the woman behind the counter. "Troy ever mention a boy named Sam?"

She shook her head. "Not that I recall."

"Is there anyone else I could talk to about him, someone who might know where to find him?"

"Not that I know of. Troy was a real loner, you know? He did his job and left. He never hung around with the other guys."

Ben took out his wallet and handed the redhead a business card. "I'd really like to speak to him. If you think of something that could help me find him, Ms....?"

"Ferber. Tracy Ferber."

"Ms. Ferber. If you think of something that might help us find him, I'd appreciate it if you'd call me on my cell."

"Okay—" she read his name on the card, gave him a flirty glance "—Ben."

Claire fought the urge to roll her eyes. She felt Ben's hand at her waist, directing her toward the door, then they were outside heading for the car.

"That was a big fat zero," she said as she settled in the passenger seat and buckled her seat belt. "Unless you were looking for a date."

"Funny. We got a lead. Bridger may be headed home and that might mean he's moving south."

"But we don't really know."

"That's the way it works, Claire. You collect the bits and pieces, keep adding to them, see which ones fit, which ones don't. Pretty soon you begin to get a picture."

But all of that took time and time was something they didn't have. "Where to next?"

Ben started the engine. "I'm going over to his apartment. I'll talk to the landlord if he's there, try to get him to let me in. If that doesn't work, I'm going in anyway. I've got his address programmed into the GPS. I'll drop you off at your place on the way."

Claire leaned back in her seat. "Not a chance. There might be something there. I want to have a look."

Those blue eyes pinned her where she sat. "You understand I'm going in—one way or another?"

"Just drive, frogman."

Ben Slocum actually smiled.

Five

Troy Bridger lived in a run-down neighborhood not far from LAX. The apartment building had cracks in the plaster—probably earthquake damage—and the blue paint had faded to a washed-out gray. Unit four sat on the bottom floor, the curtains partially open. There was no on-site manager and no one around.

The sun was moving west, the afternoon waning as they walked up on the porch and looked through the windows. The apartment was cheaply furnished, but Ben could see no one was living there.

"I'm going to take a look inside," he said. "Why don't you wait for me in the car?"

"If you're going in, so am I. I might find something you miss."

"Breaking and entering's a crime, angel. You'd be smarter to stay out of it."

Her chin went up. "I'm going."

Ben just shook his head. "I'll go round back and find a way in, come back and open the door. Whistle if someone's coming."

Her pretty green eyes widened. "I don't know how to whistle."

Amusement slid through him. At least Claire Chastain was keeping him entertained. "You'll think of something."

He headed around the corner to the rear of the building. Behind the apartment, each ground-level unit had a small fenced yard. Bridger's had enough dog crap to tell him that Pepper had definitely been in residence.

Using a credit card, he opened the cheesy lock on the back door into the kitchen. The good news was, the place hadn't been cleaned. He made his way into the living room, past a worn tweed sofa with a couple of springs sticking out, and opened the front door for Claire.

As she walked inside, her nose wrinkled at the musty, unpleasant smell. "It looks like he's been gone awhile. Thank God the cleaning crew hasn't been in."

Smart lady. "Doesn't look like the cops have been here, either. Maybe the landlord wouldn't let them in without a warrant."

"The Robersons convinced the police Sam ran away, so they probably didn't try to get one."

He made a quick sweep of the living room and bedroom. "I don't see any sign of a kid being here. Sam disappeared eleven days ago. If Bridger took him, they must have headed straight out of town."

"Let's make sure," Claire said.

He nodded. "I'll look in here. You take another look in the bedroom."

Claire disappeared into the other room while Ben made a slow sweep of the living room, looking for anything that might have information they could use. All he saw were old movie-ticket stubs, dirty Kleenex, candy wrappers and empty foam cups. Nothing of any value.

Reaching into the pocket of his jeans, he took out one of the small brown paper bags he carried for evidence collection, tucked the cup inside for a DNA sample.

He wandered into the kitchen, found an overdue electric bill on the counter. The wet garbage had been carried out, but a lot of paper trash remained. He used a pen to poke through litter here and there, looking for any scrap that might lead to Bridger.

His eye caught a haphazardly stacked pile of what looked like opened, discarded mail. Bridger's name was on the envelopes and flyers, most of which were advertisements. All but one. A VISA credit card statement. The card had recently been canceled. This was the closing statement. No charges. No money owed.

It had been mailed to unit four but the name on the envelope wasn't Troy Bridger. It was Troy Bennett.

Bingo.

He refolded the piece of paper, stuck it back in the envelope and shoved it into his hip pocket. Looking up, he saw Claire walking back into the living room, her eyes wide, her face as pale as cotton.

Ben started toward her, caught her shoulders to steady her. "Claire, what is it?"

She looked up at him, moistened her lips. "Blood..."

He urged her over to the sofa, sat her down on one of the sagging cushions. "Stay here."

Blood. It didn't mean anything. It could be anyone's blood. There was no reason to think it was Sam's. Still, a knot formed in his stomach as he rushed into the bedroom.

Nothing in there. But in the bathroom, the sink was

covered with a dried, dark brown substance that could only be blood.

Using his pocket knife, he scraped enough blood off the porcelain into another bag for a sample. There was a fine spatter on the walls, but nothing else in the room besides dirt, mold and rust around the bathtub.

He spotted pieces of a broken glass in the corner and felt a hint of relief.

The color was back in Claire's face when he returned to the living room.

"I'm sorry," she said as she stood up. "Was it really—"

"It's blood, but there's no reason to think it's Sam's."

"No, of course not. I was just… It scared me."

"I found pieces of a broken glass. Looks like that's what happened. Someone cut himself and bled into the sink. Doesn't look like enough to be fatal. I took a sample. We'll see what it shows."

"Maybe the police can match the DNA or something, find out Bridger's real name."

"They have to have something to match the DNA to. Bridger would have to be in the system. Can take a while to find out." He rested a hand at the small of her back as they started for the door. "The good news is I found an old VISA bill in the name of Troy Bennett."

She stopped so suddenly, the curve of her bottom came up against his groin. "Oh, my God, that must be his real name." Ben stepped back, the firm roundness feeling way too good.

"Not necessarily. Sometimes a guy like that uses half a dozen aliases."

"Oh. Are you giving the card number to the police?"

"I'm giving the number to a friend in Houston. The card's been canceled, but with any luck, he can tell us where it was used last."

"What about the police?"

"Not yet. If Bridger's got my son, I don't want the police accidentally tipping him before we can get to him. We don't know anything about this guy. We don't know what he might do."

"I didn't think of that."

"Come on. Let's get out of here." There were things he needed to do. More pieces of the puzzle to find and fit together. More information he needed in order to find his son.

On the way back to her apartment, Claire sat quietly as Ben phoned Tyler Brodie and got the name of a private lab he and John Riggs occasionally used when they were working a case. She waited in the car while Ben went in to drop off the blood sample he had scraped out of the sink, fidgeting, wondering if they would be able to get a result before the end of the day.

A few minutes later, Ben climbed back into the car.

"How long will it take them to get the DNA?" she asked as he started the engine.

"They'll have the blood type by tomorrow morning at the latest. Getting the DNA and running it through CODIS will take a couple more days."

"CODIS...that's the criminal offender database. I've dealt with it in my work." Social Services had to know as much as possible about the people they were trying to help. The system gave them badly needed information.

"It only works if the DNA from the blood belongs to someone in the system. If that's the case, they'll be able to tell us who it is."

She glanced out the window, saw the sun sitting low on the horizon, the afternoon slipping away. "Sam's blood type is O-negative. He took a fall off a skateboard, cut his arm and had to have stitches. I went with Laura to the emergency room."

"O-negative. Same as mine." Something flashed in his eyes. Not relief that the boy was his. Something a father might feel when he spoke of his son. "They would probably have taken a sample of his DNA when he went into the foster care program."

"Yes, that's right." Claire didn't say more. She didn't want to think that the blood belonged to Sam, that he might have been seriously injured. There had been no sign of a child, she reminded herself. Chances were the blood was Troy's.

As soon as they got back to her apartment, Ben went to work on his laptop, trying to find something on the name Troy Bennett. He also called his friend in Houston, a guy named Sol Greenway, he had told her, a computer expert, and put him to work, as well.

Now Ben was pacing, waiting to hear back from his friend. Clearly, Ben wasn't a patient man.

His iPhone rang. He picked it up from where it sat next to his laptop and pressed it against his ear, looked at her and shook his head. Not the lab or Sol Greenway.

"Brodie. What's up?"

She couldn't hear what Tyler Brodie was saying on the other end of the line but Ben's face looked grim when he hung up the phone.

"What is it?"

"Brodie talked to the cops." Ben stuck the phone in his pocket. "They said Sam's teachers knew he was unhappy. The police are sticking to their theory that Sam's a runaway. They're checking local hangouts, places where kids congregate who've left home."

"I could talk to them again, try to convince them. I know it's Bridger. Laura said he promised he would

find a way to pay her back for what she did to him."
She glanced away. "And he wanted to hurt me, as well."
She looked back at him. "Maybe this time the police
will listen."

"Look, Brodie's going to check the runaway angle,
too. He says he knows some of the lowlifes who lure
these kids into working for them. They use them for
drug mules, get them to steal. Traffic them. He'll find
out if any of these guys have seen Sam."

Claire's heart jerked. "Traffic them? Oh, God, Ben."
Her eyes filled and she started shaking. She had blocked
that kind of possibility out of her mind. She couldn't
stand to think of Sam being sexually abused, suffering
in some terrible way.

She felt Ben's arms go around her, drawing her
against his powerful chest. "It's all right. We don't know
that's happened. From the start you've been convinced
Sam didn't run away, that it was Bridger who took him."

She looked up at him, into his strong, handsome face.
"What if I'm wrong?"

"Are you?"

She swallowed. She was risking Sam's life. Claire
shook her head. "No." She eased away from him, felt
the loss of his warmth.

"Then we keep looking for Bridger. My instincts say
you're right. Bridger wanted revenge against Laura.
With her dead, he wants payback from you. He went to
see Sam on at least two different occasions. Sam was
desperate to escape and Troy used that desperation to
convince the kid to go with him. We just have to figure
out where he's gone."

His cell rang again. Claire watched his expression,
read his determination to find his son. She thought of
the way he had tried to comfort her. She hadn't ex-

pected his sympathy. Ben Slocum didn't strike her as a sympathetic man. But he had surprised her at Bridger's apartment. Surprised her here. There was no mistaking his concern.

He ended the call. "That was Sol. Troy Bennett worked as a crane operator in Vegas. He lived with a woman, an exotic dancer named Sadie Summers. His old VISA bills show he left town about six months ago and came to L.A."

"How does your friend Sol know all that?"

Ben's mouth edged up. "Sol doesn't say and I don't ask. But I need to talk to Sadie Summers."

He started for the bedroom, but Claire caught his arm. "I'm going with you, Ben. We're in this together. I promised Laura."

"Fine, get on the phone and charter us a plane out of Santa Monica. It's only a little over an hour flight. If we get going, we can be back late tonight."

Claire didn't argue. She had money in the bank, enough to rent the plane. She got on the internet and found a charter company, arranged for a flight from the Santa Monica airport to McCarran Field.

"We're all set," she called out as she walked down the hall. "The plane'll be ready to leave in an hour." Ben's door stood open. She stopped in the opening. He stood beside the bed, naked to the waist, a yellow oxford-cloth shirt lying on the bedspread ready to be put on.

Claire just stared. Her heart was pounding, the blood rushing to her head. It was impossible to look away from all those perfect muscles. Impossible to keep from thinking of sex, which she hadn't had since her breakup with her former boyfriend, Michael Sullivan, five months ago.

Rarely before that, since he was gone so much.

"Keep looking at me like that, angel, and we're going to have to add a couple hours to our departure."

She stared into those ice-blue eyes that were anything but cold and felt light-headed. "A couple of hours?"

"I'd prefer to take the rest of the day, but we have things to do."

Her face heated up. "Oh. Oh, my God." Turning, she hurried back down the hall, embarrassment washing through her. She couldn't believe she had gawked at him that way. It wasn't like her to let a man's appearance affect her. She was interested in brains, not brawn. Well, usually.

In her bedroom, she grabbed a small overnight bag out of her closet, tossed in a change of underwear, a clean T-shirt, a sweater, her makeup bag and travel kit. By the time she walked into the living room, her composure had returned.

Ben was unplugging his laptop, putting it in its case.

Claire lifted her chin. "If you didn't want to be stared at, you shouldn't have left your door open."

Ben's mouth edged up. "Actually, I didn't mind at all. In fact, I'm hoping you'll return the favor."

Heat slid through her as she thought of those amazing eyes running over her half-naked body. She wondered if he found her attractive. What kind of woman appealed to a hard man like Ben?

"As you rightly pointed out," she said, staring at him down the length of her nose, "we don't have time for those kinds of distractions."

"Yeah, unfortunately." He grabbed his laptop case and the black canvas duffel he'd brought with him, though clearly he'd only packed enough for the night. "I doubt we'll be staying, but you never know what might turn up."

She grabbed her overnight bag and they headed out the door.

Less than two hours later, she climbed down off the wing of their chartered Cessna 310 and crossed the tarmac next to Ben, toward the rental car she had arranged. The sun had set, but the lights of the casinos were so bright it didn't seem dark in Las Vegas.

"Since you insisted on paying for the plane," she said, "I used my card for the car."

Ben flicked her a glance. "A liberated woman. I figured."

But she wasn't sure he liked it. The guy had *macho* stamped in invisible letters on his forehead. Macho men weren't usually attracted to independent women. She told herself it didn't bother her.

They climbed into the Toyota Corolla she had rented from Hertz. Ben plugged the address he had for Sadie Summers into the GPS and started the car. It occurred to her that if the meeting went anything like it had at Warner Construction, Ben would probably make more progress with the stripper if he went alone.

Claire didn't suggest it.

Six

It was chilly in Las Vegas but the cool fall weather didn't deter the millions of tourists who prowled the casino strip. Ben avoided Las Vegas Boulevard, taking a less-crowded route from the airport to an address on the west side of town. A couple of times as he drove along, his glance strayed to Claire.

Ben knew women and there'd been no mistaking the sexual interest in those big green eyes when she had caught him half-naked in his bedroom. He hadn't missed the way her breath quickened, the pulse that throbbed at the base of her throat. It was good to know the growing attraction he felt for her was returned.

But Sam was the priority for both of them, and even if the time were right, he wasn't sure the lady would invite him into her bed. Claire was uptight and reserved. She wasn't the type to have sex with a man she barely knew.

On his side, Ben didn't want the problems that came with sexual intimacy. He wasn't good at the morning-after niceties. As far as he was concerned, by morning both parties had gotten what they wanted and it was over.

He was pretty sure that wasn't the way Claire approached a physical relationship. She'd want more, and he wasn't the kind of guy who could give it to her.

Still, just thinking about stripping off those conservative clothes and discovering the woman beneath sent his blood pumping south, and inside his jeans he started getting hard. Shifting against his growing arousal, he turned on the radio and concentrated on following the directions to the address he had punched into the GPS.

It turned out to be an apartment in a low-rent section of Vegas. Two stories, white with black trim, a couple of scrawny trees in front. A light shone on a play area with swings and a sandbox that sat inside a chain-link fence next to the building.

"Maybe I should wait in the car," Claire said as he turned off the engine, which surprised him since she had always insisted on going everywhere he did. One look at her face and he knew what she was thinking.

"The horny redhead at the construction site wasn't my type and the last thing I want is to be alone with a stripper." She'd been uptight since their encounter in the hall that morning. It was nice to see her smile.

"Okay."

They got out of the car and made their way up to the porch. Ben knocked on the door and a minute later it swung open. Sadie Summers was a brassy blonde with a couple of kids. He could see them playing on the floor in her living room. He hadn't expected that.

"I'm Ben Slocum and this is Claire Chastain. I know it's getting late. We're sorry to bother you, Ms. Summers, but we're looking for a man named Troy Bennett. We're hoping you can help us find him."

He'd told Claire to let him take the lead, decide how much information to feed her. If Sadie Summers was still in contact with Bennett, and Bennett had Sam, he didn't want her to give the guy a heads-up and a chance to run.

Sadie propped a hand on her hip. "I have no idea where that rat bastard is. I haven't seen him in months. Troy left me holding the bag on the rent. He was supposed to pay five hundred toward the bills, but at the end of the month, he just took off. I haven't seen him since."

Ben glanced over at Claire. "Mind if we come in? I'll pay you the five hundred he owes if you'll help us find him."

Sadie's blond eyebrows went up. "Sounds like my kinda deal." She had a curvy figure, but she was dressed in sweats and a T-shirt. Ben supposed she showed off her body enough at the strip club.

Sadie opened the door and stepped back so they could walk in. "You kids go to your room and play. Mama's got company."

The kids—a dark-haired, mixed-heritage boy about five, and a little blonde girl about six—scrambled off down the hall.

"You want some iced tea or something?"

He started to say no.

"I'd love some," Claire said, nudging him in the ribs.

Sadie smiled. "I've got some made. Kitchen's right this way."

Claire threw him a look as she walked past, letting Sadie lead her into the kitchen. *Nice move,* he thought. Being friendly and forming a connection wasn't a bad idea. Maybe Claire would be an asset after all.

By the time Sadie returned to the living room, she

was smoking a cigarette and laughing. Claire handed Ben a glass of iced tea, took a drink of her own, and all of them sat down in the living room.

Ben leaned forward in an overstuffed brown chair while the women sat on the couch. "What can you tell us about Bennett?" he asked.

Sadie blew out a lungful of smoke. "Not a lot. He was kind of the strong, silent type. We met at the club. Troy was good-looking in a rough sort of way. He worked for Vector Crane as one of the operators."

"You know where he came from?" Claire asked. "Where he was born?"

"The South someplace. Every once in a while his drawl would slip out. I know he lived in Alabama for a while, but I don't think he was born there. He had a couple of brothers in Louisiana. I don't know where."

Louisiana. If Troy was going home the way Tracy Ferber had believed, he might be headed to Louisiana.

"How'd he get along with the kids?" Ben asked, watching Sadie closely.

She took a deep drag, blew out a stream of smoke. "Okay, when he was sober. He was mean when he got drunk. I think it bothered him that Billy was a mixed-blood kid, but mostly he ignored them."

"How about you? He treat you okay?"

Sadie shrugged her shoulders. "Troy knocked me around a couple of times when he'd been drinking. Once in a while he popped off how men were superior to women. He never hit the kids, but I think they were glad when he left."

Ben exchanged a glance with Claire. He could read the worry on her face. He was just beginning to understand how much she cared about his son. It touched him unexpectedly. Having a child made him see life in a way he hadn't since the day he'd found Laura in bed with another man.

He listened as Claire asked about Sadie's kids, then Claire told her about Sam and that he was missing. Ben didn't know his son, but Claire did. Hearing her say what a good kid he was, how smart and loyal, gave him a picture of the child he had fathered.

He fought down a wave of fury at the man who had taken him.

Ben focused his attention on the blonde woman across from him. "Is there anyone else in Vegas we could talk to, Sadie? Someone who might know where Troy could have gone?"

She took a drink of her tea. "There was a guy he worked with, but he's not here anymore. Eddie Jeffries. I heard Eddie quit his job about the same time Troy did. I think they went down to L.A. together."

The trail led back to L.A. Maybe they'd get lucky this time.

Ben stood up from his chair. Pulling his silver money clip out of his pocket, he peeled off five hundred-dollar bills. "You've been a big help, Sadie." He handed her the money. "Thanks."

"I hope you find the prick."

Ben gave her one of his business cards. "If you think of anything that might help, give me a call."

Sadie walked them to the door. "There is one thing."

Ben stopped and turned. "What's that?"

"I don't think Bennett was really Troy's last name."

Ben nodded. "Yeah, well, that's pretty much what I figured." From what Sol had said, Troy Bennett had been born full grown, just another alias to be discarded.

Claire leaned over and hugged the buxom blonde. "Thank you, Sadie. We're both so worried. We really appreciate your help." It was clear Claire felt a deep sense of responsibility for Sam's disappearance. The pain she suffered was almost palpable.

And yet he couldn't help thinking that some of it was deserved. If she had come to him when Laura had first given her his name, or even after Laura got sick, none of this would have happened.

Sadie looked at Ben. "Troy's bad about holding grudges. Once you've pissed him off, he can't seem to let it go. But I don't think he'd hurt your boy. At least not when he's sober."

Ben's jaw hardened. Troy Bennett had better not hurt his son. If he did, he wouldn't have to worry about going to prison.

He would be dead.

Claire was exhausted by the time the plane landed back in Santa Monica and they started the drive to her apartment. It was late but the trip had been worth it.

"Let's get something to eat," Ben said, spotting a row of fast-food restaurants up ahead. "McDonald's all right?"

"At this point anything is good." She rarely ate fast food, but she was starving. They ordered from the drive-through, then sat in the parking lot to eat so the food wouldn't get cold.

"I'm mostly a steak-and-potatoes guy," Ben said as he unwrapped his burger. "I cook for myself at home. Mostly steaks or chops on the grill and salad. It's not gourmet, but it's healthier than this stuff." He took a big bite, talked around it. "On the other hand, sometimes you just can't beat a Big Mac."

Claire smiled. She had ordered a chicken sandwich.

She wished it didn't taste so good. "You're from Pittsburgh. How did you get to Houston?"

"SEAL buddy. Houston was his hometown. He talked me into giving it a try, then a couple years later, moved away."

"I know you don't have a wife or family."

"I'm not the family type—or at least I wasn't. What about you? You born in L.A.?"

"I'm from upstate New York. White Plains. I did social work there for a couple of years after I graduated from college, but my family still lives there. I wanted to be a little more independent, get out on my own."

"Brothers and sisters?"

"No, just me. My parents and I are still pretty close. I talk to my mom every week, but right now they're out of the country." She smiled. "Mediterranean cruise. It's a lifelong dream."

"Sounds nice."

"They're crazy about each other."

He glanced away, and she wondered if it bothered him to talk about family, since he didn't have one.

"So you like L.A?" he asked.

She shrugged. "It's okay. I don't think I want to live here forever." She took another bite of her sandwich, enjoying the taste of real mayonnaise, a treat she rarely allowed herself. She was reaching for her Diet Coke when Ben's iPhone started ringing.

He dug it out of his pocket and pressed it against his ear. "Slocum." He nodded as if the guy on the other end could see, turned toward Claire. "O-positive," he said, looking relieved.

Claire felt a shot of that same relief. The lab was calling. It wasn't Sam's blood.

"How long till you get the DNA?" A moment passed

and Ben nodded. "I appreciate the extra effort. Call me if you get a match." Ben hung up and stuck the phone back into the pocket of his jeans. "One of the guys at the lab was a friend of Brodie's. He worked late, since a child was involved and he owed Brodie a favor. Be a couple more days for the DNA. They'll run it through the system, see what turns up."

"But the blood wasn't Sam's."

"No."

"If Troy's never been arrested, he won't be in the system."

"You're right. There's a chance they won't find him. We need to talk to this guy Jeffries, see if he can give us any new information."

They continued on to her apartment, Claire finishing her sandwich along the way. It was after midnight and she was bone-tired when they walked in the door. Ben didn't seem to notice. The man had boundless energy. Or maybe it was just concern for his son.

Taking his laptop out of his black canvas duffel, he went to work setting the computer up on the kitchen table. As she watched him, Claire unfastened the gold clip at the nape of her neck and shook her head, letting her hair fall free. She dragged a hand through the heavy dark strands.

"I'm going to take a shower," she said. "Let me know if you find something."

Ben looked up and those sexy blue eyes ran over her, took in her loosened hair, the shape of her breasts. "I don't suppose you want company?"

Heat slid through her, desire hot and sharp. She could tell by the way he was looking at her that he wasn't entirely kidding.

"We're working together, Ben. That's all."

"Yeah, I know." His gaze swung away from her. He finished plugging in his laptop, sat down and started typing on the keyboard.

Claire forced her legs to move toward the bedroom. She hadn't had sex since she and Michael had ended their relationship. Michael Sullivan was a well-known investigative journalist and was gone so much it was a stretch to call it more than a three-year affair.

When Michael had taken a five-month assignment in South America, Claire made the decision to end things between them.

"This isn't working, Michael," she had said. "I care for you very much, but I want more than you can give me. We both know the time just isn't right."

"I just need to get my career a little more established. Give me a few more months. I love you, Claire."

But she'd heard the words too many times. "Love isn't always enough, Michael."

He had left the next day. He'd been in touch off and on, but the calls came more and more rarely. Still, he always said he loved her and that sooner or later, they would find a way to make it work.

Claire was more realistic. Michael was a great friend, but their relationship had never been one of grand passion. At least not for her.

She had never looked at Michael the way she'd looked at Ben Slocum that morning. And Michael had never looked at her the way Ben had looked at her just now.

She had wondered if Ben found her attractive. Now she knew for sure. But she was smart enough to recognize lust when she felt it. It wasn't a feeling she'd experienced often, and definitely not something she planned to act on.

Still, as she stripped off her clothes and slipped beneath the hot wet spray, her breasts felt sensitive. Faint arousal throbbed between her legs. Claire thought of Ben and wondered what it would be like to make love with a virile, hot-blooded male like him.

It wasn't going to happen. Sam came first.

The boy's sweet, smiling face popped into her head and her heart pinched. She should have pressed harder for custody, should have found a way to keep him with her. She should have told him how much he meant to her. She had failed him so badly.

Dear God, she prayed, *keep him safe till I can bring him home.*

Seven

Eddie Jeffries was in jail. Early the next morning, Ben put Sol to work trying to locate the guy, and an hour ago he'd struck pay dirt. Though Sol was still working on information on Bridger/Bennett, he'd found Melvin Edward Jeffries in the Santa Clarita Sheriff's Station jail. Arrested for drunk driving—third offense.

"Santa Clarita's less than an hour away," Claire said excitedly as Ben used the inmate locator on the website to verify Jeffries hadn't been moved to another prison.

Finding Jeffries still there, he checked out the visitor information. "Visiting hours 10:00 a.m. to 2:00 p.m. Plenty of time. You might not be able to go in with me— only one adult per visit. But I'm a P.I., and sometimes they'll bend the rules a little if there's a good reason."

"I'd like to give it a try. If I can't get in, I'll wait in the car."

He helped her clear the empty orange-juice glasses and the plates that had held the bagels and cream cheese she had made them for breakfast.

Ben raised his coffee mug and downed the last few drops. "Let's get going."

Claire grabbed her purse and they started for the door when his cell phone rang. He recognized the number. "Brodie," he said to Claire.

"What have you got?" he said into the phone.

"Got a lead on a kid, blue-eyed, black-haired, about nine or ten," Ty said. "He's working for an ex-con named Rueben Gonzales, got him making drug deliveries. Word is he's a fairly new addition to Gonzales's crew."

Ben's adrenaline started pumping, his pulse pounding. "How do we get to him?"

"I've set up a meet, told him the kid was worth a couple of grand if he's the one we're looking for. I figured you'd be willing to pay if it's him."

"I'll pay whatever it takes." In the underworld, a runaway like Sam could be a valuable commodity—depending what Gonzales had in mind for him. His hand unconsciously fisted. "What time's the meet?"

"Noon. A bar called La Fiesta, five thousand block of Whittier Boulevard, east of the I-5. I'll meet you there."

Ben closed the phone, looked up to see Claire's eyes locked on his face. "Is it… Is it Sam?"

"I won't know till we get a look at him. Guy named Gonzales is using him as a drug mule."

Her legs seemed to give way, and she sat down hard in one of the kitchen chairs. "Oh, my God, Ben."

"Take it easy. We don't know if anything bad has happened to him. Hell, we don't know for sure it's him."

She swallowed, shook her head. "If he's… If he's been hurt or…or abused…I'll never forgive myself." She started crying, her long hair falling forward around her face.

Ben eased her up out of the chair and turned her into his arms. Her body shook as she sobbed against his shoulder. "Take it easy, baby. There's no use crying until we know what's going on."

She hung on a moment more, took a shuddering breath and moved away, her green eyes glistening with tears. "I should have come to you. I should have found out for myself what you were like."

He reached out and wiped a tear from her cheek. "So now you're sure I'm a good guy?"

Claire's chin went up as he had known it would. "Well, so far you've been great, but technically it's too soon to make a definitive evaluation."

He felt the rare pull of a grin he didn't release. "Look, you thought you were doing what was best for Sam. That means a lot to me. You may not have made the right call, but you cared enough to come to Texas to find me. You're doing everything you can to help me find Sam."

She wiped away the last of the dampness on her cheeks. "I thought he would wait, give me a chance to work things out." She swallowed. "I thought, in time, the judge would reconsider and grant me custody. I wanted that, Ben. I wanted that so much. I should have told him, let him know how much I cared."

Her lips were trembling. Worry lines marred her forehead. She was different from most of the women he knew, stronger, more concerned. He wanted to haul her back into his arms and kiss her. Hell, he wanted to do a lot more than that. But Claire deserved more than the lust he felt whenever he looked at her.

"I've got to get going. I want to take a look around, check the layout. With people like these you can't be too careful."

"I'm going with you. If it's Sam, he'll need me."

"Not this time, Claire. I can't protect you and Sam both."

He went into the bedroom to retrieve his Nighthawk .45, pulled it out of its holster, checked to be sure the clip was full, then shoved the magazine back in. Sliding the pistol back into his holster, he clipped it to his waistband behind his back beneath his black T-shirt.

He dug into his duffel and took out the envelope filled with cash he had brought from the safe in his house. Leaving two thousand in the envelope, he left the rest of the cash in the bag. He wasn't a rich man, but he wasn't poor, either. After he'd left the SEALs, the skills he'd acquired had earned him big money, most of which he had stashed away. He made a good living as a P.I., and he'd saved a lot of that, too.

He returned to the living room and found Claire pacing.

"I can't just sit here and do nothing." She followed him to the door. "Take me with you."

She was standing in the entry, her eyes full of worry, slender and elegant, so damned pretty. He paused in front of her, bent his head and kissed her, just a soft melding of lips. "Not this time, angel."

Ben forced himself to walk away.

La Fiesta was a pink stucco building in an area at the west end of East L.A. Ben was glad the meet wasn't farther into the neighborhood. Here, only half the signs were in Spanish. Farther along the street, there was no English at all.

He drove around the block, wishing he wasn't in a damned-near-new, highly jackable, bright red Honda

Accord, wishing he wasn't garnering looks from the sullen young toughs loitering on the street corners.

He spotted another new car pulling up in front of him a little ways from the bar, a black Chevy Silverado with chrome wheels and wide tires. Tyler Brodie spotted Ben, stepped down from the cab and walked over.

"Nice ride," Ben said. Ty was wearing the same scuffed cowboy boots and jeans Ben remembered, but his baseball cap was dark blue today with a gold Lakers emblem on the front.

"I just bought it. I was driving a little Toyota Tundra, same red as what you're driving. It drew too damned much attention."

Ben's mouth edged up. "Yeah, I'm sure no one notices those fancy chrome wheels."

Ty grinned.

Ben tipped his head toward the Accord. "This is Claire's car."

Brodie shoved his bill cap back, eyed the car with interest. "A red-car woman? I wouldn't have figured."

Ben couldn't stop a smile. "I guess you never know." He was starting to like Tyler Brodie. He might have a youthful, pretty-boy face, but he took his work seriously. "You think they're here?"

"Some of them will be. Not Gonzales. He'll be waiting for word we're here first." Brodie caught a glimpse of what could only be a weapon in Ben's waistband beneath his black T-shirt.

"Nighthawk .45," Ben told him.

Brodie opened the flowered sport shirt he was wearing, exposing the shoulder harness underneath. "Beretta M-9. Old habits, you know."

Standard-issue military weapon. Once a marine, always a marine. "Let's go."

Ty caught his arm. "Just one thing…I got a hunch you'd rather shoot these guys than pay them. I don't like these lowlifes any better than you do, but keep in mind this is how Johnnie and I make our living. We can do a lot more good, help more people, if we keep our information channels open."

Ben flicked a glance toward the bar, thought of the boy, thought Brodie was about half-right about taking these assholes out. "I'll try to restrain myself."

"Just so you know, Gonzales is pretty low on the food chain. He deals, but he isn't into trafficking…at least not that I know of. You got the money?"

Ben tapped the envelope stuffed into the back pocket of his jeans. "They get it if they've got my kid."

Following Brodie, he made his way in through the front door. La Fiesta was a restaurant as well as a bar and the place was busy with the lunch crowd. The smell of tortillas, meat and cheese made Ben's stomach growl. Bagels and cream cheese wasn't bacon and eggs.

Mexican pop music played in the background. Ty slowed as a beefy Hispanic with stringy black hair down to his shoulders approached them.

"This way, *amigos*."

There was no one in the bar except more of Gonzales's men. They didn't come forward to pat them down, didn't need to, since it looked like all of them were armed.

Ben's conceal carry wasn't valid in California. At the moment, he didn't care.

The others moved a little away, leaving their leader to handle the exchange.

"Señor Brodie. I see you have brought your friend." Rueben Gonzales was lean and hard, his skin as brown as old oak. A scar ran from the corner of his mouth to his ear, making him look like one badass son of a bitch.

"Where's the boy?" Ty asked.

Gonzales tipped his head toward a door at the rear of the bar and an instant later, in walked a short, fat banger pushing a black-haired boy in front of him.

For several heartbeats, Ben stood frozen. Then the kid stepped into the light and looked at Ben, and he knew the boy wasn't his son.

Ty said nothing, just stood there waiting for Ben's decision. Ben kept staring at the kid. He was older than nine, maybe ten or eleven. There was a bruise on his cheek and his lip was split. He had a shiner that was turning purple. His blue eyes looked resigned and yet there was a spark of defiance there.

The fat man moved forward and tipped the kid's chin up so Ben could get a better look. The fat guy grinned. "This one—he is a virgin. He is too much trouble so you get him cheap."

Ben's stomach knotted. He looked at the kid and blind rage struck him. His jaw turned to steel and he exploded, throwing a punch that landed so hard against the fat man's jaw it sent him flying backward over the bar. Beer glasses slid the length of the counter and catapulted into the air. A woman screamed as the guy crashed to the floor, breaking more glasses and heavy bottles of booze, groaning but not getting up.

Ben heard the unmistakable ratcheting of pistol slides. When he turned, he saw four semi-autos pointed in his direction. Ty Brodie pointed his M-9 at Gonzales.

"The price just went to twenty-five hundred," Gonzales said calmly.

Ben pulled the envelope out of his pocket and tossed it on the table. "Two thousand. That's all I brought. I'll take the kid off your hands and he won't give you any more trouble."

Gonzales gestured to his men, who put away their weapons. Ty reholstered his pistol. Gonzales picked up the envelope, opened it and thumbed through the hundred-dollar bills. "This is your lucky day, *amigo*. Take the boy and go."

The kid didn't resist when Ben put a hand on his shoulder and guided him out of the bar, wove through the restaurant, then outside to the Honda Accord. Ty walked a few feet behind him.

"I'm glad you got your son back," Brodie said once they were back to their vehicles. "For a minute there it was kind of touch-and-go."

"He's not my son."

Ty's dark brown eyebrows went up as Ben opened the door and settled the boy in the passenger seat, clicked the seat belt into place across his chest. "He's not mine, but he's someone's. I couldn't just leave him there. I'll take him to Claire. She'll know how to handle it."

Brodie clapped Ben on the back. "I'll keep looking. I'll let you know if anything turns up."

"Thanks. You're a good man, Brodie. You can watch my back anytime."

"Same here." Ty headed for his pickup, and Ben slid behind the wheel and started the engine, glad to be leaving the area.

"What's your name?" he asked the boy as he drove up onto the freeway, heading back to Santa Monica.

"Ryan." The kid's battered features turned hard. "I won't let you hurt me. I'll run away as soon as I get the chance."

"No one's going to hurt you, son. I'm going to get you home."

"I don't have a home."

Ben's gaze swung back to the boy. "No mother or father? No relatives?"

The kid didn't answer. Which meant there was someone. Just not someone he wanted to go back to.

"I've got a friend," Ben said. "She can help you find a place, people you can trust to take care of you."

The kid's chin cocked up. "Why should I believe you?"

"Because I'm telling you the truth." Ben pulled out his P.I. badge and tossed it into the boy's lap. "I'm looking for my own son. His name is Sam. You haven't seen him, have you? Black hair like yours? Eyes more like mine." He fixed one of his glacial stares on the boy. Ryan's eyes were a much darker blue than his own.

The boy shook his head. "There were other kids around, but none with eyes like yours."

"Where you from?"

The kid didn't answer.

"That bad, huh?"

"If they make me go back, I'll just run away again."

Ben wasn't sure what the authorities would do, but if the boy's home life was really that bad, he figured they would put him in foster care.

"When you talk to them, tell them the truth. Tell them what it was like there. Don't spare the details. I don't think they'll make you go back if it's that bad. I think they'll find you a better place to live."

The kid looked up at him with so much hope in his eyes Ben's chest clamped down. "You really think they'll help me?"

"Yeah, I do." Ben's gaze strayed from the road back to the boy. He wondered what Claire would say when she saw he'd brought the wrong kid home.

* * *

"Get in the goddamn truck!"

Sam tried not to cringe at the vicious look on Troy's face. "There's a law against drunk driving," he said.

"I don't give a shit." Troy reached over and cuffed his head. "Do as I say. Get in the truck before I kick your skinny little ass."

Troy's black Lab moved forward, his tail between his legs. Pepper whined and pressed against Sam's leg. Sam moved far enough away that Troy couldn't reach them. "Come on, Pep, we gotta get going."

Pepper was Troy's dog but sometimes Troy was mean to him, just like he was to Sam. He and Pep were friends. The black Lab stuck by him no matter what. Troy wasn't usually too bad a guy, except when he got drunk. When he drank, he got crazy mean. Sam was afraid of him then, and Pepper was, too. Lately he had been that way a lot.

Sam climbed into the old white beat-up Chevy, waited for the dog to jump in, then slammed the door. He buckled his seat belt like his mom had taught him, even though Troy never used his.

The engine roared to life and the truck pulled out of the gravel lot in front of The Roadhouse, spitting up dirt as the car fishtailed back onto the highway. Troy had been in there drinking beer for at least two hours while Sam and Pepper waited outside.

Before that, they'd been staying with a lady Troy knew. She was nice. She baked them a cake and let Pepper sleep with him on the bed in her son's old room. Then she got mad at Troy for getting drunk and told him they had to leave.

Sam almost wished he'd taken Pep and run off while Troy was in The Roadhouse, maybe hitched a ride with someone. But his mom was dead, and he didn't have anywhere to go.

Sam squeezed his eyes shut as he thought of his mother lying there sick in her hospital bed. He remembered the day she died, how Claire had taken him home with her, how she had let him live with her for a while.

She'd said she would help him. She and his mom were friends and he had liked her a lot. He wanted to live with her more than anything, but she didn't want him.

Not really. She had let them put him in some crummy house where the people believed their own kids were perfect and never did anything wrong. Kenny was older and he thought he was a tough guy. But Sam was smarter, and he wouldn't let Kenny push him around.

Kenny was a jerk and his sister was a tattletale, always making up stories that weren't true. He liked Suzy and Tim, but they were afraid of Kenny and the Robersons, and they would never stick up for him or even for themselves. They would just stand there and look frightened.

He didn't want to stay in a place like that. He wanted his mom, but she was dead. He wanted to be with Claire, but she had forgotten about him.

His throat ached. He closed his eyes so Troy couldn't tell he was trying not to cry. Pepper whined and nudged him, curled up against his side.

At least he had Pep.

The only friend in the world he could trust.

Eight

❧❧❧

To keep herself busy and not wonder if Ben would find Sam in East L.A., Claire went out to the carport and opened her storage locker. She had kept a box of Laura's things, stuff Claire had put away for Sam when he got older.

If she was right and the boy Ty found wasn't Sam, they would need to continue their search. She had gone through the box right after Sam disappeared, looking for photos to give the police. Aside from pictures of Sam and Troy Bridger, she hadn't found anything helpful among Laura's possessions, but there was always a chance she had missed something.

Carrying the cardboard box into the living room, Claire set it down on the coffee table in front of the sofa, retrieved a pair of scissors, cut the packing tape and opened the box.

Sam's baby clothes sat on top of a pottery plate with his handprint that Sam had made for his mom in kindergarten, and some crayon drawings he'd made that Laura had kept on the refrigerator.

Beneath them, photo albums. The one with photos of Bridger and the latest picture of Sam—photos she had given the police—Claire picked up and flipped open.

Most of the pictures had been taken with the inexpensive digital camera Laura carried when she took her son to the zoo or the time she and Claire had taken him to Disneyland last year for his birthday.

They were in order front to back, oldest to newest. She flipped to the back, to the most recent shots, including a few Claire had taken: Sam hamming it up at Christmas, Laura and Sam having Easter dinner at Claire's apartment.

She ran her finger over that one and thought of her friend. In the pictures Laura looked so normal. They didn't show the times she had drunk too much and passed out on the couch, the times she had forgotten to pick up Sam after his Little League baseball game.

They showed the Laura that was smart and funny and a very good friend.

Claire turned the page, realized two were stuck together and pulled them apart. She froze. There was a photo of Laura with Troy and two men, a picture she had never seen. She set the album down and ran into her bedroom, went over to her desk and grabbed a magnifying glass out of the top drawer.

Back in the living room, she studied the photo more closely and saw that the two men looked a lot like Troy. Enough like him, in fact, to be the brothers Sadie had mentioned. Laura hadn't said anything about the visit when she and Troy had been living together, but the resemblance and the men's ages made it hard to mistake the relationship.

She pulled the four-by-six glossy off the page and examined the men's features. Same height, around six feet; same solid, no-fat build; same dark hair, same fair skin, same face shape and eyes. Troy's were blue, she remembered, his best feature.

It was what they were wearing that was even more interesting—identical drab green camouflage T-shirts. On the front was a fist and underneath the numbers 33/6. She didn't know what the sign and numbers meant, but she had a feeling it was important.

She set the photo aside and continued through the album but found nothing more.

She closed the box and set the picture on the coffee table and looked at the clock. More than two hours had passed. Where was Ben?

Thinking of him reminded her of the brief kiss before he had left. She hadn't expected it. And as much as she tried, she couldn't forget it.

Male lips that should have been cold and hard but were warm and softer than she ever would have guessed. The way they sank into hers, the way her stomach flipped beneath her ribs.

It hadn't meant anything. Ben was just trying to distract her because she was so upset over Sam. Still, the heat of his mouth was a memory seared into her brain, and every time she remembered his kiss, a jolt of desire burned through her.

Dear Lord, it was insane. She hardly knew the man. One thing she was sure of—sex meant about as much to Ben Slocum as brushing his teeth. His after-wedding roll in the hay had clearly been a one-night stand. Which she would guess was pretty much Ben's modus operandi.

As much as she'd like to find out what sex would be like with a man she was so strongly attracted to, she didn't want to be tossed aside like an old sneaker the next morning.

At the sound of the doorbell, she raced for the door, unlocked it and pulled it open. For an instant her heart soared. Just as fast, her high hopes plunged. The boy on her doorstep wasn't Sam.

"This is Ryan," Ben said. "It's a long story. We need to find a way to help him."

Claire called the authorities as soon as she got Ryan's battered face cleaned up with antiseptic, and the boy stuffed full of the extralarge double-cheese pepperoni pizza Ben ordered from Rusty's. She was certainly getting more than her share of fast food these days.

While Ben and the boy finished off the pizza, Claire talked to a friend named Mary Wilson who worked at the Department of Children and Family Services. She told Mary how Ben Slocum, a P.I. from Texas, had stumbled upon a ten-year-old boy named Ryan Lynn who was a runaway.

According to Ben, Ryan's home life was so bad the boy would rather wander the streets doing odd jobs for criminals than stay in the place he lived.

Mary arranged to meet her, Ben and Ryan two hours later at the branch where Mary worked. There, the boy could be medically examined, and Social Services would make arrangements for him to be placed in a care facility until his situation could be investigated.

They would try to locate his family and make an evaluation, find out what was going on that would drive a ten-year-old kid out onto the streets.

Claire felt sorry for the boy, but Mary was good at her job, and she would fight for Ryan. And Claire thought that after his experiences fending for himself, he would do his best to get along in his foster home.

"This is all going to work out, Ryan," she said as they drove toward their destination. "There are people who care about kids like you. They'll do their best to find a place you'll be happy."

Ryan's eyes welled, but he didn't cry. Aside from his black hair and blue eyes, he didn't look a thing like Ben. Different nose, different mouth, different jaw. Still, Ben had paid two thousand dollars to bring the boy to safety.

It looked more and more as if Laura had been wrong. That Ben *would* make the kind of father Sam deserved.

Claire tried not to think how she had failed the child. She tried to ignore the ache in her chest when she thought of what might be happening to him. Instead, she focused on Ryan, introducing him to Mary and getting him settled.

Mary put an arm around the boy's thin shoulders. "We're going to take very good care of you, Ryan." A slight blonde woman in her early forties, Mary seemed to have a special way with kids. "I'm going to make sure of that myself."

Ryan did start to cry then, and Mary pulled him into a hug. "It's all right, sweetheart. Everything's going to be okay."

When the scene came to a close, Ben handed Ryan one of his business cards. "My numbers are all there. If you need anything, I want you to call, okay?"

Ryan nodded, looking up at Ben as if he were his personal savior. Which in a way he was. "Thanks."

Ben ruffled his hair. "Take care of yourself," he said a little gruffly. "You're getting another chance. Don't be afraid to take it."

After final farewells, they left the facility, and Ben

drove Claire home, neither of them saying much until they got the car parked and walked back inside.

Claire tossed her purse on the kitchen table. "I guess the men who hurt Ryan are going to get away with it."

"Ryan told me he'd never seen Gonzales before the meet. He didn't know the names of the guys who were working him on the street, and he was with them by choice. There's not much chance of tracking them down. And the truth is the kid is better off just getting on with his life."

She shook her head. "Doesn't seem right, though."

"There are a lot of bad people out there, Claire. Ryan's getting a second chance. A lot of kids don't." He fell silent, and she knew he was thinking of Sam, wondering if his boy was being beaten and abused.

"Oh!" Remembering the photo album, Claire hurried into the living room. "I found something while you were gone. A picture. I think it's Troy and his brothers."

"Where'd you find it?"

"I went back through Claire's things, took another look at the album where I'd found Troy's photo. I thought I might have missed something, and I had." Claire picked the photo up off the coffee table, walked back and handed it to Ben.

"You might make a P.I. yet," he said, his expression full of approval.

Claire just smiled.

Ben looked down at the photograph Claire had found. "I think you're right. These guys are brothers."

"They look a lot alike, don't they?"

He tapped the photo against his hand. "Laura never mentioned meeting them?"

"She was in a bad place when she was living with Troy. She was drinking heavily again. She knew I didn't like him. I think that's why she never said anything about the brothers' visit. She broke up with him right after."

He pointed at the photo. "You see what they're wearing?"

"Camouflage. I don't know what the emblem means."

"The fist is a white-supremacy symbol. Remember Sadie saying something about Troy not liking Billy's mixed-blood heritage?"

"That's right! And she said he thought men were superior to women."

Ben shrugged. "Well, you can't fault him on that one."

When Claire's eyes narrowed, Ben laughed.

Claire's eyebrows went up. "You're making another joke. I can't believe it."

Ben waved the photo. "Let's see if we can figure out what the 33/6 means."

It only took a couple of clicks on Google to find an article written by an intelligence operator with Homeland Security that gave them the answer.

"Says here it's a reference to the Ku Klux Klan. The eleventh letter of the alphabet is K. Three times eleven is thirty-three."

Claire rubbed her arms as if she felt a chill. "Does it say what the six means?"

Ben went back to reading. "The first era of the Klan started after the Civil War. The sixth era began in 1996. The six denotes the rebirth of the Klan."

"The Ku Klux Klan. If Troy's heading back to meet his brothers and they're white supremacists…"

"Then we've got to find Sam and get him the hell out of there." He stood up from the computer. "We need to talk to Eddie Jeffries. It's too late to see him tonight, but we can be there when visiting hours start at 10:00 a.m. tomorrow."

Ben set the photo next to the computer and turned to Claire. "Just so you know. I really liked kissing you."

Her head came up. "You...you did?"

"I was kind of hoping I wouldn't."

She moistened her lips, making him remember how sweet those full lips tasted, making him want to kiss her again. Desire curled through him and heat slid into his groin.

"We don't...don't have time for that kind of thing."

"I know." But he couldn't resist moving toward her, catching her shoulders, bending his head and settling his mouth over hers. He forced himself not to linger. Just sank in and tasted. Felt the rush of heat. Released her. "Good night, Claire."

She reached up and touched her lips. "Good night, Ben."

Claire went in to shower before she went to bed. She told herself not to think of the kiss, told herself it was just a simple good-night. But it wasn't.

Ben Slocum wanted her. There was heat in the eyes that had locked with hers the instant before their lips met, fire in the way his mouth took possession of hers. For an instant, the air seemed to crackle with sexual tension.

She couldn't let it happen. She meant nothing to Ben, just another conquest, someone to satisfy his appetites while he was searching for his son.

She wasn't a fool to be used and discarded. She might desire Ben, but she wasn't ruled by her passions, not like some women. She was a rational, thinking woman who made rational, thinking decisions.

As she climbed into bed and settled beneath the covers, she vowed to have a talk with him in the morning, set some boundaries, tell him it was time he stopped calling her *angel*. Time he took a big step back.

The doorbell rang, putting an end to her thoughts. Trying to imagine who it could be at eleven o'clock at night, Claire grabbed her robe, slipped it on and went into the living room. Through the peephole in the front door, she recognized a familiar face.

Michael? She opened the door.

"Hello, Claire." Michael Sullivan was tall, about the same height as Ben, wide-shouldered but spare, not an ounce of fat on his trim athletic body. With his dark brown hair and brown eyes, he was handsome.

"I know it's late," he said, "but I just flew back to town for a week, and I had to see you. I've really missed you, Claire." Michael pulled her into an embrace and tried to kiss her, but Claire turned her face away. "What's the matter? Aren't you glad to see me?"

Just then Ben appeared. He had pulled on his jeans, but his feet were bare and so was his magnificent chest. Claire felt a little jolt in the pit of her stomach.

"I don't think we've met," Ben said, striding forward, those pale eyes fixed on Michael's face. Michael's nostrils flared. The testosterone in the room was as thick as heavy perfume.

Claire tried to smile. "Ben Slocum, this is Michael Sullivan." She positioned herself between the two men. "Michael, Ben is Sam Thompson's father."

"Sam Slocum," Ben corrected.

Claire kept the smile on her face but it wasn't easy. "You remember my friend Laura?"

Michael ignored her, his brown eyes running over

Ben's naked torso. They stood nearly eye to eye. "What's he doing here?"

"Sam's missing," Claire said. "Ben and I are working together to find him."

Michael's gaze traveled over her silk robe, down her bare legs, to the red polish on her toes, and his lips curled back. "Looks like you're doing a lot more than just working."

Before she could stop him, Ben had a handful of Michael's striped dress shirt. "Whatever she's doing, it's none of your business."

Claire thought of all those muscles and that he was a man trained to kill. "Ben, please…"

A heartbeat passed. He let go of Michael's shirt but didn't back away.

"Michael's an old friend," Claire said, hoping to defuse the situation.

"More than friends," Michael corrected, pinning her with a glare. "At least we were."

She turned away from him. "If you wouldn't mind, Ben, I'd like to speak to Michael alone."

Ben's gaze remained locked on Michael's face. Finally, he shrugged, but the muscles across his shoulders remained tense. "If you need me, you know where I am." Padding back down the hall to his room, he closed the door.

"You notice he's sleeping in the guest room," Claire said as Michael's dark gaze followed him, "if it's any of your business, which it no longer is."

"I've been away, Claire, but that doesn't change the way I feel. I love you. I always have."

"I thought we'd talked this out, that we both understood each other's feelings."

"You said the time wasn't right. I'm here to tell you

that in a few more weeks it will be. I have to go back to Colombia to finish my assignment, but after that, I'll be back in L.A. We can set a date, get married, start living our lives together."

Claire just shook her head. "What we had was good, Michael, but it's over. I'm moving forward with my life. You should do the same."

Michael reached for her, drew her into his arms. "I need you, Claire." The door opened and Ben walked back into the living room.

"Time to go, friend. Claire needs her sleep. She's got important things to do."

Michael's jaw tightened but he backed away. "It isn't over, Claire. I'll talk to you again when I get back from Colombia." Turning, he walked out of the apartment and closed the front door.

"Your boyfriend, I take it."

Claire turned to face him. "Ex-boyfriend."

"For how long?"

"Five months."

"He wants you back. That what you want?"

"No."

"Good." Claire gasped as he hauled her into his arms and his mouth crushed down over hers in a deep, hungry kiss.

God, she tasted like heaven. Petal-soft lips, skin damp from the shower and smooth as silk. He'd known he wanted her. Until he saw her with Sullivan, he hadn't known how much.

His mouth moved hotly over hers, coaxing, possessing. She didn't push him away, but he could feel her reluctance. He didn't blame her. This wasn't part of the plan. Couldn't be.

Still, when her soft lips parted, he took advantage, his tongue sweeping in, her nipples beading beneath the silk robe, pressing into his bare chest. His arousal strengthened and he went hard beneath the fly of his jeans.

She tasted so good he kept on kissing her, and Claire kissed him back. She wasn't immune to him. He was pretty sure she'd been without a man since Sullivan left five months ago. She had needs, and Ben knew exactly how to satisfy those needs.

Claire's tongue slid over his. She leaned into him, pressed herself against his erection. Then she tore free.

Her palms trembled where they rested against his chest. "I'm not…not doing this, Ben. I can't. I don't do one-night stands, and we both know that's exactly what this would be."

His eyes ran over her, took in her rapid breathing, the hard peaks beneath her robe. "I don't think I could get my fill of you in just one night."

He didn't usually say things like that. It sounded too much like a commitment, but it was true. Claire Chastain intrigued him. And she really turned him on.

"That isn't the point and you know it. Sleeping with me would mean nothing to you, and once you're ready to move on, our working relationship would be compromised."

She was partly right. Their working relationship might suffer and he didn't want that to happen. He had to think of Sam.

"Look, angel, it was only a kiss. You don't have to get all bent out of shape about it."

"Stop calling me that. You've probably used that on a hundred different women."

"Hardly, sweetcakes." Her hackles went up, and he almost smiled. "Somehow *angel* just seemed to fit."

"Why?"

"Because there's a side of you that's still naive. I saw it the first time I met you. For one thing, just like you said, you aren't the type for a one-night stand."

"No, I'm not."

"All right. So now that you've made your feelings clear, why don't we go to bed?"

"What?"

He laughed. It happened so rarely it surprised him. "I meant in our own rooms."

Her face colored. "Oh. Yes…well, all right, then." She glanced at her bare feet. "Good night." She started for her bedroom, kept walking and didn't look back.

"Good night, Claire," he called after her softly. He didn't tell her that taking her to bed would mean more to him than just sex because he wasn't sure it would.

He had a hunch, though.

And since those kinds of emotions weren't things he wanted to feel, Ben hoped his hunch was wrong.

Claire couldn't sleep. She kept feeling the heat of Ben's mouth over hers, the glide of his tongue, the way he took complete control. Not like Michael. Michael's kisses were warm and sweet, not hot and erotic. She remembered how the muscles on Ben's chest had rubbed against her, how her nipples had begun to ache and distend. She couldn't forget the powerful erection that told her how much he wanted her.

Made her want him.

She wasn't really familiar with that side of her nature, but her response to Ben had proven it was there.

She was a woman, more passionate than she would have guessed.

Dear God, how was she going to handle being with him day after day?

Maybe he would back off as she had insisted. Maybe he would realize that she was right and a night of passion wasn't worth the price. Not when they were both trying so hard to find Sam. Ben was fiercely determined and so was she. She had promised Laura. And she had promised Sam.

Which meant she had to resist her unwelcome attraction to Ben.

As the hours crept past, her thoughts swung from the man down the hall to the boy he'd brought home with him. She kept seeing poor Ryan's battered face. Then it would turn into Sam's. She prayed that wherever he was, Sam wasn't being hurt or abused. She was terrified for him, but the clues were mounting, giving her hope.

Tomorrow they would talk to Eddie Jeffries. Maybe Jeffries could tell them something useful.

Claire prayed it would be so.

Nine

The weather changed, turning overcast and cold. A stiff desert wind blew into the L.A. basin, whipping papers along the freeway as Ben drove Claire's car north. Fortunately, the rush-hour traffic was over and wouldn't start again till later in the day. Ben made it from the apartment to the Magic Mountain Parkway turnoff in less than fifty minutes.

Keeping her distance all morning, Claire had been quiet most of the way. Now as Ben pulled into the parking lot of the tile-roofed, beige stucco sheriff's station and turned off the engine, her gaze swung to his.

"I hope he knows something."

"If he does, I promise you we'll find out what it is." Her eyes widened, and he knew she hadn't missed the threat in his voice. "You ready?" he asked.

Claire nodded. His cell phone rang as they got out of the car. It was the DNA testing lab where he'd left the foam cup and the blood sample from Bridger's sink.

"No match on Bridger's DNA," he told Claire when the call came to an end.

"I guess that's good news and bad. At least he isn't a criminal."

"Or at least not one who's ever been caught." Both of them fell silent. When they reached the door, Claire held up crossed fingers. They needed a lead. Ben opened the door, held it for Claire, and they walked inside.

People milled around the visitor waiting area; a pair of sheriff's deputies walked past.

"Give me a minute," Ben said. Claire nodded, and he went over to talk to the officer in charge, read the name on the tag on his uniform pocket.

"Deputy Montgomery, my name's Ben Slocum. I'm a private investigator." He took out his P.I. badge and flipped it open, showing his ID. "I'd like to talk to one of your prisoners, a guy named Eddie Jeffries. It's in regard to a missing kid."

The deputy's gray eyebrows went up. He was older, seasoned, looked like a no-bullshit kind of guy. "Nothing about a kid in Jeffries's file."

"He knows the suspect, the man who may have taken him. I don't know if he was directly involved in the boy's disappearance." Ben tipped his head toward Claire. "The lady's Claire Chastain. She's the social worker. I'm the boy's father."

The deputy gave him a once-over, his expression going from assessing to sympathetic. "I got kids myself. Mine are grown. How old's your boy?"

"Nine."

"How long's he been missing?"

"Nearly two weeks."

Montgomery shoved a clipboard across the counter. "The lady'll have to show ID and you both need to sign in. Leave your cell phones and empty your pockets, then you can come on back."

"Thanks."

They took care of protocol then went into the visiting area and waited for a deputy to bring Jeffries out. From what Ben had read on the internet, there were only eleven cells in the jail but the place could hold up to forty inmates. Most were kept in the station until their court dates.

Ben looked up as the door opened and a freckle-faced man with thinning red hair stepped out. According to the deputy, Jeffries was thirty-eight years old. He sat down on the opposite side of the metal table across from Ben and Claire.

"Hello, Eddie. My name's Ben Slocum. This is Claire Chastain."

Eddie eyed them darkly. "Yeah? What do you want?"

"We want to know about a friend of yours. A guy named Troy Bridger. Or is it Troy Bennett? I think you knew him as both."

Jeffries shrugged. He was nervous but trying not to show it. "I don't know much. I know he quit his job and left town."

"You know he took my son, Sam, with him?"

Eddie's complexion went pale beneath his freckles, making them stand out. "I don't know nothin' about that."

"You sure, Eddie? Because if it turns out you knew he was planning to take the boy, you're an accessory to child abduction. That's big-time, Eddie, not a measly year in jail for drunk driving."

Eddie came up out of his chair. "I didn't know—I swear it! I knew he was mad at that bitch he used to live with. *Laura.* And some damn friend of hers. Woman convinced her to kick him out for no good reason. Troy didn't take kindly to a woman's scorn."

"He thought he was smarter," Claire pressed. "Right, Eddie? He thought he was superior to a stupid woman."

Eddie was wise enough not to answer. He just sat back down in his chair.

"You say you didn't know he took the boy," Ben said. "But you don't seem surprised."

Eddie didn't answer.

"Remember, my friend, you don't help us, the cops are going to assume you were in on it. They won't just be looking for Troy, they'll be coming here for *you*."

Eddie's eyes darted toward the deputy at the door. His hands were shaking. "Troy said something once about the kid. How he needed a father to make him a man."

Ben's stomach went cold. "So Troy could have taken him."

Eddie's expression turned wary. "You said he did."

"We think he did. We need to know where he's going, where he'd be taking the boy."

"I don't know."

"Come on, Eddie. You knew him better than most. You knew him in Vegas, came with him to L.A. Where was he going after he quit his job?"

"I told you I don't know."

Ben leaned across the table, fixed his frigid eyes on Eddie's pale face. "He was headed to Louisiana to see his brothers. Isn't that right?"

"Maybe. He was real close with them."

"What was Troy's real name?"

"Bridger."

"Not Bennett?"

"I don't know."

Ben rested his elbows on top of the table and leaned

a little farther forward. "So he was headed to Louisiana. Which road did he take?"

Eddie swallowed.

"Which road, Eddie?"

The last of the man's bravado faded. Maybe he recognized just how far Ben was willing to go to make him talk.

"He had a lady friend in Phoenix. Troy had a way with women, you know? At least at first. He'd usually mess it up. Drink too much, slap 'em around. But this one woman, she always took him back. I met her once when we were down there. She was older, maybe late forties, big-titted, redheaded broad. Troy could always count on Lyla."

"And he would have to go through Phoenix if he was headed for Louisiana," Claire said.

Eddie just hung his head. "Yeah."

Her gaze swung to Ben, then back to Eddie. "What's Lyla's last name?" she asked.

Eddie's head came up. He looked resigned. "Holden. Her name is Lyla Holden."

"You got an address?" Ben pressed.

"No. Eddie and I met up with her in some bar. Now leave me the fuck alone."

Claire's pulse was still pounding when they got back into the car. "Oh, my God, Ben, we know where he's going!"

Ben started the engine. "If Jeffries is telling the truth."

"He is. I know it."

Ben nodded. "I think so, too. He's already got his ass in a sling. He doesn't want any more trouble." As they pulled into the street, Ben stepped down hard on the gas. "Which means Troy could still be in Arizona with Sam."

"We can fly commercial. There are flights to Phoenix every couple of hours and it's cheap."

"Good, I can get a one-way ticket. If Troy's already left Phoenix and I get any kind of lead, I won't be coming back."

"We're going to follow him?"

"I am. What you do is up to you."

She cast him a sharp glance. "I'm going. Just give me time to pack my things."

"First we need a location for Lyla." When Ben pulled his cell phone out of his pocket, Claire started to tell him it wasn't safe to talk on the phone while he was driving—and it was also against the law. The look he shot her warned her not to say a word.

"I need an address, Sol. A woman named Lyla Holden. She lives in Phoenix. Bridger may be holed up at her house."

Claire couldn't hear, but Sol must have agreed to help locate the woman.

"How about Bridger? Nothing came up on facial recognition?" Ben's dark look said the answer was no. "Okay, thanks." He hung up the phone, turned in her direction. "He'll call as soon as he gets an address."

"You think he will?"

"If I had to bet, I'd say yes." Ben kept up his speed and they made it back to the apartment in record time. As soon as they walked through the front door, his cell rang again.

"I'm here," Ben said into the phone. He walked over to the notepad on the kitchen counter. "Chandler, Arizona, 4523 Armand Drive. Thanks, kid." He tore off the sheet of paper and headed for his laptop still set up on the kitchen table.

"You go pack what you need," he said. "I'll get the tickets."

"Check Southwest Airlines." Claire hurried down the hall to her bedroom. "They should have the most flights." Worried Ben would leave without her if she didn't move fast enough, she raced into the bedroom and started throwing things on the bed.

When she walked back out of the room towing her carry-on, she had enough clothes packed for a quick trip to Phoenix, or longer if necessary.

Seconds later, Ben walked out of the guest room, his black canvas duffel slung over his shoulder. "We've got a one-thirty departure. It'll be tight, but if we get going, we might be able to make it. If not, the next flight isn't till five."

"Then we better hit the road."

His mouth edged up. "Good idea."

Despite hustling and getting lucky with traffic, with the extra time it took to get Ben's pistol through security, they missed their plane.

"Dammit!" Ben turned away from the boarding gate, stalked over to the waiting area and plopped down in one of the empty seats.

"LAX is a busy place," Claire commented, sitting down beside him. People of every size and shape walked past, some dressed in jogging suits and sneakers like they were out for a morning run, some sporting tattoos and piercings, a few in business suits, all of them in a hurry. Kids scrambled to keep up with their parents, who tugged on their hands or chided them to move faster.

Ben seemed not to notice. Claire could feel the frustration coming off him in waves.

"Maybe we should call the police," she said, "have them check out the address."

"If Troy sees cops, he might take Sam and run. Next time it'll be even harder to find him."

The minutes crawled past as they sat in the waiting area, Ben working his laptop, Claire on her iPad, checking her email, sending a message to Mary Wilson. She wanted to find out about Ryan, make sure the boy was okay.

It was almost time to board the plane when her BlackBerry started ringing. Claire recognized the caller ID, considered letting it go straight to voice mail, then relented and answered.

"Hello, Michael."

"Hello, Claire."

"Michael, I'm kind of busy right now, is there something you wanted?"

"I just wanted to hear the sound of your voice."

She looked over at Ben, saw him watching her, a scowl on his ruggedly handsome face. "I didn't expect to hear from you until you finished your assignment."

"I'm still in L.A. I don't leave for a couple more days. I thought maybe I could come over and we could talk."

There was a time she had yearned to talk more openly with Michael. That time was gone.

"I'm just about to get on a plane. I'm not sure when I'll be back."

A long silence on the phone. "You're not…with that guy, are you?"

She could feel Ben's hard gaze boring into her. "We're working together, trying to find Sam. I told you that, Michael."

She felt a hand on her shoulder. "They're boarding the plane. You can talk to your boyfriend later."

She gave him the same dark look he was giving her. "I have to go. Take care of yourself, Michael." She didn't give him time to reply, just ended the call and went over to where Ben waited for her at the boarding gate.

Having missed the first flight, stuck with potluck seating, Claire wasn't able to sit next to him. Fine with her. She didn't like the way her attraction to Ben kept surfacing, her heart skipping when those steel-blue eyes met hers, the way she had to try not to stare at his amazing biceps, or the shape of the muscles outlined beneath his T-shirt.

She didn't want to get involved with him, didn't want to feel this constant sexual awareness. She told herself in time she would get used to being around him, but it was impossible to convince herself.

After a short hour-and-twenty-minute flight, the plane landed at Phoenix Sky Harbor Airport. Making their way to the baggage claim, Ben picked up the bag he'd been forced to check because of his weapon while Claire pulled her carry-on over to the rental car desk to pick up the vehicle Ben had reserved.

A silver Chevy Tahoe four-wheel-drive SUV waited in the Hertz parking lot. No more compact cars for Ben.

It was after seven by the time they were ready to leave the airport. The sun went down early this time of year and darkness had settled in. Ben threw her bag in the back of the Tahoe, set his duffel down and unzipped it. He took his empty pistol out of its locked travel case, shoved the loaded clip back in and reholstered the weapon. Just watching him made her nervous.

Ben stashed the gun in the console, then punched Lyla Holden's address into the navigation system. A few minutes later, they were driving out of the parking lot, heading for the I-10 freeway.

The early-October weather was dry and warm, not the burning hot of a Phoenix summer. A slight breeze cleared the air, giving them a view of the barren desert mountains in the distance. The evening traffic wasn't too bad, thinning as they drove farther out of the city.

The GPS was taking them out to Chandler, an area south of the city. They were making good progress when Ben put on his turn signal and started moving into the right lane.

"Where are we going?" Claire asked, looking at the nav screen, which told them to continue traveling south.

"I saw a sign for a Holiday Inn at the next off-ramp. I'm leaving you there till I get back."

Claire leaned over and turned off the clicking signal. "No way. I'm going with you."

"Look, Claire, if Troy's there with Sam, there's no way to know what he might do."

"That's exactly why you need me."

He shook his head. "Forget it."

"I'll wait in the car. If something happens, I'll have the engine running and be ready to pick you and Sam up and get you out of there."

He was still shaking his head, but she could tell he was weighing her argument.

"You need to think of Sam, Ben."

The car shot past the turnoff. "I don't like it. Not a damned bit. But you're right—if there's trouble, I might need you to help me get Sam out safely."

They drove farther along the freeway, neither of them talking. After a few more miles, Ben pulled off the main highway onto a series of smaller roads that eventually led into neighborhoods less and less populated.

Though it was dark, a waning moon lit the sky, and Claire could see their surroundings fairly well. Eventually the houses became double-wide trailers on what looked like acre lots. The land was arid, sandy desert, cactus and scrub brush. Horses trod worn dirt paths in barren fenced-in pens next to the houses, and dogs barked and ran along beside the car.

The road was narrow and dusty, and as they drove farther along, the dogs disappeared in the distance behind the SUV. Spotting an address here and there, Ben slowed the vehicle. "It's got to be coming up soon."

Claire searched for a number. Spotted a couple, not the one they wanted. "I think it's one of these two on the left, but I don't see any numbers on the houses so I can't be sure which one."

Ben drove past the two double-wides, one maintained better than the other with a lawn in front. Lights were on in both houses. Claire caught a glimpse of movement behind the partially closed curtains in one of them, and heard music playing in the house with the lawn.

Ben didn't stop the car, just rolled on down the road. Eventually he pulled over and turned around, waited awhile, then drove back the way they came.

Claire's heart was pounding now, and it wasn't from sexual awareness. If Troy was in one of the houses with Sam, the boy could get hurt. Or Ben. The man might seem invincible, but he wasn't Superman and he couldn't stop a bullet.

Parking the car in the darkness about a quarter of a mile from the houses, he turned off the engine. He took his pistol out of the center console, clipped it behind his back, then popped open the plastic case on the overhead light and took out the bulb.

"Come around and get in the driver's side." He

handed her the keys, got out of the car and held the door while she hurried to the driver's side, got in and moved up the seat.

"If you hear gunshots, keep low and don't wait more than a couple of minutes. If you don't see me, just start the engine and get the hell out of here. If someone tries to get in the car, or you think something's gone wrong, start the car and just keep going."

Her heart was racing. "What…what about you?"

"We don't know who's in the house. We don't know what might happen if Troy thinks he's cornered. I don't want anyone coming after you. If Sam's there, I'm getting him out. If something happens and you and I have to split up, I'll meet you at that Holiday Inn we passed on the highway."

She could barely force out the words. "All right." When he started to leave, she reached out and caught his arm. "I don't want you to worry about me. Just go after Sam."

He started to close the car door, pulled it open instead, leaned in and gave her a quick hard kiss. "I'll be back. With luck, Sam will be with me."

Claire tasted him on her lips, realized they were trembling. "Be careful."

Ben closed the car door.

Ten

Ben made his way around to the rear of the houses, which were fairly far apart. A couple of horses stood in one of the pens, no dogs that he could see. He crept up to the window on the side of the first double-wide, pressed himself against it and peeked into the living room.

A man and his wife, older, gray-haired, sitting on the sofa watching TV. A little long-haired lapdog looked over at the window and started yapping, but the dog was too comfortable in the old man's lap to give more than a couple of high-pitched barks.

Ben backed away and headed for the second house. As he drew near, he heard male and female laughter and the sound of country music. Through the living room window, he counted seven people clustered around a big flat-screen TV, drinking beer and watching a football game.

No Sam in sight. From the photos he had seen of Troy Bridger, he wasn't there, either.

A big-busted redhead seemed to be the hostess, laughing loudly, upending a bottle of beer. *Lyla Holden.*

Quietly, he circled the house, checking the bedrooms, listening for the sound of anyone inside, listening for the voice of a child.

As near as he could tell, neither Troy Bridger nor his son was in the house.

Ben headed back to Claire.

Claire felt as tightly wound as a clock spring. With every heartbeat, she listened for the sound of gunfire. When her cell phone rang, she jumped three inches and whacked her elbow on the steering wheel. With a deep breath, she looked down at the caller ID and recognized Ben's number.

"Don't panic," he said. "I'm right beside you."

She whirled, saw him through the passenger side window.

"Open up," he said, reminding her she had locked the car. She flipped the locks and Ben slid into the seat.

"I was trying not to scare you." The corner of his mouth edged up. "I guess that didn't work."

"What happened? Did we get the wrong house?"

"Right house. No Sam or Bridger, at least that I could see from outside. Lyla's in there with six other people, four men and two women. They're watching a football game."

"What do we do?"

"Wait. Angel, you're about to find out how boring a P.I.'s job really is."

She didn't remind him not to call her *angel.* She was beginning to like the way it sounded when he said it. "So we wait until morning?"

"We wait until the game's over. Lyla's a lot more likely to answer our questions without half a dozen other people around. Start the engine. We need to get close enough to watch the house."

She started the car but left the lights off and idled past the first house, which was now dark inside, then stopped in between the two houses and turned the engine back off. The curtains were open enough to see people moving around inside.

"You might as well relax. This may take a while. Why don't you try to get some sleep? I'll wake you when it's time to go in."

Her eyes swung to his. "I get to go with you?"

"It's getting late. I'm not trying to scare the woman into talking. She'll be easier to handle if you're there with me."

"Right. I think that's a good idea."

"I don't want her to know I'm Sam's father. I don't want her getting on the horn and calling Troy, warning him we're coming after him."

"I should have thought of that."

His lips faintly lifted in the corners. "I'm the detective, sweetheart. You're doing just fine." Ben settled in to wait, and Claire tipped her seat back and tried to relax. They'd been up late every night. When she *had* been able to sleep, it had been brief and restless.

She closed her eyes, concentrated on the night sounds outside the car window, the hoot of an owl and the horses nickering in their pen, the faint sound of country music playing in the house. The next thing she knew, Ben was nudging her awake.

"Time to go."

Claire blinked and looked down the road toward the house. The lights were still on, but the music was silent. The clock on the dash said 11:00 p.m.

"They're all gone?"

"All but one. I have a hunch he's spending the night in the lady's bed. We need to get in there before they get too hot and bothered."

Claire cracked open her door, Ben did the same and they climbed out of the car. Quietly closing the door behind her, Claire took a breath to steady herself and started walking next to Ben toward the porch.

"That the doorbell?"

Inside the house, Ben heard the woman on the other side of the door.

"Maybe someone forgot something," the man's deep voice said.

Footsteps sounded. Lyla Holden pulled open the door and peered out onto the porch. She was in her late forties, pretty once, but aging badly. Her hair was her best feature, thick and wavy, a cloud of fire around her beefy shoulders. When she saw them, the smile slipped from her face. "Can I help you?"

Careful to stay partially in the shadows so she wouldn't notice his eyes, Ben flashed Claire a go-ahead glance.

"Hello, Lyla." She gave the woman a friendly smile. "My name is Claire Chastain. This is Ben Slocum."

The redhead flicked him a glance, then her eyebrows narrowed at Claire. "How'd you know my name?"

"You're a friend of Troy's," Claire said. "That's why we're hoping you can help us."

"Who is it, Lyla?" the deep voice rumbled from down the hall.

"Go on to bed, Scooter. I'll be in there in a minute."

"You don't get here soon, mama, I'm gonna have to start without you." Scooter rumbled a laugh.

Lyla ignored him. "Troy left a couple of days ago. I kicked his drunken ass on down the road."

"The road to Louisiana?" Ben asked.

Lyla nodded. She didn't invite them in, and Ben didn't press her. He could smell the beer she'd been drinking. Her eyelids were a little heavy, her lipstick smeared in one corner. She looked relaxed, a little tipsy, just the way he wanted.

"That's right—*Lou-si-ana,*" she said, pronouncing it with a Southern drawl. "On his way to see those no-good brothers of his."

"That's what we thought," Claire said, doing a nice job of bonding.

"He ain't in no hurry, though. Planning to visit some of his buddies along the way. How'd you know Troy?"

"He used to date a friend of mine," Claire said, "but she died."

"Yeah, he mentioned something about that. I guess that's where he got the kid."

Ben forgot to breathe. His pulse leaped skyward, started pounding in his ears. He forced himself to smile. "That's right. Since the boy's mother was dead, I guess he was trying to help the kid out."

"That's what he said."

"You see, Lyla, Ben's kin of his. He didn't know about Laura bein' sick till she'd already passed. We were hopin' the boy'd still be here. We've been real worried about him."

Admiration slid through him at the country note she infused in her voice. *Nice move, angel.*

"They left together, all right. How the kid got un-lucky enough to tie up with Troy, I'll never know. Guess he was desperate."

Ben's chest tightened. "Was he all right? I mean, he wasn't hurt or anything?"

"Oh, no. He was fine. Seemed like a real nice boy. Quiet, you know. Him and that dog of Troy's mostly stayed outside."

Relief slid through him. Sam was all right. At least so far. Though nothing Claire had told him about the boy made him think he was quiet. Smart, maybe. A survivor. Just trying to stay out of Troy's way.

"You know where Troy's next stop might be?" Ben asked, working to keep his tone even.

"Can't say for certain. Said he was planning to visit a friend, guy by the name of Hutchins. Duke's a real bozo. Troy said the two of them used to get drunk and high together."

"You know where Duke lives?" Claire asked.

"Somewhere down the road. Could be New Mexico. Texas, maybe. I know he worked there for a while. Troy never really said."

"Anything else you can tell us?" Ben asked. He wanted to ask if she knew Troy's license plate number, but, hell, most people didn't know their own.

"What in God's name you doin' out there, woman?" Scooter yelled. "Get in here and get this bed a-movin'."

"Damn fool's gonna get his ass a-movin' right out the door, he ain't careful." Lyla wiped the lipstick smudge off her lip. "I don't know much more. Drives some old beat-up truck. Probably break down before he gets to Lou-si-ana."

"Was Troy calling himself Bridger or Bennett?" Ben pressed, knowing he was pushing his luck.

"He's always been Bridger to me. He calls, I'm happy to tell him you're lookin' for him, but it might be bet-

ter if I don't. You're wantin' the boy to go home with
ya, right?"

He paused, considering what to say. She'd been more
than helpful so far. Maybe his luck would hold. "That's
right."

"I best keep quiet then. Troy can be mighty cantan-
kerous. Might not want to give the kid up."

Ben tried for a look of admiration. "Good idea. I
hadn't thought of that."

"Listen, I gotta go. Good luck findin' your kin."

"Thank you, Lyla," Claire said. The woman flashed
a last smile and firmly closed the door.

Ben took hold of Claire's hand to guide her through
the darkness along the road back to the SUV.

"I knew it!" Claire said as soon as the car doors were
closed. "I knew that bastard took Sam."

"This calls for a change of plans. We know where
he's headed but we can't cover half the country by ourselves. We need to call the cops, give them a heads-up
that Bridger's got the boy, get them to watch the roads,
press them harder to find him."

"I'll call while you drive."

"Don't mention Hutchins until we can get some intel
on the guy. I want to know what kind of trouble Bridger
might be taking Sam into."

Pulling her cell phone out of her purse, she pressed
the number she'd keyed in belonging to Detective
Owens, her contact in the missing-persons division.

"Hello, Detective, this is Claire Chastain. I'm in Arizona. I'm sorry to bother you so late, but I wanted to
let you know that Sam is definitely with Troy Bridger
and that he and Sam are on their way to Louisiana."

The man said something and Claire covered the

phone. "Owens wants to know how I got the information. Should I tell him?"

Ben shook his head.

"The source is confidential, but you can rely on the information being true."

He couldn't hear what Owens said.

"Thank you, Detective." Claire hung up the phone. "He wanted a way to confirm, but I think he believed what I said. By the way, where are we going?"

"Back to the Holiday Inn. It's late and both of us are tired. Once we get settled, I'll get on the internet, see if I can locate Duke Hutchins. If not, I'll call Sol first thing in the morning."

At least they knew they were on the right track. The police had believed the Robersons that Sam had run away. But Claire had been adamant that Bridger had conned the boy into going with him, and she had been right. His admiration for the lady went up another notch.

He sliced her a sideways glance. He hadn't forgotten the call she'd received from Michael Sullivan. The good news was she didn't seem to be encouraging him. Ben wasn't sure why that seemed important.

He thought of the conversation they'd had with Lyla Holden. Now that they were sure they were heading in the right direction, some of his tension eased. He was good at his job and he was determined. As far as he was concerned, it was only a matter of time until he found his son.

He carefully tamped down his worry for the boy. He had no idea what was happening to Sam, but if his thoughts started to go in that direction, he wouldn't be able to focus and he couldn't do his job. And they could only move as fast as the information they received.

He thought of the night ahead and the sleep he so

badly needed. He knew Claire was dog-tired, but also as keyed up as he was. He thought of her pretty face, slender curves and all that silky dark hair. He knew exactly how to solve the problem so they could both get some sleep.

But he was pretty sure what her answer would be if he suggested they rent one room for the night instead of two.

Claire sat quietly as Ben drove back to the motel he had spotted on the way to Lyla Holden's place.

"Nice call on Bridger," he said. "You were right all along. It took balls to stick to your guns the way you did. You kept your sights focused on the right man. I owe you one, Claire."

She ignored the feeling of warmth that ran through her. "You don't owe me anything. Bridger might not have taken Sam if he wasn't mad at me. And I want Sam to have a good home. I promised Laura. I'm just thankful we're looking in the right place."

Ben didn't say more. She knew he was as tired as she was, and though he was clearly relieved their efforts so far weren't in vain, the set of his jaw and the lines across his forehead told her how worried he was about his son.

Considering he had never met the boy—never even known he had a son—Ben had more than accepted his duties as a father. She was coming to admire him more and more.

And finding him even more appealing. Aside from the hottest body of any man she had ever known, in a rugged sort of way, he was one of the best-looking. Everything about Ben Slocum screamed sexy. From his short, slightly wavy black hair to those amazing pale blue eyes.

She had determinedly kept Ben at a distance, but part of her wanted to give in to the incredible desire she felt for him. Wanted to experience the hot sex those heated looks promised.

But Claire was smart enough not to do something as stupid as sleeping with Ben.

Eleven

———◦⟩⟨⟨◦———

Ben pulled into the motel and parked in front of the entrance. Claire got out to stretch her legs a little after sitting in the car for so long. They walked into the lobby together and up to the front desk.

A short young man with shaggy brown hair looked up. "May I help you?"

"We need a couple of rooms," Ben said. "Just for the night."

Or at least that was what Claire hoped. Ben hoped he would be able to locate Hutchins on the internet. Or that his friend would find him in the morning. Even if that didn't happen, Claire figured Ben would be too anxious to wait and would rather push farther down the road.

The desk clerk pounded on his keyboard, then turned back to them. "Sorry, sir, we only have one room left but it has two queen beds. That's the best we can do."

Ben nodded, rubbed a weary hand over his face. "Thanks, anyway." He turned to Claire. "We'll head down the highway a ways, see what else we can find."

Claire shook her head. "You're exhausted. Both of

us are. I'm not afraid to sleep in the same room with you." She ignored the way his gaze sharpened, the way it made her stomach contract.

"You sure?"

"I can trust you, right?"

His mouth edged up. "Mostly. You're safe with me tonight…if that's what you want."

A flush crept into her face as she turned back to the desk clerk. "We'll take it."

The young man slid the paperwork across the counter. Ben filled it out, and the man handed each of them a key.

"Number 203. Second floor, down at the far end of the hall. You can park down there and use your key to get into the building. Take the stairs to the second floor."

Ben stuffed the key into his pocket. "Thanks." Heading back to the SUV, he moved the car to a parking space at the other end of the motel. All the way there, Claire worried she had made the wrong decision.

She wasn't really going to sleep with Ben, she told herself. Not in the literal sense. She was just sleeping in a bed in the same room with him. But her heart was beating a little too fast, making her wonder if she would actually get any sleep.

"I hope this is a good idea," he said, reading her mind as he opened the motel room door and held it for her to walk in towing her carry-on. He walked in behind her and tossed his canvas duffel onto the overstuffed chair.

He turned on the lamp beside one of the beds. "Ladies first. You get first shot at the bathroom."

She nodded. "Thanks." Tugging her bag in that direction, she went inside and locked the door. Thank heavens there was a fan so he wouldn't be able to hear what she was doing.

She showered and brushed her teeth, then pulled on the white sleep tee with a teddy bear on the front that she had brought with her. It covered her sufficiently from neck to midthigh, but when she walked out of the bathroom and noticed the way Ben was looking at her, she felt half-naked.

There was a bottle of water on the dresser. She cracked it open and took a drink, noticed his computer set up on the desk. "Find anything?"

Ben just shook his head. "Looks like it's going to take more than just a name. Might even be an alias. I'll call Sol first thing in the morning." Ben headed for the bathroom, his expression tired and grim.

Claire was under the covers pretending to be asleep when he came back out. Through lowered lashes, she watched him, noticing he wore only a pair of white cotton briefs, figured even that was a concession to her.

He walked over to the other bed and stood with his back to her, testing the firmness of the mattress, drawing back the covers. Long, powerful legs, wide muscular shoulders that veed to a pair of narrow hips. When he turned, she allowed herself to enjoy his amazing pecs and six-pack abs.

Her eyes widened as her gaze moved lower.

"It's not my fault, angel, if the way you're looking at me is making me hard."

Oh, God! She closed her eyes tightly, pretended not to hear him.

"Seems to me it's my turn to look at you." Walking over, he jerked back the covers. Claire shrieked as a shot of cold air hit her, then flushed when she discovered her sleep tee had ridden clear up on her hips. She was wearing a pair of white cotton bikini panties, but they didn't cover much. She grabbed the hem of her night-shirt and tugged it back down.

"Very nice," he said, tossing the blankets back over her. "If I hadn't promised you'd be safe, I'd climb in there with you. I don't suppose you'd reconsider."

She looked up at him standing there completely aroused and not the least bit embarrassed. Claire's stom-ach contracted and her nipples tightened.

"We...we need to get some sleep," she said and rolled over on her side, facing away from him.

"Good luck with that," Ben grumbled, then walked over and flopped down on the bed.

Claire wasn't sure how much time passed. Minutes that seemed like hours as her mind kept replaying the sight of Ben Slocum, standing there in all his almost-naked glory, fiercely aroused. She closed her eyes but sleep remained elusive. It irritated her that Ben didn't have the same problem. It was the sound of his deep, even breathing that finally put her to sleep.

It was three in the morning when Claire awakened. Unaccustomed to the desert dryness, she reached for the bottle of water she had set on the nightstand and took a long drink. The room felt strangely quiet as she set the bottle back down. She looked over at the other bed. It was empty.

Claire jolted up off the mattress, certain Ben had left her and taken off on his own. Then she saw him on the deck outside the sliding glass doors.

He had pulled on his jeans but wore no shirt, and his feet were bare. He stood with his back to her, staring out at the desert. There was something in the rigid set of his shoulders that moved her, the way he stood with his long legs splayed as if he faced some unseen foe. He seemed so isolated, so alone.

Laura had always said that Ben was a man who needed no one, and yet there were times Claire caught glimpses of the gentler, more vulnerable man he kept locked inside.

She hadn't missed the relief on his face when Lyla Holden had told him Sam seemed all right. Ben might not know it, but already he loved his son.

Claire watched him staring into the darkness and wished she could comfort him in some way. It was foolish, wanting to comfort a man who would shun the very thought of it.

Still, she found herself moving toward the door leading out to the deck, sliding it open, stepping into the soft night and warm desert heat. The moment she did, he turned and their eyes met. Hers uncertain, his cool and remote. When she moistened her lips, his icy stare shifted, changed to a look of burning intensity.

A single instant of hesitation, then he strode toward her, pulled her into his arms, and his mouth crushed down over hers.

Heat, was all she could think. *Power and determination.* Claire swayed on her feet as need washed through her, so strong she wasn't sure if it was his or her own. Her lips parted under his relentless assault, welcomed the invasion of his tongue, and her arms slid up around his neck. He stroked deeply into her mouth even as he moved her backward up against the wall, into the shadowy darkness on the balcony. The kiss grew wetter, hotter, hungrier.

She could feel his erection, thick and hard against her belly; his hands, big and strong, easing up her nightshirt, cupping her bottom, pulling her more solidly against him. Sensation rippled through her, heat and desire, lust unlike any she had ever known.

"God, I want you," he said against the side of her neck, his teeth grazing her skin. Goose bumps rose wherever he touched. "I need you, angel."

Her breathing hitched as his hands moved to her breasts, cupping them through the soft cotton fabric. She understood his need. Worry ate at him, thoughts of the past, the woman he had once loved and the son he had never known. His ghosts were haunting him tonight, and there were times even a strong man like Ben needed to connect, to feel the closeness of someone who cared.

Claire moaned as his hands slid into her hair, holding her in place as he ravished her mouth. Her own need swelled. It was wrong, she knew. There was too much at risk. Sam's life was at stake.

But what about Ben? His child was missing, a child he might never know. Sam needed her, but so did Ben.

It took a moment for her to realize he had paused, that he was no longer touching her. When she opened her eyes, she stared into a pair as pale and hot as the tip of a flame. He was waiting, holding himself back. Keeping his word.

Claire read the need in those ice-blue eyes, and her heart expanded. Rising on her toes, she cupped his face between her hands, felt the roughness of his late-night beard and very softly kissed him.

Ben groaned and the dam of his control suddenly burst. Hard hands moved over her breasts, her belly, slid beneath her nightshirt, smoothed over the globes of her bottom. He had left the decision to her, and she had silently given him her permission. Now there was no turning back.

His fingers moved under the elastic of her white panties. Claire gasped as he ripped them away. Ben caught the sound in her mouth, kissing her deeply, taking control of her body and perhaps a little of her soul. She barely heard the buzz of his zipper sliding down, barely noticed the protection he pulled out of his back pocket, ripped open and slid onto his powerful erection.

Then he was lifting her, stroking her softness, finding her more than ready, feeling her tremble. A single deep thrust and he was buried to the hilt, drawing a low moan from her throat. For a moment he stilled, giving her time to adjust to his size and length, fighting for control.

Claire didn't want control. Not now, now when she had taken the irreversible step and given herself to him. Sliding her fingers into his hair, she pulled his mouth down to hers and kissed him wildly, deeply, urging him on, wanting what his hard body had promised. Ben lifted her, propped her back against the wall, wrapped her legs around his waist and started to move, slowly at first, then faster, deeper, harder.

Fierce, pounding thrusts sent pleasure spinning through her. She felt consumed and on fire, clinging to his neck, trembling as he took her more deeply, took her until all she could think of was the pleasure, and Ben, and how good it felt to have him inside her. She didn't expect the powerful climax that seized her, forced a cry from her lips. She shuddered with the force of it and just hung on.

An instant later, Ben's powerful body tightened and he followed her to release.

Claire. Her name rang in his head. *Claire.* He hadn't expected what she'd given him tonight. When she'd stepped out into the moonlight looking like the dark-haired angel he called her, he'd told himself to leave her alone, that she was only offering friendship. But he had needed a woman tonight, needed to feel a woman's arms around him, needed the taste of a woman in his mouth, the scent of a woman wrapped around him. He hadn't meant for that woman to be Claire.

Then he'd looked into those wide green eyes and seen something in their uncertain depths, something that reflected the same need he was feeling. Her soft kiss had been his undoing, and for a moment, he'd lost control. He'd wanted her badly, had since the morning she had talked her way into his living room. But he didn't want to hurt her, didn't want to break the trust she had given him.

He loved sex. Loved women who loved sex. Women who wanted what he had to offer and took it freely. Even then, some of them he'd wound up hurting. More than a few. He'd didn't quite know why. He'd always been open and honest, never pulled any punches.

He was who he was, and he figured that wasn't going to change.

Now everything had changed. Now he was a father.

Now there was Claire.

He took care of the condom, tossing it into the waste can out on the deck, shifted her into his arms and carried her toward the sliding glass doors. Claire leaned her head against his shoulder, her mahogany hair spilling over his chest as he made his way back into the motel room and settled her in the middle of her bed.

For several long moments, he just stood there staring down at her, wondering if she regretted what she had given him. Figuring she probably did. He'd rushed her, taken what he wanted. What he'd so desperately needed.

He hadn't expected her to be so responsive, so passionate. Hadn't figured her to climax so fast and so hard.

A red-car woman after all.

Another time he might have smiled.

"I was rough with you," he said a little gruffly. "I didn't mean to hurt you." But even if he hadn't, in a different way, sooner or later he would.

"You didn't hurt me."

"What do you want from me, Claire?"

She gazed up at him, her eyes on his face. "I could ask the same of you."

He knew what he wanted, what he had no right to. "I want more of you. A lot more. I've wanted you since you walked into my house and I asked you to make me a pot of coffee."

"*Ordered* me to make you a pot of coffee."

He didn't smile. "I'm not an easy man."

Her mouth faintly curved. "No."

"Outside just now, I didn't mean for that to happen." But it had, and he had been right. Sleeping with Claire didn't feel like just sex. There was something about her, something strong and brave and dependable that drew him. Yet she was as soft and feminine as any woman he had ever known.

"You asked me what I want," she said. "I want you to make love to me again. I want you to sleep in my bed. In the morning, I want you to forget this ever happened. I want you to pretend nothing has changed so we can go on the way we were. So that we can find Sam."

It was a wet dream come true. A woman who wanted ten-shot-tequila sex. Sex with no memory at all of what had happened. No morning-after regrets. He wondered why it bothered him.

He made no reply, just peeled off his jeans and

climbed into bed beside her. He kissed her as he lifted off her soft cotton nightshirt, ignoring the teddy bear on the front that somehow made him feel guilty. He looked his fill at her perfect, apple-round breasts, went hard again, almost to the point of pain.

His wanting hadn't lessened. He hadn't really expected that it would. Claire gave a soft little sigh as he came up over her, settled himself between her legs. Her fingers dug into the muscles across his shoulders, and his blood began to pound.

He could feel every contour of her slender, elegant body, every feminine curve. He reminded himself to go slow, that there were hours left till dawn, but the need was burning through him, hot and raging. He kissed her deeply, kissed her until she shifted restlessly beneath him, and knew her needs matched his own.

They had hours before the night was over, he reminded himself. And no recriminations in the morning.

Ben wondered if there was a woman on the planet who could actually keep that promise. He told himself it was exactly what he wanted.

Twelve

Claire rolled her carry-on down the motel hallway, heading for the rented SUV. As soon as his office in Houston had opened, Ben had been on the phone with his friend, looking for information.

As soon as they had gotten out of bed.

Claire beat down the thought. All morning Ben had been eyeing her warily, waiting for her to bring up their wild night of lovemaking. More amazing than she ever could have dreamed. She was pleasantly sore all over and relaxed all the way to her bones.

Ben was waiting for her to bring it up, but it wasn't going to happen. The man could wait till hell froze over. Until his icy eyes turned pea-green. The subject of last night was over. Closed. Finished. As if it had never occurred. She had never done anything so impulsive, never behaved with so much abandon. She wanted to forget it even more than he did.

Not to say that she ever would. A woman didn't forget a night of multiple orgasms—especially when it had never happened to her before. Ben was an incredible lover, or at least he knew how to press all her personal hot buttons. And she had a hunch he had been holding back, not pushing her for more than she was ready to handle.

As they reached the stairway leading down to the parking lot, she heard the sound of his heavy leather boots behind her. She shoved down the handle of the bag to carry it down the stairs, but Ben nudged her aside and picked it up, carted it down to the parking lot and over to the Tahoe. He tossed both their bags into the back and closed the lid.

"I looked up El Paso on my iPad," she said as she pulled open the passenger door. "It's a little over four hundred miles from here."

It was the town Duke Hutchins lived in, according to Ben's friend Sol. It had taken two hours for Sol to locate the man whose legal name was Dennis Arthur Hutchins. Apparently, only his close friends called him Duke.

Ben had been pacing the floor of the motel room by the time Sol had called him back with the information they so desperately needed.

"It's about a seven-hour trip," Claire said. "I take it we're driving, not flying."

"We know Bridger's headed for Louisiana, or at least that's the way it looks. We need to stay hard on his tail, try to intercept him somewhere along the way, hopefully in El Paso. So yes, we're driving."

"According to Google Maps, we could shave off a few miles by heading back to Phoenix and cutting over on I-70."

Ben fired up the engine. "Less traffic if we stay on I-10 and just keep going. I'll make up the time."

She remembered his Mr. Toad's Wild Ride driving and figured indeed he would.

Instead of heading straight to the freeway, he drove a few blocks from the motel and pulled into a minimart next to the freeway on-ramp. "I need some more coffee. How about you?" They had finished the in-room coffee hours ago while Ben worked on his laptop, but had come up with nothing more on Duke Hutchins.

She yawned as she cracked open her door. "I could definitely use a cup."

A heartbeat passed. He was eyeing her again, sure she was going to add a comment about how little sleep they'd gotten last night.

Not gonna happen, tough guy. They'd made a deal and she was sticking to it. She could deal with a single night of passion, handle the idea that they were adults and it was something both of them wanted, but she couldn't afford to get in any deeper with Ben.

She didn't say a word, but she couldn't stop another yawn.

They went their separate ways inside the minimart, Claire scooping up a couple of breakfast bars, a carton of orange juice out of the refrigerator section, filling a big cup with coffee and adding cream. Walking up beside her, Ben looked down at the cocoa-colored brew in her cup.

"I thought you drank it black."

"Not unless someone leaves me no choice."

He muttered something and held up the paper bag in his hand. "They've got fresh doughnuts. I got a couple of extras in case you wanted one."

She held up the breakfast bars. "These are healthier. I got an extra one for you."

They grabbed their goodies and headed for the register. Ben insisted on paying for all of it.

"You don't have to keep doing that. I can pay my own way."

"Yeah, I remember—you're a liberated woman." His gaze ran over her in a way that made her think of last night and feel like blushing. Instead, she turned and headed for the car.

They ate on the road, finishing off their makeshift meals, then settling in for the long ride to El Paso.

"Have you ever been there?" Claire asked as the vehicle roared along, well over the speed limit.

"I've been to Juarez. That's just across the Mexican border."

"What were you doing there?"

"My job."

He didn't add more. He didn't have to. He was a SEAL. Their work took them to every corner of the world. As they'd made love last night, she'd noticed a long puckered scar low on his back and another on his thigh. She knew he had left the SEALs because of an injury he'd received in the Philippines, and wanted to ask him about it. But last night was about pleasure and satisfying needs, not delving into the past.

"Juarez has been in the news a lot," she said. "Thousands of people murdered in drug-related shootings. I'm glad Duke Hutchins lives on this side of the border."

"I just hope Bridger's there with Sam when we get there."

She drained the last of the coffee in her cup. "What about the police? Do you think we should call them, tell them about Hutchins? The local police can be there a lot faster than we can."

"I've given it a lot of thought. You called Owens after we talked to Lyla. They know Bridger has Sam. They know he's probably headed for Louisiana, likely down

I-10. They'll be watching the roads, looking for a man and boy in a beat-up white pickup. The odds aren't good they'll find them, but the roads will be covered. And we can be in El Paso by dark, maybe sooner."

"The police could be at the house right away."

Ben scrubbed a hand over his face. He hadn't shaved that morning. He looked completely disreputable and handsome as sin.

"I wish I trusted them to handle it. The trouble is, if they make a mistake, maybe go in too hot or their timing is off, Sam could get hurt or Bridger could get away. If he does, he's liable to take Sam and go underground. We might never be able to find him."

Ben had made the argument before and it made a lot of sense. "I don't like the idea of the police cornering him. I'm not sure how far he's willing to go to pay Laura back."

Ben's pale eyes bored into her. "You think he might hurt the boy to get even with a dead woman?"

She swallowed, fighting a rush of guilt. "I think a lot of it has to do with me. He…um…called me once. Said if I didn't stop causing him trouble, I'd regret it."

"But that wasn't something you could do."

"I told you, Laura was my friend." She sighed. "I don't know what Bridger might do but it…it worries me."

She could tell by the set of his jaw it worried him, too.

An hour out of Chandler, Claire leaned back in her seat and dozed for a while, the lack of sleep last night taking its toll. An hour later, she jerked awake, her heart hammering, her skin flushed and her body pulsing. She'd been dreaming of Ben, remembering the erotic sensation of his mouth on her breasts.

She didn't look at him, just turned and gazed out the window, fixing her eyes on the flat, arid desert moving by outside, hoping he couldn't read her thoughts.

"You okay?"

She managed to nod. "Bad dream." But it was a very good dream, a delicious dream she was sure to have any number of times over the years.

Another fifty miles into the trip, Ben pulled off the highway to make a quick pit stop at a Chevron station.

"Why don't you let me drive awhile," Claire suggested as they walked back to the car carrying paper cups of fresh hot coffee. "Maybe you could catch a little sleep."

He looked at her over the top of his steaming paper cup. "We need to get there."

"I'll get us there as fast as I possibly can."

He hesitated a moment, then nodded. "All right." Climbing into the passenger side of the vehicle, he stuck his coffee in the cup holder next to hers and tilted his seat back. By the time Claire pulled onto the freeway, Ben was fast asleep.

Ben didn't sleep long. Just enough to refresh himself. So far, things had gone extremely well, but he didn't expect that to last. Eddie Jeffries had cooperated. He was in jail and didn't want any more trouble. Sadie had a bone to pick with Bridger—no problem there. Lyla had been charmed by Sam and wanted to see him returned to his family.

Ben had a hunch Duke Hutchins wasn't going to roll over on Bridger so easily. He hadn't told Claire the rest of the information Sol had dug up. That Hutchins had a criminal record that included assault with a deadly weapon and armed robbery. He'd been busted for sell-

ing marijuana and cocaine, spent time in half a dozen
Texas jails and finally wound up in Huntsville Prison.

He was out on parole, but there was no question in
Ben's mind the man would be armed and dangerous.

It was one of the reasons he didn't want to involve the
police. He didn't want to take a chance that Sam might
wind up collateral damage if someone started shooting.

One of the things SEALs were trained for was ex-
traction. With the right planning, he could be in and
out with Sam before Hutchins and Bridger knew what
the hell had hit them. He'd hold off bringing in the cops
until he had no other choice.

He adjusted his seat, bringing it back into position.
"Why don't you pull off at the next gas station and I'll
drive the rest of the way."

"Are you sure? You only slept a little over an hour."

"I'm good. Besides, driving gives me something
to do." *Besides sit here and think about peeling off
that cotton blouse and nibbling on those lovely white
breasts.* If he closed his eyes, he could still feel the tex-
ture of her rose-colored nipples, hard against his tongue.

Claire seemed to be doing just fine not thinking
about last night. He, on the other hand, couldn't seem
to stop.

In an oddly perverse turn, he was the one who
wanted to talk about it, wanted to hear her say how
good it was. Because it had been. He wouldn't have figured it, not with a woman as reserved as Claire.

Or maybe he would. All that bottled-up sexual energy. All that untapped heat. Making love to her was
like popping a cork on a shaken bottle of champagne.
Like riding a roller coaster on a ninety-mile-an-hour
dive. He had the scratch marks on his shoulders to
prove it.

And yet under all that hidden passion, there was an underlying innocence. Michael Sullivan might have taken the lady to bed, but he hadn't begun to give her what she needed. Not by a long shot. Now that Ben knew exactly what those needs were, all he could think of was satisfying them again.

It wasn't going to happen. They had made a deal— one night of hot, no-strings sex and nothing more. Claire was clearly sticking to it, and that meant so was he.

That didn't mean he hadn't noticed how pretty she'd looked this morning. How sexy she'd looked in her teddy-bear nightshirt with her long legs exposed and her red-painted toenails.

It didn't mean he hadn't noticed the way her jeans cupped her sweet little ass, didn't mean his fingers didn't itch to unzip those jeans, shove them down and rip off another pair of bikini panties.

Jesus, he was getting hard just thinking about it.

"There's a Shell station up ahead," he said a little gruffly. "Take the next off-ramp."

Claire pulled off and he gassed up while she went in to use the head. He did the same, then they continued down the road with him behind the wheel.

"What do we do when we get there?" Claire asked as they neared their destination, bringing his thoughts full circle back to Sam. Except for those few hours with Claire last night, the boy was never far from his mind.

"It'll be dark when we get in. Sol says Hutchins lives in a crummy apartment on the south side of town. I've already plugged the address into the GPS. We'll drive by, take a quick look at the area."

"Maybe we'll get lucky and spot Bridger's pickup."

It was a possibility. "On second thought, I'll drop

you off at a motel, then drive by. If Bridger's there, I don't want you getting hurt."

"But—"

"No arguments this time, Claire. I need to focus on Sam and getting him out of there safely."

"Time is crucial, Ben. You've driven four hundred miles at the speed of light to get here. Drive by the apartment, then you'll know what you need to do."

She was right, dammit. Finding a motel and getting her checked in took time. As far as he knew, Bridger had no idea he was being followed. A drive-by would probably be safe enough.

"The sooner we get to the apartment, the better our chances of finding Sam," Claire added, as if he needed a reminder.

"All right, but Hutchins has a record, and he's probably armed. He's a dangerous man, Claire. If something seems off or if we come in contact with him or Bridger, you do what I tell you, okay?"

"Why didn't you tell me he had a record?"

"I didn't want you to worry."

"I'm already worried, Ben. From now on, please, I want to know what's going on. That's the only way I can help."

He tended to work on a need-to-know basis, but he could see her point. "Fine, but you do what I tell you, okay?"

"Okay."

Neither of them said more till he pulled off the freeway and began following the GPS directions toward the south side of town.

As the area changed from a clean commercial neighborhood into run-down apartments, boarded-up businesses and graffiti-covered walls, he began to regret his decision to bring Claire along. He should have followed his instincts and left her someplace safe. He checked the black SEAL dive watch he'd been wearing for years, saw it was a little after 8:00 p.m.

"We're getting close," Claire said.

"Up ahead." He pointed through the windshield. "That's the apartment building on the right." Two stories. Dirty brown stucco with a black wrought-iron railing around the upper floor. A lawn that was mostly dirt and looked as though it hadn't been watered in years.

"I don't see any white pickups."

"No, unfortunately." He slowed as they approached. "That's unit five on the end upstairs."

"There aren't any lights on inside. It doesn't look like anyone's home." Claire pointed toward the building attached to the apartments. "Look! Someone's pulling out of the carport."

Ben pulled in behind a parked car, stopped and turned off his headlights. He dug a piece of paper out of his pocket, the info Sol had given him that morning, including the model and plate number of the vehicle Dennis "Duke" Hutchins drove.

"Ninety-nine black Chevy Camaro. Texas plate BQ1 BB13."

"That's it! It's Hutchins, Ben. There's no one in the apartment. We have to follow him!"

Taking Claire with him into what could be a very bad situation was the last thing he wanted. He watched the black Camaro pulling farther and farther away.

Ben stepped on the gas.

Thirteen

~~~~~⟿⟿⟿~~~~~

"Leave the damn dog inside. Get out of the truck and let's go."

Sitting in the passenger seat, Sam smoothed a hand over the dog's shiny black coat. "Why can't Pepper come with us?"

"Because he'll chase the chickens. Now come on." Troy tugged the brim of his baseball cap down over his eyes and stuffed a red bandanna into the back pocket of his jeans. He was in a hurry and Sam knew what would happen if he didn't get moving.

"Stay, Pep. I'll be back pretty soon."

Sam jumped down from the seat of the truck and slammed the door. Pepper whimpered and stared sadly out the window.

"What are you waitin' for? I said let's go."

Sam hurried around the truck, afraid to look back at Pep again. Troy could be real mean when someone didn't do what he wanted. Sam had a knot on the back of his head to prove it.

They started tramping through the powdery dust on

the bumpy dirt road, heading for the big barn up ahead. It was made of wood, and there were open windows along the sides, the kind of barn you saw in cowboy movies. There were more pickup trucks than Sam had ever seen.

Troy said they were going to watch a bunch of chickens fighting. Sam thought that sounded really weird. But a lot of people must like it because he could hear them yelling and cheering at the top of their lungs.

The moon helped them see in the dark and there were a couple of lights pointing down from the roof of the barn so people could find their way to the front door.

Walking ahead of Troy, he had almost reached the entrance when he noticed a barrel off to one side. Another barrel sat next to it. As they passed, Sam saw what was in them. His stomach rolled and his mouth went dry. The overhead light shone on feathers of every color—red, brown, gray, white, speckled. The barrel was full of dead chickens, their heads bent at funny angles, their little beady eyes dull and staring.

All of them were covered in blood.

"Those are the losers." Troy chuckled. "Don't worry, we'll be bettin' on winners." Coming up behind where Sam had stopped, Troy shoved him forward, making his feet move when they seemed to have forgotten how.

Sam swiveled his neck, his eyes still fixed on the chickens, and suddenly he understood. The chickens didn't just fight, they killed each other.

"I don't want to go in there, Troy. I want to wait in the car with Pep."

"Bullshit. This'll be good for you. Teach you to be a man."

Sam tried not to think of the dead chickens, but even if he closed his eyes he could see the mangled, bloody birds. His feet halted again and he swallowed, fighting not to throw up.

"What the fuck?" Troy shoved him hard and he stumbled. "Stop acting like a goddamned baby. You want Duke to think you're a wimp? Get your ass inside." Troy shoved him again and Sam kept walking.

All he could think was how stupid he'd been to leave with Troy Bridger. If he could do it over, he would stay with the Robersons whether they liked him or not. He would stay, even though his mother was dead and nobody wanted him.

But it was too late for that. Keeping his eyes straight ahead, Sam walked into the barn.

Careful to keep the Camaro in sight, Ben drove the SUV along the dirt road leading farther and farther out to nowhere. Nothing but cactus, mesquite and desert. Nothing but dust billowing up from the car in front of him. Good cover for the SUV but making it impossible to see where Hutchins was headed.

Then the road turned a little to the left and he caught a glimpse of light up ahead. The Camaro pulled into a makeshift dirt parking lot filled with trucks and cars. Ben parked a row behind Hutchins and turned off the engine. Fifty yards farther away, a circle of light marked the entrance to a barn.

"What is this place?" Claire asked. "What's going on?"

Ben knew the area from the time he'd spent in Juarez, knew the favorite pastime. Didn't matter that it had been outlawed. "Cockfight."

Claire's head went up. "What? You don't think Troy's here. Surely he wouldn't bring Sam to something as disgusting as that."

"You don't think so?"

She surveyed the assortment of rough-looking people making their way toward the barn. "Actually, I do. In fact, I think it would be just like him. A way of turning Sam into his idea of a real man."

They sat quietly as Hutchins got out of his car and fell in with a group heading for the barn. Two men and three big-busted, big-haired women wearing low-cut blouses and stretch pants so tight the cheeks of their asses rubbed together.

"We're going in there, right?"

"I am. You're staying here." He had never put the bulb back into the overhead light so the light didn't go on when he opened the door.

"I'm going with you, Ben," Claire said, stopping him. "Duke could be meeting Bridger, and Bridger might be with Sam. With all these people and so little light, there's no way you can spot him. I know his height and build, the way he walks, the sound of his voice. I can find him if he's in there."

"You can't go with me, Claire."

"Why not?"

"This is a damn bloody sport, for one thing. I'm not sure you can handle it."

"Other women are going in."

Ben shook his head. "Not women like you."

Another group walked past, tattoos and piercings, black leather jackets, a buxom blonde and a heavily painted redhead.

"Just give me a minute," Claire said.

Ben watched as she opened her purse and pulled out a hairbrush, unfastened the clip holding back her hair and brushed it out, back-combed it into a mass of dark silk.

She took out a tube of red lipstick he was surprised she owned and painted her full lips a fiery shade of crimson, rubbed a little on her cheeks. Unfastening the last few buttons on her white cotton blouse, she knotted the ends above her waist, then unbuttoned the top buttons to flash a little cleavage.

She cast him a challenging smile. "I'm ready. Let's go."

He tried to ignore the little jolt of lust he got just looking at her. She was right about recognizing Sam. Dressed like that she would fit in well enough. Still, he didn't like the idea. He made a last effort at discouraging her.

"What about your sneakers? Not exactly de rigueur for this kind of affair." Even in the powdery dust, the women wore platform heels.

"You're right." Climbing down from the passenger seat, she hurried to the back of the Tahoe and popped the trunk. The zipper on her carry-on buzzed. When Claire walked back to where he stood, she was wearing a pair of strappy black superhigh heels. She had rolled up the legs of her jeans, showing off her pretty ankles.

She looked more like a hooker than the angel he called her. But he had to admit it might just work.

"All right, you can come. I might need your eyes to find Sam. But you do what I tell you, and whatever I say, you play along. You're dressed like a whore. Play the part."

Those words sent his thoughts in a dangerous direction, but the moment he glanced toward the barn, his mind returned to his son and he was all business. "Let's go."

Claire wrapped her fingers around his biceps as they started walking, using him for balance on the dusty rutted road. He slid an arm around her waist to steady her and guided her toward their destination.

The noise grew louder as they drew near. At the entrance, two Hispanic men stood guard, each wearing a shoulder holster over a dark T-shirt. One was big and muscular with skin so dark it looked black, the other tall and rangy, his arms roped with muscle and lined with blue ink prison tattoos.

Ben let go of Claire and eased a little away from her in case he needed to move fast. His pistol rode at his back. He wondered if they would want him to give it up. Then again, this was Texas. Everyone carried here.

Their attention swung from him to Claire, looking her over with eyes full of lust and bulges in their jeans.

"Eh, gringo. I have not seen you here before," the bigger man said.

Ben managed to smile. "Friend of Duke Hutchins. He here yet? He's supposed to meet me."

"*Sí,* he just came in."

"How about Troy Bridger? He here, too?"

"Maybe. I don't know him." Hard black eyes slid back to Claire. His thin lips curled up in a wolfish smile. "You got a good-looking woman, *señor*. She for sale?"

Claire's face went pale. Ben kept his easy smile in place. "Not tonight."

The other man just laughed. "Good luck, hombre."

"Gracias, amigo." He wasn't fluent, but he knew enough Spanish to get by. So did the rest of the guys on his SEAL team. One of the reasons they'd been sent to Juarez. It came in handy in Houston.

"Come on, baby," he said, pulling her close. "Let's go win some money."

She laughed as if she couldn't wait, a throaty, sexy purr that made his groin throb.

"Buy me something pretty if you win?"

He raked her with his eyes. Even with the makeup and hair, she didn't quite fit in. A little too elegant, maybe. Or a little too naive. "You bet, sweetheart."

They headed for the beer concession, which was on the other side of a door leading out on the right. Ben bought a Bud in a red plastic cup and handed it to Claire so they would look like everyone else in the crowd. He made a slow, ambling loop around the barn, noticing it had four big open doors, one on each side, providing possible avenues of escape.

Then he led Claire back inside, moving toward the open area in the center of the barn, keeping her close, scanning the throng of people, looking for Hutchins or Bridger while Claire searched for Sam.

It was hard to believe people brought kids to a place like this, but they were there, standing next to their parents, some up in the rafters looking down on the matches. Bloodthirsty little bastards.

He could feel the tension in the hand Claire wrapped around his arm in a tourniquet grip. As they moved closer to the ring and the cries grew louder, he was pretty tense himself.

Claire forced her legs to move. She'd been determined to help Ben look for Sam, had told herself she could handle seeing what went on inside. Michael had once done an exposé on cockfighting, a bloody sport that was now illegal in all fifty states but still went on in far too many places.

Obviously one of those places was here.

She clung to Ben's arm and pasted on a smile, trying to pretend she was enjoying herself. The crowd was a mixture of Hispanic, white and black, the dregs of society, from what she could tell. Michael had told her it was a favorite sport in a number of countries around the world, which might have accounted for some of the Asian men she saw.

He had also said that all levels of society frequented the matches, gambling thousands of dollars, some of the purses as high as a million.

Not this one. As they drew closer to the ring surrounded by bales of straw, she saw fistfuls of money being handed back and forth as the betting went down for each match, but this crowd wasn't made up of millionaires.

In the center of the ring, a bronze rooster wearing three-inch metal spurs on its legs faced a snow-white opponent also wearing knife-sharp spurs. Their handlers were goading them, bringing them to a fighting frenzy.

The roar in the barn would have matched a World Series baseball game.

"See anything?" Ben asked, stopping next to a wooden post a little ways from the fighting.

Claire tore her gaze away from the ring just as the handlers let the birds go but not before she saw one of the steel spurs on the bronze rooster sink into the white chicken's back. Blood erupted over its snowy feathers.

"Not...not so far." She kept her gaze averted, looking up at Ben, her stomach churning, her smile carefully fixed in place. At the moment, with all the makeup and her frozen expression, she figured she looked more like a mannequin in a horror movie than a prostitute.

"Do you see Hutchins?" she asked.

"I got him spotted. Over to the left about two o'clock."

Her adrenaline took a leap as her gaze swung in that

direction. There was enough light to see him—dark blond hair, rangy build, scruffy blond beard along his jaw. She wasn't sure she could have picked him out from the glimpse she'd gotten as he drove the Camaro out of town, or watching him walk in the darkness toward the barn. But Ben had seen his photo, and he was trained for that kind of thing.

"I don't see Troy," she said.

"Keep looking." He spoke low in her ear. "Anything goes wrong, you know the drill. Get to the car as fast as you can. Give me five minutes. If I don't get there or if you're threatened, haul ass for the highway. Find a motel and leave a message on my phone where I can find you."

Claire swallowed. They'd both gotten keys to the SUV at the rental car agency. She hadn't considered she might have to leave Ben and drive off by herself. A shiver of fear slid through her.

"What…what are you going to do?"

"For now, just wait for Bridger. If he doesn't show, we'll follow Hutchins back to his apartment. I'll find out what he knows about Sam."

Those icy eyes looked hard as steel. She didn't want to think how far Ben would push to get the information he wanted.

Instead, she searched the faces in the barn, looking for Troy or Sam. At the edge of the circle of light illuminating the ring, rough-looking men and blowsy women cheered for the victorious rooster. A number of the men were armed, blatantly wearing knives hooked onto their belts or strapped to their thighs. She was sure some of them carried weapons in their pockets.

It was a dangerous crowd and it horrified her to think that Troy might be bringing Sam to a place like this.

"Hutchins is moving," he said. "Let's go."

The door on the west led to the beer stand, where Hutchins was probably headed. Guards were posted beside each open door, watching for police, she assumed, or keeping out unwanted guests.

She let Ben guide her toward the door, saw Hutchins disappear outside. Ben eased her into a shadowy corner.

"I need to know where he's going, but I need your eyes in here. Will you be okay for a couple of minutes?"

"I'll be all right." She ignored the tattooed, leather-jacketed man standing among several others a few feet away. She didn't want to think what could happen to her if Ben didn't return.

He bent his head and kissed her long and deep, sending a message to the men that she was his possession, warning them not to bother her. It was part of the role they were playing, but the heat of his mouth over hers didn't feel like acting. It didn't keep her already-hammering heart from kicking up another notch.

"I'll be right back," he said, loud enough for the men to hear, and then he was gone, disappearing quietly into the cheering throng. She scanned her surroundings, her mission clear. Locate Sam and Bridger if they were in the barn.

The shouting continued, each roar marking a bloody victory she didn't want to imagine. Instead, she kept searching the shadows, looking for Sam and Troy, praying Ben would return.

Claire stifled a gasp as she spotted them, Troy with a beer cup in his hand, his other hand resting on Sam's small shoulder. They were headed toward the east-side door that led out to a row of portable toilets. She'd only caught a glimpse of Sam as he turned away, but his body language told her he wasn't happy about being there.

Claire's insides squeezed. Sam had always been soft-hearted when it came to animals. This had to be tearing him apart.

Frantically, she glanced around, looking for Ben, hoping to see him walking back inside. No sign of him. Terrified they would get away, Claire started for the door, determined to keep them in sight. Her heart was pounding, throbbing so hard it hurt. Lifting her head, hoping to project an air of confidence as she imagined a paid-for lady would, she walked toward the door.

She could feel two pairs of eyes on her as she stepped out into the night, the men who guarded the east exit, a burly Asian the size of a house and a man of mixed heritage with angular cheekbones and jet-black eyes.

She couldn't see Troy. She had no idea where he'd gone, but she spotted Sam walking off toward the parking area.

Claire kicked off her heels and started after him, wishing to God Ben were there, afraid to call out to him. Afraid to call out to Sam for fear Bridger would hear her.

She stifled a scream as an arm locked around her neck and she was jerked backward against a man's hard chest.

"What the hell are you doing here?"

She knew the voice, knew Troy had found her. She trembled, tried to speak, but there wasn't a drop of moisture in her mouth. His hold tightened, and he started dragging her back into the shadows along the side of the barn.

"I asked you a question, bitch."

She swallowed, managed to force out the words. "I—I came after Sam."

He spun her around to face him. "Who brought you?"

"I came…came by myself."

"That's a goddamn lie." He cracked the back of his hand across her cheek, knocking her into the wall. Claire cried out when he dragged her up and hit her again. The world spun and for a moment she thought she was going to faint. She stared up at Troy, saw the hard look on his face and screamed as loud as she could.

Fourteen

Where the hell is she? Ben scanned the crowd in the area where Claire should have been waiting. No sign of her. Worry slid through him. He'd left Hutchins at the beer stand, afraid to leave Claire alone any longer, but when he got back, she was gone.

His chest felt tight. Unless someone forced her to leave, she had spotted Bridger and Sam and was following them.

Christ.

He'd come in through the west door. No sign of them there. The toilets were on the east side. Ben shouldered his way through the crowd, moving fast in that direction.

At Claire's high-pitched scream, a shot of adrenaline hit him, jolting him into action, and he shot through the open east door. Her white blouse made her easy to spot in the moonlit shadows at the side of the barn, struggling with a man who pressed her against the wall.

"Let me go!" she demanded.

"Shut up, bitch! You brought this on yourself!"

Right height, right build. He turned and Ben recognized him as the man in the photo with Laura. *Troy Bridger.* Clamping his jaw against the anger pumping through him, Ben lunged toward Bridger, grabbed him by the shoulder and spun him around, went into SEAL combat mode and pounded him with a left jab-right combination, smashed an elbow into Bridger's face, splitting his cheek wide-open and drawing blood.

"Sam's gone to the truck!" Claire shouted and started running toward the lot. "I'm going after him!"

He got a quick glimpse of her, saw that her cheek was bruised and her lip was bleeding, before Bridger swung a blow that Ben blocked. Thinking of Claire's battered face, a shot of fury tore threw him. Ben took great pleasure in elbow-striking Bridger again, then bringing the bastard down with a fist to the back of his head and a knee to the belly.

Bridger hit the ground and didn't get up.

Much as he wanted to finish the man where he lay, he started after Claire, who raced ahead of him toward the parking lot. He'd only made it a couple of steps when a gunshot cracked and pain tore into his side. The bullet spun him around and he went down, dropping onto a knee.

Heavy caliber, he figured. Enough to do some damage.

Pain ripped through him as he reached for the weapon at his back. Blood poured out of a wound below his ribs and his hand was slick with it, making it hard to hold the butt of the pistol. Through rapidly blurring vision, he saw Bridger stagger to his feet. Hutchins raced up beside him, shoving a big semi-auto into the back of his pants, and both men took off running, passing

Claire, who had turned and was racing back in Ben's direction.

She grabbed him as he swayed to his feet. "Oh, my God, Ben, he shot you! How...how bad are you hurt?"

Every instinct told him to go after his son, but he was losing a lot of blood. "Help me get to the car." He should have figured on Hutchins showing up. *Stupid.* He'd been sidetracked by his fear for Claire. He'd lost his focus in a way he hadn't since he was in BUDs, trying to suck it up and make the cut to become a SEAL. He didn't want to think what might have happened to Claire if Hutchins had been a better shot.

A crowd had begun to gather. Aiming his .45 at the curious throng, he looped an arm over Claire's shoulder and started backing away. Since knifings and gunfights were commonplace at events like these, the guards ignored them, and the sight of the weapon in his hand kept the crowd at bay as he and Claire vanished into the darkness.

No one came after them, since they were leaving the scene. The crowd just started fading away, wandering back to the betting and blood sport inside the barn.

As Claire helped him along the dusty path, he kept his hand pressed against his side to slow the bleeding, but wetness leaked through his fingers and soaked his black T-shirt. His side hurt nearly as bad as the time he'd been knifed in the Philippines.

From the corner of his eye, he spotted Hutchins's black Camaro peeling out of the lot. He didn't see a white Chevy pickup, but his vision was blurry and shapes were distorted.

"We're almost there," Claire said, her voice shaky. "Just hang on a little longer." He could feel her trembling as they stumbled together toward the car.

"We've got to stop the bleeding," she said when they reached the SUV. Ben holstered his .45 and tossed it in the console as Claire helped him climb into the passenger seat.

"I'll do what I can. You just drive."

Her hands shook as she untied the tails of her blouse and tore open the last few buttons, jerked it off and shoved it into his bloody hands. "Use this."

He watched her slide in behind the wheel in her white lace bra, had the crazy thought that she looked hot as hell, then he must have blacked out for a second. The wheels were spinning, dust flying when he opened his eyes again, Claire roaring out of the makeshift parking lot onto the narrow dirt road leading back to the highway.

"We've got to find a hospital," she said, her voice shaking.

"GPS." Tearing off a chunk of her blouse, he stuffed it into the hole in his side. "I'll find one."

The shot was a through-and-through, which was good news and bad, since it meant the bullet wasn't inside but there were two holes to fill instead of one. He ripped off another section of fabric and stuffed it in the entry wound in his back. Lucky for him, the rotten bastard had piss-poor aim or he'd be dead instead of just bleeding.

As Claire neared the highway, he reached over and hit the POIs on the nav system, pulled up hospitals and punched in the one closest to their location. As soon as they left the dirt road, the faceless voice on the GPS began to give directions.

Ben leaned back in his seat and closed his eyes, remembering those moments just after he'd walked outside the barn.

"I saw him, Claire. Just for a moment after you screamed. I saw my son."

She glanced his way and a soft sob caught in her throat. "I didn't…didn't want to leave without him. Oh, God, Ben."

"I'd be dead if you hadn't come back for me."

She turned to look at him, and he saw the tears on her cheeks. "I couldn't just leave you."

He closed his eyes, fighting not to lose consciousness. "I didn't see his face. I didn't realize it was Sam until I saw you with Bridger."

"Don't talk. You need to save your strength."

He gritted his teeth against the searing pain and his failure to save his son. "We didn't even get a fucking license number."

He felt Claire's gentle touch against his beard-stubbled cheek. "Oh, yes, we did, Ben. I memorized the number as Troy pulled out of the lot."

Ben's mouth edged up. "Good girl. Call it in." He caught the worry and triumph in her pretty green eyes the instant before he passed out cold in the seat.

Fifteen

Claire paced the floor of the waiting room outside the surgical ward of Desert Hills Hospital. Ben had just gone into surgery. She had no idea what was happening behind the closed double doors at the end of the hall. All she knew was that Ben had been covered in blood and unconscious when she had roared up to the door of the emergency entrance and slammed on the brakes, jumped out of the car and burst through the doors, shouting for help.

On the way to the hospital, she'd hit her cell number for Detective Fred Owens of the LAPD, and though he was off duty this late at night, he had answered on the second ring.

"I saw Bridger, Detective," she'd said. "Sam was with him. I got the license number of his truck." She had rattled off the plate number, told him about the cockfight, and that she was on the way to the hospital with Sam's father, Ben Slocum, who had been shot trying to rescue his son.

"I'm on it," Owens had said. "Good luck with Slocum. I'll be in touch." She had called the LAPD detective instead of 911, certain Owens would have a far better chance of getting the cooperation of the El Paso police department than she would. She prayed the local authorities would find the pickup Troy was driving before he could escape with Sam.

The waiting room was a little chilly. A heavyset black woman and her daughter were the only other occupants. They sat quietly at the other end of the room, talking in whispers.

Now that there was nothing more she could do for Ben except wait, she dug out Ben's iPhone, retrieved from his pockets along with his insurance information. The only person she knew to call was his friend Sol Greenway, whose name was in his contacts.

His voice sounded groggy when he answered. "Greenway."

"Hello, Sol. My name is Claire Chastain. I'm calling for Ben Slocum. There's…there's been a shooting."

"Jesus. Is Ben all right?"

"He's in surgery. I'm at the hospital in El Paso." Her voice broke. "I'm sorry to…sorry to bother you so late. But I didn't know who else to call."

"It's all right…it's not a bother. Ben's a friend. Just tell me what's going on."

She told him about Sam and the cockfight and the shooting and that Ben was in surgery. She told him she didn't know much more than that. Then she started crying. "I'm so worried. I just want Ben to be okay."

"Take it easy, Claire," Sol said gently. "I know who you are. I know you and Ben have been working together to find his son. Ben doesn't have any family but he has lots of friends. We're all here for both of you."

She took a deep breath and forced herself under control. "I'm sorry. I didn't mean to fall apart."

"It's okay. Sounds like it's been a hard night."

"Yes…"

"They're going to call you, Claire. Once they know Ben's been hurt, there's no way I can stop them. Odds are some of them are going to show up in El Paso. All you have to do is hold on till they get there."

She swallowed past the lump in her throat. "The name of the hospital is Desert Hills. As soon as he's out of surgery, I'll call you."

"That's good. I'll tell the others. Take care of yourself, Claire. I know that's what Ben would want."

She cried for a couple of minutes after she hung up and was glad the waiting room was as large as it was and that the woman and her daughter were far enough away to give her some privacy.

During the next thirty minutes, she heard from the owner of the company Ben worked for, Trace Rawlins, a friend named Jake Cantrell and another named Alex Justice, both investigators in his office. Justice was on his honeymoon in Costa Rica. He offered to cut the trip short if Ben needed him. She'd told him the same thing she had told the others, that there was nothing he could do until Ben was out of surgery and she had spoken to the doctors about his condition.

A woman named Annie Mayberry was the last to call. "Don't you worry, honey," she said. "Ben's too tough to let a little thing like a bullet take him out. Besides, all of us here'll be prayin' for him."

"Thank you, Annie."

"Ben's family. Family sticks together. You just let me know if you need anything."

"I will." She didn't know why, but she felt better after she talked to Annie.

Another hour slid past. Claire shoved to her feet as the surgeon, Dr. Garcia, a silver-haired man in a set of green scrubs, older, with a kind face and weary expression, shoved open the waiting room door.

"Doctor…how is he? Is Ben going to be all right?"

Garcia smiled, a good sign. "He's in amazing physical condition. He came through the surgery extremely well. There was no artery or nerve involvement, and the damage to his spleen was minor. The path the bullet traveled missed any vital organs and bones."

Her legs went weak. She sat back down in the chair. "Thank God."

"Your husband is a very lucky man."

The doctor had assumed Ben was her husband. It was easier than trying to explain their complicated situation. And being his wife allowed her visitation. It bothered her that the sound of it felt somehow right.

"Ben's lost a lot of blood," the doctor said, "but aside from that, he's doing fine. Assuming there's no infection, he'll be out of here in a couple of days."

A second shot of relief slid through her. He was going to be all right, and he would be getting out very soon. Still, it was a gunshot wound, which by law had to be reported to the authorities. She had told the doctor the truth of what had occurred, but she would have to go over the details again when the police arrived. She was hoping Detective Owens's phone call would help smooth the way.

Feeling somewhat better, she rose on legs a little less shaky. "May I see him?"

"At the moment, he's in recovery. You can see him

in a couple of hours. I'd suggest you go back to your motel room and get some sleep."

Of course she didn't have a motel room. And she wanted to see Ben, make sure he was all right and let him know she was there. "I'll wait here, if you don't mind."

Garcia nodded. "The cafeteria's down the hall. Why don't you at least get something to eat?"

She wasn't hungry. But it had been hours since she'd put anything in her stomach and she was beginning to feel light-headed. "All right. I have a call to make first. Thank you, Doctor. For everything."

"I'll let you know when you can go in." The doctor left the waiting room.

As soon as the door closed, Claire dug Ben's phone back out and phoned Sol with the news that Ben had come through surgery very well. That, if all went well, he would be released in a couple of days.

"That's great news. I'll call the others. Let me know if either of you needs anything."

"I will. Thank you, Sol." Ending the call, she dropped the phone back into her purse.

Ignoring the way her stomach rebelled at the thought of food, Claire left the waiting room and made her way down to the cafeteria. The smell of fish and fried chicken made the bile rise in her throat, but she had to eat something. She forced down a bowl of soup and drank a glass of milk, then purchased a cup of coffee to go and went back upstairs to the waiting room.

She had just stepped inside when a towering man in a T-shirt and jeans pushed through the door. He was at least six-five, with an even more muscular build than Ben, and a beautiful dark-haired woman on his arm.

"Are you Claire?" the man asked.

"Yes."

"I'm Jake Cantrell, and this is my wife, Sage. We thought you might need some company."

Her eyes welled. Sol had said Ben had friends. Apparently very good ones. "Thank you so much for coming."

Sage stepped forward and gave her a hug, and Claire gratefully returned it.

Jake led her over to the sofa, gently urged her to sit down. "Sol just called. He said it looks like Ben's going to be okay."

Claire nodded, a lump lodged in her throat. "Yes…"

"How about you?" Sage asked gently, her eyes on Claire's bruised cheek and swollen lip. "Are you all right?"

Claire swallowed. "I'm okay. It's just… It's been a really hard night."

Sage sat down next to her, and Jake took a seat in the chair across from them. "Why don't you tell me what happened," he said.

"It's a long story."

Sage reached over and took hold of her cold hand. "I gather you're waiting to see Ben."

"That's right."

"Then we have plenty of time," Jake said.

Claire looked up at him. He was amazingly handsome, the perfect match to his lovely, sophisticated wife. "You came all the way from Houston. How did… How did you get here so fast?"

"Company jet," Sage answered with a smile. "It's one of the perks of being the granddaughter of the CEO."

"Don't let her kid you," Jake said with a hint of pride. "Sage just got promoted to president of the company.

She's Marine Drilling's top dog. She earned the right to use that jet."

"It's only temporary," Sage said. "I've decided I want more time with my husband. But it's an exciting challenge right now."

Claire studied the woman sitting next to her, impressed, but not really surprised. Sage Cantrell had the poise and confidence of a woman who could succeed at whatever she wanted. And apparently, she was also a great friend to Ben. "I'm so glad you came."

"Me, too," Sage said. "We heard about Ben's son and that the two of you have been trying to find him. Tell us what happened."

For the next half hour, Claire told Ben's friends about searching for Sam, about the cockfight and that the boy had been there with Troy Bridger, who had taken him from his foster home in L.A. She told them how a friend of Bridger's called Duke Hutchins had shot Ben, and how Bridger had gotten away with Sam.

By the time she had finished, she felt drained, and the guilt she felt in failing Sam had resurfaced. Claire shoved the emotion away.

"I talked to Detective Owens," she said. "He's in charge of the case in L.A. He got in touch with the local police here in El Paso."

"That's good," Jake said. "They'll want to talk to you. Maybe I can help with that."

"Jake specializes in private security," Sage explained, squeezing Claire's hand. "He knows how to handle situations like this. You aren't alone now, Claire. We're here to help."

They had come for Ben, but they were here to help her, too. For the first time since all of this happened, Claire thought maybe everything was going to be okay.

* * *

Ben woke up feeling groggy, barely able to open his eyes. His side ached like hell, but the pain was numbed by the drugs dripping through the tube going into his arm. It took a moment to sort out what had happened and where he was. For an instant, he thought he was back in the jungle, in a makeshift triage tent being treated for the knife wound he'd received on a mission gone bad.

"Ben, it's Claire."

The soft sound of her voice floated over him. The feel of her hand gently holding on to his brought the night's events rushing back.

"You're out of surgery, Ben. The doctor says you came through really well. The bullet missed any vital organs or bones. You're going to be okay."

His eyes slid closed. *Good news. Damned good news.* He hadn't been sure how bad he'd been hit, but he knew one thing for sure. He wouldn't be in the hospital. He'd be lying dead in some ditch if it hadn't been for Claire.

"That's…good," he managed to say.

"They're hoping to release you in a couple of days."

He nodded, relieved by the words. He moistened his lips, which felt dry and chafed, and his words came out rusty. "Did the cops…get Bridger?"

Claire shook her head and he caught the glint of tears. "No."

"We'll find him…Claire. I…promise."

She managed a smile, but it looked tired and strained. "Your friends are here, Jake and Sage. They flew down from Houston."

He nodded, wasn't surprised. He was glad they were here to help Claire. He thought of how close she had come to being hurt or even killed. He couldn't remember a time he'd worried so much about a woman.

He heard the door open. Saw Jake walk in. Sage, the classy brunette Jake had fallen head over heels in love with, was beside him. Both of them looked worried, but they were smiling.

"The doctor says you're going to be okay," Sage said, leaning over to brush a kiss on his cheek.

"That's what…Claire…tells me."

"She's been really worried about you."

He'd been downright terrified for her when the shooting had started, but he didn't say that.

"I guess you didn't see this one coming, hey, Ice?" Jake said.

"Should have. Stupid…mistake."

Jake shook his head. "According to Claire, you were busy trying to save her from Bridger. She said it was a good thing you showed up when you did."

"Should have been…watching for…Hutchins. Tell me they've…got him in…custody."

"Sorry. I talked to one of the El Paso P.D. detectives half an hour ago. Hutchins is in the wind, just like Bridger."

Ben's hand fisted where it lay on top of the sheet. He wanted Bridger. Wanted Hutchins. More than that, he wanted his son.

"You'll find them, Ben," Jake said, reading his mind. "And when you do, you'll find your boy."

Ben's jaw felt tight. "Count on…it," he said before his eyes slid closed and he gave in to the pull of the drugs flowing through his veins.

Sixteen

◦⟋⟍⊙⟋⟍⊙⟋⟍◦

The stark white hospital room, its only window looking out on another concrete wing of the building, was
beginning to wear on Claire's nerves. At least the fresh-
cut flowers on the sill and lined up on tables countered
the antiseptic smells.

Most of the colorful bouquets had come from Ben's
friends in Houston: Sage and Jake; Trace Rawlins and
his wife, Maggie; yellow daisies from Sol and the office
manager, Annie Mayberry. A huge bouquet of exotics
had arrived from Alex Justice and his bride, who were
still on their honeymoon in Costa Rica.

Flowers had come from Johnnie Riggs and his wife,
Amy, and a bouquet with a silly G.I. Joe balloon float-
ing above it came from Tyler Brodie. That, of course,
was the one Ben liked best.

At night Claire returned to the La Quinta Motel, a
few blocks down the street. Sage and Jake had waited
with Claire the entire first day until Ben's condition
was stable enough he could be moved to a private room.

They'd turned out to be amazing friends. Before

they'd left, Jake had spoken to the police, clearing up the matter of Ben's involvement in the shooting. Ben had given a statement and been interviewed by a pair of detectives named Holloway and Sparks. That had led to an arrest warrant for Duke Hutchins for attempted murder. Troy was wanted for the abduction of a minor.

Sage had insisted on sending the company jet back to pick Ben up when he was discharged from the hospital, which had happened that morning. As soon as Ben was officially released, they would drive to the executive terminal at the airport, drop the rental car and board the plane.

While Ben dressed in the clothes she had brought him last night—a pair of jeans and a navy blue T-shirt retrieved from his duffel in the back of the Tahoe— Claire walked out into the hall to answer a call on her BlackBerry. Checking the caller ID, she pressed it against her ear.

"Mom! It's great to hear your voice."

"Hi, honey. Dad and I are just back from the cruise and getting settled in. The trip was wonderful. Rome was spectacular, and oh, we loved Barcelona." Her mother went on to describe all the wonders they had seen and the fabulous museums they had visited. "I wish you could have been with us."

"Me, too, Mom. Maybe next time." It certainly would have been less stressful. "I'm glad you had such a great trip."

Her dad took the phone. "Everything's good back here. How are things at your end of the country?"

No way was she telling her parents where she was or any of what she was doing. Not until this was over. Her dad had a heart condition, not too serious, but he had to watch what he ate, and stress wasn't good for him.

"Oh, just same ole, same ole." *I'm at the hospital with a man I slept with but you don't know. He's recovering from a bullet wound in his side.* "Just working hard, doing a little travel for my job." *Oh, and did I mention I was assaulted while I was helping the man you don't know search for his son—who may have been abducted by a white supremacist?*

But none of that came out of her mouth. Her dad talked a little longer, then her mom got back on the phone to say goodbye. "You're still coming home for Thanksgiving, right?"

"Absolutely," Claire said. She told them she loved them and hung up the phone.

She loved her parents, but she enjoyed her independence. And she wasn't ready to tell them anything about Ben. She wasn't sure she ever would be.

She started to stuff the phone back into her purse when it rang again. She checked the number, but it didn't look familiar. She pressed the phone against her ear.

"Hello, Claire. I've missed you."

Her fingers tightened around the phone. "Michael."

"I went by your apartment before I left the country, but you weren't home."

"You're back in Colombia?"

"I won't be here much longer. I'd like to get together when I get back, talk things over, see where we stand."

Claire's gaze shifted toward the door to Ben's room. "We stand exactly where we stood when you left the country the first time. It's over, Michael, and I'm moving on. You need to do the same."

"I love you. I'm not willing to throw what we had away."

She couldn't deal with this now. Not with everything

else that was going on. "I wish things could be different, but they aren't. I have to go, Michael. I'm sorry."

A couple of seconds passed. "I'll call you when I get back. I love you, Claire." The line went dead. For several long moments, Claire just stood there with the phone against her ear.

There was a time Michael's vow of love and his determination to make their relationship work would have meant everything. But in the months since they'd parted, her life had changed. She'd had time to consider what she wanted, discover what was important in her life. She didn't think Michael could ever give her those things.

Dropping her phone back into her purse, she reached for the door to Ben's room and walked inside. He was sitting in the chair instead of lying on the bed, his face pale and his beard heavy, desperately in need of a shave.

He looked hard as nails and more dear to her than any man she had ever known.

"What's taking them so damned long?" he asked, fidgeting, anxious to be released.

One thing she knew: Ben Slocum was not a patient man.

"Paperwork. You might as well relax. That's just the way it works. And by the way, good morning."

He didn't smile. By now she was used to that with Ben.

"I'm glad you're here, Claire. We need to talk."

Her stomach dipped sharply. She couldn't miss the black scowl on his face. "Has something happened? Did the police call? Have they found Bridger?" She didn't want to think what else that dark look might mean, or that something had happened to Sam.

"I spoke to Holloway. No news yet. They haven't found Bridger or Hutchins."

Which meant there was still no sign of Sam. "What then?"

He levered himself up out of the chair, clenching his jaw against the pain, reached out and took hold of her hand.

"I want you to go home, Claire, back to California. What happened out at that barn…you could have been the one who wound up in the hospital—or worse. I never should have taken you out there in the first place."

"You didn't have a choice, Ben. We had to follow Hutchins. He was our only lead. And it almost worked. Sam was there, Ben. We almost had him."

"*Almost* isn't good enough. Look, Claire, for the moment we're at a dead end. There's nothing either of us can do till we come up with something new. As soon as that happens, I'll be back on Bridger's tail."

"I'm not going back, Ben. Especially not now. We know where Bridger's headed. Once you're feeling better, we can go down to Louisiana and start looking for his brothers. They can lead us to Bridger and Sam."

"That sounds good, except we don't know Bridger or his brothers' real name."

"We'll find out what it is. Sol can help us. We can do it if we keep working together."

Ben shook his head. "I'm not taking you with me. It's just too dangerous. After what happened, I can't believe you can't understand that."

"I understand it. I also understand that if I hadn't been with you that night, you might have bled to death outside the barn. You might have died, and if you had, what would happen to Sam? He needs us, Ben. He's in trouble and I'm not going to abandon him."

He raked a hand through the wavy black hair he usually kept so short the waves didn't show, but now it needed a trim. She had played the guilt card, which she hated to do, but she was desperate. She could help him, just as she had before. Ben needed her, even if he couldn't see it.

"Please sit down," she said firmly. "If you want to get out of here, you had better conserve your strength."

A corner of his mouth edged up. "Since when did you get so bossy?"

"Since I saw you lying on that table in the emergency room. I figured right then, as much as you hate the idea, you need someone to take care of you—at least for the next few days."

He sank down heavily in the chair. He might be well enough to get out of the hospital, but he was hardly in top fighting condition.

"So you're planning to come back with me to Houston."

"If that's where you're going, yes."

He was quiet for a while. "You were good out there," he said softly, as if it bothered him to concede even that much. "You should have gone straight to the car when you heard the gunshot and driven the hell out of there, but I'm glad you didn't. You were tough when it counted. I owe you, Claire."

She started to say he didn't owe her anything, that they were in this together.

Instead, she said, "You owe me? Fine, then take me with you. That's what I want in payment for your debt."

His lips curved again. It made her remember how good it felt when he kissed her. It seemed a lifetime ago.

"You're a hard lady, Claire."

She smiled, certain she had won. "I'll take that as a yes."

He didn't have time to argue before the door swung open and one of the nurses walked into the room pushing a wheelchair in front of her.

"Ready to go home?" Nurse Riley, a stocky woman with curly brown hair, asked with a smile.

"More than ready," Ben said.

Exactly what Claire was thinking.

A cool October wind ruffled the leaves on the big sycamore in Ben's backyard, a welcome change after the long summer's heat. A storm was blowing in off the Gulf. Heavy black clouds rolled over the city, and the air was heavy and damp.

Ignoring the codeine pain pills the doctor had prescribed, Ben sat at the computer in the bedroom he'd converted to a study, clenching his jaw against the throbbing in his side. Though the gunshot wound was healing, it still ached like holy hell, but the pills made him sleepy and he needed to stay focused, his mind sharp as he dug for anything that might lead him to Bridger.

In the Atlas Security office, Sol Greenway was working overtime trying to come up with Bridger's real name.

Ben leaned back in his chair. The room was quiet, no classic rock playing on his iPod, no sound coming out of the speakers near the treadmill. His home gym sat forlornly beside it, the chrome weights gleaming with accusation.

His study served two purposes: a place to work cases when he was away from the office, and a weight-training area so he could stay in shape. He usually worked out five days a week, mostly heavy lifting and strengthening exercises, running on the treadmill to keep his heart rate up.

Since he got home, he'd been doing a little light-weight training, trying to build himself back up, but it wasn't enough. He'd be glad when he was fit enough to get back to his regular routine.

With any luck, that would be soon. With even better luck, he'd also find a link to Bridger that would lead him to Louisiana or wherever the bastard had taken Sam.

Seated at the computer, Ben flexed his wrists, then rested them on the keyboard and went back to work searching the internet for white-supremacist groups in Louisiana. So far he'd found nothing that pointed to Bridger or his brothers, but he'd come up with a lot of interesting information, and knowledge was often the key to solving a case.

In the hall outside the study, light female footsteps sounded. Ben looked up to see Claire walking through the open door. Pleasure at seeing her slipped through him. Ben firmly ignored it.

She'd been staying in his house since they'd traveled back to Houston in Marine Drilling's fancy Citation jet, fussing over him until it was driving him crazy.

"You've been at this for hours," she said, her hands planted on her slender hips. "The doctor told you to take it easy."

She looked so damned pretty. The bruise on her cheek was beginning to fade, and her bottom lip had healed. He was clearly feeling better because he wanted to suck on it, wanted to kiss that sexy mouth. Hell, he wanted to drag her down the hall into his bedroom and strip off her jeans and T-shirt, see what she was wearing underneath. He wanted to rip off another pair of panties.

She was driving him crazy, all right.

"I'm not the type to sit around, Claire. At least this gives me something to do besides lounge in bed and worry about Sam."

In El Paso, he had tried to convince her to fly back to L.A., but he could have saved his breath. He knew how determined Claire could be when she put her mind to it. He hadn't forgotten how she had hauled his sorry ass to the car then driven like a bat out of hell to the hospital while he bled all over the seat.

"I keep thinking we'll hear something. Now that we've given them the plate number, the police should be able to find Troy's truck and stop him."

"Lots of cars on the road between here and Louisiana."

"I know." She leaned over his shoulder to look at the computer screen and he caught the soft scent of her perfume. The ache in his side was replaced by an ache farther down.

He'd always had a strong sexual appetite. Over the years, he'd been with dozens of women. He wasn't interested in carving notches into his bedpost; he just never wanted to get in as deep as he had with Laura. He never wanted to feel the anger, hurt and pain he'd felt when he'd been stupid enough to fall in love. He didn't want to risk that kind of emotional disaster again.

At least he hadn't. Since that night in Phoenix, even with the chance of getting in too deep, the only woman he wanted in his bed was Claire.

Maybe he just hadn't gotten a big enough taste of her.

Though she damned well seemed to have gotten her fill of him.

"Have you found anything?" she asked, pulling his thoughts back where they belonged.

"It doesn't look like the fist and the 33/6 symbol on the brothers' T-shirts pertain to any particular supremacist group. Wearing it just signifies a certain belief system."

"Like a pink heart for breast cancer or a blue circle for diabetes."

His mouth edged up. "Not exactly, but you get the idea."

"So we can't track the brothers by their T-shirts."

"No."

"How many white-supremacist groups are there in Louisiana?"

He thought of the article he'd read. "The Aryan Nations just set up its new world headquarters in Converse. That's a small town south of Shreveport. Neo-Nazis, Klan, CSA and a group that calls itself The Order. They're all part of the Nations."

"CSA?"

"The Covenant, the Sword and the Arm of the Lord. They go all the way back to the seventies."

Her dark brown eyebrows went up. "Quite a name."

"They're white supremacists, anti-Semitics and polygamists."

"Great. I guess they don't like much of anyone."

"Except their many wives."

Her lips curved. She was so pretty when she smiled. Desire filtered through him and heat slid into his groin. Until the past few days, he'd been able to keep his mind off sex, but with Claire in the house, it was getting harder and harder to do. No pun intended.

"I hear you told the doctors you were my wife," he said, just to get a reaction.

Her cheeks colored prettily and her chin went up.

"*They* assumed it and I didn't correct them. It got me in to see you. At the time it seemed like a good idea."

"Take it easy. You did the smart thing." He let his gaze wander over her, thinking he wouldn't mind doing a little pretend husband-and-wife housekeeping right now. "You know that deal we made in Arizona?"

Her eyes widened. "No. I don't remember anything about any deal in Arizona."

He chuckled. The woman kept him entertained. "The deal where we had one night of hot, mind-blowing sex and promised never to talk about it again?"

"All I remember is the never-talking-about-it part. The part where we promised to forget it ever happened. You might try recalling that."

He came up out of his chair and began to stalk her, Claire backing up a step for every step he took toward her. When she came up against the wall, he pulled her into his arms.

"I don't want to forget. I couldn't, even if I tried."

She gasped as he bent his head and kissed her, settling his mouth firmly over hers, testing the fullness of her lips under his. For a moment, she pressed her hands against his chest as if she meant to push him away. Then those sweet lips softened and parted, and Claire kissed him back, her slender body melting into his.

He'd begun to wonder if she still wanted him, if her wild response in Arizona had been mostly his imagination. But the little mewling sounds coming from her throat and the diamond-hard points of her breasts said his desire for her was returned.

Ben nibbled and coaxed, deepened the kiss. God, she tasted like strawberry jam and sexy female. When she slid her tongue into his mouth, his breath hitched and so did hers. He cupped her breast through the

T-shirt, ran his thumb over the sharp little bud at the crest, heard her moan.

He wanted to pick her up and carry her down the hall to his bed, but he didn't think his side could handle it. He bit down on an earlobe, kissed the side of her neck.

"Let's go to bed," he whispered. "I'll make it good for you, Claire." He kissed her again and she swayed against him, kissed him back with growing urgency.

He figured she would have agreed if she hadn't bumped his wound just then, eliciting a sharp grunt of pain.

Claire tore free. "Oh, my God, what was I thinking? Are you all right? Did I hurt you?"

"I'm fine." That was a lie, but what the hell? A little pain would be worth it. He caught her hand, pulled her close and kissed her again. "Come on, let's go."

Claire jerked away. "No way, Ben Slocum. You aren't in any shape to have hot, mind-blowing sex. You need to get well so we can find Sam."

His groin was throbbing, aching more than his side. He was hard as granite, but, dammit, she was right. He couldn't afford to do something stupid like tear out his stitches.

She was right—again. And he was getting damned tired of it. Being a know-it-all wasn't becoming in a woman.

Well, usually. He kind of liked it in Claire.

"Okay," he said. "For now. But once I'm good to go, the deal is off. Just so you know."

"That's crazy. What if I say no?"

His mouth faintly curved. "Then I'll convince you to say yes."

"What…what about working together?"

"We've done all right so far. We'll manage."

"I'm not agreeing to anything—just so you know."

He smiled. He couldn't help it. "I've always enjoyed a challenge." He sobered. "Unless, of course, you'd rather go back to L.A." Which was suddenly the last thing he wanted.

It was insane. She'd be safe, and so would he.

Claire squared her shoulders. "I'm not going back."

Relief he shouldn't have felt slid through him. "Then as soon as I'm well, all bets are off. You're fair game, angel."

She opened her mouth and closed it again. Turning, she started for the door. "I have to go. I have work of my own to do." Leaving him frustrated and amused, Ben watched Claire walk into the hall and close the study door.

With a sigh of resignation, he returned to his desk and sat back down in his chair. His side was throbbing like a thousand hammers pounded away inside him. And yet he felt better than he had in days. Sooner or later, Claire would be his.

He waited for the little voice that told him he'd gone straight off the deep end, but the voice never came.

Seventeen

The wind blew all night and was still whipping the branches and terrorizing the shrubs late the following morning. Turning away from the window above the kitchen sink that looked into Ben's leafy backyard, Claire poured herself a cup of coffee from the dregs left in the pot. The kitchen was small but neat, with four of everything: place mats, plates, cups, glasses and silverware. Clearly Ben didn't do much entertaining.

He seemed to be feeling much better. It was good news and scary news—Ben wanted her, he had made no bones about it. He intended to seduce her. The question was what did *she* want to do?

She mulled the question over as she added some half-and-half to her cup, took a sip and winced at the bitter taste. She was wildly attracted to Ben. Just looking at his amazing body made her hot and shivery all over, embarrassingly aroused. She knew how good he could make her feel, hadn't forgotten those incredible multiple orgasms. But Ben was a loner and as soon as he found his son, he would be ready to move on.

Even now, it was hard to think of him with another woman. Getting in deeper would only make things worse.

Still, it was tempting.

Claire rolled the idea around in her head as a light knock sounded at the door. Setting her cup down on the white tile counter, she made her way across Ben's man-cave living room to peer through the peephole, saw Sage Cantrell, Maggie Rawlins and Annie Mayberry, the little blonde woman in her sixties she had met along with his other friends the first day of their return to Houston.

Claire smiled and opened the door. "Hello. Come on in. It's good to see you all."

"It's good to see you, too." Sage hugged her as she stepped into the living room, followed by Annie and Maggie.

"I could use a little female company," Claire said. "Ben's getting better, which means he's as crabby as a caged tiger."

"So he's back to his lovable old self," Annie said.

Claire grinned. "Getting close, I guess. Would you like a cup of coffee or a glass of iced tea?"

"Tea sounds great." Sage was dressed in an expensive beige suit with dark brown embroidery on the lapels, and a pair of very high brown suede heels. Annie wore a dark green pantsuit and flats, making the difference in their heights dramatic.

"I'd love some tea," Maggie said. "I think we all would." In black jeans and a lightweight turquoise sweater, Maggie Rawlins had pulled her fiery red hair into a ponytail, a few soft wisps escaping around her pretty face. She was a well-known landscape photographer. One of her pictures, a seascape at sunset, hung on the wall in Ben's living room.

"I brought this." Annie handed Claire a foil-covered plate. "I know how much His Grumpiness likes brownies."

Claire smiled. "I love them, too. Thank you, Annie."

As she carried the brownies into the kitchen, Claire glanced at the clock and realized that the morning was almost over and it was nearly noon. She poured each of the women a glass from the pitcher of tea she kept in the fridge, and the women sat down at the round oak kitchen table.

Annie took a sip and frowned. "Where's the sugar?"

"Sorry. I forgot this is the South." Claire set out the sugar bowl and teaspoons. "Ben's working in his study. Let me tell him you're here. I know he'll be glad to see you."

"In a minute," Annie said, stopping her. "Truth is, we came by to see you."

"You did?"

"We figured you could use a little moral support," Sage said. "Ben isn't the easiest guy in the world."

"The man needs a guard dog instead of a woman to take care of him," Maggie said with a smile.

Claire tossed her stale coffee into the sink, poured herself a glass of tea, carried it over to the table and joined them.

"Ben's really not so bad. He acts tough, but that's just his way of protecting himself. Actually, he's a very nice man." As if to make the point, Hercules wandered over, jumped up in Claire's lap and meowed. She stroked a hand over his soft gray fur. "See. He's a cat lover. That proves it."

Sage laughed. "I don't think most women would think of Ben as nice."

"Maybe he just wasn't nice to them."

Annie harrumphed. "You can say that again."

Maggie took a sip of her tea. "Did you know you're the only woman he's ever let stay in his house? At least that's what Trace says."

"Ben's always been a one-night-stand kinda guy," Annie said bluntly.

Something Claire had known that very first morning she'd seen him climb out of his SUV in his wrinkled black tuxedo. It was also the moment she'd been hit with a fierce sexual attraction that had only grown stronger every day.

"I know the kind of man he is," she said, tracing a finger through the condensation on the outside of her glass. "If you're thinking we're involved in a relationship, we aren't. We…umm…we're just working together to find his son."

Annie frowned. "We're talking about Ben Slocum here, right? Gorgeous blue eyes. Six-pack abs. Rock-hard body. You're not a lesbian, are you?"

"Annie!" Sage's eyes twinkled. Maggie took a drink of her tea to hide a grin.

"I'm not a lesbian," Claire said, fighting a smile of her own. "Of course I'm attracted to Ben. What woman wouldn't be? But as you said, he's a one-night-stand kind of guy. I'm not that kind of woman." Except for that one wild night in Phoenix she was supposed to have forgotten but never really would.

"Good for you," Annie said.

"Ben used to be different," Claire said. "I know I shouldn't tell you. I'm sure he wouldn't approve, but when he was younger, there was a woman he loved. When it didn't work out, he changed."

"Sam's mother," Sage guessed.

"That's right. Laura. Before she died, we became close friends."

"So you're saying this Laura is the reason Ben doesn't trust women," Annie said.

"They were madly in love, but according to Laura love wasn't enough. Ben found her in bed with another man three days after they got engaged."

Sage leaned back in her chair. "I knew there was something. I never could quite put my finger on it."

"Please don't tell him I told you. He can't handle another woman's betrayal and that's the way he'd see it."

"We're family," Annie said firmly. "Family doesn't hurt each other."

Sage reached over the table and caught Claire's hand. "Ben thinks a lot of you, Claire. When he was in the hospital, he asked Jake and me to look out for you. He said you were amazing in El Paso, that you saved his life. He said he'd never known a woman like you."

A feeling of warmth slid through her. "He really said that?"

Sage nodded. "He couldn't stop singing your praises."

"Of course at the time, he was high as a kite on drugs," Annie added.

Maggie just smiled. "I've only seen the two of you together once, but Ben was clearly protective of you. Considering he thinks women are made strictly to satisfy his appetites, you're definitely special. Of course if you ask him, he'll probably deny it."

"What will I deny?" Ben asked, strolling into the kitchen, looking ridiculously sexy in an old drab green T-shirt and jeans.

"None of your business," Annie said, and Ben grinned.

All three women just stared.

"What?" he said.

"You don't grin," Annie said. "You're the Iceman."

His grin turned into a scowl. "What are you doing here, anyway? You come by to torture Claire?"

Annie grunted. "I imagine you can handle that all by yourself."

"We just wanted to make sure you're okay," Sage put in diplomatically.

Ben ran a hand unconsciously over his side. "Better every day. I'm coming into the office tomorrow morning. I want to work with Sol, do some brainstorming, see if we can think of another way to pick up Bridger's trail."

Annie's voice softened. "You'll find your boy, Ben. I know you will."

Ben just nodded.

"You got a picture?" Annie asked.

Claire was surprised when he pulled out his wallet and slid out a photo of Sam. "I found it in an album Claire had in her living room." He turned in her direction. "I didn't think you'd mind."

"I don't mind," she said softly, feeling a stab of the old guilt for giving Bridger a reason to want revenge and not protecting the boy.

Ben held the photo out to the women.

"He looks just like you," Annie said.

Sage studied the picture. "Same black hair and those Iceman eyes. Sam's a very handsome boy."

Maggie took the photo. "He's smiling. He looks like a happy kid. You'll find him, Ben, and bring him home."

A muscle tightened in his jaw as he took the photo

from Maggie's hand and slid it back into his wallet. "I need to get back to work. Thanks for coming by."

The women watched him disappear down the hall.

"He loves the kid already," Annie said.

Claire's throat tightened. "I know." She shook her head. "It's my fault Sam's missing. I should have told him how much I cared about him. I tried to adopt him myself, but the judge wouldn't have it. I should have convinced him to give me time to work things out and find him a loving home."

Sage squeezed her hand. "You did your best, Claire."

She swallowed. "I promised Laura I'd take care of him. She didn't think Sam's father would want him, but I should have gone to Ben sooner, found out for myself. I let all of them down." Tears swam in her eyes.

Maggie leaned over and hugged her. "You'll find him," she said. "You'll bring Sam home."

She nodded, wiped away the wetness. "We just… We need a clue, something that will tell us where to look. I'm coming into the office with Ben tomorrow. He won't like it, but I'm coming anyway."

The women exchanged glances.

"You're coming anyway," Annie repeated, a glint in her shrewd brown eyes. "Even if Ben doesn't want you to."

"He can't always have things his way."

Annie grinned. Sage and Maggie smiled.

Was Ben really that hard a man? But Claire knew that he was.

The women finished their tea and headed back to work, leaving Claire alone in the kitchen. As she thought back over the visit, she started smiling. She felt as if she'd been battered by a whirlwind and yet she hadn't missed their concern. She really liked Ben's friends. And she was beginning to think they liked her. Life was just full of surprises.

If they found—*when* they found Sam, she corrected—she had a big surprise in store for Ben.

Eighteen

"I'm taking you to dinner." Ben walked out of his bedroom at six o'clock that evening, looking gorgeous in beige pants, a soft blue sweater that set off his eyes and a navy blue sport coat. "If you don't have something pretty to wear, we'll buy you something on the way."

Claire ignored the little tug of heat that slid into her stomach. She stood up from the kitchen table, where she had been working on her iPad, catching up on email and checking with her friend Mary Wilson on the boy Ben had rescued.

Mary's last email had said that Ryan was living with a family she had personally chosen and so far he was doing great. She had copied the email to Ben, who had also been checking on him.

"I went shopping yesterday," she said. "If you remember, I lost my heels in El Paso. I didn't expect to be gone from home quite so long so I needed a couple of other things, too." She'd bought a pair of jeans and a couple of T-shirts for Sam. He was bound to need clean clothes by now. "Are you sure you feel well enough to go out?"

"I'll feel the same whether I'm here or somewhere else, and the house is beginning to feel like a prison. I need to get back on my feet and this is a good way to start."

"It isn't my cooking, is it? I know I'm not great, but I thought I made a pretty decent spaghetti dinner last night."

He walked over, set his hands at her waist, bent his head and lightly kissed her. "You're cooking's fine, angel. I'm just not used to staying cooped up."

"What about Sam?" She felt guilty for even thinking of doing something that might be fun. It wasn't fair when Sam was in so much danger.

Ben clenched his jaw. "We're doing everything in our power to find him. Going out for something to eat isn't going to change that."

"I know, but—"

"If we don't come up with something concrete by tomorrow night, I'm taking the photo of the brothers down to Converse and showing it around. It's not much of a town, but maybe somebody there will know who they are."

"Aryan Nations—white supremacists. That's a good idea."

"Don't get your hopes too high. They're not a particularly friendly bunch. Even if we can get them to talk to us, they might not tell us the brothers' name."

"If they know, they'll tell you. I saw you with Eddie Jeffries, remember?"

His lips twitched. "I guess that means you're coming along."

"You bet."

"So then, how about dinner?"

What could it hurt? And the truth was, she was feeling cooped up, too. "All right, if you're sure. Where are we going?"

"Capital Grill. It's a nice place. I'll think you'll like it."

"Okay, then I'd better go change."

She was ready half an hour later in a little black sheath dress and a new pair of black high heels. The dress had cap sleeves and a low back, and she was wearing it with thigh-high black stockings. She told herself she hadn't bought the outfit with Ben in mind, but she knew it wasn't true.

She made a slow turn, showing off the dress, enjoying the way his eyes went from blue ice to hot flame.

"Maybe we don't need supper," he said a little gruffly. "You look good enough to eat." Sliding a muscled arm around her waist, he drew her close, bent his head and kissed her. For an instant, Claire thought maybe he was right and dinner could wait.

Then she came to her senses. "I thought you wanted to get out of the house."

"I do." He kissed her lightly one last time. Claire collected her sweater just in case. Ben took her hand and led her out to his Denali.

The Capital Grill was an upscale restaurant done in an elegant forties-style with dark wood-paneled walls, black-and-white tile floors and huge frosted-glass lamps suspended from the high ceilings.

"Good evening, Mr. Slocum." In a black tuxedo, the maître d', a thin man with silver-tinged dark brown hair and glasses, seemed well acquainted with Ben. "It's good to see you. I have your table ready."

"Thanks, Tommy."

As the man seated them at a linen-draped table in a quiet area of the restaurant, Claire tried to hide her surprise that Ben would be a regular in a place like this.

Ben cast her a glance. "What? You didn't think I liked nice places? Or maybe you thought all I owned were jeans and T-shirts."

Her face went warm. "I saw you in a tuxedo, but I figured it was rented. I think of you more as the rugged he-man type. Not Mr. *GQ,* though I have to say you look amazing."

He chuckled. "Thanks. The tuxedo is actually mine. There are times my job requires formal dress. But the truth is, I don't come here that often. Mostly just special occasions."

She arched a brow. "So what's the occasion tonight?"

Ben caught her hand and brought it to his lips. "I'm going to seduce you tonight, Claire. All the way through supper, I want you to think about what I'm going to do to you when we get home."

Her heart sputtered. For a moment, she forgot to breathe. "You...you aren't well enough yet."

"I'm well enough for what I've got in mind."

"I haven't said yes."

"Not yet. I plan to change that." He turned her hand over, pressed his mouth against the palm, and she felt a little quiver in her stomach.

Ben picked up his menu and opened it as casually as if they had been talking about the weather.

Claire squirmed in the seat. She was wearing red lace panties and a matching bra she had bought on her shopping excursion. Now as she thought of Ben's words, every time she moved, the lacy cups chaffed her nipples and the panties rasped against intimate places.

"Red or white?" he asked, his head bent over the wine list.

"Wh...what?"

He closed the list and she realized with a surge of embarrassment he was talking about the wine.

He turned to the waiter. "I've got a better idea. Bring us a bottle of Dom Pérignon. It's a special occasion."

She tried to swallow, couldn't. Ben Slocum was buying her expensive champagne. He was trying to seduce her. And it was working.

"What are you going to have?" Ben asked as the waiter arrived with a silver ice bucket and a bottle of French champagne. The tall, sandy-haired young man popped the cork and poured the bubbly golden liquid into two chilled flutes.

Ben's words rushed back and Claire's stomach lifted. "Fish, I guess. Something light."

His eyes ran over her, paused on the soft swells of her breasts above the bodice of the dress. "Good idea." He raised his glass. "Here's to the evening ahead."

Her hand shook. She didn't return the toast, just took a long drink of champagne. When she raised the glass again, Ben's hand caught her wrist.

"Take it easy, angel. I want you sober when I take you." He smiled, making him look even more handsome. It was so rare, it always caught her by surprise. "In the meantime, I want you to relax and have a good time."

She couldn't miss the teasing glint in his incredible eyes. He was enjoying this—far too much. Well, two could play the game.

She set her champagne glass down on the table. "You're right. There's no need to hurry. But while we're sitting here enjoying ourselves, I want you to know that under this dress I'm wearing a pair of teeny, tiny red bikini panties and thigh-high black stockings. I want you to think about how much you're going to enjoy peeling them off me."

Ben's fingers tightened around the stem of his glass, spilling a little champagne onto the white linen tablecloth. "Lady, you don't play fair."

"Yes, well, neither do you."

He signaled the waiter. "We need to order. I think this meal is going to be a lot shorter than I planned."

Claire felt a moment of victory.

Then she looked into those hot blue eyes and remembered Ben's words. She had issued a challenge, and there was no doubt it had just been accepted.

Oh, dear God, what had she done?

The rain was falling heavily when they left the restaurant, the storm revving up again. They were back at the house by ten o'clock. Not the evening Ben had in mind when he'd come up with the idea, a night that included a stop at a little jazz bar he knew for an after-dinner drink and listening to some music.

But the game had shifted the moment Claire had accepted his challenge and thrown down one of her own. He'd been hard all evening, thinking of those red bikini panties. Thinking of the passionate red-car woman he knew her to be.

They stepped through the garage door into the kitchen. Ben reset the alarm, reached for her and drew her into his arms. He kissed her softly and felt her tremble. Her fingers were stiff where they curled around the lapels of his coat.

He hadn't expected her to be nervous. But maybe he should have. The first time they'd had sex was an impulse. Claire had sensed his need and responded, sharing the comfort of her body. That comfort had turned into something wild and erotic, something neither of them had expected.

He took her hand, led her toward the living room, where he'd left a lamp turned down low. "How about an after-dinner drink?"

Claire stopped and looked up at him. "Why don't... don't you just take me to bed."

His body was already hard and aching. But he wanted this to be right. Wanted it to be good for Claire.

"Believe me, angel, that's exactly what I'm planning to do. But we don't have to hurry. We've got all night."

She seemed more nervous than before. Ben plugged his iPad into the stereo system and soft jazz poured out of the speakers. Strains of Kenny G floated into the living room. Making his way to the kitchen, he took down a bottle of Kahlua, poured the sweet coffee liqueur into a pair of lowball glasses, added ice and some of the half-and-half Claire kept in the fridge for her morning coffee.

He carried the glasses into the living room. "We missed dessert. I figure this should do." He set the drinks down on the coffee table, sat down on the sofa next to Claire. "A nice slow dance would be good, but I'm pushing my luck a little, as it is." His side was aching, but only a little. Outside, the storm was building. The windows rattled, and he heard the roll of thunder.

Claire didn't touch the drink.

"What, you don't like Kahlua?"

Her pretty lips thinned and her chin went up. "Is this your usual seduction routine, Ben? You take a woman out to a swanky restaurant and buy her champagne, then bring her home and put on soft music. You fix her a drink and dance with her and then—"

"Stop it. Stop it right now." His jaw flexed in anger. "I don't have a seduction *routine*. And I rarely bring women home. Mostly I go to their place so I don't have to wake up with them in the morning. I wanted this night to be special. I wanted you to know how special you are to me. I should have known better. Fuck it." Ben shot up from the sofa, but Claire was also on her feet.

"Oh, God, Ben, I'm sorry."

He stood rigid, a muscle clenched in his jaw.

Claire reached up and touched his cheek. "That time in Arizona…it was…it was easy. Nothing was planned, you know? It just happened. Everything just seemed right."

"But not tonight," he said darkly.

"Tonight…I wanted you to make love to me. But when we got here, I started worrying. I was afraid it wouldn't be as good as it was before. I was afraid you'd compare me to your other women and find me lacking." She went up on her tiptoes and kissed him softly on the mouth. "I'm so sorry. Please forgive me."

She thought he would find her lacking? No way in hell.

Cupping his face between her hands, she kissed him softly, planted tiny little butterfly kisses on the corners of his mouth, kissed him until his fierce expression softened and he couldn't hold out any longer.

Deep kisses followed, soft and coaxing, then fierce and taking.

"I'd never compare you to another woman, Claire," he whispered against the side of her neck. "If I did, she wouldn't stand a chance."

He caught the surprise in her eyes, along with the glitter of tears. "Ben…"

He pulled her back into his arms and kissed her. The physical attraction they felt for each other was strong. Tonight would be good. He knew it even if she didn't. Ben kissed her one way and then another, kissed her until her body softened and her nervousness slid away.

"Let me make it up to you," she said, kissing him one last time. The next thing he knew, she was reaching behind her back, sliding down her zipper, letting her little black dress fall in a heap at her feet. He watched as she unfastened the clasp on her lacy red bra and slid it off her shoulders, stood in front of him in only her tiny red lace panties, sheer black man-killer stockings and high black heels.

"You're beautiful, Claire. No man could ask for more."

"Make love to me, Ben. Make me feel the way you did the last time."

Screw the ache in his side. He'd make it good for both of them. Sliding his hands into her hair, he hauled her against him, held her in place while he ravished her mouth.

Claire shoved his jacket off his shoulders, pulled his sweater off over his head, then ran her hands over his bare chest. "You have the most beautiful body."

She pressed her mouth against his pecs, curled her tongue around a flat copper nipple and made him groan. Going up on her toes, she kissed him, slid her tongue into his mouth.

The kisses went deeper, wetter, hotter. The bedroom seemed a million miles away. They stumbled and kissed their way down the hall, through the door and over to the bed.

"We have…have to be careful of your side," she said breathlessly, and he kissed her fiercely once more.

Kneeling, she helped him out of his dress shoes and socks. He wore only his slacks and briefs, and seconds later, those were gone. Drawing her back to her feet, he cupped her breasts, took the fullness into his mouth, suckled, brought the tips to hard little crests.

"I want to look at you." Easing back a little, he let his gaze roam over the glossy dark hair spilling around her shoulders, her long legs and delicate curves, let her see in his eyes how much she pleased him.

"Leave the stockings on," he said, taking charge, unable to resist any longer. "Get rid of the panties." Deciding he liked them enough to save them from ruin, he watched her slide them down to her legs and step out of them. "Get up on the bed."

His blood raced as she settled herself on the mattress, turning his erection to granite. He hoped his raging hard-on didn't scare her again. "Part your legs for me, angel. I want to taste you."

A nervous little whimper came from her throat. "I don't think… I don't think—" She gasped as he climbed up on the bed and wedged his shoulders between her thighs. She was the sexiest thing he'd ever seen, those pretty stockinged legs parted, her eyes wide and a little uncertain.

He kissed his way to the bare spot above the top of her hose, ran his tongue over the smooth pale skin above them. Finding her softness, he stroked her, began to nibble and taste her. Claire bucked against his mouth, curled her fingers into the bedspread as he continued his assault, driving her toward climax, arousing himself to the point of pain.

Outside the window, lightning flashed and the storm

thundered. Just as his heart was thundering, slamming against his ribs. He brought her to the peak, watched her body convulse in passion, listened to her sweet cries of pleasure. It was heaven, and yet all he could think of was being inside her, taking what he wanted, what he so desperately needed.

As she began to spiral down, he came up over her, kissed her deeply, felt her arms twine around his neck.

"Ben…" she whispered, opening to him, taking him into her body, lifting her hips in welcome. He meant to go slow, but the hunger was clawing at him, vicious, relentless in its demand. His side ached as he drove harder, pounded into her with the fury of the storm, took her and took her, claiming her in some way, marking her as his.

Lust had him in its grip and yet it was more. Something primitive he didn't understand. Something that frightened him more than lying wounded in the Philippine jungle, certain he was going to die.

It taunted him as he climbed higher, took her faster, deeper, harder.

It didn't occur to him that he hadn't used protection until Claire had reached another peak and he had joined her, spilling his hot seed into her womb.

Claire lay in bed, a soft smile on her lips. Whatever happened, she would never regret these intimate moments with Ben. His hand reached for hers, curled around her fingers.

"We've got a problem, angel. I'm really sorry, but I… umm…didn't use protection. I meant to, but… Hell, I have no idea what happened. If a problem comes up—"

"It's all right, I'm on the pill. I never stopped taking them after Michael and I broke up. I don't know…

maybe I thought there was a chance we'd get back together."

Tension crept into his shoulders. "You don't still feel that way."

"No. It's over between us. It was never really right in the first place." She turned onto her side to look into his face. "You just got out of the hospital so we know you're safe. And I've been checked, too."

He nodded, seemed relieved. "Then from now on, we're good to go."

Her heart gave a little kick. "From now on?"

He ran a finger along her cheek. "I told you before, one night wouldn't be enough. Apparently, two isn't, either." He leaned over and lightly brushed her lips. He was hard, she realized. Ready to go again.

"You need to get well. We have to think of Sam."

He sighed heavily, rolled away from her onto his back. She had used an unfair tactic, but she had a hunch his wound was hurting like crazy. She thought of the scar she had seen on his lower back. It was long and jagged, puckered as if it had been treated by an amateur rather than a professional. And there was another scar on his thigh.

"I know you were injured when you were in the SEALs. I noticed the scars. How did it happen?"

He didn't answer for so long she thought he might not. Then he released a slow sigh. "We were in the Philippines. Lot of terrorist action there. I can't say much about it, just that the mission went south and I wound up in the hospital for a couple months. I couldn't do the job—not the way I wanted—so I left and eventually wound up here."

Claire leaned over and kissed him lightly on the lips. "I'm glad you did."

"Me, too." Ben moved to deepen the kiss but Claire broke away.

"You need to rest. Tomorrow we're going into the office to work with Sol. We need to be sharp when we get there."

"*I'm* going into the office."

"I'm going with you."

He came up on an elbow, his pale eyes fixed on her face. "Tell you what. We both need a good night's sleep. I know how to make that happen."

She didn't protest when he kissed her, came up over her, slid himself deeply inside. They made love again, slower this time, but in a different way just as intense.

Ben Slocum was a force to be reckoned with, a man she already cared too much about. A man who left a trail of broken hearts, and hers would surely be among them.

Claire sighed into the darkness. She would worry about that tomorrow, she told herself as she curled against his warm, hard-muscled body and listened to the sound of his deep, even breathing.

But the worry was there, tugging at the back of her mind, keeping her awake. Claire sighed into the darkness. At least one of them would be getting a good night's sleep.

Nineteen

By the time Ben's eyes cracked open at seven o'clock the next morning, Claire was already dressed, waiting impatiently to leave for his office. He yawned and hauled his ass out of bed, way later than usual for him.

It had only been a little over a week since he'd been released from the hospital. He wasn't completely recovered, he had to concede, but he was getting stronger every day.

Claire had toast, eggs and coffee ready when he padded into the kitchen, freshly showered and dressed in jeans and a dark blue lightweight sweatshirt with a Houston Texans steer head on the front. Though he waited all through the breakfast, she didn't mention the heated night they'd spent together, and neither did he.

They were back to the same old pattern, pretending nothing had happened. He wasn't sure how he felt about the night before—not that the sex hadn't been great. Better than great. Still, he hadn't had a serious relationship with a woman since Laura, and he didn't want to go down that painful road again.

They left the house and Ben drove the short distance to his Atlas Security office in the University District, arriving a few minutes after 8:00 a.m. The bell rang above the door as they walked into the reception area.

"Hey, Ice! You're lookin' good, man." Sol Greenway was the first to greet him. Tall and rangy, with a goofy grin, longish brown hair and horn-rimmed glasses, the computer whiz kid was a major asset to the company.

"You remember Claire." At one time or another, they'd all been by the house to check on him, all been introduced to Claire.

She leaned over and kissed his lean cheek. "I didn't get a chance to thank you, Sol, for everything you've done."

A little shy with women, Sol's face turned red. "Hey, no problem. Ice is back on his feet and we're just getting started. I've got some new ideas. I figure if we all put our heads together we'll find this chump and Ben's kid."

Annie walked out of the employees' lounge just then. "'Bout time you quit loafin' and got back to work."

"That's what I've been telling Claire, but she can be almost as pushy as you."

Annie laughed and turned to Claire. "So His Crankiness hasn't run you off yet?"

"Not yet," Claire said, grinning. Clearly the women liked each other. Which was never a good thing for a single man.

Trace walked out of the conference room in his usual cowboy boots, Western shirt and jeans, Jake right behind him in a dark brown suit, probably working a protection detail.

"Good to see you back on your feet," Trace said, shaking Ben's hand.

"I'm surprised you stayed cooped up this long," Jake

added. He looked down at Claire. "I see you brought the brains of the operation." Jake kissed her cheek.

"She didn't give me any choice," Ben said. But they all knew she wouldn't be there if he hadn't allowed it. He had never brought a woman into the office before.

"Maggie says hi," Trace said to Claire.

"She's really great, Trace. You're a very lucky man."

"And don't I know it." Trace turned to Ben. "So you're back to work?"

He nodded. "We need to come up with a lead. If we don't find one by the end of the day, we're headed to Converse in the morning."

Trace knew Ben had been working the white-supremacist angle. Jake was also up to speed on the case.

"You need any help you let us know," Trace said. But he and Jake both had clients of their own, and at the moment, Sol's talent was what he needed.

The kid cracked his knuckles. "Okay, let's get started." Following Sol across the beige carpet, they headed for his glass-enclosed office next to Trace's.

Aside from the reception area where Annie worked, the main part of the office was open, with sturdy oak desks for the people who worked there. Pictures of Texas ranches hung on the dark green walls, with a few new landscapes added since Trace had married Maggie.

As they reached Sol's office door, Ben flicked a glance at Claire. He had already warned her about the "don't ask, don't tell" rule that applied when any of them were working with Sol. It was a lot more productive that way.

"You ready?" Ben asked.

"You bet." Her chin firmed as they walked into the office. She was on her game, he could see, and felt the rare urge to smile.

Ben tilted his head back, trying to work the kinks out of his neck. Looking over Sol's shoulder at his computer had made a long day for all of them. Since they'd come up with nothing on Bridger, they'd decided to concentrate on Dennis Arthur "Duke" Hutchins. Though Hutchins was wanted for attempted murder, so far the police hadn't been able to track him down.

There was no way to know if Hutchins and Bridger were still together, or if they'd parted company the night of the shooting. But wherever Duke was, odds were he knew where Bridger had gone.

They started from the beginning. Duke's birth certificate said he was born in El Paso, no father listed. They looked for other family members he might have gone to for help, but his brother was in jail in Oklahoma and his mother had died of a heroin overdose when he was fifteen.

Since they were fairly sure Bridger was born in Louisiana, they skipped to Hutchins's high school records. Sol found his El Paso High School yearbook posted online, and Claire spent twenty minutes scanning class photos, hoping to spot a young Troy Bridger—or whatever his name really was.

"He's not there," she said with a frustrated shake of her head. "I don't think that's where he and Bridger met."

Ben didn't think so, either.

In his senior year, Duke had dropped out of school and joined the army. Those records showed he'd been discharged a year later over a cache of missing weapons, no charges officially filed.

"If Troy had served in the army with Hutchins," Claire said, "his prints would have been on file, right? We would have been able to find out his real name."

Ben nodded. "That's right." But Bridger wasn't in the system. "We're thinking we might find someone else who knew Hutchins in the army, a friend he might have stayed in touch with, someone he might have gone to after the shooting."

But the documents in his file portrayed him as a loner with no close friends.

"Where did Hutchins go after he was discharged?" Claire asked.

Sol pounded and clicked, watched the screen. "He went back to Texas, started working in the construction business in San Antonio."

"That's it," Ben said. "That's the link. Bridger was a crane operator. They must have worked together someplace in San Antonio."

Sol dug into construction companies in the area ten to twelve years ago, about the time Hutchins would have been working there after his army discharge. Nothing turned up that linked the two men, but Ben was convinced that was where Bridger and Hutchins first met.

They looked at his prison file, searching for cell mate names. Someone who might be out of jail and willing to give him shelter. Nothing looked promising.

Late in the afternoon, Ben phoned Detective Bruce Holloway in El Paso for an update. Holloway was a born-and-bred Texan. He understood family, and he was determined to help Ben find his son. On top of that, he was a former marine.

"Holloway."

"Ben Slocum. Anything new on Hutchins or Bridger?"

"Sorry, Ben, not so far."

"You talk to his friends? Girlfriends? Anyone who might know where to find him?"

"We've been doin' our job, if that's what you're askin'. The guy was a lone wolf. No close friends, no lady friends. His neighbors haven't seen him since the night of the shooting. It's a good bet he's left the city. I'd say there's a fifty-fifty chance he's with your man, Bridger."

"Yeah, that's what I figure, too. Keep me posted, will you?"

"You got it."

As the call ended, Ben ran a hand through his hair. His side was aching, and he was more tired than he should have been. "I think Trace knows somebody with the San Antonio P.D. I'll ask him to call, press them a little, see if they can dig around, locate anyone Hutchins might know."

The next time he looked at the clock on the wall, it was nearly 8:00 p.m. Twelve long hours and they had nothing.

"It's getting late. Why don't you go on home, Sol, get some sleep. You can start fresh in the morning."

"So we're going home?" Claire asked.

His gaze swung to hers. Until last night, those words wouldn't have bothered him. Now they made him uneasy. It wasn't much of a stretch to imagine Claire living in his house, spending her nights in his bed. That kind of thinking was the last thing he wanted.

He just nodded. "We're leaving for Louisiana in the morning. We'll need to get an early start."

She gave him a weary smile. She was as tired as he, and suddenly he felt guilty. No one he knew, man nor woman, had ever been more committed than Claire. She had been there for him when he needed her. She still was. Claire had never failed him.

But sooner or later he was going to fail her.

The notion bothered him all the way home.

Claire was exhausted, but it was Ben who worried her. His face was pale from the strain of working so hard all day, add to that the frustration of being no closer than they were before.

Ben ordered in pizza and they ate mostly in silence. As she cleaned up and put the plates and glasses in the dishwasher, her tension began to build. She wasn't sure what Ben expected. Last night had been amazing, but as before, neither of them had mentioned it. Did he want her to sleep with him again tonight? Was he expecting to have sex?

Or had he gotten his fill?

Was another night of intimacy what *she* wanted?

She knew it was, but not unless Ben wanted it, too.

"I'm going to take a shower and go to bed," she said without looking at him, afraid what she would see in his eyes. He'd been distant since they'd left the office, uncertain, perhaps, just as she was, where their relationship was going from here.

Claire headed down the hall to the guest bedroom she'd occupied since her arrival, stripped off her clothes and pulled on the terry-cloth robe she'd bought on her shopping venture, then headed for the bathroom at the end of the hall. She walked out ten minutes later, her hair swept up in a towel, her skin still damp.

In the bedroom, she discarded the towel and shook out her hair, slipped on her teddy-bear nightshirt. As she drew back the covers on the queen-size bed, a soft knock sounded at the door.

It had to be Ben and her pulse kicked up. When she opened the door, he stood in the hallway, freshly showered, his black hair still damp, looking more handsome than any man had a right to.

"I told myself to leave you alone," he said. "Better to keep a little distance. Safer for both of us. But it isn't what I want." His eyes remained on her face. "Come to bed with me, Claire."

Something sweet and warm slipped through her. "It's going to be a long day tomorrow. You need your rest. Are you sure?"

He drew her into his arms and just held her. "I'm sure." Then he bent his head and settled his mouth over hers in a soft, sweet, undemanding kiss. Ben took her hand and led her down the hall to his bedroom.

He made love to her with the same sweet tenderness, exposing the vulnerable side of himself he rarely allowed her to see. Afterward as she lay in his arms, Claire was forced to face an unwelcome truth.

She was falling in love with Ben Slocum. And it was the stupidest thing she could ever do.

Ben heard the ringing as a distant buzz in his ears. He stirred, opened his eyes, found himself pressed against a soft female body, a thick biceps draped heavily across a pale, elegant breast.

Ignoring the hard-on Claire's sweetly curved body had aroused, he eased away from her and picked up his iPhone. As he padded out into the hallway, he pressed the phone against his ear.

"Slocum."

"Bruce Holloway. They found Bridger's pickup. No sign of Bridger, Hutchins or your boy."

His hand unconsciously fisted. "Where?"

"Behind an abandoned barn off Route 96 south of Jasper. That's not far from the Louisiana border. Hood was up like he was havin' engine trouble."

"He must have gone on with Hutchins."

"Unless we get an auto theft report in the area, that'd be my guess. We've got the license number, make and model of Hutchins's car. The police are on alert."

"He's probably switched plates."

"Good chance. But they'll be watching for a black '99 Camaro with two men and a boy. Looks like you were right and Bridger's headin' for Louisiana."

Ben didn't say he was on his way there, too. He preferred to let law enforcement do their job while he did his.

"Where are they towing the pickup?"

"Jasper County sheriff's garage. It's a small town. The coroner does the forensic work. He'll take a look, see if anything interestin' turns up."

"Keep me posted, will you?"

"You know I will."

As he ended the call, Ben heard Claire's footfalls coming up behind him, felt his dark brown robe draped warmly around his bare shoulders.

"It's cold in the house. In case you've forgotten, you're naked."

He almost smiled. "I'm glad you noticed. If we had more time, I'd take advantage of that, but since they've found Bridger's pickup, we need to get going."

Her head came up. "They found the truck? What about Sam?"

"No sign of him. Best guess, both of them are with

Hutchins. The thing is, the truck was outside Jasper. It's on the way to Converse. There's a lot of back roads you can take to get there, but it may well be their destination."

"It fits with the white-supremacist theory."

He nodded. "I want to stop at the sheriff's office first. See what they find in the truck."

"I packed when we got home last night. A quick shower and I'm ready to leave."

"Same here." His mouth edged up. "I'd suggest we save water, but we need to get on the road."

She leaned into him, rested her head against his shoulder. "We're getting closer, Ben. I can feel it."

Ben thought of his son, a boy who was on the run with a convict and a child abductor, and prayed Claire was right.

Twenty

Claire watched as Ben loaded their overnight bags into the back of the Denali.

"What's all that other stuff you're bringing?" she asked, pointing to a long canvas bag and a big, heavy-duty aluminum truck box that fit behind the seat. She'd noticed the box before and wondered at its contents.

Ben gave her a long, assessing glance, leaned into the back, dragged the canvas bag over and unzipped it. Claire's eyes widened at a stash of weapons that looked as if it could arm the National Guard.

He reached into the bag and took out what looked like a machine gun. "AR 15 semi-auto. Convertible to automatic with a kit." He slid it back into the bag, opened a box and pointed to a big black handgun. "M-9 Beretta. Nine mil with a fifteen-round magazine."

He lifted out a short-barreled shotgun. "Mossberg Thunder Ranch six-shot, twelve gauge." He shoved the shotgun back into the bag, lifted out a smaller, holstered weapon. "My ankle gun—thirty-eight revolver."

He lifted out a long, sheathed knife with a serrated

edge. "My KA-BAR. It's come in handy more than once." He drew it out of its sheath, slid it in with a steely ring. "My Nighthawk's stashed in the center console. Oh, and there's a sat phone in the bag. You never know when you might be going off the grid."

"You have got to be kidding."

"In case you haven't noticed, sweetheart, I'm already walking around with the hole Duke Hutchins's bullet carved into my side. I'm not giving him a chance to finish the job."

"What…what if the police stop us?"

"These weapons are all legal, all registered. All unloaded—except for my .45." He pointed to another bag. "Ammo's in there."

Claire swallowed. "I'm afraid to ask what's in the box."

"My dive gear. I leave it in the car most of the time. I'm a frogman, remember? Oh, and a tactical vest. You never know when it might come in handy." Ben slammed the lid on the Denali. They climbed inside and buckled up. Firing up the engine, he backed out of the garage.

Following Route 59, then heading east on 190, they pulled into Jasper a little over two hours later. A town of only eighty-five hundred, or so Claire's iPad said, its only distinctive feature was the courthouse—a big oldfashioned brick building with a watchtower that dated way back to the 1850s.

The county sheriff's office was on Birch Street, a ways out of town, a beige, flat-roofed structure with white sheriff's department vehicles parked in the lot out front. She spotted a battered white Chevy pickup in a fenced-in area off to one side, and Ben parked the Denali near the entrance to the lot.

"That Bridger's truck?" he asked.

Just seeing it made her stomach knot. "That's it. I remember the dent in the front fender."

But where was Bridger now? Where was Sam? Claire ignored the heaviness in her heart as she climbed out of the pickup and let Ben guide her toward the front of the building.

Ben felt the same sense of dread he saw in Claire's face. Where was Sam? Had Bridger decided the boy was too much trouble and dumped him somewhere? Was he hurt or injured? Maybe even dead?

Ben worked a muscle in his jaw. As far as he was concerned, his son was in trouble and he was going to find him and bring him home. No other outcome was acceptable.

As he walked next to Claire across the parking lot, a silver-haired man, tall, broad-shouldered and imposing, approached from the opposite direction.

"Hello, there. I'm Deputy Carson. What can I do for you?"

Ben pulled out his badge and flipped it open. "Ben Slocum. I'm a P.I. from Houston. This is Claire Chastain. She's a social worker from L.A. I gather that's the pickup found outside town early this morning?"

"That's right. What's your interest?"

"I'm the father of the missing boy you've been looking for."

"There's a BOLO out on Troy Bridger, Dennis 'Duke' Hutchins and the boy. We've been keeping an eye out."

"I'm working the case. I'd like to see what you found in the truck."

Carson nodded. Family was important in Texas. "I

think I can help with that." The deputy led them into the sheriff's office, down a hall to an interview room. He left them seated at a table, returned a few minutes later with a large paper evidence bag.

"Wasn't much in the truck. No registration, no insurance info. Plate was still on so we knew it was Bridger's. Mostly just trash inside. Our guys have already gone over it."

He dumped the bag on the table. A beer bottle rolled a couple of inches. Ben caught it and set it upright.

"What about DNA? Bridger isn't in the system, but if someone else was in the truck besides my son, it might give us a place to look."

"We're a small department, Mr. Slocum. DNA takes time and money. We can send this stuff to Houston, have the boys down there take a look. I can tell you there was no blood in the vehicle, nothing that looked suspicious."

Relief filtered through him. "I'd still like them to make a run at it."

"All right."

But they didn't have a sample of Bridger's DNA, and Sam's would just confirm what they already knew. Then again, maybe something would turn up that would give them a lead if the trail went cold in Converse.

Ben's instincts said Bridger still had the boy with him. He'd gone to a lot of trouble to get Sam out of L.A. But now Hutchins was in the mix. If the three of them were together, Hutchins was a wild card that could change Bridger's game plan.

The deputy handed him a pair of latex gloves. "I'll give you a few minutes to take a look, but like I said, it's mostly just trash."

"Thanks." Ben looked down at the pile that included

torn Wrigley's Spearmint gum wrappers, dirty blue paper windshield washing towels, an empty Pepsi can, two Lone Star beer bottles and a coffee-stained paper cup. Taking a pen out of his pocket, he sifted through the rest of the smaller debris, including some clear cellophane candy wrappers with white printing on the sides.

"I saw some of those in Bridger's apartment," Claire said, looking down at the table.

"Now that you mention it, so did I. Guy must have a real sweet tooth."

Ben picked up one of the empty squares of cellophane, read the name of the candy. "Mud Bugs." He looked at the ingredients. "Chocolate, caramel and pecans."

"A little like pralines."

"Yeah." He read the rest of what was printed on the wrapper. "'Homemade Mud Bugs. Catahoula Candy Makers, Egansville, Louisiana.'"

"You know where that is?"

"No, but it's one more indication he's heading for Louisiana."

"Back to his family."

"Yeah. I'll have Sol check it out. Come on, let's go. It's another ninety miles to Converse. We'll do a little digging once we get there, maybe spend the night."

"I don't want to get my hopes too high, but I feel like we're getting close."

But close only counted in horseshoes. Taking Claire's hand, Ben led her out of the sheriff's office.

Converse, Louisiana, was a tiny village south of Shreveport with a couple of stoplights and a population of a little over four hundred. The residents were mostly white, typically Southern and not too happy the

Aryan Nations was planning to build a compound ten miles out of town.

Their first stop was the mayor's house, a little gray-and-white dwelling that conveniently had a sign reading Mayor's Office in the yard out front.

"The group's not even really located here," the mayor told them, a little disgruntled. "All they've got is a post office box. Anyone can have a post office box. Pastor Gulett lives over the Sabine line in DeSoto Parish. And we are more than happy he does."

Pastor Morris Gulett, the self-declared leader of the Nations, owned a twenty-acre parcel he intended to use for the compound, the mayor said. Still, Converse was the closest thing to a town in the area. Ben flashed the mayor the photo he had of Bridger with his two brothers and one of Bridger with Laura.

"Never seen any of them before," the mayor said with a shake of his head.

Since the Aryan Nations was part of the Church of Jesus Christ–Christian and heavily based its white-supremacist doctrine on their version of the Bible, they dropped into each of the several churches in the area, names like Hickory Grove, Bear Creek and Beech Grove Baptist.

None of the pastors recognized any of the men in the photos, none were happy the group was claiming Converse as its home. The owner of the tiny local grocery was no help. No one at the nearest gas station had seen the men before.

By the end of the day, Ben was sure they had made a wrong turn and Converse wasn't Bridger's final destination. He was fairly sure their white-supremacist theory had led them on a wild-goose chase.

As he started the engine on the Denali, he ran a hand

wearily over the roughness along his jaw. "It's getting late. Let's get something to eat and find a motel room."

"We're a long ways from nowhere. I looked on my iPad earlier and the closest motel is up near Mansfield. It's more than thirty miles away." Claire sounded as disheartened as he was. They needed something, anything that would help them locate Bridger.

"Good a place as any, I guess." Especially since he had no idea where they would be going from there.

They made the drive in silence, pulled into a motel called the Country Inn off Highway 171. All the place had were rooms with two double beds, which reminded him of the first time he and Claire had made love. He'd needed her that night. He needed her now.

Ben set his jaw. He didn't need anyone, he reminded himself. He was who he was, and that wasn't going to change.

"There's a café next door," he said as he carried their bags into the room. Typical cheap motel decor: old flowered bedspreads, curtains drooping a little at the windows. But the room and bathroom were clean, and the mattresses weren't sagging.

He tossed his overnight duffel on one of the beds. "You hungry?" he asked, though his appetite had waned as his mood sank from glum to completely sour.

"I'm not very hungry, but I guess I could eat a bowl of soup or something."

Ben took her carry-on and tossed it up next to his duffel. "Maybe we can bring something back here, and get to bed early."

Claire walked over and slid her arms around his waist, leaned into him. "I can't stand this, Ben. I keep thinking of Sam. We've got to find him."

His arms went around her. "I know." But Bridger had

evaporated into thin air, and unless something turned up soon, they were going nowhere. Ben stood there with Claire's head on his shoulder, trying to think of something encouraging to say, something at least half-true, coming up with nothing.

The sound of his phone ringing felt like a reprieve. Claire stepped back as he pulled the phone out of the pocket of his jeans and checked the caller ID. "Sol."

Ben pressed the phone against his ear. "Tell me you've got something."

"You are so gonna love me."

He looked over at Claire, saw the hope in her pretty green eyes.

"You know those candy wrappers you called me about?"

"Yeah, what about them?"

"The Catahoula Candy company keeps digital sales records. I found several shipments from Egansville to Troy Bridger's address in Los Angeles. A box around Christmas, another in June. I figure gifts—Christmas, maybe Bridger's birthday."

"Who sent them?"

"A woman named Agnes Bragg. She paid cash, Ice. There's a very good chance she lives somewhere near Egansville. Even better news. When I ran a background check, guess what I found? Agnes Bragg has six brothers. One of them is named Troy."

Adrenaline jolted through him. "Troy Bragg."

"My money's on it. This family is off the grid, though. Way off. Not the kind of folks you'll find on Facebook."

"You get an address for Agnes or any of the other Braggs?"

"They share a P.O. box in Egansville. That's it. Like I said, they're off the grid."

"We're on our way first thing in the morning. Keep digging, Sol. We've almost got him."

"We're gonna nail the bastard. Good luck, Ice."

Ben hung up the phone, turned to see Claire staring anxiously into his face.

"Troy Bragg?" she said. "That's his real name?"

"Looks like. Six brothers and a sister. They live somewhere near Egansville."

Excited, Claire grabbed her iPad and turned it on, brought up Google Maps. "The town's less than a hundred and fifty miles away. Maybe we should drive there tonight."

He'd already considered it. But there was nothing they could do till morning and both of them were beat. "Better to get some sleep, get an early start tomorrow."

"We're going to get him, Ben."

He drew her close. "Yeah, we are." At least they had a chance. Ben softly kissed her. "Want to celebrate?"

"Why don't we celebrate when we find Sam?" She ran her fingers through his hair, went up on her toes and pressed her soft lips over his. "In the meantime, why don't we just go to bed?"

Ben kissed her long and deep. "Good idea," he said.

But even afterward, with Claire curled sweetly in his arms, his mind remained on Sam and he couldn't fall asleep.

"Get the hell out of bed, you lazy little bastard."

Lying on his sleeping mat, Sam's eyes cracked open. Pepper scrambled out of the way as Sam dodged the heavy leather boot swinging toward him and rolled to his feet.

"Leave him alone, Troy," Aggie said. She was Troy's sister, Sam knew, older than Troy, with a big butt and bigger boobs, and long brown hair streaked with gray. Troy had told her he had brought Sam home so that she'd have a kid, like she'd always wanted.

"Sam didn't get much sleep last night," Aggie said, "what with you boys gettin' in so late from huntin'."

"Too damn bad. He's already missed breakfast, Aggie. Kid's gotta learn to carry his weight around here. Skinner's gonna show him which plants he can eat. Sam's got a lot to learn if he wants to stay alive in the bayou."

Sam's mouth went dry. Living in the swamps was the last thing he wanted. He wanted to be home in California where he could ride his skateboard and play baseball with his friends. Where he could play video games and go to the movies like regular kids.

A shiver ran down his back as he remembered the hunting trip yesterday with Troy and his brothers Scully and Mace. He'd never forget the big brown-spotted snake nearly as long as Sam was tall, slithering across the trail in front of them. A water moccasin, Troy had said. Troy said if it bit you, it could kill you.

Sam hated snakes. He hadn't known how much they scared him until yesterday.

His eyes burned. He should have run away that night at the chicken fights. He should have headed out into the desert instead of going back to the truck.

But Pepper had been waiting, and he couldn't just leave him.

"I've got some chores for him to do right here," Aggie said, resting a hand on his shoulder. She was the only one in the camp who'd been nice to him.

"I'll see he gets somethin' to eat," Aggie said. "Soon as we're done, I'll send him on out to y'all."

"All right, but don't take too long."

Aggie smiled down at him. She was kind of old, but at least she liked him. "Hear that? We'd best get you fed. How about some grits and syrup? It's still in the pot. I can heat it up in no time."

Sam just nodded. His stomach was rumbling. He tried not to think of the French toast his mom used to make, his favorite breakfast meal. He tried not to think of his mom at all.

Or Claire. He wondered if she had tried to find him after he was gone. She probably thought he'd run away and forgot all about him.

His throat closed up. When Aggie set the grits down in front of him along with the pitcher of syrup, he had to force the food past the lump in his throat.

He was never going home. He had to face the truth. Troy would never let him leave, and there was no place to run from here. Not unless he wanted to get killed by a snake or eaten by a gator. He'd seen one of those yesterday, too.

Little by little he was getting to the point where he didn't really care. Maybe he'd just take off, see if he could make it out of here on his own. Sam went back to eating his grits. He would need to be strong if he decided to run.

Twenty-One

~~~~~~~~~~~~

The sign for Catahoula Candy Makers sat in front of a long, low, metal-roofed building outside the Egansville city limits on the west side of town. The town itself had a population of twenty-one hundred, bigger, at least, than Converse. Claire couldn't keep the hope from rising in her chest as they approached the front door.

Ben held it open and she walked to the counter, where a middle-aged woman wearing a clean white apron and a name tag that read Sophie came up to greet them. She was small, with short blond hair and dark eyes.

"Welcome," the woman said with a smile. "What can I get for you today? We got the Mud Bug twelve-pack, if you're interested. Saves you ten percent. They keep real good, so you can't go wrong stockin' up."

Claire smiled brightly. "That sounds great." She hoped she could keep Ben from jumping into interrogation mode, which, with those pale eyes and the way he was grinding his jaw, would send the poor woman running for cover. "We'll take a twelve-pack."

"Sure enough," Sophie said, obviously pleased. She

disappeared into the back and returned with a white cardboard box holding twelve packages of Mud Bugs wrapped in clear cellophane, each piece twisted at the ends.

"You ain't from around here," the woman said as she wrote out the receipt. "How'd you hear about us?"

"A friend told us about you," Ben said, taking Claire's lead, thank God, and standing down, at least for the moment. "Troy Bragg. We tried some at his house. You don't know him, do you?"

She shook her head, continued writing up the order. "'Fraid I never met him."

Claire's spirits fell.

Sophie added the tax. "I know his sister, Aggie, though. She comes in a couple of times a year. Aggie loves our candy."

Claire couldn't breathe. Thank heaven Ben stepped in, because she couldn't get out a single word.

"That's what Troy told us." Ben managed a smile that looked at least halfway sincere. "We thought while we were here we'd stop by and say hello. You wouldn't know her address, would you?"

The woman laughed. "Aggie don't exactly have an address. She and her kin live about thirty miles south of here, out to Bushytail Bayou. Egansville's the closest town. Aggie and some of the others come in for supplies once or twice a year."

Finally back in control, Claire pasted on a friendly smile. "I know she has six brothers. I didn't know they all lived together."

Sophie started frowning. "I figured if you knew Aggie, you'd know about that."

"We've mostly talked to Troy," Ben said smoothly.

"He mentioned something about a big family. I can't remember exactly what it was."

The woman grinned. "Then if you go out there, you're in for a real surprise—if they'll even let you in."

A man walked out of the back room just then, tall and rangy, with silver hair, a large nose and square jaw. "That's enough, Sophie. You ain't bein' paid to stand around and gossip."

Her blond eyebrows went up and she flashed Claire a small, woman-to-woman smile. *Men,* it said. *Always interfering.* "Here's your Mud Bugs. Will that be cash or charge?"

"Cash." Ben pulled out his silver money clip and peeled off the amount needed to pay the bill.

"Thanks for comin' in," Sophie said, handing him the box of candy and his change.

The man behind the counter said nothing, just stood in stony silence, his arms crossed over his chest.

It was cool when they stepped outside, the days creeping toward November, the hot, humid Louisiana summer finally over. As she slid into the passenger seat, Claire thought of Sam and her throat went tight.

"Sam loved the summer heat," she said, remembering back to the summer before his mother died. "He can swim like a fish and he loves the ocean. He wants to learn how to sail."

A muscle ticked in Ben's jaw.

"Aggie Bragg lives with her brothers thirty miles away," Claire continued. "Do you really think that's where Sam is?"

Ben flicked her a dark, sideways glance. "Yeah, I do." He dug out his cell phone and called Sol as he drove out of the parking lot.

"Bushytail Bayou," he said. "That's where the Bragg

family lives. I need to know exactly where it is and what the hell's going on out there."

Sol said something Claire couldn't hear, then Ben hung up the phone. "We need more information."

"So how do we get it?" she asked.

"Get on your iPad. Look up the address for the Egansville post office. The Braggs have a box there. In a town this size, odds are someone will know them."

Claire plucked the device from between the seats, turned it on and brought up Google, pulled up the address. "It's on First Street. That's just off the road we're on."

The area was extremely rural. The few buildings along the way sat on big parcels of flat ground far apart from one another. There weren't many of them. It didn't take long to find the single-story brick building that served as the local post office. Ben parked in front, and both of them got out of the SUV.

Inside, old-fashioned glass-windowed brass post boxes lined the walls. The office was empty except for the wizened little man who stood behind the counter wearing thick horn-rim glasses, a yellow pencil stuck behind his ear.

"Excuse me," Ben said when the man didn't look up, just kept sorting through the stack of letters in front of him. "I wonder if maybe you could help us."

He finally glanced up, didn't look friendly. "What can I do for ya?"

Claire stepped in, deflecting the man's attention away from Ben's icy stare. "We're looking for a place called Bushytail Bayou. Can you tell us how to get there?"

"What business you got out there?" he asked Ben.

"We hope to visit some friends."

He scratched his head. "What ya do, ya go south on 121 'bout thirty miles. You'll find the road right there in the middle of town. Road follows the Black Snake River." He looked Ben over, took in the thick biceps beneath the sleeve of his dark gray T-shirt, the muscular chest and shoulders. "You one of them survivalist boys?"

Survivalist! Claire tried to hide her shock, but the picture of Troy and his brothers dressed in camouflage popped into her head. *Oh, my God!*

Ben shook his head. "Like I said, we're just meeting some buddies."

"Place ain't easy to find and them boys don't cotton to visitors lest you're one of 'em. My advice be to forget the visit and keep on a-drivin'."

Ben pretended to consider that. "I think maybe you're right. We're on our way to Natchez. It's a long drive for a quick visit. Think we'll just keep going."

Claire sighed. "Sounds like a lot of trouble, and we don't really know them that well, anyway." The last thing they needed was someone telling the Braggs they were in Egansville looking for them.

She smiled at the old man, whose name tag read Jenkins. "Thank you for your help, Mr. Jenkins."

He just grunted and went back to sorting letters into neat little piles. Leaving him to his task, they headed for the car, Claire having to hurry to keep up with Ben's long, anxious strides.

"Survivalists," she said as they climbed back into the Denali. "Not white supremacists."

"Yeah, and word gets out we're looking for them, they'll be ready for us."

"Are we calling the sheriff?"

"Maybe. I want to talk to Sol, see what he comes up

with first. In the meantime, we need a room, somewhere out of town, preferably on the road south. We need a place to stash the gear, use the computer and strategize."

"Maybe we could drive by the area first, see what it looks like."

"Hell, no. I'm not going anywhere near those guys with you in the car. Besides, I've got a hunch their compound won't be easy to find."

As Ben drove through the small rural community, he pressed Sol's number. "Bushytail Bayou is thirty miles south of—" Ben broke off the sentence and started nodding. Apparently, Sol had already found the location.

"The Braggs are involved in some kind of survivalist group," Ben told him. Sol said something. "Yeah, definitely not good news. They all live together in some sort of compound. It's bound to be guarded. I'm going to need to find a way in."

Sol said something, and a few minutes later, Ben hung up the phone.

"He's on it. He's sending area maps and intel. In the meantime, how are you coming with that room?"

Claire looked down at the Google page, open on the iPad in her lap. "There's nothing out there, Ben. No motel for a jillion miles."

"Try fishing camps. Lots of water around. People love to fish. See if there's something with a cabin we can rent."

She typed in the reference, looked up at him. "I can't believe it. Uncle Buster's Cabins. Look's like it's on a lake off road 121. They rent fishing boats and there's a small RV park. If I call from here, we might be able to get something."

"Sounds good."

She looked down at the iPad. "From the photos, the

cabins look pretty good, but there's no cell phones, no internet."

"Sat phone. We won't be incommunicado."

Claire leaned back in her seat. They were close. She could feel it.

While she made the reservation, Ben pulled into a rural market to pick up supplies for a couple of days, sandwich fixings and breakfast rolls, a couple of bags of potato chips, some milk. Claire grabbed a bag of raw almonds, picked up some apples and bananas, a jug of orange juice, a six-pack of bottled water.

As they climbed back into the car and Ben pulled out of the lot, she said a silent prayer for Sam. *We're coming, sweetheart. Be strong. Don't give up. We love you, Sam.* Her eyes felt misty, her throat tight when she finished.

Ben reached over and squeezed her hand. "We're going to find him, Claire. We're going to bring him home."

But it wouldn't be easy. Claire thought of the bullet wound in Ben's side that was barely healed, and the other scars he carried.

This time her prayer was for Ben.

Twenty-Two

*T*hey followed the two-lane road south, moving farther and farther away from Egansville, through a flat landscape of low-lying farms and wetlands. For the first ten miles, there was only a smattering of houses. The next ten were almost completely uninhabited, just miles of farmland on one side, marshy green swampland on the other.

The narrow, overgrown Black Snake River wound along on the west, slithering through a heavy tangle of leafy plants and deep woods like the serpent it was named for.

Ben hadn't spent much time in Louisiana, but he knew his way around a jungle. The Philippines had been his last mission, a major clusterfuck that had gotten one of his teammates killed and landed him and two other SEALs in the hospital. He'd been there for three months, managed to recover from his injuries, but ended up leaving the teams.

The bayou was a different kind of jungle. And still a lot the same. He'd rather not think about that.

Beside him, Claire sat up straighter in her seat and pointed off to the right. "Look, Ben, there's the turn to Black Snake Lake."

He slowed, turned down a bumpy dirt road lined with low-hanging trees and spotted another sign. He took a right that led to Uncle Buster's, a row of tidy-looking cabins right along the water, each with a small boat dock on piers out in front.

Ben slowed to a stop in front of a wooden building with a sign that read Old Fishermen Never Die, They Just Smell That Way, and climbed the porch steps to the rental office.

"Ben Slocum," he said to a short, bald-headed man with a round face and a big beer belly. "My wife called and made a reservation."

"Buster Pascal. Got it right here." He pulled a registration form out from beneath the counter.

"My wife and I are on our honeymoon," Ben said. "Any chance we could get the cabin at the far end of the row?"

Buster smiled. "Congratulations." He shoved the form across the counter. "Cabin's yours." He winked. "A man needs privacy on his honeymoon."

"Thanks." The weather here was good, warmer than it was back home. Ben filled out the form and paid the bill in cash for a two-night stay.

Buster counted the money, smiled and shook his head. "A woman who likes to fish. You're one lucky SOB, my friend."

Ben flashed him a man-to-man smile. "Won't be a lot of fishing on this trip—if you know what I mean."

Buster rumbled a laugh. "Smart man."

"I see you have boats if I can manage the time. I may want to rent one for a couple of days." He'd know more about where he was going after he downloaded the area maps Sol was sending.

"Nice aluminum flat-bottoms. Comes with a pole and gear. Take you up into the bayou. Great fishing there—bream, catfish, crappie. But I wouldn't go far. Easy to wind up lost in there."

"Bushytail Bayou?"

The owner shook his head. "Nah, I wouldn't bother. You can get there from here, but you'd have to know the way. There's lots of twists and turns. Real overgrown. You'd get lost for sure."

"Glad you warned me. I think I'll go ahead and take that boat, though." He pulled his wallet back out, paid for the boat and fishing gear. "I get up earlier than my wife. Bound to get in some time to fish."

Buster grinned. "My wife hates fishin'. Like I said, you're a lucky SOB."

Ben got two keys to cabin nine and headed back to the car. The lie about him and Claire being newlyweds had come easier than it should have, since he wasn't a marrying man. He wished to hell he could spend his made-up honeymoon in bed with her, but that wasn't going to happen.

He started the engine and drove to the cabin farthest from the office. As Claire had said, the place wasn't too bad, a small wooden structure on stilts about two feet off the ground with a covered porch out front. It had two full-size beds, a tiny kitchenette and bath.

"Look, there's a coffeemaker and bag of coffee." Claire practically swooned. "Coffee in the morning and an amazing view of a beautiful lake. This is heaven."

"Yeah, it's a regular five-star. Nothing but the best for my woman."

Claire looked over at him, and he realized what

he'd said. She wasn't his woman. She didn't belong to him. She never would. He didn't say that, though, just brought his duffel and her suitcase in from the car and tossed them up on one of the beds, stashed the weapons bag and ammunition underneath.

He took his laptop out of his duffel and set it up on the tiny kitchen table.

"No internet, remember."

He turned on the machine. "I'll be on satellite. I can tether the computer to the sat phone."

One of her dark eyebrows went up. "High-tech. Very impressive."

"Glad you approve." Before he cranked up his email, he phoned Sol, gave him their current location and told him that from now on they'd be communicating via sat phone.

"I've pinpointed the target's location," Sol said as he studied satellite photos of the area on his computer screen. "A big open space in the middle of the swamp a little north and west of you. Hang on a minute." Ben could hear him pounding the keyboard. "Satellite shows a cluster of houses...more like cabins."

"How many?"

"Looks like eight or nine. Hard to tell exactly what they're being used for."

"Can you see Black Snake Lake?"

Silence for a moment. "I see it. Looks like it's maybe three or four miles from the compound."

"I need to know how the lake connects to the location. I've got a boat, little four-stroke outboard. Unless you've found a better way in, looks like I'll be going in by water."

"I'll find the best route. Your computer up and running?"

"I'm hooking up the tether as soon as we're finished. "You come across anything new on the Braggs?"

A brief pause. "I was just getting to that."

"I don't like what I'm hearing in your voice."

"They call themselves the Bayou Patriots. Looks like about thirty members. The father's dead. Mace Bragg's the leader. He's the oldest brother. They're headquartered in the compound, but only three of the Bragg brothers live there full-time. Troy lives there off and on. The other two, Jesse and Si, live in double-wide trailers in a wide spot farther down the road. Both of them are married. They've each got a couple of kids."

"Odds are brother Troy is in the compound with Hutchins."

"And Sam."

"Yeah," Ben said gruffly.

"Believe it or not, these guys have a webpage, BayouPatriots.com. Most of the members are local, some in Egansville. One of them runs the website, posts articles on survival, how to arm and defend yourself in case of a natural disaster, or if the government tries to take away your liberties."

"A website. Twenty-first-century swamp rats."

"You got it. They hold meetings at the compound every week. From the articles on the website, these guys are heavily armed and they mean business. If they have to, they're ready to fight to the death to defend themselves against anyone they think is against them."

Ben didn't have a problem with people who believed in learning how to stay alive in a bad situation, men who could take care of themselves and their families if the need arose. Hell, he was one of them. He knew better than most that in this crazy world, anything could happen.

But taking a child without any legal right, thrusting him into a life that was completely foreign to him, was immoral as well as against the law.

Ben looked over at Claire. From the paleness of her face, he figured she was hearing enough of the conversation to understand what was going on.

"Check out their website," Sol said, "and watch your email for the intel I'm sending."

Ben hung up the phone.

"It's bad, isn't it?"

Bad enough. "Come here." When he opened his arms, she went into them and just held on. "It's going to be all right, angel. I'm trained for this. I know what to do to get Sam out safely." He'd done dozens of extractions in the SEALs. Except for the shit storm in the Philippines, all of them had been successful.

She looked up at him. "You're not calling the sheriff, are you? You never planned to call them in the first place."

"I was waiting to see how things lined up. If the cops go into a situation like this, people are going to get killed. One of them could be Sam. If I go in alone, I can get him out and back to safety before they even know he's missing."

She rested her head against his shoulder. He tried not to think how good it felt to have her there.

"I'm scared, Ben. I'm scared for you and Sam."

He smoothed a hand over her shiny dark hair. "If I believed the cops could get him out without him getting hurt, I'd let them handle it. But I can't take that chance. I won't, Claire. Not with Sam's life."

She swallowed, started to pull away. Ben caught her face between his hands, bent his head and kissed her. "Trust me, okay?"

She reached up and cupped his cheek. "I do trust you, Ben."

Wishing he could sweep her up and carry her over to the bed, spend the night making love to her, he turned away and went to work on his computer. If Sol came through with the rest of the information he needed, he would be going in late this afternoon to recon the target. There would be a quarter moon tonight, enough to light his way out of the swamp, assuming he made no wrong turns.

Tomorrow, if luck and the weather stayed on his side, he would be bringing out his son.

As the afternoon sun moved toward the horizon, Claire watched Ben prepare to leave. He was taking the aluminum boat he had rented, following the map Sol had sent of the area around the lake. There was another map showing the route from the fishing camp across a portion of the lake into Bushytail Bayou and the Patriots' compound deep in the swamp.

Since they didn't have a printer, Ben had transposed the map by hand onto a sheet of paper. It showed the main waterway narrowing to a thin channel through a tangle of narrow twists and turns. It showed most of the little tributaries that could lead him in the wrong direction. Most, but not all.

Ben would be marking his way with small pieces of orange neon tape fastened to overhanging trees and vines, the kind hunters used that wouldn't be completely out of place if they were spotted along the muddy waterways of the bayou.

She walked out to the porch as he fired up the small outboard engine and pulled away from the dock, her chest tight with worry. She hadn't even considered asking him to take her with him. She would be a detriment, not an asset, to both him and Sam. Besides, he wasn't bringing Sam out until tomorrow night.

As the time slipped past, Claire went back inside and picked up the book she'd brought with her, sat down and tried to read. When that didn't work, she set the book aside and began to pace the cabin. Finally, feeling claustrophobic and wishing she had something productive to do, she went back outside and sat on the tiny porch to watch the sunset, a flashy, beautiful display of gold, orange and pink that gave her some idea of why the people who lived out here put up with the heat and humidity of a stifling Louisiana summer.

There was always good to offset the bad.

As darkness descended and the moon came out over the lake, her worry increased. What would the Braggs do if they spotted Ben? Was Duke Hutchins there with Troy? Hutchins had tried to kill Ben at the cockfight. If he got the chance he might try it again.

And what about Sam?

If Sam was there, tomorrow night Ben was going after him. Claire wasn't sure the boy would go with him. He had left willingly with Troy in the first place. Maybe he would want to stay.

She couldn't make that scenario work in her head. She didn't know Troy, but she knew Sam. He was a smart kid, smart enough to realize the kind of life he would have if he stayed in the swamp with Troy. A kid who would figure out fairly quickly the kind of man he'd aligned himself with when he had left the relative safety of the Roberson household.

Sam loved school. He made friends easily and he loved playing sports. Still, there was no way to know for sure what he would do when Ben appeared like a specter from the dead. Exactly what Laura had told Sam his father was—a soldier killed in the war.

Claire glanced at the clock. It was nearly midnight and still no sign of Ben. Rubbing her arms against the faint chill coming in off the lake, she listened to the sound of a bullfrog croaking somewhere in the distance. A fish jumped, leaving ripples on the surface of the water.

She didn't hear Ben come up the steps, just felt his presence behind her and knew he was there. Her heart beat softly as she turned and looked up at him. He was dressed completely in dark green camouflage, his face covered with black greasepaint, making his pale, piercing blue eyes stand out even more. A band of ammunition crisscrossed his muscular chest. His knife was strapped to his thigh, his shotgun slung across his back, his pistol clipped to his web belt.

He should have looked like a stranger, and yet he seemed more familiar than any man she had ever known.

"I'm glad you're home and safe," she said softly.

Wordlessly he took her hand, led her into the cabin out of sight and closed the door. One by one, he began to remove his weapons, setting each of them down on the kitchen counter. He grabbed a paper towel and wiped some of the greasepaint off his face.

"Sam was there. I saw him, Claire. He was there with the black Lab you talked about. I didn't even have to see his face. He walks like me, moves like me. Jesus, it was eerie."

Her heart squeezed. "He seemed okay? He wasn't hurt or anything?"

He clenched his jaw. "He's lost a lot of weight. He didn't look skinny in the pictures I saw."

Worry trickled through her. "No, he wasn't thin the last time I saw him."

"They're working him hard, Claire. They had him digging a new latrine out behind the one they're using. I think it's good for a kid to do chores, develop good work habits, but they're working him like a laborer. The woman—I figure it's Aggie—she's the only one who talks to him like he's a person."

His hand unconsciously fisted. "It was all I could do not to go in and clean house, take Sam out with me by force if I had to. I knew I couldn't take the chance. I want him out safely. I need to play this right."

"How...how many were there?"

"I counted fifteen men. All camo'd up. The place is like a fortress. Twelve-foot hog-wire fences. Some kind of alarm system that runs off a generator. The men take turns walking the perimeter. They've got a shooting range, smokehouse, root cellar, meat-drying rack, vegetable garden. They're definitely self-sufficient. Aggie was the only woman I saw."

She read the turmoil in his face, his fear for Sam. His anger.

"The good news is, the bayou side is open. They see it as a line of defense, kind of like a moat around a castle. It's part of their food source, their way of life. And they're right. It's practically impenetrable. It was a bitch getting in and even harder getting out in the dark. But it can be done."

"Maybe so, but I don't see how you can do it alone. I think we should call the sheriff."

Ben shook his head. "No way. Not until Sam's out of there. After we're out and he's safe, they can go in after Troy and Hutchins."

"You saw Hutchins in there?"

"I saw Troy but not Hutchins. I overheard a couple of guys talking. Apparently a few of the men were out hunting. One of them could be Hutchins."

He took her hands, colder than they should have been. "You okay?"

She wasn't. But Ben had enough on his mind without worrying about her. "I'm better now that you're home."

His eyes remained on her face, then he turned away. "I'm going in to take a shower. I smell like a swamp."

She watched him walk away, his face still streaked with black, his features hard. He had never looked more in command, more a soldier, more a virile male, than he did tonight. She had never been more aware of him as a man.

She watched as he stripped off his clothes, noticed the puckered scar low on his back, the one on the opposite side that was pale and barely healed, the long legs, narrow hips and round buttocks. Naked, he walked into the tiny bathroom and turned on the shower.

She shouldn't have been aroused, but she was. Her mouth felt dry, her skin tingled, moisture collected between her legs. If the shower had been bigger, she would have joined him.

It was a bad idea. Ben was exhausted. He was worried about what would happen tomorrow, just as she was. She reached back and unfastened the gold clip at the nape of her neck, shook out her hair, took off her clothes and pulled on her nightshirt. The shower went off as she walked barefoot over to the counter and turned on the tap, poured herself a glass of water.

When she turned, she saw him standing in the bathroom doorway, a towel slung low around his hips. Water beaded in the dark hair on his chest, glistened on his pecs, thick biceps and six-pack abs.

Her heart was beating, drumming in her ears, her breath coming fast and shallow. His eyes were the color of hot blue flame as he strode toward her, and she knew he'd read the hunger she felt for him.

He stopped in front of her, caught the hem of her nightshirt and peeled it off over her head. He was still in battle mode, all hot-blooded male. She felt a surge of arousal so wild and wanton it made her dizzy.

"If I take you tonight, it won't be easy. I'll be rough and hot."

She looked up at him and couldn't breathe. Her heart was hammering, her body throbbing. "Yes…please."

He didn't wait, just fisted a hand in her hair and dragged her mouth up to his for a fierce, erotic kiss. The towel fell away as his tongue slid in, delving deep, bending her to his will. He moved to her breasts, cupping them, taking each one into his mouth, suckling her hard. Her nipples throbbed. The muscles across her stomach quivered.

There wasn't much room in the tiny cabin. He backed her up against the wall, kissing her hard again, then turned her toward the bed. "Put your palms on the mattress."

She understood what he wanted and heat roared through her. He bent her over the bed and she went down on her elbows as he came up behind her, reached around and touched her, found her wet and more than ready.

He stroked her, gripped her hips as he drove into her, took her in a deep, pounding rhythm, took her until she came with a hollow moan and cried his name. Ben didn't stop. Just drove into her until she came again, then turned her around and eased her onto her back on the mattress, came up over her and filled her again.

"You're so hot and wet," he said. "You feel so damned good." Grabbing her wrists, he drew her hands up over her head and began to move. Faster, deeper, harder. Heavy, unrelenting thrusts that stirred her toward climax again.

It was too much and not enough. Too hard, too fierce and not fierce enough.

She needed to touch him. "More," she whispered, freeing her hands, digging her nails into the muscles across his shoulders, wrapping her legs around his waist. "More...Ben...please."

He growled low in his throat, and took her deeper, pushed her to the edge and over. Her climax hit hard, sucking her under, dragging her down like storm waves on the lake. Ben followed her to release, his muscles rigid, his jaw clenched against the fierce orgasm that shook him.

For moments, he didn't move, just kept the weight of his powerful body on his elbows, his hard length still inside her. Then he levered himself off and lay next to her, drew her into his arms.

He didn't apologize for his roughness. She didn't want him to.

The tiger had broken free of its cage, and he was amazing.

Twenty-Three

The sun had come up, but it was still early. Across the lake, a bank of clouds loomed on the horizon, but so far the sky was clear. Claire was in the shower. Ben tried not to think of her naked, of how good it had been last night. And again this morning.

He was beginning to know her, to understand her needs. He was beginning to realize she was an even more passionate woman than he had imagined.

He liked that about her. Hell, he liked way too many things about Claire.

The coffeemaker gurgled, signaling the pot had finished brewing. He poured himself a cup, walked over to the little table, turned on the computer and brought up the maps Sol had sent yesterday. He wanted to review each twist and turn along the route, memorize each meandering tributary that led to a dead end.

It was like a maze in there, with only a single, nearly unnavigable route of entry and escape. It was the reason the Bragg brothers didn't worry about guarding that side of the compound.

Ben planned to go in again this evening. He had timed the guards' rounds, knew they changed shifts on the hour, watched the men's daily routine. They took their survival efforts seriously and everyone did their part. Sam was only nine years old but he was expected to work like a man.

Ben thought of his own childhood. He had gotten a job in the steel mill as soon as he was legally old enough. It was backbreaking labor, but he had been twice Sam's size and eventually he'd won the respect of the men he worked with. The hard labor had been good for him, had motivated him to go to college, then join the navy.

But if Bragg kept Sam in the compound, he wouldn't have the opportunities Ben had had, wouldn't have the chance for any kind of a normal life. And he would suffer the same lack of love Ben had known as a child.

He looked down at the map on the computer screen, added the information he had gleaned last night to the drawings he had made. He needed to find a spot on the bayou side of the compound where he could talk to Sam alone, get him away from the others, into the boat and out of there.

He badly needed backup, but Trace was out of town, Jake was working a protection detail and Alex was still on his honeymoon, off to Rio de Janeiro now, according to Sol, for the next few weeks.

He took a sip of coffee. Claire was right. Nothing better than a hot cup of java in the morning.

His sat phone started ringing. Ben reached over and grabbed it. "What's up?" he said to Sol.

"I've got a present for you, something you're going to like even better than the candy info."

"Yeah, what is it?"

"Backup. Guy by the name of Tyler Brodie. Says he's Johnnie Riggs's partner. Says he worked with you in L.A."

"That's right. Ty's a good man."

"Brodie called looking for you. He was in Dallas for a funeral. Annie put him through, and when he asked about Sam, I told him you'd found him in Louisiana and were trying to bring him home. I happened to mention that you could use some help and the next thing I knew, he was driving his rental car from Dallas to Egansville."

"Happened to mention?"

Sol chuckled. "The map and aerials told the tale. Getting your kid out of that bayou isn't going to be easy."

Ben felt the pull of a smile. "I really do love you, kid."

Sol laughed. "It's a seven-hour drive from Dallas. Brodie left last night. I'm surprised he isn't already there."

A rat-a-tat sounded at the door. "I think maybe he is. Thanks, Sol, you're the best." Ben hung up and went to the door. On the other side of the peephole, tall and rangy, dark-haired and pretty-boy handsome, Tyler Brodie looked more like a college kid than a former marine.

Ben felt a sweep of relief as he opened the door. "Man, am I glad to see you."

Brodie yawned. "I got in about two and needed some shut-eye. Old guy in the office rolled out of bed to rent me a cabin. I'm in number eight, right next door."

"Come on in."

Brodie sniffed the air. "Coffee. Smells great. I could sure use a cup."

"You got it." Ben walked to the counter, poured a mug and handed it to Ty. He took a sip just as Claire opened the bathroom door and stepped out in a skimpy white towel.

"Oh, my God—Ty!" Her hold on the towel went tighter. "What in the world are you doing here?"

Ty grinned. Ben didn't miss the way his eyes ran over Claire's half-naked body. "Just happened to be in the neighborhood and thought I'd drop by."

Claire laughed.

"Why don't we go outside so the lady can get dressed?" Ben suggested, nudging Brodie firmly toward the door.

"Yeah. Sure. Good to see you, Claire." They walked out on the porch and Ben closed the door.

"Sol told me she was with you," Brodie said. "I… umm…didn't realize the two of you were involved."

"We're not involved. We're working together to find my son."

He glanced back at the closed cabin door. "Nice work if you can get it." Clearly he hadn't missed the one unmade bed. Ben tried not to think of Claire bent over the mattress and him hard inside her, but his blood moved south just the same.

"I wish to hell she was back in Houston," he said, "but this is one woman who doesn't take no for an answer."

"I could tell the boy meant a lot to her."

Ben nodded, glad to move on to a different subject. "You sure you want in on this? I counted fifteen members of the Bayou Patriots prowling around in that camp. Could be more by tonight. Good chance the guy's there who shot me in El Paso. To say nothing of alligators, cottonmouths and rattlesnakes. It's not going to be any walk in the park."

Ty glanced off toward the lake and the low-lying swamps around it. "Just makes things interesting. I was in Texas for my uncle's funeral. I'm damned glad to get away from all the gloom."

"Sol mentioned the funeral. Sorry about your uncle."

He shrugged his wide shoulders. Ty was lean and lanky, but his body was rock-solid hard. "Uncle Jim was sick a long time. In a way it was a relief. My dad passed some years back, but my mom was there with her second husband. The rest of the family was there— aunts, uncles, my three cousins down from Alaska. I needed a diversion."

Ben followed Ty's gaze out over the lake toward the bayou. "May be way more than that, but I'm damn glad to have you."

"Bad news is I didn't bring my weapon. It was too much trouble to get through airport security, and I didn't think I'd need it. Sol says you wouldn't have come out here without guns enough for at least the two of us."

He thought of the stash beneath the bed. "Weapons aren't a problem. Unfortunately, we can't just go in there blasting away. We trespass on their property they've got a right to defend themselves."

"One of them shot you. Another one stole your kid. They come after us, threaten us, the game changes."

"That's right. I'm not taking another bullet. But we have to be careful. We start shooting, Sam might end up dead."

Just then the cabin door swung open. "I'm dressed," Claire said brightly, looking fresh and pretty in khaki cargo pants and a white shirt, her dark hair pulled back, the way she usually wore it. "You guys can come on in."

Ben let Ty walk in front of him into the tiny cabin. Reaching beneath the bed Claire had hastily made in a failed attempt to hide the fact they were sleeping together, Ben pulled out the canvas bag that held his weapons and unzipped the top.

Brodie whistled. "Looks like you came prepared, all right. That AR looks mighty fetching." He had a slight drawl Ben had noticed before. It was more pronounced now that he was home.

"She's all yours and that Beretta nine mil, if you want it."

"Sweet."

"Now all we need to do is figure a way to get through four miles of bayou without being seen, get Sam away from at least half a dozen armed men and find our way back through the swamp in the dark without getting lost."

Ty just grinned. "Sounds like a good time to me."

"Get back to work. You been loafin' long enough." Mace Bragg stood with his hands on his hips, glaring at Sam where he sat in the shade eating some jerky and a piece of Aggie's bread. Mace was big. He had dirty brown hair down to his shoulders he tied back with a piece of leather, and sometimes he got food in his beard.

Aggie said he was the oldest. He sure was the meanest. He'd been spittin' mad the night Troy and Duke had brought Sam into the camp. Mace said it was a stupid thing to do.

But Troy said Sam would be a big help to Aggie. He said she'd always wanted a kid and now she had one. Aggie didn't have a husband anymore. She'd told Sam her Dooley had been killed in a hunting accident ten years ago.

Sam started walking ahead of Mace, Pepper dogging his heels. *Dogging.* At home he would have laughed at the joke he'd just made. It didn't seem funny now. He followed Mace to the pit he was digging for a new out-house. The old one stunk something awful and it was full of flies and there was a spider in the corner. At least the new one oughta smell better.

As he headed down the path, he glanced at the tangle of vines and muddy, slow-moving water at the edge of the compound, and a shiver ran through him.

There were all kinds of scary creatures in the swamp. Besides the ugly snake he'd seen, there were big hairy rats, and hornets' nests as big as basketballs. Last night for supper, Aggie fixed a kind of stew called gumbo made with alligator meat. *Yuck.*

It didn't really taste that bad, he just didn't like to think of eating something that looked like a giant liz-ard. Or getting eaten by one if he ever got brave enough to run away.

Yesterday Troy's youngest brother, Luke, had shown him a gator he said was twelve feet long. It just lay there pretending to be a log, its beady eyes watching as it waited for some poor animal to get too close.

Sam jumped down in the hole and wiped his hands on his jeans. They were so dirty they were stiff, but Aggie only washed once a week, in some kind of old-fashioned white machine with a roller that squeezed the water out of the clothes.

Pepper lay down in the shade a few feet away as Sam picked up the shovel and started digging. The blisters on his hands had broken yesterday. Aggie had put on some kind of gross-smelling salve but now they were bleeding again.

"Boy's doin' the best he can," Luke said as he walked up next to Mace. He was tall but kind of skinny, the nicest of the Braggs. Him and Aggie. "He's new to all this, ya know."

"What I know is that fool of a brother of yours should never have brung him here in the first place. Now we're stuck with him. One more mouth to feed."

"Sam carries his weight."

"Maybe so, but he ain't real kin. And look at them eyes. Spawn of Satan, you ask me."

They went on arguing but Sam stopped listening. Instead, he imagined taking a long hot shower, like when he came home from an afternoon at the beach with his mom and Claire. If he closed his eyes, he could almost see the ocean, listen to the waves.

Mace leaned down and cuffed him. "Pay attention. I got more work for you when you're finished."

Sam swallowed. The beach was a million miles away. He might never see the ocean again. Maybe when he got bigger, he'd be strong enough to make it out of the bayou.

The trouble was, if the swamp didn't kill him, Mace Bragg would.

Ben and Ty spent the morning and early afternoon going over the maps and details of the mission, Ty memorizing the route so he could find his way out if something happened. Ben had drawn diagrams of the compound, the layout, the perimeter fencing. They'd discussed the guards, the shift changes, the way the bayou wove around the camp on one side.

The narrow channel was the way in, and the only way out. The biggest problem was finding a way to get to Sam. Since he didn't seem to be part of a regular routine, they would have to play it by ear.

Brodie swallowed the bite he had taken of the ham sandwich Claire had made for lunch. "Sam doesn't know you, right? How are you going to convince him to leave with you?"

That was the reason they were going in before dark. Ben was hoping he wouldn't have to go into the cabin to bring Sam out. He didn't know how many people would be sleeping in there with him, how many he would have to deal with. Better to get the boy in the boat of his own free will and get the hell out of Dodge.

"Talk to him if I can. Claire says he knows his father was in the military. He was proud of that. Claire thinks he'll be more than ready to leave. I'm hoping once he knows who I am, he'll come without making trouble."

"And if he won't?"

"Knockout drops. I've got a mild dose of chloral hydrate on a rag in a plastic bag. All I have to do is get close enough."

Once they reached the target, he'd approach the compound by water. His snorkel was in his gear bag. Ty would serve as lookout and provide cover if needed, hopefully without actually having to kill anyone. Not that he would mind personally popping Duke Hutchins or Troy Bragg.

Satisfied with the plan they'd come up with, after lunch Ty took his weapons and returned to his cabin. Wanting to be in top form for the mission, both of them slept for a couple of hours. Claire curled up next to Ben on the bed, but Ben didn't think she ever fell asleep.

The day was creeping toward time for the evening rendezvous at sixteen hundred—4:00 p.m. With the small outboard and difficult terrain, it would take at least an hour to reach the compound, longer coming out in the dark.

Ty rapped lightly, then opened the cabin door. Dressed in dark green camos and heavy military boots, a KA-BAR knife strapped to his thigh, he carried a canvas bag that held his weapons and gear.

He didn't look too young or too pretty anymore. He looked like a marine, a hard, determined man capable of getting the job done. Ben stepped back, inviting him inside. "You always fly with your gear?"

"After I talked to Sol, I paid a late-night visit to an army surplus on my way out of town. I took what I needed, left the money on the counter."

Ready to go himself, Ben set the sat phone on Vibrate and stuffed it into his camouflage cargo pants. He turned to Claire, who stood silently, her face pale and her hands trembling slightly.

Ty spoke to her softly. "It's gonna be okay, Claire. Neither of us is new to this game."

There was something in his voice. Ben took another hard look at him. His eyes were dead calm, and a there was a clarity of purpose Ben recognized in himself whenever he went on a mission.

He turned back to Claire. "If we aren't back by twenty-four hundred—"

"He means midnight," Ty said.

"If we aren't back by then, get in the car and drive to Egansville. Go to the sheriff. Tell him what's going on."

Her lips trembled. "You'll be back."

"Damned straight we will." Pulling her into his arms, he bent his head and gave her a quick, hard kiss. "See you later, angel." He grabbed his gear bag. "Let's go," he said to Ty and headed for the door.

Twenty-Four

❧◦❧◦❧

The RV park and the rest of the cabins at Uncle Buster's were mostly empty. Only a lone fisherman stood on the distant shore along the lake. Making their way to the dock in front of the cabin, Ben dumped his gear in the aluminum boat, Ty jumped in, Ben tossed him his bag, then pushed away from the dock and jumped into the stern to handle the small outboard engine.

As soon as they were far enough away they wouldn't be seen, they blackened their faces, strapped on black vest armor, pulled camouflage slouch hats down over their eyes and retrieved their weapons.

A few minutes later, the boat slipped quietly into the channel leading into Bushytail Bayou, wider here than it would be farther along the route.

Reaching into his pocket, Ben pulled out an LED flashlight, clicked it off and on a couple of times to test its strength. "If we time it right, the moon will be up when we come out. Should be all we need, but you never know."

They rode along in silence but for the roar of the engine, top speed seven miles an hour. But as the channel narrowed and started making turns, Ben slowed the motor to a soft purr. A faint sound began to reach him, a muffled jingle coming from the seat in front of him. He slowed the boat even more. "You got change in your pockets?"

Ty shook his head. "Dog tags. Sorry, I'm a getting a little rusty." He took them off over his head, wrapped them in a handkerchief and stuffed them into his pants pocket. "I like to have them with me on a mission, just in case."

"Yeah, well, I'm not letting your ass get killed, so you don't need to worry about it."

In the dappled sunlight beneath the overhanging trees, Ty's teeth flashed white against his blackened face. "That's good to know."

Ben watched the way Brodie picked up the AR, holding it as if it were an extension of his arm. He remembered the look in his eyes. "Force Recon, right?"

Ty didn't answer right away, which was an answer in itself. Clearly this wasn't something that was common knowledge. "It was a while back."

"Why'd you leave?"

"My time was up. I just… I wanted to see a different side of life. You?"

"Mission went south. Injury drove me out. I never would have left the teams if things had turned out different. I'm okay with it now."

"Me, too."

They didn't say more, just rode in silence through the murky tangle. The channel continued to narrow, clogged with lily pads and downed trees. Jagged, moss-draped branches thrust viciously into the air. They passed wild-eyed egrets and a haughty blue heron standing on one foot in the boggy water a few feet off to the right. The birds took flight as the boat moved past.

Peering through a dense wall of willows, Ben watched for the orange tape he had left to mark the way. He spotted a tiny bit of color, stayed to the right. He had memorized how far it was to the next fork in the channel, the next turn and the next, until they reached their destination. Still, spotting the markers was reassuring.

"Cottonmouth," Ty said, pointing at a big, pattern-backed brown snake draped over a branch just off to their left. "I got bit when I was a kid. Damn near died. I hate the bastards."

"Snakes and gators. I'm not fond of either."

They fell silent again as the boat turned down a nearly impenetrable waterway, and Ben cut the engine. From here on in, they would use the oars in the bottom of the boat to push themselves along, dodging dead trees and rotting vegetation.

Talking ended. They both knew they were getting close enough that if someone was out in the bayou, any sound they made could be deadly. From now on they worked with hand signals only.

More time passed, the boat gliding silently through a tangle of cypress, the water dark and muddy. Ben signaled to Brodie, pointed up ahead, used the oar to drive the boat beneath a drooping willow into a cluster of branches and cattails, hiding it from view. Over to the right, the compound came into view, nine wooden cabins scattered around an open area surrounded on three sides by twelve-foot fences.

Behind the cover of branches and leaves, both men took out their binoculars and scanned the area. Through the dusky early-evening light, Ben spotted Troy and Aggie, working in the vegetable garden. A younger, thinner version of Troy was talking to another man, laughing at something he said.

He heard the sound of gunfire and swung the glasses in that direction. The range he had spotted yesterday was off to the left, out of sight from their current position. He counted shots, figured four or five were men at shooting practice.

Brodie touched Ben's sleeve, signaled and pointed. He'd spotted Sam about three o'clock. Ben turned his binoculars, saw the boy's head moving as he worked in the pit where he had been yesterday. Ben's adrenaline spiked. He brought himself under control.

The pit was only twenty feet from the where the channel curved inland, wrapping around behind the camp. He signaled to Brodie. He'd let the guard make his next round, watch the activity for a while.

Then he'd slip into the water, see if he could get close enough to speak to his son, to get the boy to go with him. If not, he'd have to use the rag in his pocket and haul him out over his shoulder. It would make things a helluva lot harder.

He looked at the sun on the horizon. When he moved, so would Ty, positioning himself to provide cover for Ben's return with the boy to the boat.

He watched the sun sink lower and both men settled in to wait.

"Mace says you're finished for the day." Aggie walked toward him, motioned for Sam to climb up out of the pit. "Says it ought to be deep enough by tomorrow morning."

As Sam rested the shovel against the side of the hole and climbed, Pepper woke up from his nap in the shade, stretched and yawned, came to his feet and shook himself.

"You hear me? You just about got 'er done."

Sam nodded. "That's good." One more day and he'd be finished. He wondered what crummy job Mace Bragg would have for him next. Or Troy or one of the others. Sam didn't much like Pete Bragg, second-oldest, according to Aggie. He was always in a bad mood, always complaining. And there was a big-nosed guy from town named Zeke. He was a real butt hole. Always spouting verses from the Bible and talking about the world coming to an end.

Aggie settled a hand on his shoulder. Her skin was like leather, as rough as any of the men's. His mom's hands had been soft and smooth when she touched him, but he didn't want to think about that.

"Come on. I'll show you what I found this afternoon."

He followed the older woman down the trail toward the water. He was so tired it was hard to lift his feet, but he didn't want to hurt her feelings.

She crouched at the edge of the swamp. "See this right here? Them's turtle eggs. They're real good eatin'."

His stomach rolled. Turtle eggs didn't sound much better than alligator stew.

"You want me to gather them up for you?" Aggie could have got the eggs herself, he knew. She could do just about anything. But she wanted to teach him stuff so he would fit in and the others would leave him alone.

"That'd be real nice."

"I need a bucket or something."

"Walk on back to the cabin and I'll get you one. Then you can come down and pick 'em up. Just be careful to watch for gators. They love them eggs, too."

Sam sighed as he followed Aggie back to the cabin. Turtle eggs and alligators. He wondered if his friends back home would believe him if he ever saw them again.

Sam didn't think so.

His face mask and snorkel pushed up on his head, Ben sank down in the black, murky water just a few feet from the bank. He had seen the older woman walk up to the pit, heard her conversation with Sam, watched them walk to the bank just a few feet away from where he crouched in the water. Sam would be returning to collect the turtle eggs. This was the opportunity he'd been waiting for.

What he didn't know was what Sam would do when Ben appeared out of nowhere covered in mud and weeds, looking like some sort of prehistoric monster.

The chloral hydrate was in a plastic bag in his pocket, a last resort he didn't want to use. But a scream would bring the Patriot army running.

It might get all of them killed.

Standing next to a mossy tree, he used the SEAL technique of making himself invisible in the shadows as he waited for his son's return. Sam meandered down the path, a bucket in his hand, the black Lab sniffing the path behind him. Ben sank into the water, his eyes just inches away from the turtle eggs. Sam knelt at the edge of the swamp and stared down at the eggs, trying to decide the best way to collect them.

"Don't be afraid, Sam." The boy's head jerked up. "I'm here to help you. Don't scream."

Fight or flight. This was the moment. Slipping his hand into his pocket, Ben tried to read the boy's body language as he silently broke the surface of the water and rose to Sam's same height. "I've come to take you home. Claire's waiting for you. We just have to get you out of here."

Sam's muscles were rigid as he peered through the evening shadows, trying to decide what to do. "I'm your father, Sam. We have to go before they miss you."

Sam stiffened. "You aren't my father. My father's dead."

"I didn't know about you. Your mother didn't tell me. Claire came to find me after your mother died."

The boy started shaking his head and Ben flicked on the LED light, held it beneath his chin, lighting his face. "Look at my eyes. Same as yours. I'm your father." The kid's eyes widened the instant before Ben turned off the light. "Let's go."

Sam looked at the swamp and didn't move. Who the hell would? "There's alligators and snakes."

Ben slid his KA-BAR out of its sheath, let Sam see the blade. "Claire says you're a really good swimmer. I'll take care of the snakes. We need to go. Now."

Sam looked at him one final time. Then he stepped off the bank into the water. The black Lab quietly waded in beside him.

Ben shook his head. "We can't take the dog. He'll make too much noise. Send him back."

For the second time the boy hesitated. "Pep won't make noise. I taught him to be quiet. We play hide-and-seek whenever we get the chance."

Hide-and-seek. Finding a place of safety. It made his chest go tight.

The boy's eye's filled with tears. "Please, mister. Please let him come with us. Pep's my only friend in the world."

Ben's throat closed up. He'd been there. He knew

how it felt to be that alone. "Keep him quiet then. Stay as close to me as you can."

Sam nodded, his decision made. They moved through the water together, the bottom dropping away, the boy sidestroking, barely disturbing the leaves and algae in the channel. The dog swam along beside the boy through the murky brackish sludge. They were almost there. Ben could see a hint of metal where the aluminum boat waited in the heavy grass and branches up ahead.

They swam beneath the drooping cover of the willow. The boat bobbed just a few feet away.

The sound of gunfire at the shooting range had stopped.

And there was no sign of Ty.

The guy was big and beefy and he smelled like swamp mud. Ty stood immobile no more than a foot behind him, hidden in the shadows of an ancient, overgrown oak. If the guy started moving away, Ty would stay where he was.

No such fucking luck. The big guy stiffened, and his head came up. His nostrils flared, scenting the air like a dog. He'd heard something, caught some slight ripple in the usually stagnant water as a few feet away, Ben hauled the boy into the boat, lifted the dog in next to him, pulled himself over the side.

The Patriot's jaw hardened. As he opened his mouth to sound the alarm, Ty's arm wrapped around his neck and squeezed, silencing him even as he clawed to get free. An instant later, he went lights-out without a sound.

Ty lowered him to the ground, jerked his hands behind his back, bound his wrists and ankles with plastic ties and slapped a piece of duct tape over his mouth.

Dragging him behind a fallen log, he left him there and moved deeper into the swamp, heading along the bank toward the boat, careful to stay out of the moonlight, in the shadows out of sight.

Ben and the kid were in the boat when he stepped out into the open, Ben's Nighthawk pointed at the middle of his chest. Ben quickly shoved it back into his holster. There was another passenger in the boat, one they hadn't planned on. Apparently the Iceman had a heart after all.

Soundlessly, Ben pressed the oar against a tree stump and shoved the boat away from the bank, started poling toward deeper water. They needed to get some distance away from the compound before they started the engine—assuming no one discovered Sam missing or found their fallen comrade and shouted an alarm.

Ty used the other oar to pole from the opposite side. The sun had set, but rays of moonlight illuminated the darkness and lit the water with an eerie silver sheen. No one spoke as the boat slid silently along, but the kid couldn't keep his eyes off Ben. The dog lay quietly, praise Jesus, in the bottom of the boat.

They were about halfway back when the distant but unmistakable roar of an approaching engine reached them. It was still a ways back in the swamp, but moving a helluva lot faster than they were.

Ben fired up the engine.

"Sounds like the party's about to get started," Ty said, his smile grim.

"Ty Brodie, meet my son, Sam."

Sam looked up at him. "Thanks for coming to get me."

He sat down across from the boy. "That was your

dad's idea. You can thank him later. Right now, we need to get the…umm…heck out of here."

Ben pushed the speed up a notch. It was dangerous with so many hazards in the water, but the moon gave off enough light to avoid the downed trees and over-hanging branches, see the turns up ahead.

Ben was counting off the distances between forks in the channel, keeping to the right, then the left, then an-other right. Both of them knew the route by heart, and since they were traveling faster than they'd planned, Ty was damned glad they did.

A rifle shot pinged through the air. Then another hit a tree limb and bounced away. Ty reached into his bag and pulled out the AR, shoved in the magazine and pulled back the action. At the first sight of a boat be-hind them, he laid down a burst of automatic fire that flashed across the water in front it, throwing up a wall of white spray.

"I guess you found the conversion kit," Ben said above the engine roar.

Ty just grinned. He'd spotted the kit in Ben's weap-ons cache, taken the rifle apart and reassembled it when he'd been back in his cabin. "Figured we might need a little extra firepower!"

Ben's mouth edged up. Ty had begun to recognize the expression as the closest thing to a Ben Slocum smile.

They were getting near the entrance to the lake. Ben had pushed the boy down in the bottom of the boat and drawn his pistol. He fired a couple of shots behind him over the heads of the men in the boat, laying down cover as he increased the speed to full throttle.

The channel was wider here, but there were still ob-stacles in the way and if they missed a turn and went into a dead end, they were in serious trouble.

The lake appeared ahead. The boat shot into the open water and roared toward their destination. Of course at seven miles an hour, it still wasn't a helluva lot of speed. Good thing the other boat wasn't any faster.

Looking backward past Ben, Ty fixed his gaze on the mouth of the channel, expecting to see at least one boat, maybe two shoot into the lake. They'd decided if they were followed, they would head to shore south of the cabins and take a defensive position there instead of risking Claire and anyone else who might be at the fishing resort.

Nothing.

He motioned to Ben, who turned to look, both of them watching, waiting.

Nothing.

"Looks like they turned back!" Ty shouted.

Sam sat up from the bottom of the boat. "I don't think they'll come this far."

"Why not?" Ben asked.

"I heard Mace talking. He said if there was ever any kind of trouble it was smarter to stay in the bayou. He said they knew it better than anyone else in the world and it was the best place to defend themselves."

As the boat moved across the lake, all three of them kept watch for any sign they were being followed.

"Mace didn't want me there anyway," Sam said, his eyes still glued to the lake. "He'll be glad I'm gone."

Ty glanced over at Ben, whose face had turned to stone.

"You don't have to worry about that anymore," Ben said. "You got me. I want you. So does Claire."

A look of hope filled eyes as pale as his father's. "Is Claire really here?"

Ben nodded. "She's the reason I knew about you.

She loves you, Sam." Ben didn't say more, but Ty could read it in his face. He loved the kid, too.

Ty's chest filled with warmth. Sam Slocum was going home. It always felt good when a mission like this succeeded and victims were returned to their families.

He glanced across the lake. The only question was, would the Bayou Patriots return to their mud hole in the swamp? Or would they want revenge and come after Ben and Sam?

Twenty-Five

Standing at the edge of the porch watching the moon-lit lake, Claire spotted the silhouette of a boat coming toward her. She was sure it was Ben, but she could only see the outline of two people in the boat.

Her heart squeezed. Where was Sam? Had something gone wrong?

The boat sputtered to a stop at the dock, and she raced down the steps to where it bobbed in the water. Someone else was in the boat, she saw as she drew near. Her heart jerked then overflowed with love. *Sam.*

Her eyes filled as Ben swept the boy up in his arms and stepped out onto the dock. He set Sam on his feet, and the boy raced toward her, Troy's dog galloping at his heels. *Sam's dog,* she corrected, for clearly animal and boy belonged together. Running now, her cheeks wet with tears, she opened her arms and Sam ran into them, his warm body burrowing into hers as she held him tightly against her.

"You came to get me," he whispered, and began to shake as he struggled not to cry. "You're really here."

Her throat ached. He was wet head to toe, covered with algae and mud. She squeezed him tighter and fresh tears ran down her cheeks. "I'm here, sweetheart, and you're safe. Your dad's here. Everything's okay."

As he looked up at her in the moonlight, his pale eyes glistened. "I shouldn't have gone with Troy. I should have waited."

"It's all right. You've got your dad now. You don't ever have to worry about where you're going to live."

Ben walked up just then, his face still streaked with black, his camouflage T-shirt and pants wet and plastered to his powerful body. Unconsciously, his hand came up and settled protectively on his son's small shoulder.

"We have to go. I called the sheriff. He'll be going in after Hutchins and Troy, but I don't know how fast that'll happen. We need to get out of here just in case."

She nodded. In case the men came after them. They must have had trouble. She didn't let go of Sam.

Ben's voice gentled. "He's okay, Claire. He's going to be just fine." She wanted to hold on to Ben as much as she wanted to keep holding Sam.

Ben's hand stroked gently over the top of his son's dark head. "He did great out there. He really can swim like a fish. I was proud of him."

Sam looked up at his father. "Mom said you died in the war."

Two pairs of ice-blue eyes met and held. "Your mother thought I wouldn't want you. She was wrong."

"Your mother was trying to protect you," Claire explained. "Sometimes the people who love us make mistakes."

Ben smoothed the boy's wet hair one last time. "We need to move," he said.

Claire nodded, more than ready to leave. "I packed up everything just in case. All we need to do is load the car."

"I wish we had time for a hot shower," Ben said to Sam, "but that's going to have to wait."

Sam just nodded. He seemed different to Claire, more stoic, more grown-up than before he'd disappeared. She turned as Ty approached, carrying the last gear bag out of the boat.

"Thank you," Claire said to him. "I'll never forget what you've done tonight."

Ty just grinned. "Helluva lot more fun than sitting home watching TV."

Claire managed to smile, but her heart was hurting. There was so much she wanted to say, so much she owed this man who had come here to help them. But there wasn't time for that now, and even if there were, she wasn't sure she could find the right words.

She settled her arm around Sam's shoulders and they hurried back to the cabin. Ben and Ty loaded the bags and Ben's gear into the back of the Denali. Ty tossed his duffel into the dark brown sedan he'd rented in Dallas. The bills were already paid. They pulled away from the cabins, started up the dirt track to the two-lane road that would lead them back to Egansville for the rendezvous Ben had arranged with the sheriff.

It was over. And yet Ben was still in battle mode, his weapons in easy reach. She wondered what had happened in the bayou. She wondered if they were truly safe.

The sheriff was waiting for them when they pulled into the parking lot in front of his Egansville office.

Ben and Ty gave a statement of the evening's events, and the sheriff spoke to Sam.

Claire had been worried social services might want to intervene, but Egansville was a small town, and once the sheriff had verified Ben's identity and checked with the Texas police, he was happy to leave the boy with a social worker and his father. There would be plenty of paperwork once they got back to Houston, but all of that could wait.

As soon as the authorities had the information they needed, the deputies headed for the bayou, and Ben headed for home. On the way out of town, he stopped at a cheap motel so he, Sam and Ty could shower and put on dry clothes.

Claire had been carrying clothes for Sam since her shopping excursion in Houston—one of her better ideas, since Ben refused to stay overnight in the little town that was home to the Bayou Patriots. He wanted all of them safe.

The Denali led the way to Texas, Ty's rental car following in case they ran into trouble. It wasn't likely, but the internet was a powerful resource and the Patriots did have their own website. Sam slept in the backseat with Pepper as Ben drove the two-hundred-ninety-mile trip to Houston, pulling up in front of his garage at eight o'clock the next morning. Aside from a stop for an Egg McMuffin at a McDonald's in Beaumont, Sam had slept straight through.

Ben turned off the security alarm and the guys carried the bags into the house. Everything was going smoothly until Pepper danced happily through the front door behind Sam, and Hercules came meandering out of the kitchen. Herc jumped into cat combat mode, arching his back and hissing viciously at the intruder in his domain. Pepper's ears went up and a look of surprise came into his face.

"Leave him alone!" Sam demanded, coming to his dog's defense, dropping to his knees and throwing his arms around the black Lab's neck. Pepper just stood there, his head cocked to one side as he studied the big gray cat that fearlessly stood its ground just a few feet away.

"That's Hercules," Ben said. "Herc lives here. They need to get to know each other if they're going to be sharing the same house."

"I don't think Pepper likes cats. What if Pep tries to eat him?"

Ben chuckled, reached down and scooped up the big gray ball of fur. "Herc's a pretty tough old boy. I think he can take care of himself." Ben rubbed beneath the cat's chin until he was purring, then set him back down on his feet.

Herc eyed the dog, turned and walked haughtily back to the kitchen as if the animal didn't exist.

"Do you think they'll be okay?" Claire asked.

"We'll keep an eye on them for a couple of days, just to be safe. In the meantime, I think we should all get some sleep."

He cast Claire a glance that made her cheeks feel warm, but both of them knew they wouldn't be sleeping in the same bed now that Sam was in the house.

In the end, Claire slept in the guest room, Sam conked out beside her, still exhausted from his ordeal. Ben slept in his own room, and Ty stretched out on the sofa.

It was late afternoon when she and Sam wandered into the living room.

"Where's Ty?" Sam asked, rubbing his eyes.

But there was no sign of the lanky dark-haired man who had helped when they needed him so badly, just a note on the kitchen table. Claire picked it up and read it out loud.

"'Thanks for a great time. Ty.'" She smiled.

"I guess he isn't much for goodbyes," Ben said as he walked toward them down the hall.

Claire glanced at the alarm keypad next to the front door. The perimeter alarm was still set. "How did he get out without setting it off?"

Amusement curved the corners of Ben's mouth. "Guy like that, better not to ask."

"I liked him," Sam said.

"Me, too," said Ben.

Ty Brodie was on his way back to L.A. Ben would be busy making a home for Sam. There were things Claire needed to do, arrangements she had to complete, before she sprung her little surprise on Ben.

The Egansville sheriff, Lester Dumont, phoned Ben that afternoon.

"I wish I had better news," he said. "Took us a while to find our way into the compound from the road. By the time our deputies got there, the men were gone. The whole damn place was empty."

Ben flicked a glance at Claire, who was waiting impatiently for news. "I'm not surprised," he said. "These guys have been preparing for trouble for months, maybe years."

"We talked to the brothers who live down the road, but they say they weren't out there last night. Same with the local members. No way to prove it one way or another."

"I don't suppose anyone mentioned where the group might have gone."

"We've got arrest warrants out for Troy Bragg and Dennis Hutchins. The people we talked to say they haven't seen either one of them."

"According to what Sam said, Mace, Pete, Luke and Aggie Bragg were among those in the camp. He gave you names of some of the other members. They ought to be good for aiding and abetting."

"This is a small town, Slocum. Half the people in the area have kin who belong to the Patriots. I'm not stirring up unnecessary trouble."

It seemed damn necessary to Ben. On the other hand, he had his son back. And it was probably better for Sam just to move forward.

"I'll be in touch if anything turns up." The sheriff ended the call, and Ben turned to Claire, anxiously waiting a few feet away.

"They didn't catch Troy and Duke?"

"Whole bunch vanished like ghosts." He ran a hand through his hair, realized he needed a cut and so did Sam. "I'm not really surprised. Those survivalist groups all have bug-out locations. A place to head in an emergency if their home base goes down."

"It has to be in the swamp."

"Or some other swamp." And there were thousands of square miles of bayous and swamplands in Louisiana, not to mention other parts of the South.

"So what do we do, just let them get away with it?"

"I've got my son back. As long as the bastards leave us alone, I don't care where they go."

Claire looked as though she wanted to argue. Then she sighed. "Maybe you're right. It's probably better for Sam if all of this just goes away."

"The cops'll keep looking. I can't see Hutchins spending the rest of his life in the bayou. He may still turn up somewhere."

"You don't think they'll come here, do you? You don't think they'll come after Sam?"

Ben thought of his son, the fear and loneliness he had suffered, the bruises on his arms and the blisters on his hands. "These guys are extremely territorial. Their life is in the bayou. They didn't even follow us into the lake." His jaw hardened. "If they know what's good for them, they'll stay in whatever mud hole they're now calling home."

The week slid past, busy days for Claire. So far Ben hadn't mentioned anything about her moving out of his house. Maybe he'd been too busy dealing with social services, speaking to lawyers, filling out forms, talking to people in Los Angeles, taking Sam to the mandatory counseling sessions social services required after his ordeal.

Ben accepted the dictate more readily than she had expected, actually seemed glad for the help. He had never been a dad before. He was finding his way, but it wasn't that easy.

Claire had been using the time to complete the plans she had made before she'd come to Houston to find Ben in the first place.

Arrangements that had included the possibility of staying in the city if it looked as if Sam would be living there with his dad. She had betrayed Laura and Sam once. It wasn't going to happen again.

Since Sam had missed so many weeks of school and seemed anxious to return to a part of his life that offered a routine and familiar setting, on Monday of the following week, he would be attending his first day of fourth grade at University District Elementary School.

That morning, Claire made breakfast for her men— that was how she thought of them, both so much alike. Eggs and bacon, toast, juice and coffee. Milk for Sam.

She knew he must be nervous though he hadn't said anything. Sam had been unusually quiet since Ben had brought him home. It worried Claire more than she wanted Ben to know. But the counselor, and the pediatrician who had examined him, both felt certain Sam had suffered no sexual abuse.

She smiled down at the child as he ate his meal. "Big day, huh, kiddo. You ready for this?"

She'd expected him to smile back, show a little excitement. The old Sam would have.

"The kids are gonna ask me stuff. I won't know what to say."

She flicked a glance at Ben, who had stopped eating at the note of worry in his young son's voice.

He set his fork down carefully beside his plate. "If they ask, you say your name is Sam Slocum. Your mom died and now you're living with your dad in Houston."

"What about Claire?"

Ben's eyes met hers across the table. There was something there she couldn't quite read. "Claire lives in Los Angeles, son. She has a job there. She can't stay with us. Houston isn't her home."

Sam's face went pale and his attention swung to her. He almost never cried but his eyes were glistening, and she knew he was fighting to hold back tears. "You're not staying? You're just gonna leave me here?"

Her heart squeezed. Dear God, she should have talked to Ben sooner. Told him her plans, figured things out. Now it was too late.

She tried for a bright, cheery smile. "Actually, I…
umm…I'm not going back—at least not right away."
Probably never. "I've rented an apartment close by.
That way we'll be able to see each other, spend time
together, just like before."

Ben's icy eyes bored into her. "What about your job?"

"I was going to tell you. I just… I wanted to get everything in order. I…umm…found a position here."

Ben came up from his chair. "Finish your breakfast,"
he said to Sam. "Claire and I need to talk." He caught
her arm, hauled her to her feet.

Sam was out of his chair in an instant. "Don't hurt
her! She didn't do anything!"

Ben froze. Claire's heart was pounding. Clearly Sam
had seen Troy hit Laura. Or maybe it was the way Troy
had treated him on the road.

Ben crouched down in front of him. "It's all right,
Sam. I'm not going to hurt Claire. I'd never hurt her. I'd
never hurt you, son." Ben eased the boy into his arms
and held him until his small body softened and Sam's
arms went around his neck. Ben gave him a reassuring
hug. "We're just going to talk, okay?"

Sam slowly nodded and Ben released him. He looked
up at Claire with his father's amazing blue eyes. "You're
really gonna stay?"

Her heart thudded softly. She hadn't expected Ben to
like the idea of her staying in Houston. Or maybe she
had. Maybe that was the reason it hurt so much to realize how eager he was for her to leave. "I'm staying."

Sam sank back down in his chair and started eating
as if the breakfast she had cooked was the best-tasting
food in the world.

When she looked at Ben, he was standing behind his
chair, his arms crossed over his powerful chest.

"You're right," she said. "We need to talk, but unfortunately, if you're going to get Sam to school on time, we'll have to wait till you get back."

Ben scowled, looked down at the top of Sam's dark head. "Fine." He sat back down and the two of them finished their meals, then Ben loaded Sam into the Denali and drove off toward school.

Sam never called Ben *Dad* or *Father*. Mostly he didn't call him anything. Sam was settling in, trying to get used to his new life. Although he gazed at Ben with a serious case of hero-worship, he didn't know this man who had rescued him from the swamp.

He wanted to, though. Claire could see it whenever he looked at his dad. He wanted a father, just like any other boy his age. But trust wasn't that easy for a child who'd been abandoned time and again. Unknowingly by his father before he was born. By his mother, who had died and left him alone. By Claire, who had failed him.

She needed to explain all that to Ben, but she wasn't sure exactly what to say. She had rented a car when they got to Houston. It crossed her mind to head over to her new apartment, give Ben a chance to cool off a little, get used to the idea that she wasn't going to leave.

But that was the coward's way out. Clearly Ben was ready to say goodbye and move on with his life. She had known it was coming. Maybe it was the reason she had put off the discussion so long.

Her heart squeezed. For the first time Claire realized that somewhere deep inside, she had hoped Ben would ask her to stay, that maybe he harbored at least some of the feelings she felt for him.

But she had known from the start he wasn't a one-woman man, and that wasn't going to change. She just hadn't known how badly it was going to hurt.

What a fool she had been.

Ben was the Iceman. He might be a good dad to Sam, but he was hell on women.

Twenty-Six

∾

"I'll pick you up when school's over. You got the cell phone I gave you, right?" In case Sam needed him. Ben held open the door of the Denali and the boy jumped out in the parking lot of his new school, slid the straps of his backpack onto his shoulders. "My number's programmed. You remember how to use it?"

Sam nodded. "Is Claire really staying?"

Ben's jaw tightened as he slammed the rear car door. "That's what she says."

"You don't want her to?"

Hell, yeah, part of him did. The part that thought how much he liked waking up with her in his bed, making love to her in the mornings. The part that knew exactly how to arouse her hidden fires, then douse the heat and slow her passions to a tempting simmer.

The other part was terrified of the things she made him feel. He'd told himself that in another few days, a week at most, she would be gone. He would miss her, but he had a son to think of now. In time, he would forget about Claire.

Now she was staying, and he had no idea how to deal with a woman who made him feel things he swore he would never feel again.

He looked down at Sam. "Claire has a life in L.A. If she doesn't go back, she'll probably miss her friends."

Sam watched the kids streaming past him in jeans and T-shirts, carrying backpacks or an armload of books, hurrying toward the front doors of the school.

"I miss my friends. If she stays, I'll make sure she doesn't get lonely."

Ben ran a hand over the boy's dark hair. Every time he looked at his child, something tightened in his chest. From the moment he'd stared into the picture of a kid with eyes exactly like his own, he'd felt the kick. When he'd seen him in the swamp, his small hands blistered and his jeans stiff with dirt, his heart had expanded with something he had never felt before.

From the moment the kid's arms had gone around his neck, he couldn't imagine living another day without his son.

But Claire was different. Claire was a woman. He didn't need the trouble a woman would bring into his life. He'd done fine without Claire before she'd come along. He'd do fine once she went away.

Ben ignored the part of him that had felt a bone-jarring relief when she'd told him she was staying in Houston. It was just that he'd grown used to having her around. It wasn't that he admired her for her grit and determination. It wasn't that he was grateful for the love she felt for his son. It wasn't that even in a pair of sneakers with her hair clipped back and her jeans rolled up, she made him want her.

And even if those things were true, it didn't matter. He wasn't about to get tangled up with a woman.

Even if that woman was Claire.

Ben headed back to the house, drove around the block a couple of times to get his head straight before he pulled back into the garage and walked into the kitchen. He found Claire waiting. She'd known how angry he was. He wasn't sure she'd be there. Then again, one thing Claire wasn't was a coward.

Herc jumped down from her lap as she rose from her chair at the kitchen table. Pepper stood up from his place on the floor, took a long look at the cat, then lay back down and went to sleep.

Ben looked at Claire and found himself wishing she wasn't wearing her hair loose, the way he liked it. That her soft pink sweater didn't fit so nicely over her pretty breasts.

His jaw still felt tight. He didn't like surprises and this was a doozie. "So what is it? You still don't think I'll be a good-enough father?"

"I think you'll be a great father. That isn't the problem. The trouble is, all of this is new to Sam. Moving to Texas, going to a new school, having to make new friends—living with a man he's known less than a couple of weeks."

"In time he'll get used to me."

"I'm sure he will. In the meantime, he still isn't sure he can trust you. He trusted Troy Bragg and look what happened."

Ben didn't like the reminder. "So what are you planning to do?"

"Spend time with him. Have him stay overnight on the weekends sometimes—if you'll let him. His mother has only been dead a few months. I want to be close if he needs me."

"He's not your son."

Silence fell in the room. It was a low blow even for him.

Claire's chin firmed. "He might have been. If I had continued to press for the adoption. If I hadn't come to Houston to find you."

Touché. He knew she could be tough when it counted. Still, the words shook him. What if Claire hadn't come? What if she'd kept her promise to Laura, let the police handle Sam's disappearance as a runaway? Let the boy slip away and never be heard of again? His stomach knotted. He never would have even known he had a son.

If it hadn't been for Claire.

And everything she had said about Sam was true. The boy needed someone he could trust. Sam wasn't sure about his father yet. He trusted Claire, and with his mother gone, he needed a woman who loved him.

Claire moved closer, until she stood right in front of him. "I thought we were friends at the very least. You want me gone so much you're willing to deprive your son of a friend he so desperately needs? Do you want to get rid of me that badly?"

He felt as if she'd struck him. Claire was more than a friend. A helluva lot more. Too much more. That was the trouble.

"Is it another woman? Because that…that won't be a problem for me. I've got my own apartment. A job. We can work out the details so we don't…don't have to see each other very often. I've known all along you'd get tired of me and want to move on."

His chest clamped down at what he saw in her eyes. Hurt? Betrayal? Resignation?

Before he could stop himself, he caught her shoulders and jerked her hard against him, crushed his mouth down over hers. He kissed her long and deep, felt the hot rush of desire that happened whenever he touched her.

"I'm not tired of you," he said gruffly. "Hell, I can't get enough of you. That's the problem, Claire. I'm not good at relationships. I'm not cut out for this kind of thing."

Her eyes glistened. She reached up and cupped his cheek. "I hope you're wrong, Ben. Because you're in a very important relationship now. You have a son who needs your love. You're going to have to learn how to give it. You won't be able to hold it back from him. Not if you want him to be happy."

He didn't reply. She was right. She was the only woman he had ever known who made so damned much sense.

"I'm staying, Ben. Whether you want me to or not."

He watched her walk off toward the guest room, and that same feeling of relief hit him again. His son needed her, and she wasn't going to let the boy down. Nothing he said or did was going to send her back to L.A.

Claire Chastain wasn't going to walk away. Not like Laura had done. Why the thought struck him he didn't know.

As she pulled open the guest room door, she looked back at him over his shoulder. "Oh, by the way. Your son's birthday is a week from tomorrow. You might want to get him a gift." The door closed sharply.

Jesus! He'd read Sam's birth certificate. He knew the date his son was born. But he hadn't even thought of it being the kid's birthday, and unless Sam mentioned it, he wouldn't have remembered. He didn't want to think how Sam would have felt if he had forgotten.

But Claire wouldn't let him forget. She would be there if Sam needed her. If Ben needed her. He thought of her and their heated kiss and felt a shot of hunger.

It didn't matter than he didn't want to want her. It

didn't matter that he didn't want to get any more tangled up with Claire than he already was.

And deep inside, the hard truth was, he was glad she was going to stay.

Claire carried a pretty green variegated philodendron into her new apartment. Last week, she'd flown back to L.A., packed her personal belongings, loaded them into her car and started the long drive back to Houston. The movers were almost done loading her furniture when she had pulled out of the driveway.

Mr. Hobbs, her gray-haired manager, waved goodbye. They had talked before about the possibility of her moving, and he had said not to worry, renting a unit in such a desirable location wouldn't be a problem.

Now she was back in Houston, waiting for the furniture truck to arrive. Ready to start her new job, her new life.

Waiting for the regret to set in.

She had left Los Angeles, given up the near-perfect weather and living a few blocks from the beach. But in truth, she'd been ready to leave long before now. Aside from Laura, she'd made only a few close friends, most of them at work. She would miss Mary Wilson and her neighbors Penny and David, a young couple who lived next door.

After she and Michael had broken up, she'd been ready to make a change, find a new challenge. Then Laura had gotten sick and needed Claire's help. After her friend had died, there had been Sam's welfare to consider, getting him settled somewhere while she tried to secure an adoption.

Then Sam had disappeared and Claire had been desperate. Once she'd come to know Ben, she had realized living with his dad would be the best option for Sam. While Ben had been home recovering from the shooting in El Paso, Claire had started making arrangements to move to Houston.

She had made a promise to Laura. She owed it to Sam.

The only real drawback was Ben. Every time she thought of him, her heart hurt. She'd known she was falling in love with him. The moment he had stepped off the boat with Sam in his arms, she had fallen completely over the edge.

She was in love with Ben Slocum. And it was never going to work.

Determined not to think about him, Claire set the potted plant up on one end of the breakfast bar. If it weren't for Sam, she could go back to L.A., or perhaps somewhere else, but the truth was, Sam needed her.

The only real surprise was that Ben seemed to need her, too. Not that he would ever admit it.

Claire turned at the sound of a knock at the door. The apartment was on the first floor of a two-story complex with a shady yard out in front. Each unit had a single-car garage, and the unit was roomy, with two bedrooms and two full baths, a modern kitchen with granite countertops and a breakfast nook. The living room and dining area had sliding glass doors out to a small enclosed patio.

When the weather warmed up, she looked forward to using the apartment-complex pool, something she hadn't had in L.A.

The knock sounded again and she started for the door. She expected the moving van to arrive within the hour, but she hadn't heard the truck pull up. Instead, when she opened the door, Michael Sullivan stood on the porch.

"Hello, Claire."

Surprise hit her. She had forgotten how handsome he was, how boyishly appealing he could look with a lock of brown hair falling over his eyes and a smile tipping up the corners of his mouth. "Michael. For heaven's sake, what are you doing in Texas?"

"May I come in?"

"Of course." She stepped back, inviting him inside. "My furniture hasn't even arrived yet. It's supposed to be here this afternoon."

Dressed in khakis and a yellow polo shirt, Michael carefully wiped his feet on the mat and walked into the apartment. She couldn't help thinking of Ben, his face streaked with black paint and covered head to foot in swamp water, hard-edged and tough, more masculine and appealing than any man had a right to be.

"I went to see you when I got back to L.A.," Michael said. "The landlord told me you'd moved to Houston."

"Sam's here," she said lamely, as if that were answer enough.

"You said the guy in your apartment that night was his father. Why isn't Sam living with him?"

"He is, but…it's complicated."

"I realize you and Laura were close. But isn't giving up your job and moving to another state a little over-the-top?"

She stiffened. "I promised Laura I'd look after Sam. It's a promise I intend to keep."

"What about Slocum? I know the two of you traveled across the country together looking for the boy."

"How did you know about that?"

"I know a lot of things, Claire. I know about Sam's

abduction. I know Slocum and a guy named Tyler Brodie found him and brought him back. You were with them. I'm a reporter, remember?"

"Then you understand why I moved to Houston."

He glanced around the near-empty apartment. "You aren't living with him. Are the two of you involved?"

"No."

"Yes." Ben appeared in the doorway and pushed open the door. She hadn't realized she had left it ajar. Her heart took a leap as he approached her, clean shaven, his black hair cut short once more. He stopped so close she could feel the heat of his hard body, smell his aftershave.

"We're sleeping together," he said. "You're a reporter. Maybe you found that out, too."

"We aren't sleeping together," Claire said. "Not anymore."

Michael smiled at Claire. "That's good. Because I just took an assignment here in Houston. I want us to spend some time together." His gaze met Ben's. "Claire and I have a lot to talk about. I'm sure you'll be busy with your son."

Ben's eyes took on the feral gleam she had seen the night he had gone after Sam. "I'll be busy. Not too busy for Claire." He turned in her direction. "Sam's party's at six. I'll pick you up at a quarter to."

He didn't wait for a response, just turned and strode out of the apartment. Claire's heart was still pounding when Ben closed the door. She knew about the birthday party at Sage and Jake's on Tuesday night, of course. Sam had called to tell her. It was the first real excitement she had heard in his voice since he had come back from the bayou.

"Claire?"

Her attention swung back to Michael. She had almost forgotten he was there. "Would you like a cup of coffee?" she asked, determined not to be rude. "I just made a pot."

"That'd be great."

She didn't really want to talk to Michael, but he wasn't leaving her much choice. She poured him a cup, and a fresh cup for herself, and they sat down on the stools she had purchased for the breakfast bar.

She took a sip of her coffee. "You said you took a new assignment. What is it?"

"Actually, it's connected with the exposé I was working on in Colombia. Houston has a drug trafficking problem. I made a few contacts in South America, the kind of people who know what's going on. I'll be doing some digging, trying to connect the dots. If I can, it could be big, Claire. Really big."

"That sounds dangerous, Michael."

"Good stories don't come easy."

She sipped her coffee. "Is that why you came here? You were looking for another story?"

He set his mug down on the counter, reached over and took her hand. "I came because you're here, Claire. The story just gave me an excuse. I never stopped loving you. I figured if we spent time together, maybe we could find what we had before."

Claire started shaking her head. "I don't think—"

Michael put a finger to her lips. "Don't say anything. Not right now. Just say that if I call, you'll agree to see me."

She looked into his handsome face, saw the interest she had seen long ago when they had first met. And yet it didn't feel the same. "I can't do that. Not right now."

He lifted her hand and kissed her palm. "I'm not going anywhere. I'll find a way to make things right."

Claire made no reply. She wasn't in love with Michael. She was in love with Ben Slocum.

She couldn't have the man she wanted.

And she didn't want the man she could have.

Twenty-Seven

B̲en guided Sam up to Claire's front door on Tuesday evening. He hadn't seen her since last Saturday, when he'd found her in her apartment talking to her ex-boyfriend. He was still trying to wrap his head around the jolt of murderous jealousy he'd felt when he'd seen Michael Sullivan standing in her living room as if he belonged there.

"Can I ring Claire's doorbell?"

"Sure, go ahead." He could sense Sam's eagerness to see her. The bad news was, Ben wanted to see her nearly that much himself. He tried not to think what might have happened between Claire and Sullivan after he'd walked away.

Had she gone back to him? Had she kissed him? Hell, had he taken her to bed?

The thought twisted his guts into a knot. His mind flashed back to Laura the night, three days after he had given her an engagement ring, he had walked into her apartment and found her in bed with another man.

Just then Claire opened the door, putting an end to the ugly thought.

Sam grinned up at her. "Hi, Claire."

"Hi, sweetheart. Happy birthday!" She bent and gave him a hug. "How does it feel to be ten years old?"

"I don't know. I haven't been ten that long."

"Maybe you'll feel older after your party."

Sam's grin widened. It was good to see him smiling. He hadn't been doing a lot of that lately.

"You ready to go?" Ben asked Claire, trying not to notice the dress she was wearing, a soft burgundy that covered her neck-to-knee but was snug enough to show off every feminine curve. His gaze traveled down those long shapely legs, and he remembered the way they had felt wrapped around him in bed. She was wearing very high heels and he remembered the night he'd taken her in nothing but a pair of heels and thigh-high black stockings.

Christ, just looking at her made him hard, and there wasn't much chance of that changing for the rest of the evening. Ben shifted to relieve the pressure in his groin.

"Let me grab my purse." She ran back across the room and grabbed her handbag and a big present wrapped with blue-and-brown paper and a big blue bow on top. "Happy birthday, Sam."

He took the present almost shyly. "Thanks. Can I open it now?"

"Nope. Got to wait till the party."

Soon they pulled up in front of Sage and Jake's, a big pale pink colonial in the University District they had renovated. Having a party for Sam had been Ben's idea. Having it at Sage and Jake's had been Sage's.

It was November and the weather was cool. It wasn't raining but when he walked out onto the covered patio, kerosene heaters had been set up to dispel the early-evening chill. Blue-and-brown-striped tablecloths covered a half-dozen small tables, each with a football decoration set in blue flowers. Ben and Sam had been watching the Texans games together. He wouldn't have guessed how much fun it could be to share the game with his kid.

One of the tables held the presents. Staring at the pile in awe, Sam carefully added Claire's gift to the stack.

"You know most everyone," Ben said, having taken Sam into the office several times to meet his friends. They'd all been great to his son, especially Annie, who didn't have kids of her own and took on the role of substitute grandmother.

Sam's gaze wandered over the crepe paper streamers suspended from the ceiling, the party favors and colorful paper plates. "I've never had such a fancy birthday party."

"Yeah, well, don't get used to it," Ben said with the slight smile his son wasn't quite sure was teasing. "They've got a lot more money than we do."

Sam looked worriedly up at him. "We don't have any money?"

Ben grinned. It happened more lately, but it still felt a little odd. "Don't worry, we've got enough. You aren't going to have to eat any more alligator stew."

Claire's eyes widened at the mention of Sam's ordeal, but Ben had already decided to tackle the subject head-on.

Sam let out a belly laugh. Apparently the strategy was working.

"Come on, there's a couple of people I want you to meet." Resting a hand on Sam's shoulder, Ben started leading him away. When Claire didn't follow, he paused. "You coming with us?"

She hesitated, then walked up beside them. Ben ig-

nored a feeling of rightness that settled him somehow
and kept walking till he reached a familiar pair of faces.

"Sam, this is Mr. and Mrs. Justice. They're just back
from their honeymoon." Alex, a former navy pilot, was
tall and blond while his wife, Sabrina, was a cute little
redhead.

"It's nice to meet you," Sam said politely. The kid
had good manners, and he was already beginning to
fit in at school. He guessed Laura had done a good job
raising him despite everything.

"It's great to meet you, too, Sam." Sabrina smiled.
"You can call me Rina. Most everyone does."

"Everyone but me," Alex said, bending to give his
petite wife a kiss on the cheek. Sabrina flushed.

"I'm Alex," he said to Sam, extending a hand Sam
politely shook. "Welcome to the family, such as it is."

Sam looked up at him in confusion.

"We're all a family here," Annie explained as she sa-
shayed up to join them. "Some of us are a little friend-
lier than others," she said pointedly to Ben. "We just
needed a young man like you to bring us all together."

Sam seemed pleased.

"This is my sister, Rebecca," Alex said. "This is Joe,
the guy she's going to marry. And this young lady is
my favorite niece, Ginny."

"I'm his only niece," Ginny said, laughing. "Happy
birthday, Sam."

Ben didn't think the boy was old enough to like girls,
but from the look he was giving pretty little seven-year-
old Ginny Wyatt, he definitely had his father's genes.

"Wanna play kickball before you open your presents?" Ginny asked.

"Sure." Sam glanced up at him for permission. Ben
nodded and the pair raced off to play. Two other boys

from Sam's class were also there, nice kids, Ben thought as all of them started racing around on the grass, chasing after the soccer ball. Ginny, the youngest, was holding her own, but she'd always been a tomboy.

"I could use a beer," Ben said to Claire. "You want something?"

"I'd love a glass of wine."

He walked her over to the soft-drink bar that had been set up for the kids and grabbed a cold bottle of Bud Light out of the bucket of ice on the ground beside it. Finding an open bottle of chardonnay, he poured a glass for Claire. As she took the glass, their fingers brushed, and that slight contact made his blood begin to heat. Damn.

Claire took a sip and Ben tipped up his bottle. "Thanks for coming."

"Are you kidding? I wouldn't have missed it."

He walked her over to one of the tables and both of them sat down. "So how'd it go with lover boy?"

Her dark eyebrows went up. "If you mean Michael, he's here on assignment. Something about drug trafficking in Houston. He said it was connected to what he was working on before."

"That's it? That's all that happened? He told you about the story he's writing?"

"That's right. We talked for a while then he left."

"You didn't sleep with him?"

Her head shot up. "What? No, of course not."

Relief slid through him. Claire wouldn't lie about something like that. Or at least he didn't think she would.

They turned and watched the children playing on the grass. When he turned back, Claire was watching him.

"There's something I need to tell you," she said.

"I've been wanting to for some time. Somehow it never seemed right. Maybe now's the time."

"Oh, yeah? What's that?"

"It's about you and Laura."

"That's old news, angel."

"Not all of it. I think you should know the reason Laura cheated on you."

He grunted.

"Laura wanted you to have the chance to do what you always wanted. She knew as long as the two of you were together, that was never going to happen."

"Bullshit."

"Is it? How badly did you want to join the navy? From the moment she met you, she said all you talked about was becoming a SEAL. It meant everything to you, right? Then the two of you fell in love. After that, instead of enlisting, you were going to stay in Pittsburgh. You'd get a job, you said, maybe go back to the steel mill."

"We could have worked it out."

"Laura didn't think so. She thought you loved her so much you would be willing to give up everything for her. Every one of your dreams."

It was true. He had been deeply in love with Laura. He would have done anything to make her happy. His stomach was churning. He didn't like to talk about the past.

Claire was relentless. "The problem was, you were willing to give up everything, but Laura couldn't handle the responsibility. She thought sooner or later you'd come to resent her for destroying your dreams. Three nights after you gave her an engagement ring, she got drunk at a party and took one of the guys home with her."

"My ex–good buddy, Jimmy Bates. He's lucky he's still breathing."

"Laura knew you were coming over after you finished studying. She wanted you to find her, Ben. She loved you enough to set you free."

Ben's chest tightened. He set the beer bottle down on the table. "It's all bullshit. She just told you that because she felt guilty."

"You're right. She felt guilty for the rest of her life. Guilty and miserable. She never got over you, Ben. Laura never stopped loving you. That's the reason she wanted to have your baby."

"That's enough. I don't want to hear any more. Laura's dead. It's all in the past. The only thing I care about now is my son. The only woman I care about is you."

Fuck, he hadn't meant to say that. He got up from the table, downed the last swallow of his beer, set it down and walked away.

He heard the sound of the children laughing as Claire walk up behind him. "I care about you, too, Ben," she said softly.

His chest clamped down. "Doesn't matter. I told you—I'm not good at relationships."

She followed his gaze out to his son. "I'm not sure I believe that anymore."

She might not think so, but it was true. He had enough to handle learning how to be a father. He wasn't about to take on the responsibilities of learning to be a husband, too. Just the thought made the knot in his stomach go tighter.

The feeling got worse when Trace and Maggie walked in, Trace bearing cigars and, beneath his cowboy hat, a grin that stretched all the way across his face.

"We've got news," he said, handing expensive cigars to everyone within reach, even the women. "Maggie's pregnant."

They all rushed over, laughing and hugging, wishing them congratulations.

"It's a girl," Maggie said, grinning. "Trace is sure she'll have red hair." Sage laughed, knowing redheads had always been Trace's weakness. Claire seemed really pleased for Maggie, who was becoming a friend.

Ben thought of the responsibilities he was undertaking in raising a son. Claire would want children of her own. He didn't want to even think about it. He made the proper responses, then went back to watching the kids playing on the lawn.

He didn't say more than a couple of words to Claire the rest of the evening, just kept his attention on Sam as the boy opened his gifts, surprised and pleased with each new item, careful to thank the person who had given it to him.

Ben stood by as Sam blew out his candles, laughing with delight when he snuffed all ten, then helping Claire cut pieces of a chocolate cake that was decorated with a football and a Houston Texans jersey in icing on the top, Sam's name and age in big blue letters.

A few minutes later, Sam came over and thanked him in private for the iPod Ben had given him that Sam seemed to love, calling him Ben instead of *Dad*.

Ben looked forward to the day that would change.

In the meantime, he would be staying away from Claire. He wasn't ready to sleep with another woman the way he would have been in the past. But in time he would be. Down the road, he'd get past his confusing feelings for Claire, and they could be friends.

One thing Sam wasn't getting for his birthday or anytime in the future was a mother.

Ben was sure about that.

"Stop it, Aggie. You been mopin' around for weeks." Mace stood on the porch in front of his cabin in the bug-out compound. A small group had gathered around.

"He was my boy," Aggie said. "Troy brung him to me. He was mine, and you and that worthless bunch out yonder let them men come waltzing in here like they owned the place and take him right out from under your noses."

"Yeah, well, he weren't nothin' but another mouth to feed."

"He was my boy, and I want him back."

Mace flicked a glance at Troy. He was standing next to Duke, the pair of them just lookin' for an excuse to leave. Troy never was much for country livin'. 'Specially since there weren't no women. Mace had him a whore in town when he got the urge, but Troy and Duke figured they was too good to pay for it.

"I brought the kid to Aggie," Troy said. "He came with me of his own accord. He's our sister's kin now. You've always said we Braggs protect our own."

"Don't be a fool. We don't even know who took the kid or where he is."

"We've got friends in town," Troy said. "They know people in the sheriff's department. We need to find the boy and bring him back."

"Troy's right," Big Nosed Zeke agreed, always a damned troublemaker. "We let this go, people think we can't defend ourselves. They start to lose respect."

"I heard some of our members talkin'," Nate, the preacher, said. He lived on a farm down the road apiece, but he was one of the Patriots' strongest supporters. "They figure we got to settle this. They say it's a matter of honor."

Mace looked out at the group of men gathered in their secondary compound, a smaller bunch, since it was miles away from the main camp, deeper in the swamp. "We don't need no more trouble. We bring the kid back, the law'll be on us like flies on shit. Bad enough as it was."

Aggie opened her mouth, but Mace sliced her a look that warned her not to say another word. "Troy, you and Duke want to leave, then get on your high horse and go."

"Take it easy," Troy said. "We were just talking. Aggie misses the boy, that's all."

"I think Mace is right," his brother Jesse said. "I got a family to think about. I don't want no more trouble."

"Finally, someone with a brain. Talk's over. We leave the boy alone and things cool down, we'll be able to go back home."

Troy reached out and took hold of Aggie's hand. "Maybe Mace is right, sis."

For once Aggie's mouth stayed shut.

It was over, Mace figured. In time, things would get back to normal. In time his sister would lose that puckered look on her face and get back to takin' care of the rest of them like she was supposed to.

Or at least Mace damned well hoped so.

Claire hadn't seen Ben since the birthday party. He was back at work and avoiding her, just dropping Sam off a couple of times after she got home from work, not bothering to come into the apartment.

In a way, it was funny. He was the one who had said

he cared for her, made it sound as if he really meant it. She never would have said a word.

It didn't matter. Ben didn't want a relationship. He just wanted sex and that was nearly impossible with a young boy in the house. Of course he could stop by the apartment for a quickie. He had a babysitter now for Sam, an older lady named Mrs. McKenzie, a friend of Annie's. He could drop over and take her to bed, if she'd let him, which she wouldn't.

No matter how much she wanted him to do exactly that.

Michael had stopped by a couple of times. He had talked her into going out for pizza. Once he had taken her to a movie.

"My investigation is really progressing," he'd said at the Peking Palace, the Chinese restaurant they had gone to after the show. "I'll be dropping out of sight for a while, doing a little undercover work. I won't be able to see you."

"Undercover work? That sounds kind of risky. You're a reporter, not a cop. Are you sure it's worth it?"

"It's what I do, Claire, and hell yes, it'll be worth it. I promise, once this assignment is over, I'll take something easier. Something that will give us plenty of time together. We'll be able to work things out, make plans."

Once this assignment is over. Words she'd heard a dozen times. She didn't argue. The words weren't important anymore. She wasn't in love with Michael. She was in love with Ben.

Thank God work was keeping her busy. The social services job she'd taken was a management position. Learning how to teach and supervise her staff was a challenge she was enjoying. She had even begun to make a few friends. If it weren't for Sam, she wouldn't have to think of Ben at all. Eventually she would get over him.

At least she told herself she would. So far that hadn't happened. At night, she dreamed he was making love to her and woke up damp and aroused. She wondered if he thought of her half as much as she thought of him.

It wasn't likely.

He was the Iceman.

A woman was the last thing he needed.

Twenty-Eight

The office was busy, Trace in with Sol, working a case, Alex with Jake on a corporate security detail. Annie watched Ben sitting at his desk, staring out the window instead of making phone calls or working on his computer.

He'd been acting strange all week. She had even caught him reading a *Family Circle* magazine, which he had promptly dumped in the trash can beneath his desk when he'd seen her approach.

Annie came out from behind her desk and walked over to where he sat brooding, propped her hands on her hips. "Okay, what's going on? I know you've got half a dozen messages on your voice mail—I directed the calls myself."

He glanced up, his pale eyes distant. "You ask me, this new system's a pain in the ass. I liked it better when you were answering the phone. Who wants to talk to a message machine?"

"I don't like it, either. Tell your boss about it. The

point is, you need to get off your duff and get back to work. You can't just sit around mooning over Claire."

"What makes you think it's Claire? Maybe it's someone else."

"Sure, maybe it's Angelina Jolie. And I'm thinking about my hot date tonight with Brad Pitt. Let's face it, Ice. You're gone over that little gal. You're just too damned stubborn to admit it."

He just looked back out the window. "I've…ah… been thinking about asking her to marry me."

Stunned, for a moment Annie couldn't think of a single thing to say. At least that explained the magazine. She gave him a smile as bright as a sparkler on the fourth of July. "Now you're talking! She's perfect for you. I have to admit, I'm surprised you actually see that."

He just nodded. "It seems like a sensible move. We're compatible, I guess. We care about each other. We're great together in bed. And both of us love Sam. It seems like a good idea."

Annie's smile faded. "On the other hand, maybe you better think this over. You don't want to rush into anything."

"I've been thinking about it awhile. I've got a security project I need to start next week. I figure we could get married at city hall over the weekend. Have a small reception sometime later on."

"No honeymoon?"

He shrugged. "Same as. We'll be sleeping together again. Maybe we'll take a week somewhere down the road. Sam could go with us."

"Oh, boy."

"What's the matter?"

"I forgot how much you don't know about women."
Ben's broad shoulders straightened. "I know plenty."

"You know plenty about sex—that isn't the same."

"Look, I appreciate the advice, but I've got to run.
Claire should be home from work by now. I want to talk
to her before it's time for Mrs. McKenzie to go home."

Annie snorted. "Good luck with that."

"Thanks."

She was still shaking her head when he walked out
the door. Ben was in trouble, big-time. Problem was, he
didn't know it. She almost felt sorry for him. She had
a feeling Claire was about to give him a long-overdue
lesson on women.

By the time he got to Claire's apartment, Ben's
nerves were on edge. It wouldn't be that hard, he told
himself, repeating all the reasons getting married was
a good idea. Sexual compatibility, for one thing. Hell,
he couldn't stop thinking about getting her back in bed.
But he had to consider Sam. Making it legal just made
good sense.

He had to admit, after Laura he'd never thought he
would ever take the plunge, but hey, he never thought
he'd be a father, either.

The light was on over her kitchen sink as Ben walked
up on the porch and knocked on her door. When she
opened it, he saw that she hadn't changed yet from
work, still wore her hair clipped back and a conservative dark green business suit. But she'd kicked off her
shoes and her feet were bare.

Just looking at those sexy red-painted toenails made
him hard. He looked into her face and something tightened in his chest. God, he'd missed her.

He swallowed, his nerves increasing. "Hi, can I come in?"

She searched behind him for Sam. Maybe he should have brought the boy along, just for insurance. "He's at home. I wanted to talk to you."

"Come on in." She stepped back, and he walked past her, caught a hint of her soft perfume and resisted hauling her into his arms and kissing her.

"Nothing's wrong with Sam?"

"No, it's nothing like that." He was starting to sweat. He could feel it running down the middle of his back. "You wouldn't have a beer, would you?"

She didn't reply, just walked over to the refrigerator, took out a Bud and handed it over. "What is it, Ben?"

"I need to ask you something. Can we sit down?"

She cast him a wary glance. "All right." He hadn't wanted her to stay in Houston. He'd hurt her. She didn't trust him the way she had before. He'd have to be patient, explain things so she understood.

They walked into the living room and both of them sat down on the sofa. He wanted to reach for her hand, but he didn't. He should have bought a ring. Why hadn't he? He tried not to think of Laura and what had happened after they'd gotten engaged.

"I've missed you, Claire."

She sat up straighter. "If you think you can walk in here and charm me back into bed, you're wrong."

He shook his head. "That's not it at all. Well, not exactly. The thing is, I think we should get married."

Her eyes widened.

"Just hear me out, okay? I know I said I wasn't good at relationships, but I figure I'm better with you than I am with other women. We're great in bed and both of us love Sam. You want to spend time with him. If we're living together, you'll be able to see him all you want. We could get married by the justice of the peace. You know, just something quick and easy, no fuss, no muss. If you think about it, it's a logical solution."

He didn't expect it. Wasn't prepared when her pretty eyes narrowed, her hand shot back and she slapped him hard across the face.

She was on her feet, trembling as she pointed toward the door. "Get out of here, Ben. Don't come back. I don't ever want to see you again."

He rubbed his cheek as he stood up from the sofa. The lady packed a wallop. "Claire, I'm sorry. I didn't say it right. I know if you just—" He caught her wrist before she could nail him again.

"Get out! Get out now!" She started crying, left him standing in the middle of the living room and ran off down the hall.

Ben stared after her. His heart was painfully throbbing. He felt as if he couldn't breathe. He could hear her in her bedroom crying, but he couldn't make himself go after her.

He hadn't meant to hurt her. He'd just wanted… What? Claire in his bed? Things back the way they were? He should have known she'd want more from him than he would be able to give her.

Christ, she deserved more. A helluva lot more.

He looked down the hall, at the door she had closed behind her. She'd meant every word she'd said. She didn't want to see him again.

Ben walked to the front door and let himself out. It was over. He should be relieved. He was never cut out to be a husband.

He ignored the pressure in his chest. He'd get over

it. He had a son to think of. He should have known it would never work.

He should have known better than to fall for another woman.

Claire threw herself into her job. She went to work early and stayed late. Ben hadn't called. She hadn't seen him since he had tried to convince her what a good idea it would be if she married him. After all, it would be so *convenient* for both of them.

She had talked to Sam on the phone a couple of times, but she wasn't ready to face the boy. She couldn't manage to act as if nothing had happened between her and his dad.

She hadn't seen Michael, either. And though she was no longer in love with him, she was worried about him. He was working on a dangerous story. She didn't want anything to happen to him.

On Wednesday of the following week, she caught a flight from Houston to White Plains to have Thanksgiving dinner with her parents. Her mom and dad were great, showing her the photos of their anniversary cruise through the Mediterranean. She and her mother had cooked a traditional turkey dinner and it had been a fun distraction. All the while, Claire had pretended her move to Houston was a great idea and everything was fine.

The pretense had made those few days among the most stressful of her life. The truth was, as much as she loved her parents, she'd wanted to be back in Houston, sharing the holiday with Ben and Sam. Or having them there with her, meeting her parents and enjoying the traditional meal.

It was never going to happen.

On Sunday morning, she caught an early flight back to Houston and arrived more exhausted than she'd been before she'd left. Monday morning, she went to work early and stayed an hour late just so she wouldn't have time to think of Ben.

A light rain was falling as she drove back to her apartment. When she got there, she tossed off her navy blue suit jacket, poured herself a glass of white wine and carried it into the living room, too tired even to change.

Sitting down on the sofa, she tucked her legs up under her and took a sip. She was beginning to relax when a knock sounded at the door. With a weary sigh, she set her wineglass down, walked over and pulled it open. Annie Mayberry and Sage Cantrell stood on her porch.

"May we come in?" Sage asked, also wearing a business suit. Annie had come from work, as well.

As tired as she was, Claire was always glad to see the women she considered friends. "I just poured myself a glass of wine. Would you like one? Or maybe a glass of iced tea?"

"Wine would be perfect," Sage said, following her toward the kitchen.

"I could use a little bracer, myself," Annie said.

Wondering if there was a reason the women had come, Claire poured the wine, and they all sat down at the dining room table.

"Your place looks nice," Sage said, glancing around at the pale green sofa and chairs, her glass-topped dining table, taking a sip of the chilled chardonnay.

"Thank you. It's coming along. I haven't had much extra time to spend decorating."

"I guess Sam talked to you," Annie said. "He told us you went to your parents' house for Thanksgiving."

She nodded. "We'd been planning to get together for the holidays."

"I hope you had a good trip," Sage said.

"I enjoyed seeing my parents. But I wasn't particularly good company."

Sage set her wineglass down on the table. "Because of Ben?"

Claire's chest tightened at the mention of his name.

"I guess Ben really blew it," Annie said bluntly, and Claire realized the women knew about Ben's marriage-of-convenience proposal.

"Ben was just being honest," Claire finally said. "He wants a mother for his son. I guess he thought I'd make a good one."

"Ben was just being Ben," Annie said. "Which means he wasn't being honest at all. At least not about his feelings. When it comes to his emotions, I don't think even Ben Slocum knows what's going on in his head."

Claire sighed. "Whatever he's thinking, I can't do it. I can't marry a man who doesn't love me. Not even for Sam's sake."

"That's the irony," Sage said gently. "I think Ben loves you very much."

"He's sick over what happened," Annie added. "He can't work. He can't think. He's focused his entire attention on Sam just so he won't have to think about you."

"That...that can't be true."

"Oh, it's true, all right," Annie said. "The poor kid doesn't know quite what to do with all the attention."

"That's partly my fault. After what happened, I couldn't face him. I pretended to be happy the whole time I was with my parents. I wasn't ready to pretend with Sam." She looked at Sage. "Maybe you could talk to Ben, tell him I'd like Sam to come over. Maybe he could spend a night this weekend."

Sage reached over and caught her hand. "None of this is your fault, Claire. Ben's in love with you. He just doesn't know how to handle it."

She started shaking her head but a lump was swelling in her throat. "In a way, I feel sorry for him. He's built such a wall around his emotions." She wiped her eyes. Dammit, she was tired of crying over Ben. "I knew what he was like. I knew better than to fall in love with him."

"Maybe you should just go ahead and marry him," Annie suggested. "Sooner or later, he's bound to get his head out of his behind and figure things out."

She almost smiled. "I'm not sure what Ben feels for me. Whatever it is, I'm not willing to take that kind of chance. It wouldn't be fair to any of us."

Annie opened her mouth to argue, but a knock at the door stopped her. *Busy night,* Claire thought as she got up from the table, walked over and pulled the door open. Two men in dark suits stood on the doorstep, a good-looking Hispanic in his late thirties, and a blond man with a pale complexion and slightly ruddy cheeks.

"Claire Chastain?"

"That's right."

The men flipped open their badges. "Houston Police. May we come in?"

Her heart started pumping. "Yes, of course."

"I'm Detective Castillo and this is Detective Richmond. I'm afraid we have some bad news, ma'am."

Her hand came up to her heart. "What is it?"

"A man was found murdered this morning. We believe his name is Michael Sullivan."

She sagged. Detective Castillo caught her, guided

her over to the sofa. Sage and Annie both rushed into the living room.

"I'll get her some water," Annie said, hurrying into the kitchen then returning, pressing a glass into her trembling hand.

"What...what happened?"

"We aren't sure yet. The investigation is ongoing. We found your business card in his wallet. There was a note on it that said to call you in case of emergency. We need you to come down to the morgue and identify the body. Can you do that?"

A tight sound escaped from her throat. She managed to nod. Michael was dead. *Oh, God.*

"While you're there, we'll need to ask you some questions. We can drive you or meet you there."

"I know where it is," Annie said, taking charge. "Sage and I'll drive her down."

Castillo nodded. "All right. We'll meet you there." The men left the apartment, and Claire wiped at the wetness on her cheeks.

"I told him it was dangerous," she said. "Michael thrived on danger. He lived for it. He couldn't give it up."

"He was a friend?" Sage asked gently.

"Ex-boyfriend," Annie supplied, swinging Claire's gaze in her direction. Ben said Annie always knew everything. No one ever quite knew how.

"We lived together for a while. I loved him once. I can't believe he's dead." Fresh tears welled. Sage went into the bathroom and brought out a box of Kleenex. Claire grabbed a tissue and blew her nose.

"Are you sure you can handle this?" Sage asked.

Claire rose shakily to her feet. "Michael's dead. I don't really have any choice."

Twenty-Nine

"We got a problem." Trace walked out of his glass-enclosed office just as Ben was leaving for the day.

"What is it?" He needed to get home. Mrs. McKenzie would have supper ready for him and Sam. He didn't like to make them wait.

"Mark Sayers just called." Sayers was a detective friend of Trace's. "You know that journalist you mentioned? Claire's old boyfriend, Michael Sullivan? They found him dead this morning in an abandoned warehouse."

"Jesus. Does Claire know?"

"Detectives just left her house. She's on her way to the morgue to ID the body. The thing is, Ben, according to Sayers, the guy wasn't just killed, he was tortured. This is going to be really rough on her."

Ben didn't hesitate. She might not want to marry him, but right now she needed him, and he was going be there, whether she liked it or not. He headed for the door. "I'm on my way."

* * *

Inside the Harris County Forensic Science building, Claire left Sage and Annie in the hall and walked woodenly beside Detective Castillo through the door leading into the refrigeration area of the morgue. Rows of stainless steel boxes held the remains of dozens of people. One of them was Michael.

Her throat closed up. Of all the endings she had ever imagined, she wouldn't have guessed she'd be standing in front of a refrigerated box preparing to say a final farewell to the man she had once hoped to marry.

"Are you ready?" Detective Castillo asked.

Claire moistened her lips and nodded. A man in a white lab coat grabbed the handle, opened the stainless steel door and wheeled out a metal table. A white sheet was draped over the body, covering it from head to toe.

She moved closer, stared down at the outline of the man who had been so vibrant in life and now lay so silent.

Castillo stood beside her. "I need to warn you, Ms. Chastain, Michael's death wasn't easy."

She looked up at him, her breath coming shallow and fast, not quite sure what he meant. Castillo nodded, and the black-haired lab tech pulled back the sheet.

"Oh, my God!" She almost didn't recognize Michael's battered face, his cheekbones smashed, cigarette burns on his forehead, one of his ears missing. There were bruises on his neck, more burn marks on his chest. She whirled away from the grisly sight, took a stumbling step backward, turned and felt hard arms go around her.

"It's all right, angel. I've got you. You're okay."

She swallowed, couldn't speak. *Ben.* She clung to

him, slid her arms around his neck and just hung on. She was shaking. Ben pressed her tighter against him.

"It's…it's Michael," she said. "Oh, Ben."

He looked over her shoulder, down at the man on the cold steel table. "It's Sullivan," he said to the detectives, followed by the rustle of fabric as the lab tech pulled the sheet back up over Michael's battered and tortured body. "Let's go."

She let Ben take charge, let him guide her out the door, passing Sage and Annie in the hall.

"I'll take care of her," he said, and as fractured as she felt, as raw and grief-stricken, she knew a moment of relief. Ben was there. Everything would be all right.

As he led her toward the door, Detective Castillo caught up with them. "Hold up a minute, Ben. I know how hard this is on her, but we need to ask her some questions."

"Tomorrow, Castillo." The detective was head of the gang division. Ben seemed to know him, had probably worked with him before.

"Now would be better," the detective said as Ben urged her forward.

Claire took a deep breath and stopped. She looked into the detective's face. "I want you to find the men who did this. I'll help any way I can."

Castillo nodded, led them into an interview room and closed the door. Ben sat down next to Claire. He reached over and took hold of her hand. "You sure you can handle this?"

"You saw what they did. They tortured him, Ben."

"I'm sorry, baby."

"Thank…thank you for coming."

He just nodded.

The interview didn't take long. She didn't know

enough to really help. She repeated the few things Michael had told her, that he was working on a story that dealt with drug trafficking, that he had made connections with people in Colombia. He had hinted they were linked to people here. As upset as she was, she couldn't think of anything more. She could hardly remember her own name.

She swallowed, tried not to think of Michael's smiling face the last time she had seen him, or the brutalized face in the morgue. "He said…said the story could be big. That's all I know."

Castillo asked a few more questions, but it was clear Michael hadn't really confided in her.

"I wish I knew something more helpful. I should have paid more attention." But much of the time they had been together, she had been thinking of Ben.

"You did the best you could," Castillo said.

"What…what about his body?"

"Will you be handling the funeral arrangements?"

"No. I—I can give you his parents' phone number. They live in California. They'll want to claim the body and make arrangements for the…the funeral."

And they wouldn't want anything to do with her. Not since she and Michael had ended their relationship. They faulted her entirely for the breakup.

Castillo shoved to his feet. "I'm sorry for your loss."

Claire swallowed, nodded. Ben helped her out of her chair and guided her into the hall. She felt weak and disoriented, slightly sick to her stomach.

"I came with Sage and Annie," she said. But they were already gone.

"I'm taking you to my house."

She shook her head. "I don't want Sam to see me

like this." Her face tear-streaked, her makeup smudged. "He's had enough grief. Please, Ben."

He clenched his jaw. He knew she was right. As soon as they got into his car, he phoned his house. He told Mrs. McKenzie he would be late getting home and asked the babysitter to spend the night.

Ben drove her back to her apartment and escorted her up to her door, took her key and let her in. He led her down the hall to her bedroom and began to strip off her clothes. She stopped him before she was completely naked.

"I can't, Ben. Not tonight."

He stepped back as if she'd given him another slap. "Jesus, Claire, do you really think I'm that bad? Don't you know by now, I'd never do anything to hurt you?"

Not on purpose. She knew that. She went into his arms and they closed tightly around her. Her heart ached with love for him.

For long moments, they just stood there, Ben holding on to her, Claire with her head on his shoulder. He tipped her chin up, brushed a soft kiss over her lips then moved off in search of something for her to wear. He found her nightshirt, handed it to her and turned away while she unhooked her bra and pulled it on. Drawing back the covers, he waited while she slid between the sheets.

"Try to get some sleep. I'll be out on the sofa if you need anything."

"You don't...don't have to stay."

"Yeah, I do." He started for the door, then turned back and paused. "Were you still in love with him?"

She swallowed, tried not to see Michael's shattered, bludgeoned face. "No. We were just friends."

Some of the hardness left his features. His shoulders seemed less tense as he walked out the door.

Fatigue washed over her. She was tired clear to her bones. Yet every time she closed her eyes, she saw Michael's face, the crushed bones, the cigarette burns, the hole where his ear had been cut away.

Her stomach rolled. She was afraid she might be sick. She must have made a sound because Ben appeared in the doorway.

"You all right?"

She tried to nod but a sob welled up in her throat. Ben didn't hesitate, just walked over and climbed into bed beside her. Stretching out on top of the covers, he pulled her into his arms.

Time seemed to blur. She could feel the warmth of his hard body, hear his even breathing. As her eyes drifted closed, she felt safe and protected. The odd thought occurred that she felt loved.

Claire wondered how that could be.

Lying on the weight bench in his study, his body drenched in sweat, Ben pressed the three-hundred-pound bar a couple more times, then set the barbell on the rack above his head. He was back to his normal workout routine, hitting it hard this morning to work off some of his frustration.

Just after dawn, he'd left Claire sleeping and returned home. She'd taken Michael Sullivan's death hard, but he knew her well enough to know that seeing anyone suffer the way Sullivan had would upset her badly.

He'd stayed with her last night, but he hadn't wanted to be there when she awakened. He didn't want to know what he would see in her eyes when she looked at him.

He'd been an idiot to think she would marry him.

Claire would want love and commitment. She'd want happily ever after. He wouldn't have the vaguest idea how to give her those things.

He glanced at the door, surprised to see his son standing in the opening. He got up from the weight bench, grabbed the towel off the rack, mopped his face and slung the towel around his neck.

"You're up early." He'd sent Mrs. McKenzie home when he'd come in this morning. Sam had still been sleeping. "You hungry?"

Sam eyed the heavy weights. "You're really strong. Do you think I will be, too?"

"If you work at it. Staying in shape isn't easy."

"Mrs. McKenzie said you stayed with Claire last night. She said Claire was feeling bad."

"Claire felt bad because one of her friends died."

His expression turned somber. "Is she okay?"

"She will be. It takes a little time."

He looked as if he knew exactly what that meant. "If you stayed at her house, you must not be mad at her anymore."

He mopped at a trickle of sweat that ran down his chest. "I wasn't mad at her." It was the other way around. And after the way he'd botched things, he didn't blame her. "We've both just been busy."

"So she can come over sometime?"

Did he want her to? From the hopeful look on Sam's face, he didn't have much choice. "If she wants to." Though he wasn't sure she would.

"Claire likes you. Whenever I go over there, we talk about you a lot."

Interest trickled through him. "That right? What's she say?"

"She said you loved my mother very much. Did you?"

He had, but it seemed like another lifetime. "Yes. But it was a long time ago." He thought of what Claire had told him. That Laura had ended their engagement in a way that would force him to go on with his life. To go after the dreams he would have given up for her. He hadn't believed it at the time, but more and more he wondered if it could be true.

Was it possible to love someone that much?

Had Laura sacrificed everything for him?

Had he spent all these years keeping his emotions locked away for the wrong reasons?

"I'm gonna jump in the shower," he said. "Then I'll make you something to eat."

"Okay."

"You can watch TV till I get dressed, then you need to get ready for school."

"Do you think someday you and Claire might get married?"

The words tightened a knot in his stomach. No chance of that happening now.

"I don't think Claire wants to marry me."

"If she did, would you?"

"I think you'd better go watch TV."

Sam grinned and headed for the living room, flipped on the Disney channel.

Kids, Ben thought. They took some getting used to.

After a breakfast of French toast and bacon, Ben took Sam to school. He usually rode the bus, which made Ben a little nervous, but Sam was making friends and he wanted the boy to fit in with the rest of the kids at school.

Once in a while Ben liked to drive him. He enjoyed watching him mix with the other kids as they all poured into the school building. He liked the feeling of being a father. Sometimes he still found it hard to believe.

After he dropped Sam off, he thought about calling Claire, see how she was feeling. In the end, he just went into the office and started working on the security plan he had been hired to design for the Hamilton Medical Center.

Trace would take care of the alarm system, but it was Ben's job to work out the number of security guards that would be needed, figure where they should be stationed and organize their routine.

He hoped he'd be able to concentrate enough to get the job done.

Claire worked hard all day, trying not to think of yesterday, trying not to wonder what progress the police had made in solving Michael's murder. Michael had been searching for information. That was his job as a reporter. But digging so deeply into whatever he was working on had managed to get him killed.

She thought of Ben and the way he had come for her last night, how he had been there when she needed him. Ben always seemed to be there when she needed him.

She was thinking about him when she got home from work. This time of year it got dark early, but she had left the porch light on and a lamp turned on in the living room. As she pulled up into the driveway, she noticed the front door standing slightly ajar.

Claire frowned. She'd locked it before she'd left that morning. Living in the city had taught her to be careful. Instead of pulling into the garage, she put the car in Park and turned off the engine, got out and walked up to the door. She wasn't foolish enough to go inside until she knew it was safe, but she shoved the door open a little and looked into the living room.

Her heart jerked and started pounding. Oh, dear Lord! Hurrying off the porch and moving a safe distance from the apartment, she pulled her BlackBerry out with a trembling hand and dialed 911.

"My name is Claire Chastain. Someone broke in and vandalized my apartment." She gave them the address and answered the dispatcher's questions.

"Wait outside till the police get there," the woman said. "They're on the way now. Don't go inside till they get there."

"I won't."

"Stay on the phone with me while you're waiting."

"Okay."

She was trembling when the white-and-blue patrol car rolled up. Two officers climbed out, one tall and thin, wearing aviator-style glasses, the other shorter and almost completely bald.

"This your place?" the shorter policeman asked. Officer Renick, his name tag read.

"Yes. I'm Claire Chastain. I noticed the door standing open as I pulled into the driveway. The whole place is destroyed." Her chest clamped down. Everything she owned was ruined. A little shiver rolled through her. "Why would anyone do such a thing?"

The officers didn't answer, just drew their pistols and walked toward the house. She heard them inside, moving through the rooms, making sure no one was still in there.

"Looks more like vandals than burglars," the bald cop said when he walked back outside. "But we need you to go in and take a look, see if anything's missing."

She nodded, took a steadying breath and followed the men back into the house.

"They did some pretty major damage," the thin cop said, shoving his glasses up on his nose as he glanced around.

The understatement of the year.

Claire felt sick at heart. The place had been torn apart, the sofa turned over, the cushions ripped open. The lamps were knocked to the floor, the shades bent and torn. The kitchen looked just as bad, the dishes shoved out of the cupboards, shattered on the floor, the toaster tossed clear across the room.

She took a shaky breath. First Michael, now this. She felt like crying, but she had done enough of that lately.

She headed down the hall just as her BlackBerry started to ring. She dug it out of her purse, recognized Ben's number and pressed it against her ear with a shaky hand.

"It's Ben," he said, as if she wouldn't know his voice. "I…ah…just called to see if you're okay."

She tried to control the quiver in her throat. "I'm okay but someone…broke into my apartment. The police are here."

"What the hell?" His voice hardened. "I'm at the office. I'll be there as fast as I can."

"I'm okay, really."

"Just hang on till I get there."

The same feeling she'd had last night swept over her. Ben was coming. Everything would be okay. She hung up the phone and leaned against the wall.

"Anything missing in the living room?" the officer asked.

"Nothing I noticed offhand." She went into the bedroom. It looked the same as the living room, the covers pulled off the bed, the mattress slashed open, stuffing pouring out on the floor. She'd only hung a couple of pictures—a landscape photo Maggie Rawlins had given her as a housewarming gift, and a photo of her and her parents—but they were ripped off and tossed on the floor. Her desk had been rifled through, as well.

"My laptop is missing."

The officer wrote that down. "Anything else?"

The TV was still sitting on her dresser, though the drawers were all pulled out and the contents dumped on the floor.

"How about your jewelry?"

She made her way over to the mother-of-pearl inlaid jewelry box her parents had given her on her sixteenth birthday and flipped open the lid. The box was empty.

"My jewelry is gone. I had some nice gold necklaces and gold earrings, a couple of rings, one with opals, one with sapphires." The sapphire ring had been a gift from Michael. It was all she had left of him. Her heart squeezed. "They weren't worth a fortune but they were valuable to me."

The officer made a note. Down the hall, heavy footsteps sounded. She turned to see Ben walking through the bedroom door, a grim look on his face. For an instant their eyes met, hers frightened, his worried.

His gaze went from her to the two police officers. "What'd they take?"

"Laptop. Her jewelry. That's it so far."

He looked at Claire. "Any money in the house?"

"A little in a jar in the freezer. I didn't look there." They walked in that direction. The jar was there, but the money was gone. She walked back into the living room, feeling dazed and shaken, her gaze going over the destruction in her apartment.

Her heart beat dully. "They found my jewelry and my money. Did they really think they would find something valuable inside the cushions on my sofa?"

Ben surveyed the chaos in the room. He was standing so close she could feel the warmth of his body, comforting somehow.

"Meth heads," he said. "Or someone had a bone to pick with you. You had any trouble at work?"

"No. I'm not taking cases, and I haven't been there long enough to make any enemies."

He stood beside her as the officers took her statement. They wrapped things up and headed for the door.

"You have someone you can stay with tonight?" Officer Renick asked.

"She's staying with me," Ben said. He turned to Claire, waiting for her to protest, those ice-blue eyes on her face. "I'll bring you back to get your car in the morning."

She knew she should argue but she didn't. There was nowhere else she wanted to be.

The moon shone through the branches as they walked outside. She watched the patrol car taillights disappear into the darkness as the police drove away.

"You got some kind of insurance?" Ben asked.

She looked up at him. She was so glad he was there. It was dangerous to feel that way. More frightening than her apartment being vandalized. "I have a renter's policy with State Farm."

"You need to call them right away. They'll give you the name of a company that can clean up this mess."

She looked back at the apartment. "I need to collect a few things."

Ben walked her back inside, waited while she packed an overnight bag with clothes she picked up off the floor and a couple of business suits that were still hanging in her closet, enough for a couple of days.

As they left the building, she paused at the bottom of the front porch stairs. "You don't think they'll come back, do you?"

"Depends on why they were here in the first place." He didn't say more, but she knew him well enough to be sure he was thinking about it, drawing some sort of conclusion.

Ben waited while she drove her car into the garage and closed the automatic door, then helped her into the Denali.

She felt safe sitting next to him. She always felt safe with Ben.

It was her heart that was in danger.

Thirty

Sam was watching TV with Mrs. McKenzie when Ben got back to the house. The boy grinned when he saw Claire and ran to give her a hug.

"I asked Ben if you could come over, but I didn't know you were coming tonight."

"Claire's staying for a couple of days while they do some work on her apartment." He cast her a glance, still waiting for her to argue. He'd been surprised she had agreed without a fight.

She just looked down at Sam, and though her face was pale, she gave the boy a smile. "I hope you don't mind sleeping on the sofa."

"I don't mind."

"I made lasagna," Mrs. McKenzie said. "There's plenty for company." She was a small woman, rotund, with silver hair and tiny wire-rimmed glasses. She looked as though she had stepped out of an ad for homemade jam. Sam loved her. Ben was damned fond of her, too.

"Mrs. McKenzie, this is Claire. She's...a friend." She

was way more than that. Not his girlfriend. Not exactly. But something close to it. He wasn't sure when he had started thinking of her that way.

He wasn't sure what word Claire would use to describe their relationship. Or lack of one.

"It's nice to meet you, Mrs. McKenzie," Claire said warmly. "Sam thinks a lot of you."

"It's just Emma, and that's real nice to hear." She patted the boy on the head. "You take care of your guest tonight, and I'll see you tomorrow." She waved and headed for the door.

"How about some dinner?" Ben asked, looking at Claire for agreement as much as Sam.

Sam vigorously nodded. "I'm starving."

Claire looked pale and not the least bit hungry.

"You need to eat," he said, encouraging her, and finally she nodded.

Ben served the meal, including the crisp green salad Emma had made, and they all sat down together. It felt the way it had when he had first brought Sam home and Claire had been staying at the house with them.

He thought about the last time he had taken her to bed, the hot sex they'd had at Buster's cabin. He thought about all the days since then that he had wanted her and not been able to have her.

He looked at her, noticed the way a few strands of dark hair had come loose from her clip and floated against her cheek. He noticed her soft blue cashmere sweater and how it curved over her pretty breasts. Arousal slipped through him, tightened his groin.

He wanted her just as much as he had when she had been in the house before. And his bed was going to be just as empty.

He waited till they all finished eating then shoved

back from the table. "Time for you to put on your paja-
mas and brush your teeth," he said to Sam. "Say good-
night to Claire."

He did so politely, the way he always did, then disappeared into his bedroom to get dressed for the night
he would spend on the sofa.

Ben wondered what Claire would do if he came to
her tonight. He rubbed a hand over his jaw at a memory
of a slender palm burning his cheek and wondered if
she'd hit him again or invite him to join her.

"The cleaning lady was here this morning," he said.
"Clean sheets all around. I've got a T-shirt you can borrow if you need one."

"That would be great. I'd…umm…like to wash my
underwear before I wear it. I can't stand to think of who
might have handled it."

He remembered her sexy red bikini panties and his
blood heated. "Go ahead."

He watched her head back to the bedroom to retrieve
her things, walk past him into the laundry room to start
a load of clothes.

The nights had been long without her. Now that she
was back in his house, it was going to be a long night
again.

Sam was asleep in the living room when Claire threw
her clothes into the dryer and padded down the hall in
search of Ben. She found him sitting at the computer
in his study.

"What are you working on?" she asked, only a little
self-conscious in the olive-drab T-shirt he had loaned
her with just a pair of bikini panties underneath.

When he looked up and saw her, his shoulders tightened. She wanted to walk over and massage the tension away.

"I'm reading the exposé your boyfriend wrote for the *L.A. Times*."

A chill slid through her. "Ex-boyfriend. Why are you doing that?"

"Because, angel, your friend was tortured. Whoever did it either wanted payback for something he did, or they wanted information. If they were looking for something they thought he had, that could also be the reason they trashed your apartment."

"I thought they were looking for something to sell."

"Could be. Could be they were looking for something else and what they took was just a bonus. Since the vandalism occurred a day after Sullivan was killed and I'm not a big believer in coincidence, I'm trying to figure out what your friend was working on."

Claire straightened. "Oh, my God, you think what happened could have something to do with Michael."

"If they were pressing Sullivan for information and didn't get it, they might think you have it."

"But I don't have anything. I only went out with him a couple of times."

"Unfortunately, no one knows that but you."

"What…what should I do?"

"Be careful. Don't go off by yourself. Tomorrow I'll talk to Castillo, tell him what happened at your apartment. There's a chance it was just what it seems, a drug addict looking to make enough for a fix, or a bunch of destructive kids. But we need to find out."

Claire said nothing.

"Listen, baby, it's been a long day. Why don't you try to get some sleep?"

She nodded, but didn't walk away. Even with Michael's death and the vandalism, there was something she had to know. Something she'd been thinking about for more than a week.

Ben looked up, surprised to see her still there. "What is it?"

"I've been thinking…. The other day…when you made your ugly proposal…"

He frowned. "I'm sorry. I didn't mean for it to be ugly, just practical."

"Well, I've been thinking about your *practical* proposal. If I'd said yes, what did you plan to do about women?"

His frown deepened. "Women?"

"We both know you have a voracious appetite for sex. To the best of my knowledge, that involves women."

He shrugged. "I like sex. I'm pretty sure you do, too."

"That isn't the point. You aren't a one-woman man. Were you planning to fool around on the side? Maybe you thought if you were discreet—"

He was out of his chair in an instant and pressing her up against the wall. "I wasn't planning to cheat on you. I don't believe in that. I haven't been with another woman since I met you. I sure as hell wouldn't do it after we were married."

She swallowed, surprised by his answer and the fact she knew he meant it. "I just… I was curious." She tried to move away, but he didn't let her go, just bent his head and kissed her. A deep, wet, ravishing kiss that turned her body liquid and warm. His tongue was in her mouth, tasting and coaxing, and she melted against him.

She could feel every hard muscle, feel his powerful erection, and though she told herself to resist, he was Ben and she loved him. And she ached for him to touch her the way he had before.

"I want you, angel. God, I want you so much."

"Oh, Ben. I want you, too."

He kissed her again, softly his time, then more deeply. She loved the way he kissed, loved the taste of him, the feel of his hard body. No man could ever compare, not for her.

Lifting her into his arms, he carried her down the hall into his bedroom. In an instant, the borrowed T-shirt was gone, her panties stripped away. She helped Ben take off his clothes, then naked, he carried her over to the bed.

The loving started slow and easy, in seconds turned hot and wet, deep and erotic. He knew just how to touch her, how to stir her body until she couldn't think of anything but him, couldn't stand another moment without him inside her.

He drove deep, took her hard, drove her to frenzy. She bit down on her lip to stifle a cry as she reached a climax, then another. A few minutes later, Ben followed her to release.

Afterward they lay entwined, Claire nestled against his side. She traced a finger over his powerful chest. "I should go. Sam might wake up." Thank heaven he was a deep sleeper.

Ben pressed a kiss on her forehead. "Not yet." For a while he just held her, and she wondered at his thoughts. She was back in his house, but nothing had changed. Leaning over, he kissed her again, came up over her and slid himself inside. This time they reached their peak together and slowly drifted down.

Ben didn't stop her when she eased out of bed, grabbed his T-shirt and her panties off the floor, went into the bathroom. When she walked back out, he was wearing his jeans and nothing else, standing in front of the door, blocking her escape from the bedroom.

"We're good together, Claire."

She reached up and touched his cheek, felt his late-evening beard. "I know."

"Will you think about it?"

She didn't have to ask what he meant. She had been thinking about his "practical" proposal for days. But until that very moment, it hadn't occurred to her that she might actually accept it. Now as she looked into his hard, handsome face, she thought how much she loved him, thought how lonely her life would be without him.

And what if Sage was right and Ben really did love her? Would it be possible for them to be happy?

But what if Sage was wrong and the reason Ben was marrying her was exactly what he said. A practical solution to the problem of sharing Sam?

Could she live with a man who didn't love her? Claire knew she could not.

And yet she heard herself saying, "I'll think about it," as she turned and walked out of the bedroom.

Ben drove Claire to work the next morning.

"Don't you think you're overreacting?" she said.

"It'll only be for a day or two, till Castillo gets a line on things. We need to be sure the break-in isn't connected to Sullivan."

"I'm staying at your house. No one knows I'm there. Surely it's safe for me to drive myself to work."

"I'll pick you up at five. And don't go out to lunch by yourself."

Claire sighed. "All right, I'll do it your way for a while, but it if looks like a burglary, I'm driving myself and moving home as soon as my apartment is ready."

"All right, fine."

The morning passed uneventfully. No phone calls, no

one following the car or watching the building as they had driven away. Ben was being ridiculously cautious, but he'd always had a protective nature. It was one of the things she loved about him.

Sitting in the employee lounge eating the brown-bag lunch she had made herself that morning, Claire thought of Ben's "practical" proposal. It wasn't the hearts-and-flowers kind of marriage proposal she had dreamed of. It wasn't promises of eternal love and devotion.

But she would be sleeping in Ben's bed, and he would be making love to her. He would be a faithful husband, and both of them could take care of Sam. In time, maybe he would even come to love her. Was she brave enough to try?

He had asked her to think about it. Claire couldn't seem to stop.

As he drove to his meeting at the Texas Café, Ben's attention kept wandering. Claire was considering his proposal. He should be frantic. Why wasn't he? If she married him, he would have to settle down, give up his freedom, give up other women. But now that he was a father, he had to settle down anyway. And though he had a strong sexual appetite, he had never been into counting coup, the way some guys were. He just hadn't wanted to risk a deeper commitment.

It doesn't get any deeper than marriage, buddy.

But it did. Love was the dangerous part and he wasn't marrying for love. He was just being practical. The plan suited him perfectly.

He pulled into the Texas Café and spotted Danny Castillo's plain brown police car. As head of the gang division, Castillo knew everything there was to know about drug trafficking in the city.

Ben shoved open the door to the café, and a tall, knockout blonde named Ashley Sommerset walked over to greet him. "Hey, Ben."

She was Maggie Rawlins's sister, married now to a Houston multimillionaire named Jason Sommerset. She didn't have to work, but she was studying to be a chef. She loved the café, and her husband indulged her.

"Hey, Ash. How's the family?" Ashley had a baby, a little girl less than two years old.

"Great, how about yours? I hear your son is living with you now."

He felt a rush of pride. "That's right. His name is Sam." It took all his willpower not to pull out his iPhone and flash a picture of Sam around like one of those old geezers in the park showing off his grandkids.

"Bring him in sometime," Ashley said. "I'd love to meet him. I'll make him one of my special chocolate shakes."

"That'd be great. Sam loves ice cream."

"Detective Castillo is already here. He said you'd be looking for him."

He headed in the direction she pointed, slid into one of the pink vinyl booths and ordered a cup of coffee.

"How's the investigation coming?" he asked, not mincing words.

Castillo took a sip from his steaming cup. "From what the body showed, it looks like it may be the work of a guy named Diego Santos. Those cigarette burns on the forehead are his trademark. He likes to look his victims in the eye while he's burning them."

"You got him in custody?"

"Not enough evidence to arrest him. It's all just hearsay, rumor and word on the street. We'd bring him in for questioning, but we haven't been able to find him."

Not good. "What about motive?"

"We think Sullivan may have dug a little too deep. Pissed some people off."

"Last night Claire's apartment was vandalized. Any chance Santos was torturing Sullivan to get some kind of information, something Sullivan had that Santos wanted?"

Castillo sat up a little straighter. "Sullivan's apartment was trashed, too. If they tore up Claire's place, maybe they didn't find what they were looking for."

Tension rolled through him. "Hard to believe Sullivan didn't give it up, considering what they did to him."

"Unless he gave it to Claire and was trying to protect her."

Ben didn't like where this was going. "If Claire's got it, she doesn't know it. She's told you everything she remembers."

The waitress refilled Castillo's cup and walked away. "Her laptop was the only thing taken. They could be looking for emails between her and Sullivan, something that would help them locate whatever it is they want."

"Sullivan was in her apartment a couple of times. If he was being followed, they'd know where she lived."

Castillo mulled that over. "If they come after her, can you keep her safe?"

Ben thought of the torture Michael Sullivan had suffered, and his stomach burned. "You can count on it."

Ben picked up Claire after work, but he didn't take her home. Claire was only a little surprised when he headed for the shooting range.

"Castillo says Sullivan's apartment was trashed just like yours. That means someone is after something. They wouldn't have hit your place if they'd found it.

That means they might come after you. I want you to know how to defend yourself."

"I don't know, Ben. I've never shot a gun."

"You'll do fine."

"Are you sure this is necessary? They don't even know where I am."

"No, but they might find out. My house has the best alarm system money can buy. You'll know if someone's coming in, but if they're serious about getting to you, they'll still get inside, and you'll still have to stop them."

Claire was nervous, but Ben was determined, and she had to admit, she had always been curious.

"Just relax," he said. "This is my ankle gun— six-shot, .38 revolver. It's very easy to use."

First he showed her how to load and unload the weapon, how to cock it, instructed her in all the safety aspects she needed to know. "It's only loaded with five bullets, so the chamber beneath the hammer is empty. That way it won't go off if you drop it. When you cock the weapon, the cylinder turns and the gun is ready to fire."

She worked with it for a while, then they were ready to shoot. Her hand shook as Ben showed her how to hold the weapon, then moved behind her to steady her aim. With that big hard body and all those amazing muscles pressed against her, she could barely concentrate. She shifted against him and heard his soft curse.

"You make me crazy, you know that?"

"What?" She looked at him over her shoulder, saw his mouth curve up and his eyes dancing. She gasped as he leaned forward, let her feel his erection.

Claire laughed.

"You think that's funny, huh? I'm trying to teach you to shoot."

"It isn't my fault. Well, not exactly."

"It's exactly your fault," he teased. "Now let's try it again."

She was still smiling as she aimed at the paper target, relaxed for the first time. She missed the first two shots, hit the third, fourth and fifth.

"Not bad. Let's try it again."

She fired and reloaded until Ben was satisfied she could aim and hit what she was shooting at.

Finally he took the gun from her hand and they headed back to the house. She should have felt safer, but she didn't.

Thirty-One

~~~

Though no one knew where she was, Ben was still guarding her like a rottweiler, driving her to work, insisting she have lunch in her office, picking her up after the office closed.

At night, either she or Ben helped Sam with his homework before they ate supper. Afterward, they played board games or watched TV. Once Sam was asleep, Ben would come into her bedroom and they would make love. In the morning he drove her to work and the routine started all over again.

Ben barely let her out of his sight, and the terrifying part was she liked it. She liked being part of a family. She loved having Sam in her life. She loved being with a strong, protective, sexually attractive mate who satisfied her in bed. She loved Ben.

But she didn't like sneaking around the way they were. It was time to do something about it.

On Friday night, Sam was having a sleepover with his new best friend, Marty James. Marty had been at Sam's birthday party, and they had grown closer since then. Ben was sitting at the kitchen table after supper cleaning his pistol. Watching him, Claire took a moment to summon her courage, then walked up behind him.

"What kind of gun is that?"

"Nighthawk .45." He pushed the button and the clip dropped out of the bottom into his hand. He checked to be sure it wasn't loaded, then handed it to Claire. "You did good with the revolver. I'll teach you to shoot this one, too."

She looked it over, handed it back, searched his dear, handsome face. If she was ever going to do this, it had to be now. "A woman wouldn't need to know how to shoot a gun if she were married to a man like you."

His eyes shot to hers, assessing the look on her face. "It wouldn't hurt. Like I said, you were good with the revolver. No reason you couldn't handle a gun like this."

She glanced away. "Maybe so."

Ben grabbed her hand and dragged her down on his lap. "You're talking about marriage. You've been thinking about it. Are you saying you'll marry me?"

She kept her features even, determined to make it appear as if this were as unimportant as he had made it seem, but her insides were quaking. Saying yes to a man who didn't love her was the most terrifying thing she had ever done. She took the same tone he had taken when he'd made his "practical" proposal.

Claire shrugged her shoulders. "We're sleeping together anyway. It's hard with Sam in the house."

He shifted a little beneath her, letting her feel his arousal. "It's hard with *you* in the house, angel."

She couldn't quite muster a smile. Her heart was throbbing dully, aching inside her chest. "I wouldn't have to spend the money the insurance company is giving me to replace the furniture in my apartment. We could use some of it here, make things more comfortable for the three of us."

"You could put it in the bank. I'd pay for anything you wanted to do to the house. I know it's not very female friendly."

Her heart was pounding. She could feel tears threatening behind her eyes. Dear God, she couldn't cry. She didn't want him to know how difficult this was for her.

"I wouldn't change much," she said casually. "Maybe just some ruffled curtains in the kitchen, a few things like that."

"Maybe we'd sell this place and buy something bigger, give us a little more room."

"Could we afford it?"

"We could."

Her throat tightened. A bigger house wasn't what she wanted. She wanted Ben to love her. "That…that might be a good idea."

"What about next week?"

What did it matter? It was only the rest of her life.

"Sure." She forced an upbeat note into her voice, but her heart was hurting, squeezing inside her chest. "We could go down to the courthouse on my lunch hour."

She was going to cry if this didn't stop. She'd always imagined a white wedding gown and an orchid bouquet, a flower girl and a ring bearer. Walking down the aisle on her father's arm to join the man she loved at the altar. A man who loved her in return.

She thought of her parents and how disappointed they would be to miss her wedding. They didn't even know Ben existed. She thought of the romantic honeymoon she had imagined, walking on the beach in the moonlight, drinking champagne and making love, and her heart squeezed even harder.

"We'd need someone to stand up with us," Ben said.

"Maybe Sage and Jake." Her voice sounded strained. She prayed Ben wouldn't notice. "Or if they can't, we could ask Trace and Maggie."

"I'll talk to them on Monday." His eyes were on her face, pale eyes, cold some people said, but she knew they were hot as flame. Something shifted in his features, something was there that hadn't been there before.

Maybe he was getting cold feet. Maybe he would save them both by saying no. "You still want to do it, right? Because if you've changed your mind—"

"Jesus! No, I haven't changed my mind. I want us to get married. Are you saying yes?"

The lump in her throat was so big she wasn't sure she could talk around it. She should be happy, but her chest was aching, her heart throbbing.

She loved him so much.

All Ben wanted was someone he enjoyed in bed and a mother for his son. "Yes."

He stood up with her still in his arms. "You won't be sorry, angel. I promise."

But Claire was already sorry. She wanted a man who loved her with all his heart.

It didn't matter.

She was going to marry Ben.

Monday morning, Claire sat behind her desk at the University District Neighborhood Center. Her job was to coordinate public relations for the different centers in the Houston area, supervise and train volunteers.

One of those volunteers, Carol Blankenship, the receptionist, walked into her office just as Claire's cell phone started ringing. She picked it up off her desk, recognized Ben's home number and pressed it against her ear.

She recognized the voice but it wasn't Ben—it was Mrs. McKenzie, the babysitter. "Emma?" She held up her hand when Carol started to say something about the ribbon-wrapped package she held in her hand. "What is it? Has something happened to Sam?"

Carol set the package down on the corner of Claire's desk and walked back out of the room.

"I'm sorry to call you at work," Emma said, "but I am just sick as a dog. I don't know if I ate something or what, but I had to go home. I tried Ben at his office, but the call went straight to his voice mail. Same with his cell phone. I figure he must be out on a job. I don't know what to do about Sam, Claire, but I won't be there when he gets off the school bus."

Claire looked at her watch. It was almost time for the bus to arrive. "Don't worry about it. I've put in a lot of overtime since I started." *Trying to keep my mind off Ben.* "I can leave a few hours early. I'll be there when Sam gets home."

"Are you sure?"

"Of course. Take care of yourself and I hope you're feeling better soon." Claire ended the call and walked out into the reception area. "Is John here?" One of her colleagues at the center. "I've got to go home early. I'm hoping he can give me a ride."

Ben wouldn't like it, but at least John was a man, and once she got to the house, she could set the alarm, and she had Ben's revolver if she needed it. Maybe it was good he had taught her to use it.

John appeared a few minutes later, car keys in hand. Claire grabbed the package off her desk, wondering if it was something Ben had sent, hoping it was, and headed out the door.

It didn't take long to reach the house. John dropped her off in front and she waved as she walked up on the porch. Once she got inside, she reset the alarm, gave Pepper a couple of pats, then went into Ben's bedroom to unlock the gun safe in the drawer next to his bed.

Ben had had lengthy discussions with Sam about weapons. He had told the boy how dangerous guns could be and promised to teach him how to handle a pistol as soon as he was old enough.

Of course Sam knew about the shooting in El Paso, and Ben had even shown him the bullet hole in his side to make the point.

Still, they kept the weapons locked up unless there was a reason to have one of them out. Just to soothe a little of Ben's ire, she made sure the pistol was in easy reach.

Claire checked the time. Sam was due home any minute. Glancing out the window, she saw the big orange school bus pull up at the corner. Hurrying across the living room, she turned off the alarm and opened the door.

Sam waved and ran toward her. Pepper barked and wagged his tail as Claire walked out on the porch to greet him. She didn't noticed the white van parked on the street until the door slid open and a lean, dark-haired man jumped out.

Her heart jerked as she recognized Troy Bragg, and fear tore through her. "Sam!" Claire had taken only two steps before a man came up behind her, wrapped an arm around her waist and dragged her back against his hard body. He pressed a pistol against the side of her head.

"You want the boy unharmed, keep quiet and keep walking."

She didn't know the voice, but she figured Duke Hutchins. She was shaking all over as she watched Troy manhandle Sam, binding his wrists, slapping a piece of tape over his mouth. Troy hoisted him up and tossed him into the van.

"Keep walking."

From the corner of her eyes, she recognized Hutchins's face. She considered screaming, but Duke had shot Ben without the slightest qualm, and Sam needed her. One thing she believed with all her heart—Ben would find them. He wouldn't give up until he did.

All she had to do was keep Sam safe until Ben could get there.

Claire climbed into the van. Troy jerked her wrists behind her and used a plastic zip tie to bind them. Tearing off a strip of duct tape, he pressed it over her mouth and shoved her down on the floor behind the seats.

Sam lay next to her, his face pale as glass, his small body shaking and cold as ice. She wanted to reassure him, pull him into her arms, but with her hands tied behind her, all she could do was press herself against him. She turned her head to look at him over her shoulder, stared into his frightened eyes, and tried to silently tell him that everything would be all right. She prayed he would know his father would come for him, just as he had before.

The only problem was she had no idea where Troy and Duke were taking them.

Or what would happen to them when they got there.

Ben hit the button on his voice mail to play back his messages. He hated the damn machine. He liked it better when Annie handled the calls, wrote out the name and number on a slip of paper. Annie knew which calls were important, which weren't and those that were urgent enough to track him down. A goddamn machine couldn't do that.

He listened to a couple of calls and wrote down the phone numbers, one a former client that could be important. All the while he was thinking of Claire, anxious to see her, tell her he had talked to Jake and that he and Sage would be happy to stand up with them at the courthouse one day this week. He couldn't believe how excited he was to be marrying her.

It was crazy, considering how hard he had worked to avoid any sort of commitment, but as far as he was concerned, marrying Claire couldn't happen soon enough.

The third message was from Emma. She was sick, she said, and had to go home. Since she couldn't reach him, she was calling Claire at the office to see if she could meet Sam's bus.

Uneasiness slid through him. He didn't want Claire in the house alone. As soon as the call ended, Ben phoned her cell. Her BlackBerry rang and rang, but she didn't pick up. He phoned the house. No answer there.

He checked his watch. Sam should have been home by now. His adrenaline was kicking up, making his heart beat faster. He phoned Claire's office.

"I'm looking for Claire Chastain. This is Ben Slocum. Is she there?"

"Claire left early," the receptionist said. "Something about being home when Sam got off the bus."

His stomach tightened. "How'd she get there?"

"John Conrad gave her a ride. John works here."

"Let me talk to him."

"I'll put you through."

But Conrad wasn't any help. He had dropped Claire off at the house. He had watched her go inside. Ben was up and heading for the door before the call had ended. He drove like a madman the few blocks home.

When he pulled up in front of the house and saw the door standing open, saw Pepper lying on the porch looking forlorn, he couldn't breathe. He turned off the engine and ran inside, saw no sign of Claire or Sam and dialed 911.

That was when he saw the ribbon-wrapped box. It was sitting on the kitchen counter. Claire's name was on the top, but she hadn't opened it yet. Ben took out his pocket knife and sliced through the ribbon, lifted off the lid.

Inside the box was a note that read, "We want the flash drive."

Beneath it was Michael Sullivan's ear.

Thirty-Two

$\sim\!\!\sim\!\!\odot\!\!\sim\!\!\odot\!\!\sim\!\!\sim$

Ben waited for Danny Castillo on the front porch of the house. He had talked to the detective on the phone, given him the scant details of Claire and Sam's disappearance. The uniforms were there, a couple of detectives milling around. The forensic guys had gone through the house and taken the box with the ear to the lab.

Ben had called Jake and told him what had happened, or at least what he thought must have happened. Jake and the rest of the Atlas gang knew about Michael Sullivan's murder and that the police believed Diego Santos was involved. Ben told Jake about the box left for Claire, the note inside and Michael Sullivan's butchered ear.

He tried to stay focused, tried to think clearly, the way he would if this were just another case. But he kept seeing Sullivan's bludgeoned face, the cigarette burns across his forehead. He kept thinking of Claire and what they might be doing to her. He kept thinking of Sam and what might be happening to his son.

He heard a car pull up and then another. He looked

out to see Jake's black Jeep and Alex's fancy BMW. Trace's Cherokee pulled up behind them. All three men got out of their vehicles and started walking toward where he stood on the porch, one taller and brawnier than the others, one blond, one in a white straw cowboy hat. Seeing their fierce expressions, their determination to find his family, made his throat feel tight.

He took a deep breath, fought to steady himself.

"Where's Castillo?" Jake asked as he climbed the stairs to the porch.

"On his way. The cops were here, detectives are just about finished. Crime scene guys took the ear. I don't know how the box got inside the house. Nothing looks out of place. Claire's purse is on the table with her cell phone inside. She'd opened the gun safe next to the bed, but she hadn't touched it. The forensic guys didn't find any evidence of a struggle. I don't think Santos and his men ever came into the house."

"What's your theory?" Trace asked, forcing Ben to concentrate as he hadn't been able to do since he had seen the front door standing open.

"They had to be watching the place, but I never saw any sign of them." He shook his head. "I should have been paying closer attention. I should have figured they'd find her. I should have been more careful."

"Okay, so Santos and his men were watching the house," Jake said. "What about Sam? How does he fit into this?"

He tried to think. Couldn't get his mind to function. *Sam.* He had just found his son and now he had lost him. His stomach knotted. *Claire.* Jesus God, what were they doing to Claire?

"They'll torture her," he said, his mouth so dry he

could barely force out the words. "They think Claire has the information they're looking for, but she doesn't."

"Ben, you've got to focus," Jake said. "I know how much you love her, but you've got to clear your head."

Ben stared at his best friend as if he had never seen him before. For several seconds he just stood there. *I know how much you love her.*

Claire was gone, maybe hurt, maybe dead. Jake knew the truth. The rest of his friends probably did, too. He couldn't lie to himself any longer. "You're right, I love her. I'm crazy in love with her. I didn't tell her. I couldn't say it. Jesus, why didn't I tell her?"

Jake grabbed his shoulders and shoved him hard against the outside of the house. "All right, goddammit, you love her. You've said it. You've accepted it. Now get your fucking head on straight, and let's go find her and your boy."

Ben took a shuddering breath, looked up at Jake, and everything seemed to fall into place. He had to find Claire and Sam. He had the men he needed to help him do it.

"Sam was on the school bus. They must have known what time he came home every day. When he got off at the corner they were waiting. They must have figured Claire would come out of the house to get him."

"How did they know Claire would be home?"

How had they? "Good question. Emma got sick. She called Claire at the office. Santos knew the address of her apartment. Sullivan had her business card in his wallet so Santos knew where she worked. Maybe someone at the office tipped him that she was staying with me. When she left early, they called, told Santos she would be here by herself, waiting for Sam."

"We need to find out," Trace said.

"If they wanted Claire," Alex asked, "why did they take Sam?"

"Leverage," Ben said, his brain finally beginning to function. "They figured if they threatened the boy, Claire would tell them where to find the flash drive." He ignored the sick feeling in his stomach. He was thinking again and he wasn't going to let his worry get in the way.

A brown Chevy unmarked police car rolled up and Danny Castillo got out, tall, black hair combed straight back. They all knew him, all had had dealings with the detective at one time or another.

Ben watched Castillo striding toward the porch, a grim look on his face.

"We talked to the people at Claire's office," he said. "Some kid dropped off a box tied up with a ribbon no more than fifteen minutes before Claire left to go home. The receptionist said Claire took the box with her when she left."

"That's how it got inside the house," Alex said. "Claire carried it in. She didn't have time to open it."

"We've had uniforms canvassing the neighborhood," Castillo said. "One of the neighbors saw an older white van parked on the south side of the street just down the block from the bus stop. It was there about half an hour before the bus was due to arrive. She couldn't see who was driving, and she didn't notice if the van was there when the bus actually drove up."

"We need to interview the employees in her office," Jake said, "find out if one of them tipped Santos that Claire would be home alone."

"We've already pushed them pretty hard," Castillo said. "On the surface it looks as if they didn't know anything about Claire's troubles or have anything to do with Santos."

"Maybe not," Trace drawled, "but if Santos wanted the information bad enough, he could afford to pay whatever it cost to get it."

"What do you think is on that drive?" Alex asked.

Castillo shook his head. "Whatever it is, it's important."

"What about Santos?" Ben pressed. "You have any idea where we can find him?"

"We've been looking since Sullivan was murdered. So far no sign of him. Odds are he's gone underground."

Ben's jaw hardened. He couldn't stand to wait any longer. "I need to get going. I've got people I need to see, guys who might know where Santos is holding Claire." Informants, guys he paid for information. He needed to round them up, put them to work. He needed information and he needed it fast.

"I've got calls to make myself," Jake said.

"We all do," said Trace, "We've all got people who might know something."

"Let's meet back at the office at twenty-one hundred," Ben said, "unless someone comes up with something before then." Eight p.m. It sounded like an eternity.

The men dispersed back to their cars. Ben climbed into his Denali and fired up the engine. He was on track now. Single-minded. Completely focused.

He was going to find Claire and Sam. And he was going to kill Diego Santos.

Claire had been riding in the cramped position for hours. Her shoulder ached, her back throbbed. Her wrists were scraped raw from the plastic bindings, and her hands felt bloodless and numb. It was at least a six-hour drive from Houston to Egansville, farther on to Bushytail Bayou.

Even worse, Claire had a bad feeling the men weren't taking her back to the compound. Ben believed they had fled to a secondary location, a place they went to in case of an emergency. It would be deeper in the swamp or in another place altogether.

A shiver rolled through her. She hadn't eaten anything since the yogurt she'd had for lunch and she was beginning to feel light-headed. She had tried to gauge which direction the van was traveling, thought they were heading northeast, but she couldn't be sure. She really needed to use the bathroom, but with the tape over her mouth, there was no way to communicate her wishes.

Finally the van pulled into a service station in the middle of nowhere and Troy slid open the door. Reaching inside, he ripped the tape off her mouth. He did the same to Sam.

"I figured you'd need to use the can. Duke will walk you over, bring you back and then take Sam. If you try to scream or make any trouble, I'll take the boy and leave. You'll never see the kid again."

She weighed her options. She could scream or try to escape, but Hutchins was armed and she didn't think he would hesitate to shoot her. He certainly hadn't thought twice about shooting Ben.

She looked up at him. He was taller than Troy, about the same height as Ben and solidly muscled, thin-faced and hard-edged, with shaggy black hair and a beard that needed trimming. He was maybe mid-thirties, the same as Troy.

Hutchins looked around the gas station. No cars in

sight. The attendant was inside the run-down building. The bathrooms were in the back.

He cut the plastic bindings on her wrists and jerked her forward. "Let's go." Claire stumbled and would have fallen if he hadn't been holding on to her. Hutchins hauled her upright and dragged her toward the women's bathroom behind the white stucco building, opened the door and shoved her inside.

"Make it fast."

She hurried, looking around while she was inside for some way to leave a note. But her purse was still in Houston, and the bathroom was empty except for a roll of toilet paper and the dirty paper towels on the floor.

With a calming breath, she walked back outside, rubbing her wrists to try to get the circulation going. Once they reached the van, Troy rebound her wrists but left the ties a little looser this time, helped her up into the van while Hutchins took off with Sam.

"I'll leave the tape off," Troy said, "but you say a word or make any trouble, I'll truss you up like a Christmas goose. You got it?"

She nodded. It wasn't long before Sam was back in the van lying beside her. They could talk, but she didn't dare say much. Keeping her voice below the level of the engine noise, she looked into Sam's frightened face.

"Your dad will come," she whispered. "All we have to do is wait."

Sam blinked as if he were fighting tears and glanced away. She had a hunch he was thinking the same thing she was. *How is Ben going to find us?*

"He'll come," she promised. "No matter what."

This time Sam nodded, and she thought he looked a little less afraid.

* * *

The eight o'clock meeting led nowhere.

"No word on the street," Ben said as they sat down at the conference room table, each carrying a mug of coffee. "No one's heard a fucking thing."

"Same here," Jake said. "Guy's definitely lying low. I've called in some markers. Sooner or later, something's bound to turn up."

"I tracked down the kid who left the box," Trace said. "He was a teenager who happened to be ridin' his bike in the area. Said a guy paid him twenty bucks to deliver the box to the Neighborhood Center. From the kid's description, the guy was Hispanic."

"Santos?" Ben asked.

"Probably one of his lackeys."

Alex raked a hand through his dark gold hair. Frustration turned his *GQ* good looks hard. "I took another shot at the employees Claire works with at the center. Either they're all professional liars or they've never heard of Diego Santos or anyone who works for him."

Ben's fingers tightened around his coffee mug. "Then how the hell did they know she'd be home?"

Alex set his coffee mug down on the long mahogany table. "Might be they were watching her office. When she left, they followed her back to your place."

"Makes the most sense," Ben said. "But I was at her office morning and night, even drove by a couple of times during the day, and I never spotted anyone."

"I know none of us are big believers in coincidence," Trace drawled, "but maybe this once, they got lucky. Maybe they found out Claire was stayin' with Ben. Maybe they got his address and just happened to be driving by, checking things out, when Claire showed up."

Ben rolled it around in his head. Didn't like it.

Couldn't make himself believe it. "Too many maybes for me. I'm going back out, prowl the streets a little more, see if I can dig up something we can use."

"Keep us posted." Trace rose as Ben pushed up from his chair.

"Call me if you find Santos and need some backup," Jake said.

"Same goes." Alex clenched his jaw.

"We'll be there if you need us," Trace finished.

Ben just nodded. Walking out of the conference room, he headed for the door.

It was getting late. He spent most of the night driving the streets on the dark side of Houston. In his black SUV, with his black hair and swarthy complexion, he could move around without drawing much attention. He set up meets with more of his informants. They showed, but said no one was talking. Santos was powerful, and a real badass. No one wanted to end up like Michael Sullivan.

Unable to face the empty house, Ben returned to the office. He slept a couple of hours on the couch in the employee lounge, but was wide-awake before dawn, restless to get started even as tired as he was. He made a pot of coffee, poured some into a go-cup and drove back to his house.

Maybe they had missed something. Maybe Claire had left some sort of clue. Maybe Sam had.

He fed Hercules and put out food for Pepper, but the dog refused to eat. Clearly the dog was as distraught over the missing boy as Ben was.

For nearly an hour, he searched the empty house, looking for something that would give him a lead. Trying not to blame himself, knowing if he went down that road he would be as useless to Claire and Sam as he had been yesterday before Jake had squared his ass away.

But the house was as void of clues as it had been before. Going back outside, Ben walked the area around the perimeter, then headed for the school bus stop at the corner.

One of his neighbors had noticed the white van parked near the stop. It occurred to him that maybe Santos's men hadn't come to the house because they had followed Claire or somehow knew she would be there. Maybe they had found out about Sam, knew how much he meant to her, planned to take him and trade her for the disk.

It wasn't a bad theory. He walked to the corner, prowling the sidewalk, people's front lawns, checking the street. About where the van had been parked, the sun reflected off something in the gutter. Ben reached down and picked up a piece of paper, the clear cellophane crackling in his hand.

He recognized the sound, and his heart started pounding. He spread open the candy wrapper, read the familiar white lettering. *Homemade Mud Bugs. Catahoula Candy Makers, Egansville, Louisiana.*

Relief and fury hit him at the same time. It wasn't Santos. She wasn't being tortured. Troy Bragg had come for Sam, and Claire had tried to stop him. Bragg had taken her with him to whatever godforsaken rat hole he and his clan were calling home.

Santos didn't have her, but she was still in terrible danger. Both of them were, but especially Claire. His stomach knotted at the thought of the Bayou Patriots, thirty-odd men and very few women. Thirty horny, caged-up motherfuckers and a beautiful woman like Claire, helpless against them.

As Ben headed for the car, he pulled out his cell phone and started making calls. Jake, Trace, Alex and Sol were waiting in the office when he stepped inside, ringing the bell above the door.

"All right, we know who's got them," Ben said as he approached. "We just need to find them. Time to go to work."

"Copy that," Trace said as all of them headed for the conference room. Ben didn't miss the hard, determined looks on his best friends' faces.

Thirty-Three

~∽⊶⊷∾~

Ben settled back in the copilot's seat as Alex's twin Beechcraft Baron dropped lower, winging its way over a dense green landscape ribboned with water and very few roads. Jake and Trace sat behind him. The nose and fuselage of the plane was full of their gear.

The ground came up. The wheels lightly touched down on the tarmac as Alex made a perfect landing at a small airport near Deerfield, just over the Catahoula County line where Ben hoped word of their arrival wouldn't reach the Patriots before he and his friends could get to them.

Back in Houston, Sol waited at his computer. The kid had access to satellite imagery that could pinpoint areas Google Maps couldn't begin to reach. If the position of the satellite was right, he was hoping to get some video footage this time.

First, though, they needed a starting place, some indication where to look for the Bayou Patriots' bug-out compound. They had to know if it was somewhere in the area or someplace altogether different.

They'd discussed going to the sheriff, talked over the pros and cons. But the only people who had known Ben and Ty Brodie had pulled Sam out of the compound, knew Ben's name and where he lived, were people who worked in the sheriff's department.

Information had been provided to the Braggs. Whether on purpose or accidentally, the result was the same. Claire and Sam were missing, and Ben had no doubt Troy Bragg and his clan had taken them. He couldn't chance letting Bragg escape again.

A pair of rental cars were waiting, a dark brown Chevy Tahoe, different color but otherwise the same as the one he had rented in El Paso and driven to Houston, and a white Jeep Grand Cherokee. They needed room for men, weapons, ammunition and miscellaneous gear, and he wanted a backup vehicle in case of trouble when they headed into the compound.

They piled into the two SUVs and drove to a motel on the edge of Deerfield that Ben had reserved on Hotels.com. They had to move fast. If word got out that four strangers had arrived in the area, it might reach the Patriots. If the group figured the men were there in search of the woman and boy, they would bolt like scalded dogs to a new location, forcing Sam and Claire to go with them.

These men knew the swamp, most had lived around here all their lives. The only way to get to them was to take them by surprise.

Sol had discovered the double-wide trailers Silas and Jesse Bragg and their families lived in a ways past the turnoff to the Bushytail Bayou compound. He had also discovered where the two brothers worked.

Silas managed a sporting-goods store in Egansville, but Jesse drove heavy equipment for E. and J. Construction, currently working on a project in Deerfield. The plan was to wait for Jesse to finish his shift and head for home.

Ben was going to make sure he didn't get there.

"Claire!" Sam bolted toward her as Mace led her away, but Troy slung an arm around his neck and dragged him back.

"She'll be fine. No one's gonna hurt her. Pete's just gonna talk to her awhile, get to know her a little. He's lookin' for a wife. Woman could do a lot worse than my brother Pete."

"She can't marry him. She's gonna marry my dad!" Sam had overheard Claire and Ben talking. He would have a mom and dad, something he wanted more than anything in the world.

Troy spun him around. "You better get this straight, boy. You live here now. Aggie's your kin. Claire'll be living here, too, but she'll be marrying Pete."

Sam's jaw tightened. "My dad's coming, just like before. He's a SEAL. You'll be sorry you took us away."

Troy chuckled. "He's not gonna find you. He got lucky last time, but we're deeper in the bayou now. Me and Duke ain't leaving for a couple of weeks. Your daddy comes, we'll feed him to the gators, and the sheriff won't find a trace."

A shiver ran down Sam's spine. "I hate you." A blow to the side of his head sent him reeling.

"Your mama taught you better than to disrespect your elders. I won't put up with it and neither will anyone else."

Sam thought of his mom and tried to remember what it was like when Troy lived with them. His mom liked the way Troy looked, Sam guessed, a little like Ben when Troy shaved and kept his hair trimmed instead of letting it grow, but he had always had a bad temper. Mom hadn't let him stick around very long.

Sam glanced across the compound to where Claire sat in the shade with Pete Bragg. Pete looked a lot like Troy, same blue eyes and dark hair. All of them did, but Claire wouldn't be interested in a loser like Pete and she sure wouldn't want to live out in a dung hole like this.

His chest clamped down and his eyes burned. This was all his fault. If he hadn't gone with Troy in the first place, Claire wouldn't be here, and neither would he. What if they made her marry Pete like Troy said? What if Ben couldn't find them? What if he came and they shot him and threw him into the swamp?

"Get on out there," Troy said, nudging him down off the porch. "Aggie's workin' in the garden, and she could use your help."

Sam cast Claire a last, regretful glance, then started for the garden. *This is my fault,* he thought again as he trudged through the dirt and fought to hold back tears.

Jesse Bragg sat in a chair in room 126 of the Deerfield Motel, his arms and feet bound with plastic ties, a rope tying him to the chair. He was six feet tall, dark-haired and blue-eyed like the rest of the Braggs, with a thin scar on his chin. Now a bruise darkened his cheek and his lip was split.

When Ben had taken him down on his way to his pickup truck after work, it was over before Bragg had time to put up much of a fight or sound an alarm. The scuffle had begun after they got inside the motel room. Bragg had started it, but Ben had enjoyed the punches he'd thrown in return a little too much.

Fortunately for Jesse, Trace had been there to stop him from doing a whole lot worse.

"I don't have time for this," Ben said, crowding Jesse enough to make him uncomfortable. "I want to know where they've got my woman and my boy. You can make this easy or hard. Either way, you're gonna tell me what I want to know."

"Give the guy a break," Alex said, stepping in to play good guy. "Jesse has a family of his own. He knows how worried you must be." He turned to the man in the chair. "We need to find them, Jesse. Claire and Sam are Ben's family. What would you do if someone took your family and disappeared?"

Jesse swallowed. "I tried…tried to talk them out of it. Silas was against it, too. Even Mace thought it was a bad idea."

"Tell us where they are," Alex said, "so we can bring them home."

"I can't do that. They're my brothers, my friends. We took an oath."

"Did your oath include kidnapping an innocent boy and a woman?" Ben asked.

"I told you it wasn't me. It was Troy and Duke. They stirred everyone up."

"Why'd they take the woman?" Jake asked. "What do you plan to do with her?"

"Nothin' that'll hurt her. They're plannin' to marry her off to one of my brothers. Nate's a preacher, and it ain't like she's never had a man between her legs."

Ben's fist shot out and slammed into Jesse's face, knocking over the chair and sending him crashing to the floor.

Jake grabbed Ben and dragged him away before he could lift up the chair and hit him again.

"Take it easy," Jake warned, but his hard look said he wouldn't mind punching the guy himself.

Unclenching his fist, Ben pulled himself under control. They needed information. That was the reason Jesse was there.

"I've had enough of this," Ben said as Jake set the chair upright with Jesse still in it. "Let's go get his wife and kids, bring them back here. We'll have a little fun with the woman—just like your brother is planning to do with mine. We'll let Bragg watch while we're at it. Maybe let the kids watch, too."

He'd bring them back if he had to, but only as a threat. Hurting women and children wasn't part of his plan.

Alex shoved himself between them, playing good guy again. "We all know how you feel, Ben, even Jesse." He turned. "You've got to tell us, man. Ben's tied up in knots over this. He's going to find your bug-out spot whether you help us or not. In the meantime, your wife and kids are going to be the ones to pay."

Jake moved in for the kill, giving Jesse the out he needed. "If your friends give you any trouble, you tell them we threatened your family, your wife and kids. Tell them you had no choice."

Jesse surveyed the four hard men standing around him. He moistened his lips. "You go in there...you aren't gonna kill them?"

"We're going in and bring out my lady and my son," Ben said. "We won't hurt anyone unless we have to."

"Ben's a SEAL," Jake added. "He's done dozens of extractions. No one has to get hurt."

Not unless they tried to stop him. If they did, he'd do whatever it took to get Claire and Sam out of danger. But he didn't say that.

"This is your last chance, Jesse," Alex said. "You need to tell us. You need to do what's right."

Jesse hung his head. Seconds ticked past. No one said a word. Finally, he looked up. "There's a way in off the road."

"Which road?" Ben pressed.

"Same road outta Egansville that led to our first camp. The turnoff's ten miles south of the one you take to Bushytail Bayou. You can get there through the swamp, but you'd have to know the way and you couldn't make it in at night."

"Go on," Ben said.

"Road's hard to find. The turnoff's completely overgrown. You have to know where it is to find it."

"How many men are in there?" Ben asked.

"Ten, maybe twelve. Too hard getting in and out, and it's harder livin' that far from town. You can make it with a four-wheel drive, but it's real rough goin'."

Trace leaned down and cut the man's bindings. "You're gonna make it easy, Jesse. You're gonna show us the way."

Jake jerked him out of his chair. "You're going to do what's right. And you're going to keep your family safe."

"Make her take off them clothes, Mace. Man don't buy a pig in a poke. Gotta sample the goods a little first."

"Get away from me!" Claire slapped Pete Bragg's hand away as he reached out to touch her cheek. Since the men didn't approve of a woman wearing jeans, she was dressed in a worn cotton print dress that Aggie had loaned her and she had taken in by hand to fit.

Mace reached out and roughly caught her chin, forcing her to look at him. "What's the matter? You don't like Pete? You think you're too good for him?"

"I— I'm already engaged to be married to another man."

"Yeah, well, your man ain't here, and he ain't gonna be." He turned to his brother. "You need to give her a day or two. She ain't used to the way we do things here. Aggie'll talk to her, get her straightened out. Woman needs a man to take care a her. A couple of days, she'll come around."

"What if she don't?" Pete asked. He looked like all the other Braggs, not unattractive if it weren't for his shaggy hair and ugly brown beard.

"You can wait till hell freezes over," Claire said. "I still won't marry you."

Mace drilled her with a glare that sent a shiver down her spine. "Fine, you don't want to be a wife, you can be Pete's whore. Service a few of the others, too. Choice is yours."

All the blood drained from her face. She would have to marry one of them, or all of them would take her. For a moment, she thought she might faint.

Aggie's arm settled around her shoulders, steadying her. Claire took a deep breath as the woman led her off toward the cabin she was staying in with Aggie and Sam.

"Don't you pay no mind to Mace. We got good Christian values here. I'll see to it you get yourself a husband of your choosin'. Don't you worry about that."

Her stomach rolled. Oh, God, what if Ben didn't find them in time? Claire moistened her trembling lips. So far Aggie had been an ally. She couldn't afford to lose her. "Thank you."

Aggie patted Claire's back as they walked up on the porch of the one-room shack, and Sam ran up to her.

"You didn't say you'd marry him, did you, Claire? You're still gonna marry Ben?"

Sam had asked her about it that morning, told her he had overheard them talking. He had asked if it was true and looked up at her with so much hope in those pale eyes so like his father's it made her heart hurt. It made her glad she had said yes to Ben. It wouldn't be the kind of marriage she had always dreamed of, the kind based on love, but there would be caring and it would be enough.

Aggie shooed Sam away before she had time to answer. "You go on now, this is grown-up business. You go check on the chickens, make sure they're in for the night and the henhouse door is closed. We don't want some fox getting into the coop."

They went to bed early in the swamp, a little after the sun went down, which this time of year was right after supper. Lamps provided the only light and oil was costly.

"Go on," Claire said softly. "Everything's going to be okay." But her hope was rapidly fading. She had learned this was not the same place the men had taken Sam before. It was deeper in the bayou and nearly impossible to find.

On top of that, Mace Bragg had sentries guarding the compound, two men on each shift now instead of just one. They were heavily armed and ready for trouble.

Claire thought of Ben and her heart squeezed. Dear God, even if he found them, she wasn't sure he would be able to get them out without getting killed.

She turned and forced her feet to move through the door. The cabin was the largest of those built around the clearing, with a kitchen equipped with a wood-burning stove and a long table and benches where Aggie fed the men.

The place was so crudely constructed that in the daytime she could see light coming in through the cracks in the rough board walls. At night, she slept on a pallet on the floor while Sam slept on the rope bed next to Aggie.

The cabin was steamy with the smell of pork and vegetable stew. Biscuits were baking in the oven. She helped Aggie serve the men, then washed the tin plates in a big pot of boiling water heated on the stove.

Earlier, Aggie had put her to work washing the men's laundry. It was done the old-fashioned way, immersing the clothes in a huge cauldron of boiling water, scrubbing the garments with homemade lye soap, then running them through the wringer of an old-style washing machine with a hand crank and hanging them up to dry.

It was a hot, brutal job that left her back aching and her hands red and rough, but at least it had kept her busy.

The dishes were done, darkness had settled in and the lamps were being snuffed. As she lay on her pallet, she heard Aggie speaking softly to Sam, settling him in bed beside her for the night.

Claire stared up at the ceiling, a thick lump building in her throat. Since her arrival, she had studied the terrain, hoping to find some way to escape, but the bayou surrounded them on one side, armed men guarded the other.

The lump in her throat grew thicker. What kind of a life would they live in this terrible place?

Closing her eyes against the urge to weep, Claire pretended she was lying next to Ben.

Thirty-Four

Leaving Jesse tied and gagged in the motel room next door, Ben, Jake and Alex spent the day making plans. Using Jesse's information, Sol was able to locate the road into the compound via his satellite link. Trace downloaded photos that revealed the narrow, heavily overgrown dirt track winding deep into the bayou.

Satellite imagery showed eleven men inside the perimeter hog-wire fence, matching Jesse Bragg's info, two females, and a smaller individual who had to be Sam.

The compound was set up much like the first, with rustic cabins around an open area, outbuildings and a garden. There was no sign of movement along the road leading into the compound, no sign of anyone guarding it.

By nightfall they were fairly certain which cabin Claire and Sam were being held in and were ready to go in after them. With time of the essence, they couldn't recon the area beforehand. They would have to make

do with Sol's intel and the information reluctantly provided by Jesse Bragg.

Faces streaked with black greasepaint, dressed head
to foot in night camouflage, tactical vests, and carrying
semi-automatic pistols, stun guns and flash grenades,
they loaded into the SUVs, armed for the confrontation
they hoped to avoid.

Ben drove the lead vehicle, the Tahoe, Alex riding
shotgun toward the hidden road leading into the compound. Jake drove the Jeep, Trace at his side, Jesse
Bragg bound and gagged in the back, an asset in case
he was needed.

By the time they reached the coordinates that marked
the turnoff into the muddy, rutted lane, a half-moon
had risen, making the night a little too bright, but giving them the ability to move more easily through the
dense, boggy terrain.

According to their intel, the compound was three
miles deep in the bayou. It sat in a clearing next to a
branch of the Black Snake River that slogged along beside it, brimming with alligators and poisonous snakes.

The plan was simple. En route to the compound,
Trace would use the sat phone to call the Egansville
sheriff and the Houston P.D. He would bring the authorities up to speed on what had happened so far, telling them they had located Claire and Sam, and giving
them the location of the secondary compound.

Ben figured it would take the deputies an hour to
get organized and reach the camp, plenty of time to get
Claire and Sam to safety—or arrive in time to rescue
them if the plan went south and he and the others were
hurt…or killed.

Once they reached the compound, Jake would position himself in a location allowing him to use the

Pneu-Dart X-Caliber tranquilizer rifle he had used on missions before. A former Force Recon Marine sniper, Jake would fire sleep darts to take out the perimeter guards while Ben, Trace and Alex cut through the fence.

Trace and Alex would provide backup and take out whoever happened to get in the way—hopefully without killing them—while Ben went in and brought Claire and Sam to safety.

That was plan A. Get in and get out without the Patriots knowing what the hell had happened, then waiting in a safe location for the sheriff to arrive. Both Troy and Duke were wanted men. The other men in the compound were guilty of aiding and abetting a kidnapping at the very least.

The Braggs had gotten away with breaking the law before, but Ben couldn't let it happen again. Claire and Sam wouldn't be safe until Troy Bragg and Duke Hutchins were in prison.

Of course, on any mission there was always a plan B. That was the plan they would use if plan A turned into a major clusterfuck. That plan included defensive firepower and trying to keep everyone alive while the Patriots, armed to the teeth, rained hellfire down on top of them.

Ben focused on plan A.

The Tahoe bounced over a rock, then tipped sideways as it came out of a deep, muddy rut in the narrow dirt lane.

"Helluva road," Alex grumbled, bracing himself for another jarring pothole.

"Good way to keep people out," Ben said.

Alex grinned, cutting dimples into his cheeks. "Most people, at any rate."

Ben's smile looked grim. An army of a thousand men couldn't keep him from going in after Claire and Sam.

"We're about a half mile out," Alex said, checking the GPS. "Look over there. Seems like a good spot to park."

Ben pulled the SUV off the road and turned it around, then backed into the foliage beneath the branches of an overhanging tree. He and Alex dragged a few palm fronds and a couple of dead branches over and tossed them onto the bumper, hiding the vehicle completely.

Both of them piled into the backseat of the Jeep. Ben fixed his gaze on the landscape outside the window, keeping a sharp watch for unwanted company as Jake continued another quarter mile to their insertion point. As they bounced along the rutted road, the men checked their earbuds and mics, and armed themselves for the mission ahead.

Alex slung the AR-15 over his chest, the weapon Ty Brodie had used, while Trace checked his Beretta nine mil, and Ben dropped the clip on his Nighthawk .45 then shoved it back in.

They traveled another quarter mile before Jake pulled the Jeep into a low spot beside the road, turned the vehicle around and parked it in the deep, leafy foliage where it wouldn't be seen. The men unloaded, leaving Jesse in the back. With a "go" nod to the others, Ben disappeared into the darkness, the men spreading out behind him, traveling the last quarter mile on foot.

The familiar rattle of flash grenades hanging from his vest, the stun gun in a pocket next to them, Ben moved through the thick, wet foliage, the ground soggy beneath his high-top boots.

"I'm in position," Jake said through Ben's earbuds.

"Roger that," each man replied. Ben, Trace and Alex moved to locations thirty yards apart and dropped down in the undergrowth to wait for the guards to appear as they made their rounds inside the fence. Minutes ticked past, an eternity as Ben waited for Jake to take out the guards so Ben could get inside the compound to retrieve his family.

That's the way he thought of them now. Claire and Sam meant everything to him. He couldn't imagine life without them. Claire belonged to him, and so did Sam, and he would give his life to protect them.

Through the heavy foliage, he saw the two guards approaching as they completed a round inside the fence. For a moment, they stopped to speak, then started moving, passing each other and continuing on their way. As the distance between them increased, Ben heard the faint thud of Jake's rifle, saw the first guard stiffen, slap a hand to the back of his neck and go down.

For the time it took Jake to reload his single-shot air gun, the second guard stood immobile, surveying the heavy foliage through the darkness outside the fence where the faint sound of the shot had come from. Then the soft thud came again and he went down as if he'd been cut off at the knees.

"Move out," Ben said into his mic. Trace and Alex rose like specters out of the deep green grass, all three of them moving carefully toward the fence.

"Hold!" Ben said into the mic, his foot on the edge of a rudimentary booby trap, a hole dug into the earth lined with rows of deadly sharpened sticks. Rudimentary but lethal if you happened to stumble into one.

"Watch for booby traps. These guys mean business." Moving a little more slowly, testing each step, they converged at the designated point along the fence line and set to work. No alarms here, just empty cans tied to the fence. In seconds, Ben had cut the wire and bent it upward, making a hole for them to pass through. They were inside.

While Ben checked to be sure there was no one around, Alex positioned himself in the shadows next to an outbuilding close to the fence, his AK ready to lay down cover fire if needed. Crouching low, Ben and Trace moved toward the cabin the satellite had shown Sam and Claire going in and out of that afternoon.

Moonlight passed in and out behind the clouds, lighting the way across the compound. No sign of a Patriot. Reaching the opposite side, Ben pressed his back against the rough wooden wall of the cabin, his gun in both hands and pointed upward. He motioned to Trace, who moved into the spot he vacated as he slipped inside.

Finding only three occupants, Ben holstered his .45. Claire lay sleeping on the floor near the corner, while Sam slept next to Aggie on a lumpy mattress over an old-fashioned rope bed. The back door was closed.

Ben started to move just as the older woman stirred, and he froze. Inching into the shadows, he went still, making himself invisible inside the room.

Long seconds passed. Little by little, Aggie relaxed back into slumber and began to snore softly. Ben gave an inward sigh of relief. He looked down at Claire and an ache throbbed in his chest. In a shaft of moonlight coming in through the window, she looked beautiful, her dark hair spread over the pillow, a trace of tears dried on her cheeks.

He wanted to tell her how much he loved her, tell her

how much he regretted not saying the words before, but there wasn't time for that now.

Sinking down on a knee beside her, he placed his hand gently over her mouth. Claire's eyes popped open, wild with fear. Then she realized who it was, and those pretty green eyes filled with tears.

Ben held a finger against his lips, warning her to silence, then took her hand and helped her to her feet. She was wearing a worn cotton nightgown and her feet were bare. She looked exhausted and afraid, and love for her welled in his chest. Bending his head, he pressed a quick kiss on her mouth, then motioned her back against the wall and moved toward Sam.

Ben froze next to the bed. Aggie's arm lay possessively across the boy's chest, and though the woman was sound asleep, Sam shifted restlessly. Any minute he was going to wake her up.

Fuck. Drawing his .45, he leaned over the bed and clamped a hand over Aggie's mouth. When her eyes shot open, he showed her his weapon, motioned her out of bed and onto her feet.

Sam stirred and opened his eyes. "Dad!" The boy shot out of bed and ran toward him. Ben's throat tightened. Until that moment, he hadn't realized how much he had wanted to hear that word.

"It's all right, son," he said softly, keeping his voice even and his gun on Aggie. "Go over there with Claire."

Sam's pale eyes went to the older woman, barefoot and dressed in her nightgown. "Don't hurt her, Dad. She was nice to us."

Ben reached out and stroked a hand over his son's sleep-mussed hair. "We just need her to be quiet until we get out of here."

With perfect timing, Trace appeared in the doorway, weapon drawn. Ben holstered the Nighthawk, used a plastic tie to bind Aggie's wrists and feet, then stretched a piece of duct tape over her mouth. He lifted her into his arms and set her gently in the middle of the bed.

"Bye, Aggie," Sam said as Claire pulled him against her and urged him toward the door.

Trace went ahead of them, checking to make sure it was clear, his pistol in both hands. Ben signaled for Sam and Claire to move out of the cabin, staying close to his side.

It all happened in an instant.

A man walked out of the cabin next door, the tip of his cigarette glowing in the darkness. From where he stood on the porch, he couldn't miss seeing them, and when he did, he started shouting the alarm. Jake fired a sleep dart from his position on the hill, hitting the man in the neck, and he went down, but the camp was already in motion.

Half-dressed men streamed out of the cabins, weapons at the ready, some of them firing though they didn't have a target. They had drilled for this moment, practiced for the day their camp might be invaded.

Ben shoved Claire and Sam back inside, out of the line of fire, and slammed the door. "Stay in here and stay low!" Across the clearing, Alex laid down a spray of automatic-rifle fire, giving Trace the cover he needed to reach safety behind the woodshed.

Outside the cabin, bursts of gunfire rattled across the compound. Ben strode over and dragged Aggie off the bed. He cut the plastic ties binding her wrists and feet and hauled her toward the door. Ripping off the duct tape, he pushed her out onto the porch, his gun pressed into her ribs.

"Tell them to hold their fire."

Aggie straightened, didn't hesitate. "Stop shooting, you fools. You're gonna get somebody kilt!"

Looked as if killing somebody was exactly the plan, but Ben didn't say that. "Tell Mace to come forward."

Aggie flicked Ben a measuring glance, caught the hard set of his jaw. He had a feeling she'd been expecting him, maybe even approved in some way that he had come to save his family.

"Mace, you heard the man. Get yourself out here."

Only a few seconds passed before the oldest Bragg stepped out of the safety of his cabin. He was big and thick-chested, with a long, shaggy beard. "You Slocum?"

"That's right."

"Let my sister go and we won't kill you."

"You've got armed men, Bragg, but so do we. Here's the way it's going down. I've come for my boy and my woman. We have your brother Jesse and your sister, Aggie. Three of your men are already down and the sheriff's on his way. We let Aggie and Jesse go as soon as the sheriff arrives. In the meantime, we all hold our fire and wait."

Silence ensued. Mace backed up a few paces and disappeared inside the cabin. Ben stepped back into the shadows, Aggie beside him, figuring Mace and the men were talking it over, trying to decide what to do.

"You think he'll agree?" Claire asked.

"We'll soon find out."

Mace stepped into the open doorway. "How do we know you got Jesse?"

"How do you think we found this place?" Ben called back.

Mace cursed. "Stupid son of a bitch."

"He had a family to protect. So do you, and so do I. You got nowhere to run—not this time. And the sheriff'll be here any minute. We wait and we all stay alive."

Even with the faint rays of moonlight, it was too dark to see Mace's face.

"Gotta talk to the rest of the men." Turning, he stepped down off the porch, apparently convinced no one was going to shoot him, crossed the open area and disappeared into another cabin.

Ben moved backward, hauling Aggie back inside the cabin. "Hold your positions," he said into his mic.

Time slid past. The longer it took the better the chance the sheriff would arrive and end the standoff.

"They're gonna put us all in jail, ain't they?" the gray-haired woman said.

Ben looked down at her. "Troy and Duke for sure. No way around it. Maybe the rest of you can cut a deal. Sam says you treated him and Claire well. That'll be in your favor."

She looked over at Sam, her features softening. "Boy loves you. So does the woman."

Ben's chest clamped down as he followed her gaze to his family. Sam stood in front of Claire, both of them facing him, Claire's hands resting gently on his son's shoulders. Sam's gaze followed Ben's every move, and there was no mistaking the trust in the eyes so like his own.

"I love them, too," he said gruffly.

Claire's gaze shot to his, then drifted away. He wondered if she believed him. He didn't think so. He would find a way to convince her as soon as they got out of this hellhole.

Mace's deep voice echoed across the clearing. "We'll wait for the sheriff."

Ben breathed a sigh of relief. "Good call," he said. To a man like Mace, his word was his bond. It was almost over.

Unfortunately, *almost* could be a deadly word.

Claire leaned against the rough wooden wall, her arms around Sam, who shivered in front of her though it wasn't cold in the cabin. Ben was keeping watch out the window, Aggie crouched next to him on the floor below the sill.

For an instant, he turned and his eyes met hers. The icy shade stood out even more against the black greasepaint on his face. He looked big and hard and male. More capable than any man she had ever known. She loved him so much.

I love them, too, he had said, and she knew that in a way he meant it. He loved his son and he cared for her. He had come for her, as she had known he would. And though she hadn't been sure he would find them, she had known with an unshakable certainty deep in her soul that he would come after them. He might not love her the same way she loved him, but he would be good to her. He would make a home for her and his son.

Her throat tightened. All they needed was to get out of there.

Something shifted in the air inside the cabin. Claire turned to see the back door swinging silently open and Duke Hutchins moving into the shadows at the rear of the room. Claire caught the glint of a pistol, the barrel coming up, pointing at Ben's back.

"Ben!" She didn't stop to think, just launched herself at Hutchins, knocking him sideways, his pistol discharging as Ben whirled and fired two quick shots in return.

Claire screamed as Duke's pistol roared again and Ben slammed backward against the wall. Hutchins teetered and crashed to the floor, his gun spinning away.

Shaking all over, Claire raced toward Ben, her heart trying to tear through her ribs.

He caught her against him. "I'm all right, baby. Hutchins is down. I've got a vest. I'm bruised, but I'm okay." Sam ran to them and Ben pulled both of them against him.

Shooting erupted outside the cabin.

"Get down!" Staying low, Ben peered out the window, checking the area in front of the cabin. He rubbed his chest where the bullet had struck as he made his way to where Hutchins lay on the floor.

Claire was certain the man was dead until he started moaning. Crouching, she hurried to the bed, dragged a pillow case off a pillow and tore off a strip. She handed it to Ben, who pressed it against the wound in Hutchins's chest.

"I'll tend him," Aggie said, bending low as she crossed the room in her nightgown and knelt beside Ben. "I got some blame in this. When Troy brung the boy here, he said he didn't have no kin. Sam was the son I never had and I wanted to keep him. I didn't know he had family till Troy brung him back and Sam told me. I'm glad you come for him."

Aggie tore off another strip of cotton and pressed the

material over the wound to help slow the flow of blood. She looked down at Hutchins.

"You never was one of us, was you? You just come here to stir up trouble. Troy's my brother, but you always had a way of turning him bad. You're lucky this man didn't kill you."

Outside the cabin, the shooting had ceased. New sounds reached them. Engine noise, wheels churning up mud, then the single quick bark of a siren as the sheriff's vehicles reached the gate. Claire crept to the window, peeked over the sill and saw the gate standing open and a line of white SUVs pouring into the compound.

Spotlights lit the clearing. As the deputies streamed out of their cars, men emerged from the cabins, their hands in the air. Jake, Trace and Alex walked into the clearing, their weapons no longer in sight. Jake hauled Jesse Bragg along with him.

As Ben walked out on the porch, a movement caught Claire's eye. Troy Bragg bolted out the back door of the nearest cabin, running hard toward the darkness and safety of the bayou.

"Son of a bitch!" Ben took off after him. One of the spotlights swung toward Bragg, illuminating his lean figure running flat out toward the swamp. In the round circle of light, Claire saw Ben tackle him, bringing him down hard in the mud at the edge of the bayou. Deputies raced toward the struggling men as Ben dragged Troy to his feet and punched him hard enough to knock him back into the mud.

The deputies grabbed Troy and hoisted him to his feet, pulled his arms behind him, cuffed him and hauled him back toward the clearing. Claire figured Troy was lucky the deputies were there to keep Ben from giving him the beating he deserved.

Ben walked toward her, mud all over his clothes and his knuckles bleeding. He climbed the steps leading up to the porch, and Claire threw herself into his arms.

Ben's hold tightened around her. "It's over, angel." Sam ran up and threw his arms around his father's waist. Ben smoothed a hand over his son's dark hair. "Time to take my family and go home."

Claire looked into his hard, beloved face and burst into tears.

Thirty-Five

It took two hours to mop things up.

Since the clearing wasn't big enough for a medevac to land, Duke Hutchins rode away in the back of a sheriff's SUV. Troy Bragg was hauled off in handcuffs, covered in mud, his nose bleeding and his lip split. Mace and Aggie were taken into custody, while everyone else was read his rights and released on his own recognizance.

The Bayou Patriots all had strong ties to the Egansville community. And the men had mostly been pawns in Troy and Duke's scheme. Ben figured the two would serve time, if Duke lived. Mace, Aggie, Luke, Pete, Jesse and the others would probably cut a deal.

All Ben wanted was to take Claire and Sam and go home.

The problem was, once they got there, Claire's life would still be in danger. Diego Santos and his band of cutthroats still believed she was hiding information she had received from Michael Sullivan. And they were willing to kill in order to get it.

Ben mulled over the problem as Alex landed his plane in Houston and taxied to the executive terminal. As soon as he shut down the engines, Jake opened the cabin door, and they all climbed out. Ben was reaching for one of the gear bags when his cell phone started ringing. Caller ID said the number belonged to Danny Castillo.

"Slocum," Ben answered.

"I hear you found Claire and your boy," Castillo said.

"That's right. We just landed in Houston. We're on our way home."

"That's good news and I've got more."

"Yeah? What is it?"

"Undercover cops located Diego Santos last night. When they tried to bring him in, he resisted, and there was a shoot-out. Santos and two of his top guns were killed. Looks like your lady is safe."

Relief slid like whiskey through his veins. "That *is* good news. Thanks, Detective. Maybe now our lives can finally get back to normal."

"Maybe yours can. My job never ends."

Ben chuckled. "I guess not. Thanks for the call."

Feeling as if a weight had been lifted off his shoulders, Ben hung up the phone. "Santos is dead," he told Claire. "Happened last night. Perfect timing, if you ask me."

Claire sighed with relief. "Thank God."

"Exactly." Ben slid an arm around her waist and another around Sam's shoulders. "Let's go home."

There were things he needed to say to his family. Important things he hadn't been able to say before. It wouldn't be easy for a man like him, but he was determined to make things right.

Ben couldn't wait to get there.

* * *

It was late morning by the time Ben reached his house, everyone got cleaned up and settled in. While Claire went into the kitchen to make a badly needed pot of coffee, Ben led Sam over to the sofa in the living room and urged him to take a seat.

Sam looked up at him, his eyes big and worried. "You aren't mad at me, are you?"

Ben frowned. "Why would I be mad at you?"

"If I hadn't gone with Troy in the first place, he and Duke wouldn't have come back and taken Claire."

Ben slung an arm around the boy's shoulder. "None of this was your fault, son. I just called you in here to tell you…how much I love you. You never have to worry about being alone again. And I wanted you to know how much I liked it when you called me Dad."

Sam looked up at him. "I didn't mean to. Claire said you would come, but I was afraid you wouldn't find us. When I saw you by the bed, I was so glad to see you it just popped out."

Ben smiled. "I'm really glad it did."

"So it's okay if I call you Dad from now on?"

Ben hugged him, his throat a little tight. "From now until forever."

Sam grinned and Ben ruffled his hair. "Go get some sleep, okay? You've been up half the night."

The boy yawned. He'd slept on the plane, but after so much excitement it wasn't enough. He glanced toward the sofa, where he had been sleeping while Claire was staying in the house.

"Why don't you use your own room?" Ben said. "From now on, Claire will be sleeping with me."

Sam looked up at him solemnly. "You're going to marry her, right?"

"That's right." *If she'd still have him.* The more he thought of the way he had asked her to marry him, the more he worried she might have changed her mind.

"I'm glad."

"Me, too."

Sam padded down the hall to his room, went in and closed the door.

Ben took a breath for courage, thought about what he planned to say and headed for the kitchen.

Claire filled Hercules's bowl with dry cat food, then returned to the kitchen counter to check on the pot of coffee she was brewing. She hadn't been able to sleep on the plane. She kept seeing Duke Hutchins pointing his gun at Ben, remembering the raw terror she had felt when she'd thought Ben had been shot. He was badly bruised where the bullet had hit, but the vest had protected him.

As she reached for a pair of mugs, she felt him come up behind her, settle his big hands at her waist. Sliding her hair to one side, he bent his head and kissed the nape of her neck.

"You okay?"

She set the mugs down and turned into his arms. "I knew you'd come for us. I didn't know how long it would take you to find us, but I knew you'd never stop looking."

"I would have searched the rest of my life." He very softly kissed her. "Troy and the others…they didn't… hurt you?"

Claire shook her head, remembering the hard work, what Mace and Pete Bragg had planned for her, trying not to think how much worse it could have been if she had been forced into some sort of sham marriage.

"You got there in time. Pete Bragg wanted to marry me, but I told him I was engaged to another man."

Ben caught her chin, forcing her gaze to his. "Not anymore."

Claire felt the blood slowly drain from her face. She stared up at him. "I thought…thought you wanted to marry me. I thought we were going to the justice of the peace. Just something simple—you said that's what you wanted."

Ben shook his head. "That's what I thought I wanted, the reason I made that ugly proposal."

Panic slid through her. "It wasn't really ugly. It was… It was practical. That way we could both be with Sam."

"It was ugly and selfish. If I hadn't been such a fool, I would have told you I loved you. I would have said that I'm so crazy in love with you it hurts to think of spending another day without you as my wife. But I didn't say those things."

Her heart squeezed. She couldn't figure out where this was going. Dear God, was he going to change his mind? She couldn't bear to think of a future without him.

She forced herself to smile. "It doesn't matter what you said. We'll both be able to be with Sam. It was a good idea. It still is."

"It was a stupid idea. I don't want to marry you because of Sam. I want to marry you because I love you. I want to marry you because I can't live another day without you. That's the way I feel, Claire. What I need to know is how you feel about me. Do you love me? Because I want to marry you more than anything in the world."

Relief hit her hard, then a surge of joy. Her eyes welled. Claire threw her arms around Ben's neck, her heart beating so hard she was sure he could hear it. "Oh, Ben, I love you so much. It seems like I've loved you forever."

The tension eased from his powerful shoulders. Ben kissed her long and deep. "I don't want to go to the justice of the peace. I want us to have a big fancy wedding with all the trimmings. I want you to wear a long white gown and carry an orchid bouquet. I want your father to walk you down the aisle and your whole family watching. I want our friends there when we say our vows. I want them to know how much I love you and how proud I am you're going to be my wife."

Claire started crying.

Ben's arms tightened around her. "I love you, angel. I was just afraid to tell you. I was a coward, but I'm not afraid anymore."

Claire swallowed and shook her head. Ben Slocum was the bravest man she had ever known.

He eased back to look at her, wiped away the wetness on her cheeks. "Will you marry me, Claire?"

Fresh tears spilled over. How many nights had she dreamed of this moment, dreamed of saying yes to a man who truly loved her.

Claire smiled up at him. "I'd be honored to marry you, Ben. You and your son."

Ben kissed her, a long, deep kiss meant to show her how much he cared. And though she might have doubted it, somewhere in her heart she had known, the moment he had stepped through the cabin door in camouflage and greasepaint, exactly how strong his love was.

Claire looked up to see Sam standing in the kitchen.

"So is she gonna marry you, Dad?"

Ben grinned. "Yeah, son, she is. She's gonna marry both of us."

Sam shot a fist into the air. "Yes!"

Pepper barked his agreement, and Claire and Ben both laughed. Ben was a man of danger and adventure. Claire looked forward to the adventure the three of them would share.

Epilogue

Two Weeks Later

Ben carried a box out of Claire's apartment and loaded it into the back of the Denali. Trace shoved a box in after it, Alex piled a suitcase on top and Jake shoved in a basket filled with household cleaning supplies.

"That's about it," Jake said. "I think we got the last of her stuff out of there."

Most of the furniture had been put into storage until they found a bigger house. At the moment, Claire was so wrapped up in making wedding plans they hadn't had time to look.

It had been two weeks since their return to Houston. Ben had wanted to get married right away, but a big wedding took time to plan. Claire had picked Valentine's Day, corny but, hey, the lady was a romantic, and anything she wanted was fine with him.

All Ben wanted was to put the wedding band that matched her engagement ring on her finger so that a-holes like Pete Bragg would know damned well she belonged to him. Ben was going to be grinning ear to ear on his wedding day, looking as besotted as Alex Justice had on his.

Ben no longer cared. Deep down, maybe he had known Claire was the woman for him the morning he had first seen her waiting impatiently on his front porch. She had come into his life and changed everything. Because of Claire, he had a woman and a son he loved, a family who loved him in return.

She walked out of her apartment, turned and locked the front door. "That's everything. Jake got the last of it."

"You ready to go?" Ben asked. Sam was staying with Mrs. McKenzie while they packed the last of Claire's things. Claire would be staying in his house until the week before they were married. Then she'd be staying with her parents while they were in town for the wedding. Ben was already dreading the week without her.

"Let me check my mailbox one last time." She went over and unlocked the glass-windowed box along a row that belonged to other tenants, looked curiously down at the six-by-nine manila envelope she took out, and walked back to him. The envelope, dog-eared and covered with postmarks, looked as if it had traveled cross-country.

"This went to my California address," she said. "It was forwarded to my apartment. It took a couple of weeks to get here."

Ben moved closer, looked over her shoulder as Claire ripped open the envelope and took out a piece of paper. "It… It's from Michael. The note says, 'Call me when you get this.'" She turned the envelope upside down and a plastic flash drive slid into her hand.

"Oh, God, Ben, this must be what Diego Santos was looking for."

Jake walked up just then. "What is it?"

"Might be the information Santos tortured Michael Sullivan to get."

Alex whistled as he joined them. "Let's take it down to the office, see what's on it."

"Good idea," Trace agreed. He, Jake and Alex headed for Trace's Jeep Cherokee, piling in while Ben and Claire climbed into the Denali.

Being a Saturday, the office was closed. They all poured through the front door, and Ben led Claire over to his computer, started it up and plugged in the flash drive.

There were three files on the drive. Ben clicked on the first one. They watched as the screen filled with numbers.

"What is it?" Claire asked.

"Ship names and arrival dates," Ben said.

Alex's blue eyes fixed on the screen. "Looks like merchandise coming in from Colombia."

"Colombia would fit," Claire said. "Michael was down there for months doing a magazine feature on drug trafficking. He said he came to Houston to continue the work he started down there."

"There's a product list for each shipment," Ben said. "Could be drugs." Ben clicked on the next page.

"It's drugs, all right," Jake said. "Cocaine and plenty of it."

Ben opened another file.

"Whoa!" Trace's eyes widened. "Will you look at that?"

Ben leaned back in the chair. "Account numbers in the Cayman Islands. And look whose name is on them."

"Congressman Ted Reynolds," Jake said.

Alex peered down at the screen. "Wasn't Reynolds the head of the Longshoremen's Union before he got elected?"

"Sure enough," Trace drawled. "Which would give him the kind of connections he'd need to pull off a shipping operation this size."

"Michael knew Reynolds," Claire added. "He mentioned being invited to his home for a party. I didn't even think of it until you mentioned his name."

"Maybe that's how Sullivan got the info," Ben said. "Went into Reynolds's home computer and downloaded his personal data."

"Michael was good," Claire said. "One of the best investigative journalists in the country. If he had any idea Reynolds was involved in a drug operation, he would have looked for a way to get the information."

"So Sullivan downloads the info and Reynolds finds out," Jake said. "Then he hires Santos to get the flash drive back."

Ben thought of Michael Sullivan's bludgeoned face. "Maybe Sullivan gives Santos the one he had, but he was smart enough to have made a copy and sent it to Claire."

"Maybe he sent the drive to the old address on purpose," Trace said, "figuring it would take a while to get back to Houston. Give him some time."

"Or he was in a hurry," Claire said, "and my old address was the only one he knew without having to look it up."

"Could be," Alex agreed.

"Either way, we need to call Richard Haskins," Jake said. Haskins was head of the DEA in Houston, a man Jake and Ben had both worked with before. "We need to get this to the Feds before Reynolds hires another hit man to come after Claire."

Ben's stomach knotted. He wanted Claire safe. He wasn't about to lose her again. "Call him," he said darkly, and Jake picked up the phone.

By the end of the following day, Congressman Theodore Reynolds was in custody. Though the man had been released on a ten-million-dollar bond, Reynolds now knew the police had the disk Sullivan had made, which meant Claire was no longer in danger.

"I guess it really is over this time," she said that evening after supper. Sam was already in bed for the night, and the two of them were sitting together on the sofa. "I think Michael is resting easier knowing he didn't die for nothing."

"And I'm resting a helluva lot easier knowing you're safe."

Claire turned and slid her arms around his neck. "I love you so much."

Ben pulled her into his lap and kissed her. "I love you, too, angel." He was surprised how easily the phrase slid off his tongue. Thanks to Claire and Sam, he was a different man than he had been—freer, more at peace with himself, his world a far brighter place than it had been before.

He thought of the morning Claire had shown up on his porch desperately needing him to help her find his son. The son he hadn't known he had, by a woman he had both loved and hated.

Ben looked at Claire and thought how much he loved her, thought of his son and knew what a lucky man he was to have found him. He thought how the two of them had helped mend his heart, and silently thanked Laura for the gift she had given him.

Ben wished her peace in her eternal slumber.

* * * * *

Author's Note

~~~~~~

I hope you enjoyed Ben Slocum and Claire Chastain in *Against the Edge*. I really enjoyed writing their adventure. Later this year, *Against the Mark* will be out. Johnnie Riggs's friend, former Marine, Tyler Brodie, first appeared in *Against the Night*. You met him again in these pages.

In *Against the Mark,* Ty meets his match when Haley Warren comes to him for help in solving her father's murder. It's a fast-paced, high-action tale I'm hoping you'll enjoy.

If you haven't read the other books in the series, look for the Raines brothers in *Against the Wind, Against the Fire* and *Against the Law,* as well as their friends in *Against the Storm, Against the Night, Against the Sun* and *Against the Odds.*

Till next time, very best wishes and happy reading.

Kat